LAND OF LOVE
AND DROWNING

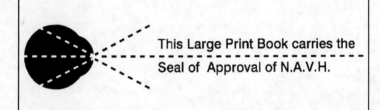

This Large Print Book carries the
Seal of Approval of N.A.V.H.

LAND OF LOVE AND DROWNING

TIPHANIE YANIQUE

THORNDIKE PRESS

A part of Gale, Cengage Learning

GALE
CENGAGE Learning·

Farmington Hills, Mich • San Francisco • New York • Waterville, Maine
Meriden, Conn • Mason, Ohio • Chicago

GALE
CENGAGE Learning®

Copyright © 2014 by Tiphanie Yanique.
Frontmatter map by Meighan Cavanaugh
Thorndike Press, a part of Gale, Cengage Learning.

LIBRARY OF CONGRESS CATALOGING-IN-PUBLICATION DATA

Yanique, Tiphanie.
   Land of love and drowning / by Tiphanie Yanique. — Large print edition.
     pages ; cm. — (Thorndike Press large print core)
   ISBN 978-1-4104-7278-6 (hardcover) — ISBN 1-4104-7278-7 (hardcover)
   1. Magic—Fiction. 2. African Americans—Fiction. 3. African American families—Fiction. 4. Saint Thomas (United States Virgin Islands)—Fiction. 5. Large type books. I. Title.
   PS3625.A679L36 2014b
   813'.6—dc23   2014025475

Published in 2014 by arrangement with Riverhead Books, a member of Penguin Group (USA) LLC, a Penguin Random House Company

Printed in Mexico
2 3 4 5 6 7 18 17 16 15 14

For Beulah Smith Harrigan

AMERICA / THE MAINLAND /
THE CONTINENT
↑

✻ THE VIRGIN ISLANDS ✻

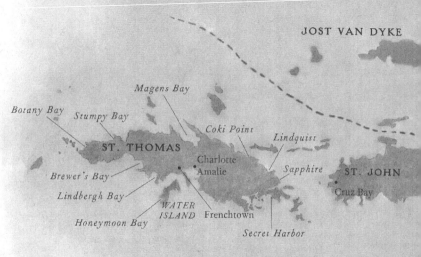

JOST VAN DYKE

Magens Bay

Botany Bay   Stumpy Bay

Coki Point   Lindquist

ST. THOMAS   Sapphire   ST. JOHN

Charlotte
Amalie

Brewer's Bay   Cruz Bay

Lindbergh Bay

WATER
ISLAND   Frenchtown
Honeymoon Bay

Secret Harbor

← PUERTO RICO
AND OTHER
BIG ISLANDS

The U.S. Virgin Islands

Freedom City   ST. CROIX
(Frederiksted) ·

DOWN ISLAND
↓

Flash of Beauty

ANEGADA

TORTOLA

AFRICA, ASIA,
AND EUROPE →

Coral Bay

The British Virgin Islands

Christiansted

© 2014 Meighan Cavanaugh

■ ■ ■ ■

FREEDOM

■ ■ ■ ■

The greatest hazard to sailing in the
Virgin Islands — if not in the whole
Caribbean — was and is Anegada.
— DAVID A. MELFORD

1.

Owen Arthur Bradshaw watched as the little girl was tied up with lace and silk. He jostled the warm rum in his glass and listened to the wind.

The storm outside wasn't a hurricane. Just a tropical gale. It was the season for storms. Lightning slated through the heavy wooden shutters that were closed but unfastened. The thunder was coming through the walls built with blue bitch stone. There was no one outside walking in the rain. That sort of thing was avoided.

A scientist visiting from America had brought the lace and the silk. They were all at the house of Mr. Lovernkrandt, an eminent Danish businessman. Denmark was giving up on the West Indies and America was buying in, but Mr. Lovernkrandt was not leaving. The scientist was tying the girl up. He was demonstrating an experiment that had become stale on the Continent, an experiment of electricity. The little girl was very beautiful. And she was very little. And she was very afraid. She was also very brave.

Captain Bradshaw thought on his daughter, Eeona, who was not unlike this American girl. Only Eeona was more beautiful and at least as brave.

The people who had come together to make Captain Owen Arthur Bradshaw could be traced back to West Africans forced to the islands as slaves and West Africans who came over free to offer their services as goldsmiths. Back to European men who were kicked out of Europe as criminals and to European women of aristocratic blood who sailed to the islands for adventure. Back to Asians who came as servants and planned to return to their Indies, and to Asians who only wanted to see if there was indeed a western side of the Indies. And to Caribs who sat quietly making baskets in the countryside, plotting ways to kill all the rest and take back the land their God had granted them for a millennium.

Owen Arthur had been raised from a poor upbringing to a place of importance and ownership. He was the captain and owner of a cargo ship. And now he was among the important men who sat in this living room and watched through the haze of the oil lamps as a girl was hoisted off the ground via lace and silk and a hook in the ceiling. The little girl's body jerked as the American scientist tugged. Her body jerked until she was a few feet off the ground, but she did not cry out. Owen Arthur Bradshaw was not sure how much longer he could bear to watch. But it was essential for him to be at this gathering. The host, Mr. Lovernkrandt, was a rum maker and Owen Arthur had always shipped rum. But with American-ness would come Prohibition, and Owen Arthur needed to ensure he was included in any of Lovernkrandt's nonliquor endeavors.

He pressed his own earlobe between his thumb and forefinger. Success and solvency should have been on his mind, but Owen Arthur could not help but watch the Ameri-can girl with a father's tenderness. This little girl was pale-faced and blond, and Owen's little girl, Eeona, was honey-skinned and ocean-haired. But still he looked at this strange little girl as though looking on his own child. The first half of him desired that he had created this little girl. She was a pretty yellow thing. The lower half of him desired the girl. How young could she be?

He put his mouth to his glass and tilted it until the warm sweetness met his lips. *She will outlive me,* he thought to himself. And who was the "she" he was referring to? Perhaps his wife, who was just then sitting at home doing the sewing that it seemed God had created her to do. Or perhaps he was speaking of his mistress, who was at that moment sitting in her home playing the piano he had bought her, making a music that only God or the Devil could bless. Or perhaps he was actually speaking of his daughter, whom he loved like he loved his own skin. Perhaps he was speaking of the little girl to whom the scientist was now attaching cords of metal. Perhaps the little girl was, in a way, all women to him, as all women might be to a certain kind of man.

Owen Arthur is right. All these shes will outlive him, though he cannot bear the thought of his women going on. He knows his daughter will live forever, in the way all parents do, simply because parents generally die first. But Owen will not die of old age. Owen will die of love. The Danish West Indies will become the United States Virgin Islands and then this patriarch will die. And perhaps these things are the same thing.

"Behold," the American is saying in his strange accent. He hands the girl a glass ball and then whispers to her, "Do not drop it or I will punish you." She does not make

14

a move to suggest she has heard. She only takes the glass ball in both her hands. And then the first miracle happens — her hair begins to rise. The storm outside begins to howl.

"Christ, have mercy." This is what the Christians whisper. The Jewish and Muslim men for whom these islands have been a refuge, mutter "Oy, Gotenu" and "Allahu Akbar" under their breaths respectfully. Yes, America will bring us progress. Here is progress before us.

Lightning claws through the window, as though hunting. And Owen Arthur watches the girl's hair rise toward the ceiling until it is sticking up like so many angel horns.

Oh, the stories these men will tell of this night. How they will embellish one part, shrink the other. How they will make this night real again and again, some in Arabic or Danish or Yiddish or English, others in that Caribbean language that tourist guide-books will call "Creole." The story will become more real than the night itself because the story of it will last, while this wet night will soon be over. And here we are putting it down, so that it may last forever.

But Owen Arthur thinks on his firstborn. His only child, thus far, who has survived to life. His honey-skinned Eeona. Her hair, too, has a life of its own. He has combed it himself and knotted it into braids and found that he can get lost in its forest. He collects the pieces of her hair from the brush and burns them himself, so that no one can steal them and put a curse on her. Owen himself is not a hairy man, he does not even sport the sideburns so popular for men of this time and place. His daughter has the glorious hair on her head but otherwise she, too, is smooth all over.

Eeona is so beautiful that many call her pure and they think on the virgin hills. Or they call her pristine and they think of the clear and open ocean. Or they might use terms such as *untouched* or *undefiled,* but then they are cautious because they know that their words alone might spoil her. So on damp nights men imagine that they are angels and may touch her as they please, but when they wake, they sign themselves with the cross. And if available, they pat handfuls of holy water on their chests. They do not really wish to pollute little Eeona. They only wish to witness a bit and then return, like a tourist might.

The American scientist takes the ball from this other little girl in this parlor. Now he prepares for the real triumph. He will make the little girl into a miracle. The scientist raises the vial to the little girl's face. The little girl is wise as little girls must be. She does not flinch, but she closes her eyes. The scientist touches the vial to her nose. White lights spark like lightning about her face. She cries out, but the men clap louder. They have seen electricity! They have seen the future!

"Mr. Lovernkrandt," the scientist says, "you must try." The vial is passed to the man of the house, who has been standing near a window that is fastened but not sealed — the legs of rain kicking at his back. He steps forwards, and with great hesitation that might be called trepidation were he not a wealthy man, he presses the vial to the brave girl's nose. He feels the shock in his hand and up his wet sleeve and lurches away. "Mercy," he exclaims so loudly that no one hears the little girl cry out again. His face is hot. For a moment he had thought he would be paralyzed. But he had survived.

Owen feels the rain sneaking through as kisses from a tiny mouth. Now he raises his hand. "I should like to try," he says. The American scientist smiles as Owen Arthur steps forward. He passes Owen the vial. Owen walks toward the little girl. She is suspended so that he and she are level. Their eyes meet. He bends toward her and caresses her earlobe gently, for he enjoys the feeling of that soft skin. "Men are foolish when pretty girls are involved," he says loud enough for all to hear, and then he dashes the vial onto the floor.

The great men snort. Many look away, ashamed that they had not had Captain Bradshaw's integrity. "My apologies, Mr. Lovernkrandt. I seem to have broken the American's instrument. I am afraid I have ended the game." Owen thinks on the major shipping deals he must have lost now. Thinks on how his business has depended on Lovernkrandt's rum for more than a decade. But then he thinks on something else. "I fear most that it is past this little girl's bedtime." He touches the girl's hair then tips his hat and takes his leave into the storm.

Science is just a kind of magic, and magic just a kind of religion, and Owen Arthur knows all about this because Owen owns a ship and men who spend their lives on water know that magic is real.

Owen stands in the rain, the lightning brightening the way ahead of him. Lovernkrandt's house, so well positioned at the center of town, is not far from the opening of the sea. Wherever Owen goes, the sea will be at his side either way. A small wall of stone has been built to block the bay. So it is no longer really a beach but a proper harbor. Still, it would be nothing at all for Owen to walk to the ocean right now. He has done it before. He swam in this harbor as a boy. The ocean, look now, is coming to him. The waves are bounding over the seawall, leaping, like animals, like little girls.

Owen cannot decide to which house he will walk. If he keeps the sea on his right, then he will go past the market square where entrepreneur ladies sell their produce and straw creations. There, Rebekah lives in a small house with her sons. None of these sons are his, yet.

If he puts the sea on his left, he will pass the smaller fish market where men haul in the catch of the day before dawn. Beyond, Owen's wife, Antoinette, lives in Villa by the Sea. It is a wealthy but modest estate where their daughter and their cook, Miss Lady, and their groundskeeper, Mr. Lyte, all live. The house is at the shallow edge of the harbor. The living and dining rooms are separated from each other by a line of linen curtains, which makes the house feel like a ship at sail. From the Villa by the Sea balcony the captain can see his own ship docked farther into the bay.

Now Owen Arthur thinks of the little girl's hair rising into the air and he faces the beach. He waits until his whole body has received the rain. Then he goes toward his Eeona, because the little orphan girl reminded him of her. Owen cannot see into the future, but he can see into the past, and this is a magic we all have. As he walks, the sea is at his side, but the rain is at his back, pushing him toward his only child. The waves slip over his shoes.

When Owen arrives, he goes to his wife, who is telling a story to little Eeona in the parlor. This family will know itself through stories told in time and others told too late. In this way they are no different from any other tribe. "Holy Ghost," his wife cries when she sees him wet, as though he'd been drowning. "Lady!" Antoinette calls. "A towel, a change of clothes for the captain. Quickly." Eeona has no restraint. She runs to her father and he picks her up and puts her to his chest, even though he will make her wet and they will both be sick over this. When Miss Lady comes from upstairs with the towels, she knows to bring two.

At this moment it is only the one child and she is in love with her father. It is no large thing that this daughter will, in time, kill Owen Arthur. No large thing at all. Family will always kill you — some bit by bit, others all at once. It is the love that does it.

In her womb mother Antoinette is carrying another child. But she does not want more children, so this child, like the three before it, will be made to know the island ways of washing the womb. But women do not always have their way. This child will survive and will be the last of Owen's children. She will be called Anette.

Anette Bradshaw will be as different from her elder sister as water is from land. The elder sister will be so stunning that men will scare of her. But not Anette. Boys will stick to the younger sister like the slick of mango juice. A trinity of men will feel the love of her like casha bush burring their scalp in sleep. Anette's own image will grace the silver screen. The islands will drop the BOMB because of her say-so. But baby Anette has not come as yet. Right now it is only Eeona and Papa, with Mama there watching.

2.

ANETTE

Don't mind I ain born as yet. I is the historian in this family. Teacher of history at the Anglican school where all the fancy families does send their children. So is me could really tell you what happen on Transfer Day. If anyone know the history is me. Nowadays people think historians are stuffy types, but history is a kind of magic I doing here.

Is March 31, 1917. The islands of St. Thomas, St. John, and St. Croix, getting transfer from Danish to American rule. Denmark decide it don't want we. America decide it do. One find we unnecessary because they way up in Europe. The next find we absolutely necessary because they backside sitting on the Caribbean. Just so we get pass from hand to hand.

The day of the Transfer our men there trying to keep they dignity. Making declarations: "We are pleased to be among the brave and to have our land be among the free." But for true, money been tough and trade poor. We Bradshaws was wealthier than most, though we not as wealthy as some. Don't worry what Eeona and them old wives going to tell you. Others much more mighty than we. When he propose marriage, Papa surely had promise Mama all the riches the Caribbean could offer. But all she come to know of these riches is Villa by the Sea, a maid-cook, and a man-about-the-house.

The cook, who is also the maid, name Sheila Ladyinga. She didn't love we, but she did always look out. The man-about-the-house name Hippolyte Lammartine, and he a good man despite the foolishness that he throw on me later. Mr. Lyte and Miss Lady, they was called by all who know. But Mama Antoinette, she had want what we read in novel them British ladies have, what the governor wife have. A butler. A cook and cleaner — separate. Nanny for each child. A wet nurse. Mama had to give we she own breast. Is like Mama was a radical or something so. She don't want to give over everything for children. She want to give over to she self. The times ain right or Mama Antoinette ain right. I can't say. We can't say. But she what she could do was sew. Had a way with the stitch. Teach Eeona all she know. Ain had the occasion to teach by time I born and reach. But still. Mama had talent. I know. All the old wives say so.

On Transfer Day everybody gone to the military Barracks and wave toonchy American flags and wonder if our V.I. could ever become a U.S. state. Only now that I is a historian myself, I could look back and really see that it was a funny thing happening that day. The land and the people like we going separate ways. The land becoming American, but we people still Caribbean. Eeona always say Papa was British and Danish, but anybody could watch the picture of him and see that he part Frenchy and plenty Negro.

But look. In America, they have a dream. People from all about the place come together and now they is one nation. It dougla-up, just like the Caribbean. Correct? And the island intellectuals who was writing then, they thinking is only a matter of time before all of we Caribbean going to be part of the United States and then the United States, with the Caribbean as figurehead, like what on ships, going to be a shining beacon to the free world. That what some fools was thinking on Transfer Day.

At the Barracks you seeing men with money wearing blue linen suits. The women dress in white linen with red shawls and big white hats. But watch, they have a few who dye up their white dress until it bright yellow. Them protesting. For real, protest! Yellow is the color of we islands — sunny. In

America, yellow mean coward. But not for we. Yellow mean brash. Yellow mean happy and free. These in yellow want we to stay Danish or go join the British Virgin Islands or even be independent like everybody saying going to happen with Puerto Rico. But watch, even them protesters in yellow having a good time. They protesting but they done lose, might as well enjoy the bacchanal.

Eeona, she still a girl and she done pretty, so pretty she could sink ships. And she done the type that see sinking ships like the only thing worth doing. Mama sew she a red dress — which ain scandalous since she still a young girl. Eeona wearing a straw hat that bleach white like bone. Back in them time children was well behaved, quiet. But Eeona was a something else. She like a mannequin for Mama. As far as Mama concern, Eeona there just to receive compliment that belong to Mama. Like Mama sew and stitch the child and not the dress alone. That day Eeona ain even allowed to lift she head, just in case she beauty end up snaring somebody and distracting from the formalities. So she keep she head low; watch Papa foots as he stroll through the crowd.

Everybody giddy-like. You could just read the newspapers from that time to know.

"So-and-so son going to America for adventure," say one. "Fulano de tal son going to America for university," say a next. Mama and Papa hearing this but they ain have no son going no place for no reason. Mama ain want no more children, she want to make she glove and dress and make she self the head fashion lady that other fashion ladies depend on. Papa want a son, but he need Mama for this. But Mama only need fancier fabric and industrial sewing machine. All of that easy to come by in America, but close to impossible here on island. Mama ain figure out how to get all what she want.

In the Barracks everybody nyamming down some pick-up saltfish. The place smelling like ocean. The talk keep talking: "Our family is moving to Atlanta, Georgia. My husband has taken a position . . ." Mama couldn't stay and listen to that, so Eeona get jerk this way and that. Lose Papa legs. Mama stand by the Frenchy women selling straw bags. These woman faces brown even though they white like white people. The Frenchy woman-them poor, but they have a fashion. They make their nice hats and their simple clothes and back in the day they was from a French island. Even we know that French mean fancy. Don't mind that our Frenchies poor. Mama lime

26

by them, gripping Eeona until some other woman of Mama class stroll by and Mama hook she self and Eeona on to these.

Now the Barracks coming loud and garrulous. They close to the Yard. That place always rough. Even during the Prohibition anybody could get a shot of rum from time daybreak start. So is a real bacchanal going on this morning. Like a carnival. Man-them singing "The Star-Spangled Banner" with a quelbe flute leading. Woman, like Mama, clapping dainty.

The brass brand finally and officially begin to play the Danish national anthem. Twenty-one guns shoot out from the boat in the harbor. Each fire pound through Mama Antoinette stomach, for she pregnant and is me in there. The Danish flag inch down. Some of the man-them actually weeping. The guns go off again. The new anthem start up and everybody get quiet-quiet. Papa ease up to Mama and Eeona, stand by them at this important time. Don't say nothing 'bout where he just reach from wandering.

That American flag go soaring up, and Papa soar up Eeona to his shoulders so she could watch America up there on the gazebo stage. Eeona too big for going on anybody shoulders, you hear. She a girl, but she 'bout to be woman any minute, getting her bleeding soon-soon. People watching the flag and people watching the woman-child and both making them stare and stay hush. Mama Antoinette pull Eeona dress so it cover the knees at least. Mama say: "Observe, Eeona. That is freedom." And you could see even now from the pictures in the archives, how them men looking sharp in their military uniforms. Gold buttons glinting. Mama could see that freedom does be well dressed and fashionable. And that's what happen. Danish West Indies become United States Virgin Islands. And just so, we go from Danish to American like it ain nothing. Like it ain everything.

3.

The evening after the Transfer, Antoinette and Owen Arthur quarreled in Antoinette's bedroom. Eeona awoke from a nap of damp sheets and went to squash her tender ear against the door that linked her room to her mother's. Miss Lady, who knew everything, came in and slapped Eeona's behind and sent her off — though Miss Lady stayed to listen herself.

Papa's voice was loud and insistent. Mama's voice was soft and appeasing. This is how they always fought.

28

"Nettie, I understand you snubbed the Baskervilles because they said they are sailing for New York."

"I did not snub them, Mr. Bradshaw."

"Is it that you are jealous?"

"Please excuse me for repeating, but I did not snub them."

"Madame Bradshaw, it has become clear that we cannot leave the sea. It is my business. Our livelihood."

"What business, Mr. Bradshaw? Tell me. How exactly is the business going? Or am I merely a woman and so therefore unable to understand that there will be no real business without the rum . . ."

"Antoinette. Please. I am a ship captain. This is the sea I know. What would you have me do on the mainland?"

"It is not that I am interested in moving per se, Mr. Bradshaw."

"Madame Bradshaw?"

"I am only concerned that those of us who do not move to the Continent still be allowed access to the niceties of our new country. Are we not to be American citizens?"

"Yes, of course. In time."

"American women may vote. Here, our men will be less than women even. Here no one will be able to vote at all. But if we are

29

on the mainland, we will vote, we will gain the things we desire, fabrics of silk or lace . . ."

"Now, Madame Bradshaw, you have just said that you don't need to be in America. You are losing your logic. You are going into one of your episodes."

"You will not speak to me like that! I am not a small girl. I've carried how many of your children in my womb as they hurried toward death? I don't want us to move permanently. It is only that I had hoped we would have access to the Negro artists and actors of New York, and perhaps I could contribute my dresses for the stage and perhaps Eeona might take singing lessons like a proper lady. We need not live there forever, but we must do what we can to bring these things here. You are a ship captain. Is this not in your power, Owen . . ."

"Hush, Nettie! What is this nonsense about Negroes? Your episodes are making you ramble. You speak of our child, but your influence is causing her to have your same wildness. She is becoming bold, going beyond herself."

"What are you saying?"

"What am I saying?" he shouted, gathering himself. "I am saying that you must forget this. We must first demonstrate good character."

"Good character? Did America not look us in the mouth before the buy?"

"Stop this, Antoinette. Stop this now. As a St. Thomas seaman I stand to benefit greatly from this transfer of nations. Can you not see already how all the other islanders are coming here? It is like when they built the canal. Half of St. Thomas went because Panama was the promised land. Now we are the promised land."

"I don't want to be half an American. I want full and free access. You knew I wanted this when we married. You even said then . . ."

"You mustn't believe all the things you are told." He shook his head, but softened when he saw his wife's desperate face. "Oh, Nettie. Negro theater? That is an American thing. We Bradshaws are British and Danish for goodness' sake."

"We're hardly British or Danish, Owen." And now she glided her hand along her own brown arm. They were not arguing anymore about leaving or voting or access to the arts. They were having the argument they always had. She would align herself with whomever would have her. She had heard that there were rich people of all complexions in

31

America, ones who might fall for her fashions and not worry about her pauper personal history.

It was like this when she was having one of her episodes. The episodes were a state where she wanted and hungered and that took many slights of magic to calm. The doctor said it was a nervousness brought on by the pregnancies and miscarriages. A woman's wildness.

But instead of appeasing her, Owen switched off his charm to face her challenge. "Go back to Anegada where I found you, Antoinette Stemme. That dry atoll where there are more lobsters than people. Go marry your fisherman instead of this ship captain. Maybe he will row you to America."

"My mother married a fisherman, Owen Arthur. It would do you well to be careful with your words."

"Your mother is dead, Antoinette, and so is your fisherman father. I am the man of this family and we will become American by staying right here on the island. With or without your consent."

"I am your wife. From whom else do you seek consent?"

"Please, Nettie. You want too much. You always want to go and go. You are a lady. You must be still. Consider your condition . . ."

"Is there someone else to whom you have committed to staying near? Someone else keeping us away from moving or visiting even?"

Then something broke. Not a dainty glass, but an entire dresser crashed to the floor and the photographic portrait of the couple on their wedding day on top of it. Owen Arthur Bradshaw streamed downstairs and he called for Mr. Lyte, the Frenchy groundsman who was also their fisherman, to bring him a glass of rum. This is how the husband and wife always ended their bouts. Antoinette would then call for Eeona, who would go to her. And Antoinette would say, "I shall make you a skirt of linen. Be still. Be my doll."

But when baby Anette comes, it will be different yet again. By the time Anette is old enough to know why Papa and Mama are fighting, there will be no more fighting between Papa and Mama. Because there will be no more Papa and Mama at all. Then Anette will be the sister who muddies the family water, just like a wave overtaking a mound of loose sand.

4.

Madame Antoinette S. Bradshaw was still early in her pregnancy. It was also early, only weeks, into Americanness. Antoinette was the type of woman who only became ill when lying in the morning sun. It was an irony, of course, that a woman who had thrown away so many babies was a woman whose pregnancies were relatively sweet journeys. Antoinette Bradshaw looked the most lovely when she was pregnant. Her hair did not fall out. Her nose did not spread. Her feet did not swell. Her breasts did not burn and her back did not ache. She did not lose her bladder. None of these things that average women experienced. Instead she became queasy in sunlight, and, as if she were regressing, she would seem spritely and fresh-faced, like a girl.

Normally, her bleeding was clockwork. To the day, to the hour. And that was how she knew, the morning of the family leisure voyage, to take her special bush tea so the not-yet-baby would wash out of her. Any sickness that came as a result, she would blame on the sea. The voyage was a husband's kind of penance, a slight giving in. *The Homecoming* would not take them to America, but Owen was the ship's captain and he could take them somewhere, take them to the British islands and the Spanish. A bit of adventure to calm his wild wife. He hoped the child in her might be a son. But now Antoinette was on the ship and her blood was coming. She stood and looked for her living daughter.

Eeona herself had only just started to bleed, and Antoinette had decided that if Eeona did not pitch away her virginity, for she was a girl too aware of her beauty, they would marry her off early. Antoinette and Owen Arthur had already been bickering about sending the child away. Antoinette thought the neighboring British Virgin Islands would be a good place for a young lady's education or perhaps Puerto Rico, where Antoinette herself had attended finishing school. But strangely Owen had mentioned Britain or Denmark, maybe even America, and though Nettie fancied his ideas, she didn't quite understand her husband's desire to send their daughter so far away. Especially without them. In the meantime, the girl needed womanly education — one gained from an elder woman kin. For Antoinette, the most vital lesson of womanhood was knowing how to rid yourself of an unwanted child before it became a child.

"Make haste," Antoinette snapped. The child was so fast with her father.

Eeona had been sitting on a sack of sugar that was about her size. This was not a work sailing trip, so the ship was not stocked with all the ship hands and the livestock to feed the ship hands. Eeona had seen the ship like that. She had also seen the ship empty with no one but herself and her father. She liked it both those ways. She did not like it now, with her mother at her father's side. Though Eeona did like that the kitchenhand and the deckhand stared at her until the ship matron would tug them by their aprons into the bowels of the ship.

Her father had taught her to swim in the open ocean. And now Eeona wanted to glide naked in that very sea and then collapse into her father's arms. But not with her mother around. Eeona hadn't given any thought to things like how she would bathe with her mother here. If she had, she would have begged to stay home, keep the villa with Miss Lady. They had not had a family sail since Eeona had begun puberty, since her secret had appeared.

On this trip they would port up at many small islands, lounge on the beaches, and pay visits. Antoinette's elder cousin, who taught French in the neighboring British island of Tortola, would host them for a week. She would teach young Eeona some smart things to say in that lovely language. An old comrade of Owen's would meet them in Fajardo, at the tip of Puerto Rico. Puerto Rico was where Owen had sent Antoinette during their engagement, so she could learn to serve tea and coffee, to sit like a lady. These visits were now exploratory, for perhaps Eeona would end up in one or the other. They were also places Antoinette knew and loved, but they would not visit the place she knew and loved best, which was Anegada. The place where she had learned to walk and talk and swim — the place where she was born. The place where she had had her first kiss and first love. It was just there, but they didn't sail in that direction. It was true that her parents were already dead. But it was also true that the lobsterman she had almost married was quite alive. That man had promised Antoinette a life of labor and love, but Owen Arthur had promised her leisure and liberty. Since making her vows to the ship captain, Antoinette didn't dare visit, for she knew the danger of old fire sticks, how quickly they alight. Owen, wise, never offered to bring her when he docked there. They were sailing elsewhere.

Now Antoinette called to the deckhand to lower the rowboat. Where was Eeona? The mother snapped her fingers and Eeona slugged over. "My child, stop being molasses." Eeona climbed into the rowboat with her mother, and they were lowered down toward the sea.

They rocked unsteadily and Antoinette opened her arms to Eeona, who seemed unafraid. "Balance yourself," Antoinette said into Eeona's ear as their rowboat slapped onto the sea. Antoinette undressed herself then looked at her daughter. "You, as well."

The child looked around. There was *The Homecoming* looming large beside them. There was the ocean around her. She should swim away. She was a very good swimmer, which was extraordinary in these islands, especially for a girl. She should call to her father. She should tell Mama Antoinette that she was ill and must go back up. That she had her monthly period and so should not be so close to water for fear of sharks. Miss Lady had given her this warning, but her mother, an Anegada woman and so a seawoman herself, didn't believe in those fearful excuses. Eeona couldn't think fast enough. "May I wash your hair, Mama?" The child stroked her own hair as though it were a pet. This kind of distraction worked on her papa.

"No, Eeona. My moon is full now." Antoinette paused. "Right now." And then the blood, the almost-baby, began to drain out of her.

Though Eeona also bled, it was not with the command her mother seemed to have. Her bleeding came unexpectedly and left unexpectedly and was generally a nuisance. She stared at her mother with awe. She squeezed her thighs together, to hold her own brightness in.

Antoinette's face was set and cold as she pressed the rags between her own legs. Readying for the gurgle and the pulp. "Bleeding is not a curse," she said to her daughter. "It is a blessing." She checked the cloths and pressed them to herself again. "But it is only a blessing if you own it."

Eeona wanted to be brave. So she began to unbutton her dress. Beneath her dress Eeona was wearing pantaloons that puffed around her hips. She held her breath as she took those off. Then she waited for her mother to look at her.

"Eeona," Antoinette said, "soon you will have desires . . ." It was the beginning of a lesson. But Eeona would not sit. Instead she pushed her pelvis out.

Antoinette looked. She had been trained to be a lady, so she knew how to retain her composure. Now she simply sucked in air. Then she reached out her hand to touch her daughter. She wasn't quite sure of what she was seeing.

Here was Eeona's secret: The hair growing between her legs wasn't brown and bushy like her mother's. It wasn't black and wiry like Miss Lady's. It was gray and thin. Like an old lady's. Like the little wisps at Papa's temples. In Eeona's mind they were from Papa. Their private secret in her secret private place. No one had seen, except Papa. He had told her then that it meant wisdom, just before they'd stood on the ledge of *The Homecoming* together like castaways and dived into the sea.

"Let me see," Antoinette now said sternly. "Let me see what is wrong." *Perhaps it was just ash,* the mother thought madly, as though the daughter might be smoldering in her intimate places. But no, the gray color did not come off in Antoinette's hands.

Eeona sucked in her own breath. Since she could remember, only her father had ever touched her there.

Mama Antoinette forgot her own body. She pitched her blood-spotted cloths into the sea and scooped seawater into buckets.

With fresh rags she rubbed a log of soap into suds. She spread Eeona's legs and began to wash her there. "What have you done, Eeona? Why did this happen?" She dipped the cloth into the bucket again. Eeona said nothing. Perhaps her mother would get the gray off. The girl didn't want it gray, despite what Papa said. She wanted hers dark like Mama's or Miss Lady's. She also wondered.

Oh, but she knew. She knew. She had liked it when Papa kissed her there. She knew she shouldn't, but she had. Now, she would shrivel into an old lady all over. Or she would become plump at the belly — forever pregnant like Mama. Eeona just stood there as Antoinette scrubbed harder. Eeona wanted to tell Mama that the scrubbing hurt, but she didn't. The cloths Antoinette had cast out were gone, but Eeona stared at the spot where they had settled into the sea as her mother went at her as if Eeona were the deck of a boat.

Eeona's skin became raw until the color that came on the cloth was the dark rust of blood. Antoinette had forgotten her own bleeding, which had slowed, which had stopped, the child inside her no longer in danger.

"This cannot be real," Antoinette whispered softly. The hair had not revealed itself to be brown or black or even a saving yellow.

Instead, the hair between Eeona's legs now glittered clean like silver and Eeona felt her mother's breath on her like a lover's. Now Eeona found the silver curiously beautiful, but she knew she should be ashamed of this thought. She held her breath and tried to drown the feeling. And in a way this is how she would be for long after. Either trying to bury herself under a foot of earth or trying to burst free from under a foot of water.

Above them on the deck was the ship's matron. At this moment her job was to guard this side of the boat so that Madame Bradshaw and Miss Bradshaw could bathe without the men stealing a peek at them from the deck. Now Owen Arthur approached and looked to walk past her. "Captain, the ladies are bathing."

He nodded and stepped forward.

"Captain."

The matron was not large, but she was wiry and younger than Captain Bradshaw, who stepped again.

"Captain, the women," the matron said, this time sternly as though she was not speaking to the captain at all.

Owen cleared his throat. "And whose women are bathing?" The matron looked at the captain. "Your women, sir," she answered, understanding the intention of his question. He nodded and walked around her. She turned to see him go. He spoke back to her, without turning: "Keep your post." The command was gentle and gruff at the same time. The matron turned, so that now she was guarding Mr. Bradshaw as well.

Owen leaned over and peered down at his wife and daughter, the ship on one side of them, the sea on the other. His eyes filled with tears. "Christ Lord," he whispered, and did not feel it was in vain. He wanted to call to his women. He wanted them to look up so he could see his wife's breasts out in the open like this. So he could witness Eeona's tight belly.

Owen Arthur had not, after all, won the lucrative sugar shipping deal with Mr. Lovernkrandt. Instead, with liquor soon illegal, Captain Bradshaw had squeezed out some hauls of strange things — a shipping of shoes from Santo Domingo, bull bones from Ponce, oil in barrels from Port-of-Spain — the bones being his most frequent cargo. For now, his only faith was his love for his wife and daughter. But he knew there was

43

something wicked in his wanting to see even a harmless part of his daughter's body in the same way he wanted to see his wife's.

But perhaps it was not Eeona whom he lusted for at all. Antoinette, with her sewing, was not often obliging. Perhaps he just needed to visit Rebekah more often. Mrs. Rebekah McKenzie, the piano teacher and market lady. Her husband, a Navy man, had disappeared for good a few months ago. The meté was that Rebekah had disappeared him.

Owen had been with Rebekah at times when her husband shipped out. He remembered how being with Rebekah had been like walking on the land after a month at sea. He'd even bought her the piano. It was made in Florida, and he'd picked it up on a haul to San Juan. But now, watching his daughter and wife, Owen felt somewhat calmed. He'd been with Rebekah recently. That time he'd tried to claim her. "Mine," he'd said to her open legs, "Mine" to the smooth of her shoulder. He could do that. Own a woman. Look how easily he'd tugged Antoinette from that lobsterman on Anegada. Now he would own a woman who might bear a son for him, damn the American law and its rule of legitimacy.

He looked down at the little boat one last

time. He could see the bodies
and daughter against each o
courtesans, then a glint of silver.

Down below, in the small boa
little to separate her from the ocea
had stopped crying. Now she loo... nard
at her mother and spoke harder. "Stop,
Mama." Antoinette finally ceased but her
alarm solidified. Now the women faced each
other, hard as mountains.

5.

EEONA

My mother was jealous of me. Mama would
often take me to her rooms where there was
a mirror. She would bid me sit up straight
beside her before the looking glass. She
peered from my face to her own as if searching my face for a history of herself. She was
very pretty, but I was the more lovely. I say
that only because it was a fact.

My mother also feared for me. She feared
that I would become a woman who depended on her beauty and so did not de-
velop her skills and talents. It was not
enough to be beautiful, she said. A woman
must be able to create beauty. Mama made
sure I learned to weave straw, sew clothes,
and crochet bags. These were all skills that

I do believe, however, that Mama's stories also had their power. Their telling was also a skill, albeit one only displayed for me. The story of the Duene was used to warn me. If a woman was not self-possessed, she was in danger of the wildness. I knew my mother suffered from this. Episodes, we called them. Papa described the episodes as a bit of rebellion and impetuousness. My mother, as everyone knew, had run away from her island of Anegada to marry my father. She had barely known Papa. Mama had wild and wandering tendencies. I always knew I had the same.

In order to tell her story, Mama would sit in her rocking chair. It was a fine rocker, made by hand from a strong stick of mahogany. It was one of the things I was most sorry to see go when the drowned lands took my father. In the big drawing room, lamps would flicker about us. Our shadows would reach long behind our backs. Often, Miss Lady stood over me braiding my hair for bed. My father would sip a short glass of rum and watch my hair being tamed. I have always known that my real skill is my own beauty, despite what Mama said.

When Mama began to tell a story, Papa

would rise and take a turn around the room. This would be terribly distracting to me. The sound of his sipping his drink made me want to place my own finger in his mouth. Now that I understand envy, I understand that perhaps he was jealous of this time that Mama had with me. With his free hand Papa would stroke his earlobe. When on his stroll, he would arrive at the door and lean against the chest where Mama displayed her treasured porcelain figurines. Then he would slip out of the room.

Mama never asked if I wanted to hear a story. She would be unassumingly sewing an accent onto a dress and then she would look up at me. She began with the female Duene who live in the sea of the Anegada Passage. They sink ships with their singing. They are tall with thin angular legs that push like fish through the water. On parts of their bodies they have scales the colours of precious metal. This hides a bit of their bursting beauty when they come to land.

The men live only on the land of our sister island, St. Croix. The males are as chiseled as stones and as brown as bark. They wait on the land for the mating season when the women come to them. The Duene men live mostly in Frederiksted, where the inkberry trees grow wild and hide them. They do not swim. Sometimes Mama would say that the men hide extra legs in their breasts. That they are arachnids, like Anancy. Sometimes she would say that they hide wings in their shoulders, and that they fly.

There is only one thing the men and the women have in common. Their feet face backwards. This is so it is difficult for humans to track them. The Duene do not want us to follow them because they protect the wild things from our destruction. The women protect the sea. The men protect the land.

Mama said that even when you see the Duene you cannot tell which way they are going. They will seem to be running away from you just as they are rushing forwards to chop you down. Though the Duene will not harm humans who do not harm the land or the sea, it is best to avoid them because one does not always know when one is doing harm. The Duene have no mercy. They will drag you by your hair into the sea. They will pluck your extremities from your body as we pluck petals from a flower for love-me, love-me-not. The Duene do not love us. They love only themselves and the wildness, Mama said.

Here, she would pause in her sewing to

48

look directly at me. "The wildness is many things besides a gathering of trees or a pooling of water."

I came to understand that the wildness could be inside of me.

6.

Madame Antoinette Bradshaw, wife of Owen Arthur, mother of Eeona, was at the Lovernkrandt house for a ladies' tea party. Mrs. Liva Lovernkrandt, the wife of the former rum maker, had just returned from a month in America. At the tea she wore a large floppy hat made of what Mrs. Lovernkrandt called felt. Everyone had to lean forward to get a better view of her. She was also wearing a dress without a girdle, which caused her to resemble a sack of yams. Later the women would giggle at her behind her back. But not Antoinette.

"New York," Mrs. Lovernkrandt began, pausing to sip her tea, "is the classy capital of this new world." She rested her teacup into its saucer. "Look, ladies. Look at these classy fashions." She retrieved an armful of magazines and spread them out on her new coffee table. The other women hurriedly picked up their teacups to make room. The magazines were glossy, with bright colors.

The women on the covers wore lipstick that was red, and smiled with big straight teeth all showing. Their skin looked all one pale color, like a skinless Irish potato. They wore high heels. They exposed not just their ankles, but their entire calves, their entire knees. On one cover the words "Snag Mr. Right!" were written along the bottom. The model on that cover was displaying a little box held with a garter against her thigh. She was retrieving an actual cigarette out of the box. It looked like she might set the words on fire.

The women at tea leaned over the magazines but didn't touch them or open them. Mrs. Lovernkrandt leaned back and gave her guests her floppy gaze. She smiled, but with her mouth closed, more demure than the American women. Then she called for her own maid to bring out the "animal." It took two people. The maid carried it by one arm and the Lovernkrandt's man-about-the-house led it by the other. The ladies around the table gasped: "Oh my. Is it alive? Keep it away from me!" But Mrs. Lovernkrandt stood and walked up to the furry specimen. She slipped her arms into its body.

"Imagine!" she exclaimed. "A coat made from little soft animals. You feel like a Viking lady gliding across the Arctic. And you need one of these with how cold it is in New York City. Colder than Denmark, I'm sure."

The other women looked skeptical but Antoinette leaned forward. "What kind of animal is it?"

"Fur," said Mrs. Lovernkrandt, and she ran her hand down the front of the coat.

"What does a fur look like?"

Liva Lovernkrandt was ready for Antoinette. She knew it was Madame Bradshaw who would be the most curious, the most envious. "A mongoose, Antoinette. Just like a mongoose." But, oh dear, she was beginning to sweat underneath the coat. Liva slipped out of it and gestured for it to be taken away. "And they have shoes made of snake's skin and eyeglasses rimmed with the backs of turtles," she continued, now dabbing her perspiring brow with a handkerchief. "Antoinette, you can only dream. Perhaps next time I depart, I should take the gloves you embroidered for me."

The other women turned to nibble the imported digestive crackers and sip the tea, for they were all aware that Antoinette Bradshaw had never been to America, and wouldn't it be something if her gloves got there and she never did? But Antoinette's mind was already dreaming. Oh, it was

51

unfair that women could dream at all. There she was, the very Madame Antoinette Bradshaw, wondering what it would take to create coats of mongoose hair. Would American women wear that? Might she convince Liva Lovernkrandt to take more than one pair of gloves, perhaps a chest of gloves, to give as gifts to stylish New York ladies? The gloves might serve as a kind of announcement. Or perhaps Antoinette and Owen would, after all, send Eeona to the States for a fancy finishing school. Antoinette would insist, absolutely insist, on accompanying her daughter. Then Nettie would invent a reason to stay for a while. First, she must master mongoose coats. Then the women who wore her gloves would commission her. Later she would make garters rimmed with the backs of sea turtles. Ones that every woman of class would want to wrap around her thigh. Now Antoinette looked down at the woman on the magazine, the one ready to blaze. Mr. Right was not the only thing worth snagging. When Nettie left the Lovernkrandt house, she went to take the hot-pepper tea so this damn hardheaded baby would finally burn out of her.

7.

ANETTE

Let me tell you something I know about Anegada. Because I learn plenty somethings with this hard head of mine. I don't remember nothing of my life before I turn four years old. But I don't need memory. A historian, that's me after all. I ain never been Anegada, but I know enough.

In all my years I have never want to chase a child. I had want every child I ever conceive. But not every woman have that in she. I can't speak for those women. But I know that Anegada wasn't no place to do nothing except make love. I mean, you know the place? You seen even a postcard of Anegada? It too pretty. Like heaven and hell marry up and birth all the beauty goodness and badness could possibly make. You hearing me? When you raise up in that place, like how Mama had raise up in that place, you only know about beauty and how to make it. And lovemaking is a beauty making.

So it ain nothing to imagine that Antoinette Stemme had come pregnant when she young. Probably for a nice boy, a lobster fisherman, who have legs like bronze. And if this is so, you can't blame she. Everybody

53

loving and beautifying and the man sweet and tender. Besides they have maybe fifteen girls and fifteen boys on the whole island. Of course, they going to meet up and mix up and mate up. And all of them is the most beautiful people you ever dream.

And we could just imagine what is they life back then. Fishing is life. Eating lobster twice a day is life. Swimming is life. That sound like leisure for any of we in the big city of Charlotte Amalie, St. Thomas. But for them then? No. Because there ain no hospital in Anegada. No doctors. If you deading, you going to dead. Can't blame nobody. No police, no lawyers, no court. Because that's the place. Perfection but with a hole in the middle. Is not a island really. Is a atoll. You listening?

So when a young captain get he young ship catch on the coral . . . what? Even if we just making this story up, we could easy say that is like the Anegada girl named Antoinette is a siren. And her mother and father love she like the land and they want the best for she. They done realize the girl have vision for she self beyond what the atoll know how to manage. So they convince the captain, and it don't take much for the young captain Bradshaw. Sure, he know that she have the other boy baby in she body. But the girl sweeter than lobster. The captain, he know 'bout bush. He the kind of man know all about woman things. Swift as anything captain and girl wash that other man baby away. The captain ain know that he teach his wife the very thing she going use against him for the entirety of they marriage.

So he gone with her. Love her till the day he dead, but also he own her in a way. Because of what he could make her do. Leave her fiancé. Get rid the not-yet-baby. Leave her Anegada land and never return.

I ain saying this is the way it happen with my parents. This ain true history. I just saying that given what we know about the place and about the time, my version seem to have a truth somewhere. Is just a story I telling, but put it in your glass and drink it.

8.

Antoinette lay in bed and knew she was awake. Her eyes wanted to open but she resisted. She knew what would happen. Instead, she lay with her arms spread wide open as though she were about to scoop up a child. Her legs spread wide as though to take a lover. Both these postures were the problem. Even though her eyes were closed, even though the mosquito nettings draped down, tenting the bed, the orange glow of the sunshine still seeped through her eyelids. She could hear the sea outside the window. She could hear the eager humming of the mosquitoes just outside the net.

Antoinette curled her fingers into a fist. That is how small the child inside her was now. She had bled red blood and still the child, no bigger than her fist, remained. She must win this one. This one was stubborn, but she must win. There was already one child. She'd done that — given Owen the girl. Enough.

You see, Antoinette had vision. With another child she would surely lose herself. How did other women do it? Seven children. Twelve children. Even her mother, married to her fisherman on that tiny atoll, had had only her.

And just then, as Antoinette thought of her dead parents and the island of Anegada where the sun set at her feet, her eyes fluttered open before she could stop. The light hit her full-on. The nausea that came was fast and hard. She raked the netting aside and leaned over the chamber pot. She pitched out last night's supper, now reddish, even though they'd had mutton with mint jelly and fungi with avocado pear. She flopped back onto the bed, breathing hard. Her eyes slit, half open, letting the sun come at her gently now.

She was married well, despite her brownness and meager upbringing. She had a daughter and a house and a maid-cook. She had a man-about-the-house who also brought fish to their door. And they were all Americans now. They would be allowed American passports someday soon. Eeona was growing up fine, just fine. Owen had taken a mistress, but what landed man did not have an outside woman? Genteel women such as Madame Bradshaw were supposed to be still. Perhaps Antoinette Bradshaw was just selfish.

But Antoinette made a fist again. This time she raised the fist into the air and slammed it down into the soft of her belly. She cried out. But she did it again. She cried out again but still she struck herself again and then again. Suddenly Miss Lady was at the door, knocking and knowing. "Madame Bradshaw. I could come in? You having the illness?"

Madame Bradshaw was infamous for how quickly she could lose a baby. Bed rest, the doctor had said when she was carrying the one after Eeona. But she lost that one despite the bed. She'd drowned that one in her womb actually, but who could prove that? Fresh sea breeze, the doctor had said for the next, but Antoinette had pitched that one, too. Then bed *and* fresh air he had said, so Antoinette had been made to stay in bed all day and all night with the windows flung open. That baby made it to the quickening. But then stilled. Was stilled.

"I'm fine," Antoinette called to Miss Lady, but Miss Lady flowed in anyway. She had tea and bread, which she left on the nightstand. She gave Madame Bradshaw a hard look. "This one must be a girl. Stubborn," she said, before taking away the chamber pot. Antoinette narrowed her eyes. Miss Lady knew Antoinette had other plans besides children. But Sheila Ladyinga could at least pretend as though she didn't know — that would be more proper. She must be on Owen's side, as the women in this household always would be. Antoinette leaned up on her elbow. And what was in this tea? Likely something to make this baby strong. Antoinette stopped drinking the tea. The bread was malleable. She ate and dreamed.

She daydreamed of her and her husband walking around the milk-and-honey streets of New York City in bright green iguana-skin shoes. But slowly it came to Antoinette that she had not heard Owen Arthur come in last night. Perhaps he had been with his tart. The witch, that obeah woman, Rebekah. Rebekah who could have baby after baby after baby and still play that piano and still sell lime and mesple in the market. A low-class market woman who had simply married well and whose husband had left her. But not Antoinette. She might have entrepreneurial dreams but she would not lower Bradshaw as Rebekah had lowered the McKenzie name. True, the McKenzie name was not as high as Bradshaw to begin with. The McKenzie men married well, but there wasn't a ship captain among them. Either way, Antoinette's endeavors would cause her family to rise, not recede.

Antoinette sat up and went to her writing table. She wrote a note telling Liva Lovernkrandt that she was coming straightaway to pay a visit to discuss private business matters. She called for Miss Lady to deliver it. Sheila Ladyinga could read; Antoinette would not have had a maid who could not. So Miss Lady could be trusted to knife open the note and believe that indeed Madame Bradshaw was going to Mrs. Lovernkrandt's just now. And Miss Lady could be trusted to relay this false information to Owen if questioned. Madame Bradshaw was not going to the Lovernkrandts' immediately. She was going to that very Rebekah McKenzie. Owen's witch woman.

9.

In the market Antoinette Bradshaw took her time through the sugar apples and the hot peppers. When a lady of a fancy house, even a fancy house in not fancy Frenchtown, came to the market, she was usually accompanied by her maid or daughter. But here was Madame Bradshaw, mistress of Villa by the Sea, wife of Captain Owen Arthur Bradshaw, wandering calmly through the open-air bungalow by herself. Carrying only a little basket. One that might hold some lime, some guava — not much more. The St. Thomas market was not the sprawling thing one could find on the big islands of the Caribbean. Here there might be two dozen women selling produce. Half a dozen men selling cane. Here the walking market women, their baskets on their heads, called out to Antoinette by name. "Best plantains, Mada Bradshaw. Ready for frying. You don't want fry, I have ones for boil."

As she eased through the market, Antoinette was aware of where Rebekah was and Rebekah was aware of her. Women who have a man between them always are. Even in the crowded market, filled with the aggressive selling of provisions and the passive selling of sugar, Rebekah and Antoinette had already seen each other and kept each other firm in the corner of an eye. But Antoinette took her time. It was a hot day. She refused to break out in a sweat.

Many of the market women sat beside their produce, a linen cloth spread beneath them and their wares. The buyers looked down on these women, and when they turned away, the market women had to witness the retreating backsides. But not Rebekah McKenzie. Rebekah had a table. One that sat in her little yard at night and that her sons hauled out to the market every morning. Rebekah sat behind her table in an actual chair, more like a privileged bank clerk than a market woman. When Antoinette reached Rebekah's table, Rebekah said to her what she had been saying to everyone else: "You must buy some lime if you want mesple. Today, lime marry to mesple."

"I know quite well who is married to whom."

Rebekah smiled. "Of course, Madame Bradshaw. Is me does forget sometimes."

"Do your best to remember, Miss McKenzie." It wasn't true that she was *Miss*

61

McKenzie. Rebekah had married Benjamin McKenzie. But her husband was dead or at least he was like dead — run away on a naval ship or dead in a Puerto Rican rain forest, so the stories poured. But Rebekah was not like Antoinette. Rebekah was a woman who managed to do as she pleased. Even though her husband's brothers did not drop a dime and did not drop in for visits, they could not take away what she had gained. She had the McKenzie house. She had the McKenzie marriage. Her sons had the McKenzie name.

In the same yard where Rebekah stored her table, she also grew her fruit. She sold what she didn't use in the market. She played her piano in her parlor. She took in pupils, daughters of the wealthy, though never the daughters of men she slept with, which meant not Madame Bradshaw's daughter. Besides, Rebekah loved the market. Loved the noise and the interaction. Loved the power. Loved using the power she had. In the market she was more than a woman selling lime and mesple. She was a doctor, a kind of doctor, and her specialty was women problems.

She had a power that came from all those people who had made Owen Arthur Bradshaw, all those people who made all of us.

Knowledge of the mustard from Scandinavia. Knowledge of the nutmeg from West Africa. Knowledge of the sesame from China. Knowledge of the sea grape from the Arawak. So Rebekah could do things. She could make the blood in your body course saltwater — burn you from the inside out. Erode your womb as if it were tin until the eggs inside rattled like a beggar shaking a cup. She could make a stingy husband's pockets turn to dust, his fingernails turn to dust, then his mind slowly turn until the coin crumbled out of his ears. She could get a woman from St. Thomas to New York City safely, even on a drowning ship. Every woman on island knew what Rebekah McKenzie could do. Of course, she could get rid of what Antoinette wanted riddance from.

"I need to lose a little fruit." Antoinette spoke quietly and looked the other way.

"Did you try the mash of dirt with nutmeg and pepper sauce? That worked before."

"Nothing turns this fruit into juice." Antoinette rolled one of Rebekah's limes around in her hand.

Rebekah made change for someone else and passed that person a bag of limes and mesple. "Try the tea with soursop and sea grape. Follow with a soak in scalding salted water."

"This is a hard lime." She looked at Rebekah now. She leaned over the table, squeezing the lime she now held in her hand. "Don't make me beg, sister." For, of course, that is what they were. Women loving the same man. They had this in common, like two daughters sharing one father.

Rebekah looked at Antoinette's hands, which were now sticky with sour pulp. "I'll see you this evening." Then she passed Antoinette the sweetest mesple on her table.

Oh, but what happened that evening was not enough because nothing would be enough. Afterward, Antoinette lay in her own bed at Villa by the Sea. She had gone to visit the Lovernkrandts for just a brief visit to chat with Liva about the possibilities of iguana shoes and mongoose stoles. Then she'd gone to Rebekah's. Rebekah had put her hand on Antoinette's stomach and then pulled it away as though she were burnt.

Now it was night and Antoinette lay in her bed, but this time she was not alone. The doctor had come. Not because Antoinette had lost the baby. But because Antoinette had walked the whole way home from

Rebekah's, forgetting her sidesaddled mule tied up outside of the McKenzie house where everyone would know. Antoinette had walked up the grand stairs to her own house, then turned and flung herself down. But Antoinette didn't even twist her ankle. She didn't even retain a bruise. Nothing at all happened to the baby.

But the madame of the house flinging herself down her own steps was dangerous enough. So the doctor had been summoned and the pregnancy Antoinette was trying to keep from the world was discovered and announced. This doctor was the same one who had prescribed bed rest before and salt air after, then both. Now he prescribed the best-worst thing of all: Someone must be with Madame Bradshaw at all times. And while Madame Bradshaw slept, someone must be more than near her; someone must be touching her. She needed the feeling of another heartbeat, of another pulse, the doctor said. This would calm her nervous episodes and keep her and the baby alive.

So that night Owen Arthur stayed with his wife and did not go to his mistress or out with his daughter. He stayed in the bed with his wife and held her close to his chest so she could feel his heartbeat. In the past he had resisted touching her even in the earliest stages of pregnancy for fear of her miscarrying. But in truth he loved how nymphetish her body became when with child, as though she became a child herself.

Now Antoinette rested against his chest. His bare chest, naked of any hair as it had always been. Antoinette felt she would surely lose everything now. Everything, except perhaps her man. Fine, then. She would relinquish. Because at least in this she had bested someone. Blasted Rebekah, who couldn't even help her get rid of the child.

But Antoinette was not entirely right. Rebekah was also in her own house that night. The house with the red shutters and the piano Owen had bought. Her sons were asleep, except for the one in her belly. She was also carrying Owen's child. In this, she was not bested by Antoinette after all. Rebekah's husband had been gone for just under a year. Everyone would whisper that this new child could not be legitimate. Rebekah, too, had tried to lose the baby — for its own sake. But even Rebekah's stews and teas and prayers had not worked. And then when she had seen Antoinette she knew why.

10.

"I spit up blood," Antoinette had said when she'd gone to Rebekah looking for obeah. "When I vomit, it's always maroon." Rebekah had touched Antoinette's belly. Rebekah's hand felt smooth and cool. But then the obeah woman had snatched her hand away and smacked her own chest in surprise.

"Fine," Rebekah said. "Fine. You leave me no choice, woman." But she wasn't speaking to Antoinette. Rebekah was speaking to the spirit of the child who would become the redheaded woman. This redhead woman who would stain Rebekah's son's soul. Together those two children would be the whole awful story.

Rebekah went into her room. She removed her right boot. She gripped a piece of brown hair from her own ankle and plucked it out.

Antoinette took the strand of animal hair that Rebekah gave her.

"Put it under your tongue," Rebekah had directed.

Antoinette did not hesitate.

"Now we wait," Rebekah said.

The coarse hair rested under Antoinette's tongue. She waited for it to dissolve or grow legs and crawl out of her mouth. She listened to the sounds of people passing and calling for each other.

"Anything?"

Antoinette shook her head.

"Give it."

Antoinette slipped the hair out of her mouth. It was slimy, but it was also silver now. Was that the obeah? Antoinette thought on her living daughter, on Eeona's silver, and wondered what this might all mean. Would Antoinette go home, feel the familiar cramps, and then see the child, a stream of blood and silver and nothing more, pour out of her? Would some curse be transferred to Eeona?

Rebekah looked at her own hair in Antoinette's palm. She was alarmed by its sparkle. This has never happened before. But she knew it meant something bad for both her and Antoinette. This one was old, ancient.

"This child will kill you before you kill her."

"Why? I tell it not to come. This child is disobeying me already."

Rebekah turned away. She reached into her bosom for the money Antoinette had given her. She knew Madame Bradshaw's name was Antoinette, though she would never call her that. Rebekah even knew that Owen Arthur called Madame Bradshaw

"Nettie," for he had called Rebekah that more than once in the storms of their lovemaking. "Madame Bradshaw, you won't be mother to this one."

11.

Every night for the next many months, young Eeona was made to lie all night in her own bed, which was now on the other side of the house. The room beside Mama's was being readied for the new baby. Eeona lay alone and seethed. She was old enough, a marriageable age herself, to know better. But she was livid that she and her father had not swum together at night for so long. They had not danced on the balcony at dusk for so long. He had not taken her for walks at dawn for so long. All that time he now gave to Mama. "Your mother is the madame of this house," he had said to her when she'd searched for him that first lonely evening. "I have to be with her in this time of need." The resentment grew in Eeona's own body like a tumor, or like a child.

Antoinette's stomach grew like a continent. Owen stayed beside her, as the doctor ordered. Despite desiring her early expectant body, he had never made love to his wife when he knew she was pregnant. He always feared losing the child. Besides, if Antoinette ever made it to a rounding in the belly she would no longer seem as nubile to him as in the first months of her condition. This is the stage when Owen had always desired the narrowness of his daughter's body and so would go elsewhere to relieve himself. But now Rebekah was pregnant, too. Nothing narrow there. He had been ordered to stay with Nettie and he wanted to stay. Perhaps this might be the hoped-for boy in her womb. So now the husband and wife made love, for the doctor had prescribed this as well. She was large as a ship, and Owen steered like her captain. He found he enjoyed the new swelling and the heat that spread inside. Owen never muttered Rebekah's name when making love to his wife. "I own her" was mantra'd in his head, but he never let that escape either.

The one time Antoinette went to the market that season, Eeona and Miss Lady both went with her. But she didn't go again until the baby was born. For that one time Nettie had seen Rebekah, selling sweet pepper and nutmeg. And Nettie had seen Rebekah's own slope of belly, just a bit larger than Antoinette's. Madame Bradshaw had not known about the other pregnancy.

For fear of causing more nervous episodes in the madame, no one had even let the meté slip. But now Antoinette knew what had happened. She had not won out over Rebekah. They were both in this together.

The morning that Antoinette finally felt the steady contractions, Owen Arthur was inside her. She moaned and he, mistaken, thrust harder. She let him finish because she was a good wife, after all. When he slumped beside her, she turned to face him. "You made the baby come."

There in the bed, it felt like the Earth was pounding out of her. When the baby did come, it wailed as though on fire, and its hair was red as lobster. Antoinette looked the child in the face. "Oh," she said. "If I had known it would be you . . ." The child was red all over. Her lobsterness reminded Antoinette of a time before nannies and maids and a husband with a ship. Reminded her of Anegada. So she gave the baby a trick name.

When Owen came in, Antoinette allowed him to take their daughter. Owen held the child, not so disappointed at her femaleness as he had thought he might be. Instead, he wondered if this one would help diffuse the dangerous love he had for the other. He thought of a name like Francesca or Liberia

71

that might give the girl some freedom. But Antoinette spoke clearly. "I've named her Anette. After me." Instead of a middle name, Antoinette had Stemme, her maiden family name, put on the baby's birth certificate. Naming is a parent's first sorcery.

She gave her breast to Anette. But the red-haired baby gnawed at her mother instead of sucking. Though Antoinette dabbed her breasts with a soothing salve, her nipples still cracked and bled. So raw, they looked like the inside of a snapper fish. Antoinette, determined as ever, thrust the nipple into the child's mouth and they cried together.

It might be said that Anette clamped on because she knew her mother would go. She didn't even get a chance to hold on to her father. Owen Arthur didn't even leave Anette anything when he left. Not even a piece of land. That was what every island man knew he should leave. For in the beginning there is the water but in the end there is only the dirt. Owen left his wife and children nothing but the sea.

12.

EEONA

It was I who corrected Anette's English, for even as a child she spoke like a Frenchy. It is true that my hair was dark and thick and full of vinelike curls, but it was I who tamed her picky hair with the burning hot comb. I was a well-bred girl. I did not have to go to Puerto Rico for finishing school, as Mama had to when she married Papa.

After Anette was born, there was an entire week where it was only Papa and I at the dining table. He passed me each dish. He conversed about his business with me. He openly expressed his troubles with the ship itself, which was aging, and with the shipping, which was tedious and lacking in decent profit. I sipped from his glass of prohibited rum. I was the mistress of Villa by the Sea those days. Papa smiled and said that I had a head for running things and that I would make a fine madame.

Even after Mama was recovered, it was I whom Papa escorted down Main Street during holidays and holy days. Mama stayed home with baby Anette and pretended she did not care. I wore the gloves Mama made for me and I would proffer my gloved hand, as many mouths trembled and leaked saliva when they kissed it. Little girls would follow me, caressing the skirt of my frocks, hoping that touching even my clothing would grant them any bit of my beauty. I believe Mama was greatly bothered by this all.

Mama and baby Anette joined Papa and me for the Anglican church service. Still, I stood beside Papa. He always kept a handkerchief ready to wipe away the sweaty embraces of the other parishioners who rushed to give me fellowship before the organ quieted. Papa cared for me in this and many ways. Even the altar boys shook the bells and lifted the host to the bishop's mouth with a grace I knew was for me alone. These appeals were in vain, for I belonged only to my father.

Baby Anette was no beauty. She burnt with fever regularly, as if she knew this was the means to smuggle Mama's attention. Now Anette is a history teacher and studies the past, but perhaps then she knew the future. Perhaps she knew Mama would leave us. Either way, Anette became Mama's new doll. This left Papa and me to ourselves. Only now, I was a young woman.

After the sun set, Papa would teach me the waltz and the seven step on the balcony. Linen curtains separated the balcony from the house and also shielded the balcony from the elements. They billowed in and out with the sea breeze. "Yes, my lovely. One, two, three, four, five, and six and seven. One and two and three. Good!" I would wear Mama's housedress and feel it was a ball gown. Papa would swing me about on his toes and then shuffle side to side. He held his hand high and stiff, clutching me like a Frenchy man clutches his old-shoe wife. After all, though we were supposedly not Frenchy, we did live in Frenchtown. We danced on the balcony overlooking the harbour, where *The Homecoming* lay awaiting Papa's command. We swam in the sea, nude as the Lord made us. The ship a large shield from prying eyes. I would imagine that it was only we alone in this family. No Mama, no baby sister. I knew this imagining was vile, but I could not help myself. My mind wandered and plotted.

"I love you, Papa."

"I love you, my own."

By breakfast it was a hushed rendezvous that we kept from Mama. I knew the stories. Miss Lady, who like many on island at the time, couldn't swim, said she saw frightful ghosts floating in from off the ocean. Mr. Lyte, a Frenchy and so a swimmer by standard, said it was Captain Bradshaw and a mermaid mistress. Still, that Sheila Lady-inga and Hippolyte Lammartine both did agree that the woman in the apparition had hair that waved like a nighttime ocean. Papa and I, obscured by the blowing curtains of the balcony or the body of the boat, knew the special truth: Louis Moreau would not be the first man whom I kissed.

Now Papa Owen's ship sits buried by the Anegada shoal. My Villa by the Sea still stands, though not by that name. Now it seems that anyone can walk among our bedrooms after a paid meal. Even the balcony where Papa and I danced can now be rented for banquets. On the walls now are pictures of Frenchy men hauling boats, or photos of Charlotte Amalie before the American flag. But there is not one picture of Papa and me alone. There is no evidence of us, white bed gowns and house slippers, with the wind blowing into our sea-wet faces that were pressed cheek to cheek.

13.

Anette Stemme Bradshaw will grow to be a history teacher, but she never knew the miraculous truths about her own early history. By the time she is old enough to be told the story of herself, her parents will be dead.

But when she was a baby, she was cherubic and red. Her skin was red and her hair was red and to some it seemed like an awful thing. Red skin was attractive enough. Red hair, however, might be a genetic recession.

Something like albinism — which the island had only seen once in a nicely behaved but too quiet child who didn't live past six years. Anette, however, would live. The red hair, of course, was a trait from Antoinette's line. On a child the red hair was one thing, but on a grown Anegada woman it could be something else — something arresting, something bewitching.

To some, Anette's childhood red hair was not an entirely awful thing. It was a sign of her sunny disposition — for wasn't the sun a big ball of fire? And Anette was a devoted smiler. Even as a baby she seemed to have a knack for people — as if people were her hobby. She smiled before she was one week old and even Miss Lady had to admit that it was a real smile and not gas, for the newborn had looked directly at her mother's beaming mouth and responded.

Baby Anette walked at ten months, which was not unusual because all our children walked before a year. But Anette also spoke at ten months. Which was almost impossible. And yet, it was true. She could walk and talk, and she had a sense of humor and a sense for people, all before she was one year old.

But there is no legacy of any of this. Families who are determined to keep their legacy make legacy arrangements. They put their names on things that carry on after they are gone: books, buildings, boy children. Owen Arthur did not come from legacy and neither did his wife. It is true that they were each persons of great determination. But their determined lives crossed with the bulk of a nation, and that nation watered them down into something softer than they had hoped. They had had spoons of silver and a rattle made of real gold for baby Eeona. But by the time Anette arrived, the world had changed. American Prohibition was spooking the rum makers into running. Continentals were arriving with their own ships of tourists. So different from the Danes, British, and Frenchies, these new whites built homes up in the hills. Built inns at the edge of the island. Built the Gulf Reef Club on the little island in the harbor. Far away from we, the people.

Antoinette would catch hold of hurricane Anette. Grab the chunky baby and whisper "Anegada" into her ears. "Sweet lobster," she would say. "Hidden as the horizon." "My little Duene daughter." Then she would release Anette and send the girl flowing.

When Anette was just eleven months old, Antoinette took the child to the sea. It was not a beach in the town area, for that would have been too public. Beaches were social places. But Antoinette didn't want anyone telling her she was doing the wrong thing. Virgin Islanders of the time tended to have a healthy fear of the water. With the exception of Anegadians and St. Thomas Frenchies, most of us did not even know how to swim. Even seasoned ship hands were known to drown as easily as anyone who worked on land. Owen, with his secret Frenchy heritage, had learned to swim early. But this was considered a cowardly skill for a captain. Captains were to go down with their ship, not be saved by their own stroke. Still, Owen had taught his eldest daughter by throwing her over the side of *The Homecoming* when she was five. "Don't fight!" he had shouted to her as her lovely limbs chopped the water. "If you fight water, you will drown." He said this just before he dived in beside her. Then he held her and showed her how to make the water give. Swimming, it seemed, was a seduction.

But when Anette had learned to talk so early, it had scared people. What would we say of her actually swimming before reaching one year? But as Antoinette was born on the Anegada atoll, she was a swimmer. Then so would Anette be. Anegadians were all sea people.

At Antoinette's request, Mr. Hippolyte arranged for a cart and mule to take the mother and little daughter to the country and then beyond the country. They were heading to a beach where a thirty-foot drop had just been discovered. An American Navy man had swum out and then suddenly had found himself in the deep sea. The drop, which before had just been an old wives' tale, was confirmed. We old wives, who had always known, nodded to ourselves.

Because of the drop, it was a dangerous beach and so no one would be there. It was also a beautiful beach, where the water was as clear as rain in your palm. And whoever owned the land around the beach didn't bother trespassers. Already some beaches on island were closed off, owned by someone, protected with a lashed chain.

Mr. Lyte drove the mule himself. People passing called out to them, and Antoinette called back that they were going in the country to air the baby. It took mother and child and manservant a few hours to get to the country, and then to the eastern countryside, and then to the beach that didn't yet have an official name but would later be called Coki.

80

It was just them alone. Just Hippolyte and the lady and the infant. The man tied the mule and fed it. The mother took out a small shawl and nursed her child with un-necessary modesty. Then Antoinette pulled out a big piece of cloth and laid it out on the sand and she ate the soft bread and sweaty cheese she'd packed, chewing the bread to mush for the baby. They all shared the water. Mr. Lyte went back to the mule.

With the groundsman at a decent dis-tance, Antoinette removed the baby's clothes. Then Antoinette stripped herself, so no wet clothes would reveal her doings. Drowning the child is what the island would declare. But Anette clung to her mother as the two walked into the sea like a myth.

Yes, we believe in the beach. We have always believed in the beach. Beaches are places of baptisms and funerals. Of bac-chanal but also of solitude. But we did not consider the sea itself, even at its best behavior, as a place for babies. And also, it was January and no right-minded Virgin Islander swam in the winter sea. But Re-bekah had said that Antoinette would not mother this one, and so Antoinette under-stood that Anette needed to be taught everything a mother could teach and as soon as possible. The waves were not the

81

usual Caribbean calm. They were proper waves, large and white-lashed and buoyant. The baby was paddling on her own within the hour. Under the water with her eyes open and legs and arms coming and going and her mouth in a smile. The waves embracing her completely, then releasing her to the air for breath. Anette was a natural for the sea. Like any Anegada child.

They dried off on the sheet and then went back in and then dried off again and then went back. In between, Antoinette draped herself with the sheet and held Anette by the hand looking for sea fans. When Antoinette saw a large conch shell, she lifted it for the child.

"You can hear Papa in the shell," she told Anette. What they could hear was the sea itself. Little Anette pressed her head to the shell. The sound made her feel sleepy. "Good night, Papa," she said to the shell. Antoinette nursed the baby into a nap, touching her hair and face gently. No one else touched the child this way. When Anette awoke, the two went back to the sea.

Hippolyte watched them all along, despite the lady's nudity. He needed to watch, because of the drop in the water and because of the isolation of the beach. And yes, Madame Bradshaw was a pretty woman. He watched from close enough so in case a current came he could catch them. But far enough so that he could not see the cleft in the clavicle or the bowl of the breast.

Hippolyte Lammartine was a man to be trusted. He kept all the family's secrets — until the day he told all. Little Anette was much too young to remember this day. When later Eeona would tell her, "Don't go near the water, you'll drown like Papa," Anette would believe. She never knew that her mother had already taught her how to swim.

But here is the truth. Mother and child were baptized again and again on a beach that seemed to belong to no one. Except that day when it belonged to them alone.

14.

EEONA

Papa intended to give me the scholarly education of proper young ladies. Mama argued for a place in America, but only if she could chaperone and stay on in the event I gained interest from a suitable suitor. Papa insisted to her that the current finances would not allow for such an expense. There would be passage and then lodging for four, as Mama would not leave little Anette, and Anette would of course need a nanny. I, however, knew that Papa just wanted me close. Mama wanted me as far away as possible.

Tortola was more rural than our island. It was much closer than America, closer even than Puerto Rico. Also, Mama had a cousin there who would see to my education and sieve the suitors who would come.

I did not cry until I was on the boat and St. Thomas was just a gathering of hills in the distance. Then I gave the sea my tears. Men walked back and forth behind me. I considered jumping over, simply so one of these men might save me. I did not risk this only because it dawned on me that, relieved of the longing pain in their chests and their loins, they might be delighted to see me drown.

I would miss wild Anette who could climb trees and manage other unladylike things. I would miss my mother's stories. As for my father . . . there were no words for missing him.

My French tutor was an elder female cousin who would organize a series of *entretiens* with any well-bred French visiting the island. Still, she could not keep away suitors of all kinds. Men filled the porch steps with fruits and flowers.

I chose Louis Moreau after six months of choices. I had been away from Papa and Villa by the Sea all that time. Moreau was from a real French family, and so with him I would be a real madame. He was not from our islands, so he was easily manipulated. I was not supposed to sail from Tortola to Anegada with Louis. Such an adventure alone with a man was forbidden. Still, I wanted to be a woman who made my own life, found my own place, not one who must ask for it like Mama.

Louis and I sailed to Anegada without telling a soul. It was only a day trip; we would be back by sunset. The elder cousin was old and overlooked the simplest things, such as whom I ventured out with and for how long. On the small vessel Louis and I kept to ourselves, as lovers do. Someone shouted that Anegada was nigh and I looked out in vain for the land. Louis took my hand in his and pointed my fingers. The island looked like the horizon itself.

Tortola, where I had been staying, is mountainous, like St. Thomas. The hills are as steep as walls. The island of Anegada, however, is not an island at all. It is a ring of coral skimming just above the water. It is scarce in trees and plentiful in sand. A submerged reef surrounds it eight miles out.

This is why it is so dangerous.

Our vessel had to dock far off at the edge of the reef. A rowboat came to meet us and take us closer to land. Still, even the rowboats were unable to negotiate the shallow coral. Dark men took me and the other women up in their arms and lifted us out to carry us to shore, so our dresses would not be wet. When my carrier held me, he trembled with care. You would have thought I was a case of china dishes.

On the sand, I could see that the sky over Anegada was a huge dome. Everywhere I turned the firmament was there, landing at my feet.

"Monsieur Moreau," the people called, nodding their heads but looking only at me. Then I saw the brashness of this adventure. Though Papa, Mama, and I had sailed a number of times aboard *The Homecoming,* we had never sailed to Mama's homeland. I had not fully considered that perhaps Mama would have close family still on the island and that I might be recognized. "Good afternoon," one woman said to me as Louis and I walked. Her eyes were shining from beneath a head of hair as red as the setting sun. She seemed startled to see me. I lifted my head to show my breeding and stave off any questioning. Doing this, however, made a smile come to her face, as if she now knew exactly who I was.

"Miss," she said to me, "you from Anegada."

How could she have detected anything? I was wearing the European single petticoat, which shielded my shape. I was leading a Frenchman. She wore pants like a man and led a donkey. "You are mistaken," I said, turning to Moreau. He raised his eyebrows and I raised mine in return.

"I'm not mistaken," the woman went on. Her eyes pooled in her face. "I know a Stemme when I see one."

I wanted to correct her; I was a Bradshaw. I was my father's child. My mother had been the Stemme.

"You just like those Duene stories they tell the children," the woman said. "Take this here," and she passed me something the size of a baby wrapped in a clean rag. "Is like you arrive for mating season. Some Stemmes does leave for love, others does come." I could not respond to such audacity, but this grown woman just patted the bundle she'd given me. "Don't wait," she said, before walking on.

Moreau guided me towards the beach without making comment, though from his face I could see his bemusement. I opened

87

the woman's offering after a respectable distance. It was red and clawed, though its belly was bursting with meat. I came close to dropping it on the ground out of fright. "Lobster!" I exclaimed. I had not before had the opportunity to eat or touch one.

"The people here are so pleasant," Moreau said. "This was probably that poor woman's lunch."

I nodded, not wanting to add anything more to that conversation in the event he began to envision me in men's pants, leading a burro.

We continued walking over ground that was not ground at all, but coral. It was as if we were walking on the bottom of the ocean. Mama had never spoken much about Anegada. "I cleaved to my spouse," she had said, as though Papa were her new fatherland. If Papa had not whisked her away, perhaps I would have been like a Duene daughter, as it went in my mother's stories. I would walk right into the ocean. I would walk on the coral bottom as if walking on land.

Now Louis stretched out his long arm and gesticulated across the beach that was named Flash of Beauty. "Like you," he said.

The waves on the beach seemed thick, as though we were in the middle of the ocean, not simply sitting on the sand. I would not have been entirely surprised to see a lovely woman raise her head from those waves and come towards us with mangrove legs and backwards feet. I could not dream why my mother had left this place. Though even as I began to dream, I knew the reason. She left for Papa.

The sea fans were bright purple. I stooped for one, and shaking it of its sand, I held it by its bulbous root and fanned myself. Far off into the water the waves stood tall and frothed white before crashing and then subduing. "The reef," Louis said, pointing. "The Spanish named this island Anegada, the drowned land, because it has a history of drowning ships. Thousands of ships, and they remain here, under the ocean." He pointed out to where the waves crashed far beyond the shore. "Unless you know where the reef begins, you will crash into it and sink your ship. When we own the land, people will only come if we show them how."

As we set our blanket down for the picnic, Moreau told me of his plans to build a golf course and resort on Anegada. He spoke of the entire land as if it were his already. I could not help but wonder what would become of the woman who had gifted me the lobster. "But Flash of Beauty," he said, as if in conciliation, "we shall keep it as a refuge for women and fish."

I looked at him then. His hair was straight and his legs were long. His mustache curled towards his ears. His nose arched towards his mouth. I decided that I was going to marry him. He would be interesting to look at for a long time. With him I would have Villa by the Sea and perhaps have all of Anegada. I would be a generous madame and convince my husband to release another beach for men and arachnids. We would allow native people to trespass without permission. Yes, Moreau would do. Then I would do as I pleased.

I did not see the point in waiting.

With both my hands, I loosened my hair out of the bun that held it. My hair waved out around my face and crashed down over my shoulders. I drew close to Moreau until our faces were close and my hair touched his face.

Perhaps he now leaned over me. Perhaps I leaned over him. It does not matter. Our mouths touched and his filled with the ends of my hair. My hair hid us like a wave. He reached into his damp breast pocket and pulled out a silk kerchief. Inside was my diamond-and-pearl engagement ring.

"There has not been a marriage on Anegada for ten years," he whispered.

15.

Jacob Esau McKenzie had been so young, not much more than three, that for his whole life he was convinced that the visit from the ship captain had not been for real. The memory came to him at odd times. When someone told him he was handsome, when dancing, when gazing on a picture of Anette Bradshaw.

That night his mother was fixing up the house nice. Lemongrass bush arranged in vases as if it were flowers — the place smelling minty. She bathed Jacob special, soaked him like she was thawing him out. Dunking his head under again and again; singing what she did. A melody for the dipping. A hum for the scrubbing. His other brothers had been sent off on long errands with too much money so they would waste more time.

"Jacob, the most loved," Rebekah said, and finished drying the little boy down with a rough towel, clumps of vanilla bark in the cloth like burrs. "Your eldest sister studying in Tortola. The redhead sister stop suckling but still keeping she mother busy. So now your father coming back to we." But Jacob didn't have any sisters that he knew of, and so he didn't pay his mother much mind. She was always whispering and humming things that had nothing at all to do with him.

The father who came wasn't the one from the Navy photo on the living room wall; "McKenzie" in black on a white rectangle over his chest. The father who came was tall with sea-gray eyes. He smelled of the ocean.

This was Owen Arthur's first time seeing the baby boy who was not a baby anymore but a boy.

"Esau," Rebekah said, as she presented him to Owen. "Because he is your beloved son." His primary name was Jacob, but that was so he would be hers first.

Owen had not been with Rebekah for all this time, but he had sent money for the son that was his. He had been distracted with his hurting business and the tightness of banks and with Eeona and with sending Eeona away. Now standing in front of him, his only son looked like a grain of sand. He'd so hoped Rebekah would give him a boy child, but now he wished it wasn't a son after all. He needed another daughter. For already he knew that baby Anette, despite her pluck, was not diluting the ill love he had for Eeona. He noticed now that Esau and Anette looked alike. The same something in the mouth and around the eyes.

Owen knew that this son could never openly inherit anything from him, that he could not carry on the Bradshaw name. But he would help Esau as the boy grew. He planned for the boy to come up knowing who his father really was; it would be one of the open secrets so easily kept on any island. When he died, he'd leave Esau all his experience and a third of his money. All this Owen would do once the shipping business became steady again. When Lovernkrandt or any someone put the proper faith in him and his ship. For now, he stared at Esau and then smiled at Rebekah. The faithful feeling of wanting Rebekah was coming over him and it was a relief. She was wearing her boots as always, though she would take them off to make love to him. She only took them off to do that magic.

The two adults spent many minutes just looking at Jacob Esau and at each other. They sat in opposite chairs in the small sitting room. The shutters were closed so the red of the insides was given only to them; the muted white side exposed to those in the street. Rum was becoming near impossible to procure on island anymore, though Owen knew if anyone had a taste, it would be Rebekah. Still, he restrained himself and rubbed his earlobe instead. Rebekah sat erect, her long dress billowing out and covering the ground around her in all directions. The two adults had not made love with each other for three years.

After tea was offered cautiously and rejected kindly, after his earlobes became raw, Owen finally reached out to touch Jacob Esau's face. The man's rough hands scuffed across Jacob's nose and his eyelids. Cupped his jaw and traced his head.

"You are very handsome, Esau," the man said. "But of course, you would be." And then the adults looked at each other. "Play for me, Reba," the man said.

Jacob Esau's mother went to the piano. She lifted its cover gently and sat on the bench. She let her fingers touch the keys first without sound. And then very quietly. Giving a sound almost like silence. Before the ears even knew the song was playing. Feeling it first just under the skin where the hair grows, Rebekah eased a pained song of sweetness into the room. She pressed the pedals only very lightly with the tip of her right foot in its black boot.

Owen loved to hear her play. There wasn't

anyone on island who didn't. He would never say it out loud, but Owen would have traded ten minutes of her piano playing for any one of the shirts Antoinette embroidered for him. Rebekah's piano, which he'd had shipped from America for her, could sound like a drizzle, could sound like a storm. It was wet, her music. As a seaman, how could he want it any other way?

Now Owen Arthur picked Jacob Esau up and began waltzing with him. Swinging him around until Jacob Esau laughed and laughed. He flashed this father all his teeth. The scene layered and lasted until Jacob Esau fell asleep in the arms of the ocean-dancing man. And when he woke, he was alone on the settee. He wandered around the small house quietly because there was only quiet in the house.

In his mother's room he saw this other father leaning over the high bed. His mother's arms were meeting and crossing at the top of the man's back. He knew her arms well. But there were her legs at the lower part of the man's back. One perfect smooth brown foot. The toes pointing and flexing into the air silently. And the other foot was not a foot at all. But a hoof. A hoof all the way up to what should be his mother's ankle. A bone-colored cleft in place of toes.

Thick brown hair all the way up to the knee. And this foot did not touch the father's skin or move at all, but remained stiff just over this father's tight back.

Jacob, who was never called Esau except today, eased out of the room. Chanting in his head, "You are not real. You are not real. You are not real." And lay back down on the sofa in the sitting room. Waiting to fall back asleep and wake into his real life.

Did his mother know that he saw? Did her instructions as he grew up to keep his head high and his eyes to the ceiling show that she knew? But in time, Jacob forgot that he really knew. Forgot that it wasn't a bad dream. Forgot that his real-real father was not Benjamin McKenzie. Forgot his mother's hoof foot. Forgot that he had any sisters at all.

16.

Eeona had been only seventeen when she became engaged to Louis Moreau III, the son of a landowner from the countryside of Guadeloupe and a woman from the seaside of Nice. He would take Eeona back to his Guadeloupe and let her finish her studies before babies came. It would be important that his wife speak both French and English comfortably — especially if she was to be an asset with the wives of the men patronizing the golf course he would build on Anegada.

A month after the furtive proposal, Eeona was still seventeen when her parents finally paid her a visit on Tortola. Mama brought lace doilies for her cousin as a gift. Little Anette hid behind Mama's dress, shy of this lovely older sister she barely remembered. The cousin coaxed Anette into the kitchen with sweets. Then the parents shut themselves up with Eeona in the sitting room and asked if she was still a virgin. They had heard about the clandestine visit to Anegada and the beach called Flash of Beauty. We all had. Eeona had looked at her father sitting with both his hands tugging on his earlobes. She had sobbed then, forced tears about being deflowered by Louis Moreau on the small Anegada. It was a lie, but during Eeona's entire performance, she kept her teary eyes on her father. Did he see that she was a woman now? Fit to be a madame? Was he jealous?

As far as the Moreau boy was concerned, Antoinette wasn't concerned at all. The mother wanted the daughter married off. Period. Perhaps young Moreau would even love Eeona. Then Eeona would be saved from her irascible beauty. And Antoinette would only have little Anette left between her and her real life. The recent one in her womb was already washed away. Easy this time.

What Antoinette worried about was her daughter's silver secret and how a premarital lover might respond. Eeona was secretive but her mother knew she also tended to the silver with a soft baby brush — she might be silly enough to flaunt it. Perhaps the Frenchman had kept his eyes closed out of fear or modesty during their first knowing? Oh, but he would soon become bold and wide-eyed and he would see. He might assume the silver hair suggested infertility. Or an overly mature nature. Either way, it was a risk to marriage and the mother knew she must keep her daughter away from the lusty fiancé until they were sanctified.

When the parents finally opened the parlor door, little Anette walked cautiously to her sister and began babbling incoherently.

"I've taught her a few Latin phrases," said the cousin proudly. "She's a natural with language."

Eeona pursed her lips, for her own French progressed slowly. She didn't bother to embrace her baby sister, but instead stood and went to her room. Anette could be heard crying, then Mama was comforting. The parents took both their daughters back to St. Thomas the next morning.

The evening they returned to Frenchtown, Owen Arthur came to Eeona's room. This was something he had not done since she had left the nursery. This was not a thing that fathers did. He didn't knock. He simply opened the door and there was Eeona sitting at the edge of the bed in her flowing nightgown. The hair on her head bursting around her like a halo. Owen would have stopped and run. Stopped and kneeled. Either one, if he were a lesser man or a better man. Instead: "I've tried other waters," and he was walking toward her. "But I need," and he was close to her now.

Eeona stared at her father and did not move. What she missed those months in Tortola was here, but now she was afraid. "Papa," she said, keeping her voice steady. Would he really own her now? With Mama just on the other side of the house? Would he not wait until they could sail away together? Leave Moreau and Antoinette the house and the Anegada golf course. Owen held his hand up flat, as if to say "Stop," or as if to say "I praise you." Instead: "I need you to marry this man and go away with him," and then he shook his head as though he did not believe himself. "I always wanted Europe for you. They say there are others like you in Paris. Women of splendor. Your own beauty will not be such a burden."

"But Papa, there are no others like me." She controlled her voice, for that, too, was part of her beauty. "Do not send me away, Papa."

"My own, I already have." He turned to the door.

The things in her that Eeona understood receded, the things in her that she did not understand seeped in — her episodes, they would be called later. "But Owen," she said like a woman, "what about the silver? You always said it was yours."

Owen did not turn back to face her. Instead: "Your mother has almost finished your wedding dress."

Eeona stood up and embraced his back. He turned to her. Their faces too near. In this way he could not remain composed. In this way the woman whose lips were close could not have been his child. How could he send her away? The skin on his cheeks was tingling. He took her waist in his hands. "We have always known that this is not the way of a good father or of a good daughter," he said.

Eeona was barely a woman, really. She was a child. Her mind was storming. Would Papa kiss the silver? Right here in her mother's own house? Eeona took his face in her palms, feeling her strangeness rising like a tide.

Owen Arthur's heart beat so slowly he thought he might die right there. "There is nothing good I can give you," he said. "For your own sake. There can be no more of this."

Eeona's heart beat so hard she could feel the pulse between her legs. "Then I wish you would die, Papa. I wish you would just die."

And then Owen, released as though from a shackle, streamed from the room.

The telegram came the following evening: "*Homecoming* wrecked on Anegada reef. Two survivors. Captain not among them."

As simple as that.

17.

The Homecoming went down on a day that had been bright and young. What they said happened to the ship was something that could happen to any ship ringing the coral atoll of Anegada. Except that this captain knew Anegada well; after all, it was where he had found his wife.

Every family of note from the U.S. Virgin Islands and the British Virgin Islands had a relation who went down with the ship. More than one family lost their breadwinner. More than one woman lost a lover. Eeona, still seventeen, lost both. Instead of planning a wedding, she helped her mother plan Papa's funeral. Anette could not have understood, but still she played quietly, tending the doll her mother had made her. Feeding it, dressing it, holding it to her chest, putting it gently to bed. In general, giving it the love no one had time to give her those days.

The two deckhands who survived the wreck were pulled ashore by the lobstermen of Anegada. The deckhands told the stories of how in the past the captain had always sighted Anegada in the distance because he said it looked like the flat chest of a child floating in the water. But this time the captain must have been called to the island, as though by a siren. "That does happen," so the living men said. *The Homecoming,* which had shipped rum, which had shipped the food that fed St. Thomas, shipped the money that floated Tortola, had been shipping nothing more than a cargo of bones. A ship full of bones and all of it sunk to the shallow sea bottom.

We can imagine what will happen to the cargo on *The Homecoming.* How the bones will be released from their sacks by nibbling fish. How for years fishermen will pull up mandibles with their lobster catch. How for generations children will find femurs in the sand.

Eeona's pearl-and-diamond engagement ring was returned to Moreau — whose father now forbade him to marry Eeona as it was clearly a burdensome financial venture. Moreau saved the ring and put it on the finger of a full-bred French woman whom he followed back to Nice — abandoning his Anegada dreams. Whenever Louis Moreau sat alone in a quiet place to drink a bottle of wine, he tasted Eeona in it. In company, he would whisper her name into champagne flutes, for she was that color — champagne. A muted color and mysterious for that. Even his pretty French wife thought he was mad. She never knew who Eeona was, though she heard the name often.

And though *The Homecoming* crashed miles away on the shoals of Anegada, Owen Arthur Bradshaw's body was finally found washed up from the sea on the bay right there in St. Thomas's Water Front. His face was liquid but the rest of him was unmistakable to anyone who had seen him naked in life. Antoinette wept and believed that her husband must have been trying to get back to her. But it must be said that he was equidistant between Villa by the Sea and Rebekah's red-shuttered house. And of course, Antoinette was not the only woman of his heart who was there at Villa by the Sea.

Most said drowned. But the Frenchies knew that Owen Arthur was a man of the sea and men of the sea don't just drown. They walk into the sea with stones in their fists. They drink and bow into a heavy wave. They are smashed in the head by a loose anchor and heaved into the sea.

From Anegada came the stories. Someone had seen the little side boat gliding away empty as the big ship sank. Someone else had seen a large beautiful bird circling a figure eight just as the boat began to rumble. It was whispered that the murderess was a woman with backward-facing feet and hair like the sea. Perhaps it was the captain's witch mistress, who knew magic and knew love and knew that they were one and the same, despite any sin.

Eeona, who knew she could sink ships, could only blame herself.

Owen's mates came in from around the closer islands. Mama Antoinette didn't fling herself into the arms of any of these, as we'd all imagined she must do to save the family's wealth. No, that Antoinette had her own ideas. No men even boarded at Villa by the Sea, which was too full of women for it to be decent. Male mourners stayed in the new Grand Hotel, right there in town, which otherwise catered to visiting Americans.

During the wake, Owen Arthur's bloated body lay in his marriage bed with a linen spread to hide the sea-mauled face. It was noted by Liva Lovernkrandt that Owen's buttons were still sewn tightly on. Antoinette felt there had been no point in removing the buttons from his clothes. Nor did it make sense to cut out his pockets. He didn't need this help to swim easily up the River Jordan. Clearly her husband had been swimming. Or drowning.

The captain's daughters, one too young and the other too shocked, also failed to tie his toes together so he wouldn't turn into a jumbie and haunt them. But Owen Arthur would have haunted them anyway. This is what parents do.

Three months after the funeral Eeona was still seventeen when Antoinette grasped her hand and said, "You are now the mother of

Anette and mademoiselle of Villa by the Sea." Antoinette packed one small bag full of the lace gloves that were her trademark. "I will return with iguana-skin shoes," she announced, before she boarded the big boat and gushed off to New York toward her own slippery freedom.

So before Eeona turned eighteen, she was no longer rich, no longer engaged, and no longer studying French in Tortola. But Eeona was still lustfully beautiful. Only now beauty was just about all she had.

18.

Antoinette had not been swept away to America on a whim. Staying at Villa by the Sea was not an option, really. The family needed money. She had considered returning home to Anegada. But her parents were gone now. Perhaps her lobsterman was there and perhaps he had resisted marriage. But Antoinette had two children, both for the man she'd married over him. Really, there was nothing there in Anegada except beauty. And that wouldn't pay one expense. Rebekah had once told Antoinette that she would not mother Anette. As a widow, Antoinette now knew this was a harkening that she would leave the island. More than a harkening, it was a kind of permission.

It was Liva Lovernkrandt who told Nettie about the Negro designer who wanted pretty, high-colored girls to sew and design for him. Actually, Liva had offered it as an option for Eeona, who everyone knew had lost her fiancé and her father and her future. It would have been rude to suggest that Antoinette needed the work.

But once in Manhattan, Antoinette found that the Fashion Institute for Coloreds was only a grave of an office. One woman sitting at the typewriter but not typing, just there at her casket of a desk in order to tell Nettie, "The position is not available. Don't you know, there is nothing available? Not even for the whites." Then the woman turned aside to cough a spittle of blood delicately into a colored kerchief.

There were no jobs in our United States of America. There was no milk and no honey. Instead there was a Depression. The streets were paved, but with litter as much as anything. And at night men would throw food out onto the streets and then other human beings would descend on the garbage like rats. Handsome women wore the designs from Liva Lovernkrandt's magazines, but the dresses seemed to rattle instead of ring. The city was tall and dreary, and even the rats were hungry.

The buildings were impossible mountains and carried ill-mannered people up and down as if they were freight. The food was more expensive than any food in the Virgin Islands. And the cold was colder than any cold Mama Antoinette had known.

19.

ANETTE

This my first memory. Not history book or library archive, or even imagination. My own actual memory. Mama lying in bed. She beautiful and brown but still she look like a cloud. Like she going to just float off. Eeona tell me to step back. Mama gone, she say quiet-quiet. But I know I seeing Mama right there. "Dead," Eeona say now, less quiet. "Dead like my doll?" I ask. Eeona look at me funny, but nod. Then I put my hand flat on Mama chest. In that place where my head always used to rest. And just so, Mama breathe. I make she breathe. I look at Eeona. "I bring my mama back to life!" I say. But Eeona just looking vex and shaking she head. Like I ain do enough. Because is true, when I look back, Mama ain breathe again.

I so confuse because Mama reach back

from America just to go again, but gone in a worse way. I want to ask Eeona why, but Eeona now marching up and down the room and talking some nonsense about a brother. And I thinking maybe he dead, too. Gone. Or maybe he coming to help we now that Mama gone. I go to Eeona and stand up strong in front she, make she stop pacing and chatting. "Sister Eeona, why God ain save Mama?"

Eeona answer fast like she been waiting for this question. "God is not in the business of saving. You must do that yourself." And is then I know that, yes, I could have save Mama. If only I had really think harder when I touch her chest. If I only had really believe.

Then Eeona march out the dead room. She turn back and call for me to follow. She close the door and watch me tight. She speak tight. "We can still salvage your education and your decency. I make that commitment." As if I care about any of that.

20.

There was no money. There was debt. Not only to Lovernkrandt, but to other businessmen who had helped Owen secure his new cargo. Financial assistance was needed but it would have been too disrespectful, so instead the women of Antoinette's circle gave flowers. Endless useless flowers. The villa smelled like a whorehouse. The walk to the cemetery lacked the proper austerity — might have been a Carnival troupe what with all the shades of purple in the petals. Eeona made little Anette and Miss Lady leave all of the flowers at the grave. Those that were delivered directly to the house stayed until they stunk.

The evening all the flowers finally died, Miss Lady placed a cup of tea beside Eeona and stood there until Eeona, swimming in her thoughts, looked up. "I have my own children," Sheila Ladyinga said to Eeona. "My three girls almost grown up but they still needing me." Three daughters? Almost grown up? "I going to get some cook and clean work at one of the hotels. You need to sell Villa by the Sea, Eeona." She could leave off the "Miss" because she had braided Eeona's hair. She had wiped Eeona's backside. "The Yankees already come around asking. Get you some money to start." Miss Lady didn't say "start over." She was kind that way.

Everything was happening fast-fast. Eeona felt as though she were an earth full of standpipes that had been turned on full.

Her head filled with liquid and became heavy. She opened her mouth to let it out. Water came. But in a drip, like saliva. She was not a standpipe. Eeona was just a girl who had never come around to forgiving her father for being her father or forgiving her mother for being his wife. Now everything that Eeona was — favorite daughter, desired debutante, even young miss of Villa by the Sea — had fled from her. And here was Anette needing her for mooring.

21.

EEONA

Before she died, Mama had taken my hand and then had spoken quite clearly. "You have a brother. Your father's outside child. Esau McKenzie. Same age as Anette. Please. Watch out for Esau and Anette."

I twisted my hand from hers and stepped away. I had not wanted to think at all about Owen Arthur having another woman and that woman not being me. Nor was it clear if Mama meant for me to care for this unknown brother or to be careful of him.

22.

It was their last evening at Villa by the Sea. The last supper of sorts. Miss Lady, who was not a Miss at all but a Mrs., brought Eeona and Anette a loaf of warm butter bread and some cheese that she had bought fresh that morning. She picked them some lemongrass bush from the yard and they all three had tea. For a month now the house had been emptying out of furniture. Already the living room and parlor were caverns. The things that had been their things had been hauled away by hand, by burro, and by man-pulled wagon.

After supper, Miss Lady left them. She already had a job, working in the new Gull Reef Club hotel over on Water Island. She would be a cleaner there, later a cook, then eventually head chef. "If you need anything," she'd said to Eeona before turning and walking out, never offering the second half of the sentence.

Anette's little bed had been sold off, so when she became sleepy, she hummed herself into slumber right there at the remaining supper table. But when she awoke, it was dark and quiet except for the crickets and the singing tree in the backyard. The house was a large one, but she went where she used to go when seeking safety. Eeona was there in Mama Antoinette's high mahogany bed. Anette climbed the little bed stairs. Eeona felt the small warmth of a new body and moved from it.

In the morning Eeona nearly screamed to see Antoinette lying in the bed beside her, for Antoinette's body had been buried over a month now. But then Eeona realized that it was only the runt copy of Mama, the baby daughter now shook awake from sleep. And Eeona felt annoyed that this little sister thought it was her place to sleep in the same bed with her.

No one had put down money for Antoinette's bed and no one would, for Antoinette's disease was a contagion. After the family left, Mr. Lyte, who had not been paid by the Bradshaws for almost a year now, would burn the bed into ash.

That morning the sisters packed their belongings. That done, Eeona dragged Antoinette's rocking chair to the veranda and began rocking. It was the chair where Antoinette had nursed each child and the chair where she had sat to tell stories. Eeona rocked like it was a spell. Like maybe she thought the chair was a boat and she could, if only she rocked hard enough, get it out to the water and across the harbor. It was frightening for a little child to watch Eeona, serious-faced, rocking in a frenzy, lost in a daydreaming episode. So little Anette did not watch. She turned and looked at the sea. The sky was open and clear, and had a tint of yellow in the air, showing how perfect the sun was. But Anette saw the sad clouds coming from across the harbor with their bundle of tears.

They each had eaten a mango and some kenips for breakfast but now it was afternoon. They were hungry but there was nothing to eat in the house. Mr. Lyte arrived with a burro and pulled their bundles onto its back. The dark cloud arrived with him.

The wind picked up. When their belongings were well tied to the burro, Eeona stood — the chair still rocking. She stepped down the stairs and Anette followed. Eeona walked with her back so straight one would have thought she was headed down to a great martyr's death.

The rain came like a sheet across the water and whipped toward them and then over them. And then it was gone before they'd even had a chance to contemplate escaping back into the house. But now they were sopping. Just so, they walked beside the burro, and Mr. Lyte tried to talk and little Anette tried to listen but Eeona would not speak. Speaking would make this ritual real and it was not real. Could not be real to Eeona.

Anette had always sat with Mama during church and so she had heard of the pillar of salt. The girl had understood it as a parable of not letting go. But she did not want to let go. So she did look back to see the rocking chair pumping furiously in the left-behind wind.

Eeona's severe walk kept them moving slowly. The shame made more shameful by the indignity of making their way in wet clothes. They made their way to the little flat Eeona had secured, a flat the size their parlor had been. They left all the dead and dry funeral flowers behind. They left the rocking chair. They left the house and the land. They left it or it had been taken from them. Same thing.

For Eeona, this day was like the end of her days. No mother, no father, no land, no Villa by the Sea. Nothing for which she could say, "You belong to me."

For Anette, this day would become the beginning. It was the same memory as Eeona's but the feeling was opposite. No mother, no father, no villa, no land. Nothing for which she could say, "I belong to you."

23.

ANETTE

While my friends was learning to play marbles, I was learning from Eeona how to sit like a lady. How to curtsey. How to walk with my back very straight. How to sip tea from our chip-up china cups. How to talk in so-called proper English.

But we was living in Savan and we wasn't rich no more. I used to get tease for wearing rubbers to grammar school. Now the boys pay plenty money to play basketball in rubbers. But back then the shoes was poor people's shoes and that was that. My friend Gertie couldn't defend me with words, but she defend me with she fists. Even in grammar school Gertie knew how to fight. I mean, is fight she coulda fight. She talk rough, talk like Eeona had never wanted me to. Is Gertie she self who convince me to go to that party years later where I meet the man of my life.

I was the young Bradshaw sister. I didn't remember Papa at all. I was too small when he drown on the boat. Too small when Mama come back by boat to drown in she own blood. I wasn't born by Transfer Day, but I born when everybody done decide we all going to be American. And then I was a orphan in fast time. So those two things, orphan and American, always seem the same to me.

Eeona say she sell the house and everything in it, for food and a few months on the flat. She say that's all that was left once the debt to the Lovernkrandts was paid. Then she say the house burn down — face tight and funny like she self might have flick the match. Eeona tell me we forbidden to go to the place where the villa used to be because of some law Lovernkrandt make against us.

But in truth they say Frenchtown is for boat people. I don't trust them things, boats. Boats kill off both my parents. I had just want to be really alive for as long as possible. That my goal. To live. To be up under a man who love me 'til death do us part. To make babies so I could keep on living after I dead. Eeona believe in ladylikeness and lineage. But I ain so.

Let me tell you a story. One day a boy in my third-grade class name Franky make me a fake villa out of aluminum. Like for a doll so, with no roof. You could just sit a dollie down in it and start playing. Inside had a toonchy pair of chairs, a table, a love seat. He had carve tiny flower designs onto the front door. He good with he hands. Could have been an artist maybe if life was different.

The Franky boy present the dollhouse to me with a puff-up chest one day after school. The villa was fastened onto a wood board but I was very careful, so afraid it going fall and crumple or scratch. I carry it home, up the little hill. I don't look up or down the street, just keep my eye fastened on the little house and looking through the little window at the little love seat. I there wondering if my sister could make me some little pillow to be like a bed. She get the stitching skills from our mother. I thinking Eeona going to like it, since she always going on about our Villa by the Sea. In fact, I worry she might thief it from me. When I reach our flat, I look into the window at Eeona taking a siesta, I see her lovely hair spread out all around her face.

But when she wake, is as if she could have smell it. She walk right into the kitchen. She barely glance at me doing my sums before walking over to the aluminum miniatures.

"How did you come by that?" she ask. She just wake, but already she evil like a needle.

"Franky Joseph gave it to me."

Her eyes look startle, as though I slap she. "Little Franky Joseph is not of our class.

You will return his offering tomorrow morning. Take it off the table. Put it on the floor."

The next morning I walk the toy house back to school. It a kind of walk of shame. I had really want that house. All night I been playing games in my head. Seeing me eating at the dollie table. Seeing me sitting on the dollie settee. Seeing me in that house like it own me.

Outside of the schoolroom, I ain have to find Franky. He find me. The aluminum shimmering in the morning sun. "Why you ain keep it home, yes?" He voice, poor thing, was hopeful. As if he think maybe I bring it back to show it off to my friends. When I tell him that my sister making me give the fake villa back, you could have see in his eyes that he understand. He stand up watch me like he know something about me that I ain even know. Then he take the house from me and fling it in the bush. It crumple onto itself. It stay there in the sun for months. Winking at me whenever I walk to school.

These things don't go away easy, I tell you.

When I reach home that day, Eeona sit me down saying is time she tell me 'bout boys. But it ain no birds and bees she talking. She tell me I am not to mess with no boy beneath my class and especially no boy name Esau. We poor but we acting rich and so I don't know what class we claiming. And I can't see what so bad about friending up a boy even if he have a funny name. Eeona say is not the name, is the boy. But it have a hundred boys on island and I ain know one name Esau.

24.

Rebekah McKenzie was watching her sons swim in the sea. The beach was called Coki and was famous for its undercurrent. Infamous for swallowing people down its thirty-foot drop. Rebekah chose this beach because not many other people would be there. Parents still did not bring their small children to this beach. No one had claimed ownership since an American Navy man drowned a generation ago, and it still seemed a place of solitude. The water was rough and beautiful, and the bay was far away from civilization. Rebekah would not go in the water unless she must. She would never take off her high-laced boots or her long white dress. She sat on the beach, her legs bent under her, her back erect, and watched them. Her boys. Glints of gold in the ocean.

Up the beach, another woman had

brought her girl. She also did not want to be seen. But not because she was afraid of revealing her body's silver secret. The bathing suits of the time were modest, but she wasn't even wearing one of those. She wore light cotton short pants and a matching shirt, which she could bathe in if needed. She simply wanted some peace from her male admirers and their envious women. There was no one else on this beach; well, no one but that one other family who were kind enough to stay down the other end. That family was just flecks of brown far away in the sun.

Anette had been begging and begging for a beach day. All the other children went, why couldn't she? On St. Thomas there were many calm, children-friendly beaches. But Eeona did not allow her little sister into the water at all, so the rough waves did not matter.

"You may slip your feet into the water, but nothing more," Eeona told her. She didn't need to say this, since she'd said it so many times before. "The sea will kill you, as it killed Papa." Little Anette did not know that she already knew how to swim. And Eeona was not teaching or telling. Instead, Eeona was sitting on the beach, struggling through needlepoint — a skill her mother had been expert at.

Anette was in a sack of a dress, something Eeona had patched together with scraps of red. Her hair, as always, was shooting off her head like flames. The little red girl stooped to put her face in the ripple of a wave when her sister wasn't looking. She quickly scooted herself back up the shore and sat on the beach to collect shells. Next to her sister, the shells were the prettiest thing on the beach. Anette didn't remember being on this beach and learning to swim. She didn't remember her mother holding a conch shell to her ear. But now she picked up such a shell and ran it over to Eeona. Eeona put down her stitching. She clenched her fist and pressed her ankles together. Perhaps her own episodes were coming on. Either way, she was ready to leave. Ready to scream at the child for harassing her. The smell of the saltwater. The sand under her feet. Anette, so uncomely compared to what Eeona had been. It all made Eeona miss her father and her mother and even Louis Moreau.

"A conch shell," Anette declared.

"More specifically," Eeona said tensely, "this is a queen conch."

Eeona grabbed the pink shell from Anette and held it to Anette's ear. Now Anette's eyes opened wide. She listened intently as though being given directions or told a secret.

"Be quiet and you will hear the ocean," Eeona said, which is what Papa had taught her.

"I hear Papa in the shell," said Anette.

Eeona looked at Anette as though the child had spoken another language, one with sharp screeches for vowels. "Pardon me?" Eeona asked, alarmed. But Anette only looked far off and seemed to continue to listen intently. "Anette, it is time we make our way back to town."

It was the red dress that caught little Jacob's eye from the other end of the beach. The girl's dress was an awkwardly long length, like his mother's. And the girl had a burn of red hair on her head. Red like stewed cherries. The little girl was wandering toward him, while the lady with her packed up their things. The girl was safely away from the ocean, but Jacob had this sudden feeling of wanting to save her. He knew how to swim, a gift his mother had bestowed. Early on she had considered drowning him and so had pitched him in the sea at six weeks old. But newborn Jacob had been young enough to remember the womb. Swimming was not only natural but immediate. Rebekah had taken it as a final sign, a final witchery the world had won — she would love the boy and let him live. But Jacob also wanted to save the girl because Jacob had those saving tendencies. They would flare up later when he was an Army man and then again when he was pressed to choose between love and life. Now he ran toward the girl who was carrying the big shell.

Eeona was packing them up quickly. Rushing to leave, leave, leave. She didn't see the little boy with the sand-colored skin approach Anette.

Jacob had run to the girl, but now that he was before her, he didn't know why. "You might drown," he said, as though it was impending.

"I know," Anette said, without looking up at him.

Anette was almost eight. And Jacob was only just eight. She was wearing red. And red was his favorite color.

"Can you swim?" Jacob asked.

Anette still didn't look at him, for she didn't like her answer. "My sister won't teach me."

"I can swim," said Jacob. By which he meant, I can save you if you need saving. As the youngest child in his household, he had never been allowed to do that.

Now Anette turned. "You can swim!" she said. And she said it with determination as if, like a witch, she had wished it. Jacob nodded, receiving this. Then she offered the queen conch to his ear. "Do you want to listen to Papa in my shell?" Jacob leaned and let her press it against his ear. Anette liked how he did this. How she held this beauty for him and he didn't recoil.

She lowered the heavy shell. Jacob smiled. "Mama say I come from the sea," he said, not understanding himself. "That's me in your shell."

"Me, too," Anette said.

Then Jacob's mother and Anette's sister saw them and ran to save them each. Rebekah and Eeona knew each other immediately and so immediately knew the other's child, as well. They snatched their respective eight-year-olds away as though the other woman and the other child were a disease.

"But Mama, I was just telling her what you tell me," Jacob whined, as Rebekah dragged him by the waist of his shorts. He was a child, so he didn't look back just then. He said the words to his mother. It wasn't the little girl he really cared about, not yet.

"I just tell her I from the sea," he tried to explain.

"Not everything I tell you is for everyone else to hear," Rebekah said, dragging him away and calling to the other boys.

"But she say she the same as me, Mama. That's true?"

He asked again and again. But Rebekah understood the power of a flood, the power of dirt heaped down a hole, so she began to tell a story. One she hoped would push out the memory of that little girl and her little-girl words. It was meant to be a harmless story, but even stories that seem harmless are never without their danger.

"The Duene live in the sea." (This little girl had not even swum in the sea.) "They have long hair." (The little girl had picky red hair.) "They walk backwards." (The girl had feet facing forward.) Rebekah told the myth as she gathered her sons one by one and marched them the long way home.

But before they left the sand and sea, Jacob did look back. Because his mother did not take him to church, he had not heard of the pillar of salt. It happened. He did not turn to salt exactly, but something in him did become preserved. He looked back and saw the little girl in the red dress being pulled away from him, but looking back at him as well. And from then on, it was clear what would be.

Back in Savan, Eeona decided she had to do something. Mama had said "watch out" for the boy and Anette. Perhaps the first thing she should do was to send Anette to the cousin in Tortola. This was honoring Mama's wish, wasn't it? Wasn't it a clean solution to all problems? The Tortola cousin was older, feeble even, but Eeona could say it was just for a visit and then a visit would turn into years. Or what of that bright-eyed Stemme woman in Anegada? But even if that woman took the child, all of St. Thomas would judge Eeona for sending her sister to Anegada to be a fisherman's concubine. But there was also the orphanage on the less familiar island of St. Croix. Someone had written about it in the *Daily News* and it seemed a clean place. And St. Croix, Eeona had heard, was a large piece of land where no one would even know who little Anette Bradshaw really was and to whom she belonged.

And then Eeona would be able to start. Start over. In the meantime, the mentor Eeona had decided on was off island. She was rootless, that Liva. But this was fine, because Eeona had to sew herself a blue dress, which she knew caused women to calm in her presence.

Liva Lovernkrandt returned from her most recent New York visit just when Eeona was adding a lace hem.

25.

The McKenzies of St. Thomas were all men. They were descendants of a Catholic slave owner who gave all his land to his one hairy bastard son. Y chromosomes were all that was ever passed down. The men were all huge, full of muscles before they made their tenth year. They could make baby boys from age nine to ninety. But this masculinity didn't come free. In every litter there were a few who weren't quite right.

The McKenzie oddness was a mysterious thing that made some of the McKenzie boys never learn to dance well or read even the simplest books. Still, there were those who could calculate your birthday and the hour you were born and then tell you when your world would end, or those who could play any instrument you put their fingers to. McKenzies were hard to love, though, because they never hugged or smiled much or seemed to need anyone — not even one another. The women were all outsiders, mothers and wives. Breeders of a race of men.

The McKenzie men were never senators, were never doctors; they were never journalists, never major contributors to Caribbean or even Virgin Islands history. They had two truly extraordinary qualities — they always had sons and they always married well.

With the exception of Rebekah, the McKenzie wives and mothers were of the richest, highest families, which kept the family light-skinned — easy to pass for Portuguese or Sicilian when traveling to the U.S. So the McKenzie boys who at least learned to read continued to carry on these ultra-male genes, matched with all the wealth and caste St. Thomas and the other Virgin Islands had to offer. Many of the men became successful — though never all on their own merit. Always with the help of a well-connected and rich-born wife.

Nowadays our McKenzies tend toward jobs such as police officer and security guard, fireman and military man. Those public jobs weren't always available to natives, though Benjamin McKenzie, Rebekah's husband and the legal father of all her sons, did manage to make it in the Navy. But still the McKenzies were always a family of class and coarseness. Every debutante sank her face into a silk-covered pillow and dreamed it was the hairy belly of a Mc-Kenzie man. Every businessman, black, white, mixed, Frenchy, or mulatto, longed for endless grandsons and so sold portions of his soul to see his daughters married and McKenzied.

With Rebekah, however, Benjamin Mc-Kenzie had not married well at all. He had married out of infatuation, which was rare among McKenzies and was most definitely the work of Rebekah's enchantment. And when Benjamin left her with man children — we must say man children, and not boys, they were gruff those lads, even before puberty — Rebekah did not despair. Indeed, most on St. Thomas assumed that Rebekah had sent him away on a wind — and they were correct. The other women who married McKenzies envied her. She had managed a hat trick. She had the McKenzie name and the McKenzie sons, but she had escaped the McKenzie man.

It must be said that Jacob Esau McKenzie became the favored child. He'd come of romantic longing, not a longing for security. Yes, she'd tried to kill him, but if you ask even we old wives, we'd say that was out of worry and love. The love mostly won. But still there was the worry. Rebekah made

Jacob go barefoot so his toes would not fuse into clefts as hers did, which was an Athy trait, from Rebekah's line. But the big worry was over Jacob Esau not really being a McKenzie. Would he go unsupported by the McKenzie uncles when the time came for him to go to college or get a job? Would he be denied the good match in a wife? True, not being a McKenzie meant Jacob Esau wouldn't suffer the prepubescent hair and deep toddler voice of his brothers. He was hers and Owen's, but for all Rebekah's knowledge, she did not know really what this mix might mean. It was Owen who'd once told her the story of the Duene.

To be fair, it is all maddening. These myths that conflate and grow into one another. Do the Duene men only live on the land of St. Croix? Do the Duene women only live in the sea of Anegada? Even myths must have their rebellions. Even we old wives must have our secrets.

What Jacob Esau had was an incredible confidence that would later make him a leader in the Army and presumptuous with another man's wife. He could play the piano. He loved stewed cherries for their taste (both sweet and tart) and their color (deep red). And more important, unlike any other McKenzie man, he would fall madly and obviously in love.

This last one Rebekah knew. After all, Jacob was not a McKenzie. He could love and be loved. And if a man can love, it is only a matter of living long enough before he does. Rebekah knew this, but she was determined to prevent it. Her husband was gone. And her lover was gone. All she had were her sons. If she could help it, the only woman her Jacob would ever love would be her.

To this end, Rebekah kept all her sons away from the Roman Catholic Church, despite the McKenzie baptisms. In that church there were women. Lovely young women with veils on their heads, just waiting for some man to lift and kiss them. Worst, there was Mary. The Virgin dressed always and forever in blue. Rebekah hawked up and spat when she thought of this. Mary was no virgin. Mary had fucked before marriage and then had convinced everyone, even her clueless boyfriend, that God had impregnated her instead. There was also Jesus himself, with all his nakedness on the cross and lovelorn face begging.

"Don't take a person into your mouth unless you are willing to commit," Rebekah told Jacob when he begged to receive the Sacrament like his friends. "It's called

Communion for a reason. You *commune.*"

But these islands are just too beautiful. You walk out of your own front door into cathedrals. You step down your own stairs up toward an altar. God speaks from the bougainvillea bush, from Mountain Top. You go to the beach and swim in holy water. The beauty, like God's face, is ubiquitous and it is blinding. Of course, Rebekah would lose. Jacob would commune without her say.

We sometimes say their love began with music, but as with all things, it began with water. And as with all things of importance to us, it began on a beach. It began that day when Jacob saw Anette in her stewed-cherry dress, and Anette put the shell to his ear, and they each heard their father speak the sea.

26.

Eeona had pinched and managed to buy a burro for traveling in style to market and Mass. This one was smaller and more stubborn than the almost grand beast the Bradshaws had owned. The ass came with the name Nelson. Eeona, always thinking that a given name had great importance, didn't change the name even though she found it frivolous. To go to Mrs. Lovernkrandt's for tea, Eeona tied thin cerulean ribbons around Nelson's ears, so they might arrive in class. The donkey's ribbons matched Eeona's dress. But then there at the Lovernkrandt gate she saw an actual automobile parked like a sphinx. Sure, she'd seen them, the motorized donkeys, carrying their masters up and down Main Street. But she had never been so close to one before. It seemed a dangerous omen. And it was.

As she entered the parlor, Eeona saw immediately that this Lovernkrandt woman was sitting in her mother's rocking chair. Eeona hadn't sold the chair, but had simply left it at Villa by the Sea. And now here it was. If Liva had the rocking chair, perhaps she had other Villa by the Sea pieces. Perhaps all the fine women of the island had a signature piece of the home that should have been Eeona's now molded into their own. Eeona, of course, was no longer privy to the goings-on of the high-bred women and their families.

Watching this woman, her mongoose face and pasty complexion, sitting in a prized part of Villa by the Sea, Eeona had the vulgar urge to loosen her hair, as if she were drawing a sword. But she remained mindful that this woman was to be her benefactor.

Mrs. Lovernkrandt did not take out her

fur coat for Eeona, but she spoke of her travels. The woman even spoke, imagine, of Anegada, where part of her people had been from generations ago. Eeona revealed nothing of her own old adventure on the atoll. Though, if we are being honest, everyone knew of Eeona's failure with the young Frenchman.

"They are so small-island-thinking there," Mrs. Lovernkrandt said of the atoll. "But . . ." And now she smiled and looked out the window just over her shoulder. "I can see my grandfather now, knee-deep in the ocean. The sun is setting behind him and he is just a silhouette with a machete, chopping a lobster into pieces." She sighed. "Backwards and beautiful. But not New York City. The city is just ugly and forwards." New York had become Liva's most frequent excursion. "The music, the art, the theater — it all rages on despite the depressive state of things," she said, seeming to forget that Eeona's mother had been to America but returned just to die. Instead, Mrs. Lovernkrandt leaned forward with her eyes wide open. "And some of the art is by the American Negro."

Mrs. Lovernkrandt, a mulattress herself, was generally of a nutmeg color. When she returned from New York, she was very pale, as though there were milk under her skin instead of blood. She looked almost like a white woman. And truth be told, her Danish husband had told the Americans that his wife was of Portuguese descent in order to dampen any Negroid suspicions. Now Mrs. Lovernkrandt always wore a hat when outside and she always sought the shade.

Sitting in her parlor with Eeona, Mrs. Lovernkrandt seemed conspiratorial. "Your mother, rest her in her grave, had always wanted to see the newest fashions."

Well, perhaps Antoinette had seen them. Perhaps the Widow Bradshaw had touched and smelled it all. But it didn't matter, because that happened far away from here and so we can't be sure. Instead, Liva Lovernkrandt spoke about the black men scatting on stage. She had seen black women dancing like Africans, which, truth be said, was quite similar to how everyone danced on the island.

"American Negroes," she said, with awe, as though these were a new breed of people. Which, in a way, they were. Just as we were. Indeed, we were now a version of them.

Eeona held her back stiff and straight, and this severity, as it often did, caused her pain. Often she would crumple into bed after she had allowed herself to be witnessed in public. But she could never let anyone see her as anything other than the lady she had been raised to be. Should have been. Would be again. She listened to the tap of the rocking chair as Liva told her silly stories.

When the man-about-the-house poured more bush tea, he rattled Eeona's cup. He could not look at her in the eye. He gave her the back of his neck. He gave the side of his face. Eeona could hear his sharp swallow of breathing. She could not blame him. He was in her presence. She had felt the same thing when she was alone in her own company. Her blue motherly dresses did often calm men, but not entirely.

Eeona waited to speak until he had left the room, for fear she might give the man a heart attack with the close proximity of her voice. She didn't look at the rocker, plain in her peripheral vision, but straight at this woman who would save her. "You have very fine help, Mrs. Lovernkrandt."

"Yes, and I would much appreciate it if you kept your hair pinned up or I'll have to keep him in hiding whenever you pay a visit. You know how you Bradshaw women are." She sighed. "I so prefer having a male servant to a woman. Perhaps it's because I only had sons." She paused, leaning forward in the rocker to sip her tea and, perhaps, consider her words. Mrs. Lovernkrandt knew that Eeona no longer had any kind of servant and, at the rate she was going, might never have any children either.

Eeona heard all the things unspoken. She tensed but waited.

"Well, Eeona, lovely, it is time you called me Liva."

A good sign, but still Eeona knew she must be careful. The most significant reason for selling Villa by the Sea had been in order to repay Captain Owen Arthur Bradshaw's debt to this woman's husband. Now Eeona lifted her chin as though looking down on her own words. "Liva, thank you. My visit is more than a social one." She knew how to charm a man but she was less skilled with women. "Perhaps, in memory of the business long between our families, you might provide some guidance for me."

Liva's smile seemed sour. "Lovely Eeona. Your mother always did say you were clairvoyant. I have, I won't deny it, been considering you."

Eeona felt the stiffening in her spine release with a small sigh. She readied herself for an offer and for her own life to begin. Liva continued. "Tell me now. What are your skills."

Poor Eeona hadn't thought deeply on this.

She supposed the woman would want her the way any woman liked pretty things. She could be a doll, a daughter. Eeona smiled, giving herself a moment of time to swim her own brain. "Crochet," she said quickly. "I can crochet quite well. I am good with baskets made of dried palm. I am also learning needlepoint."

Liva nodded eagerly, the chair swaying, as though she'd hoped for all this. "And what of your younger sister. Is she not in your care? Unfortunately, I have no need for the both of you."

"I am just now organizing for her send-off to Puerto Rico," said Eeona in a flash, though the letter she was writing was to St. Croix, the orphanage.

"Finishing school in Puerto Rico! As your mother did." Liva clapped with giddiness into Eeona's discomfort. The chair shook. "To wash off some of Anegada's backwardness before marriage. Though Antoinette did seduce your father, despite her small-islandness. Yes, well, so many of us tried for your father. Oh, no worries, my dear. She won fair and square. I've always admired your mother for that. It's a Stemme thing, you know — the men falling for you." Throughout all this, Liva rocked the chair like a tune, a mood music to her chattering.

"Oh! But how wonderful you were able to secure your sister a place. You must tell me your secret. We will have secrets, you and I."

Well, the woman did seem to be on Eeona's side. "That would all be very fine, Mrs. Lovernkrandt. Liva."

"Good. Good. Well, it is true that I shall be traveling again soon, this time alone. Travel I must, you know. I was born for New York. I see that now. When I'm there, I don't even stay with my sons. The younger ones only have a toonchy bachelor flat between them. You remember them, don't you?"

"Splendid young men," Eeona said, though she only remembered the Lovernkrandt boys as a scrum of young Danes who grew shy in her presence. But now she could see how perhaps the boys, grown men by now, might fight over her attentions.

"Well, yes. The eldest is married, you know, of course. We had the wedding here." Liva's eyes opened in amusement or embarrassment, Eeona couldn't be sure. Eeona hadn't even been invited to the wedding. The rocking halted for a brief moment, but recovered. "My younger boys are now engaged to blue-blooded girls. Sisters, imagine! I think their father is in the railroad business. Well, here it is, Eeona deary. It just won't due to have a man not my husband with me when I travel alone." Liva leaned back in the chair and fluttered her hand to the door through which the servant had disappeared. "Now see how your query is so timely. You can come along instead. A kind of handmaiden."

It took Eeona a minute. *Handmaiden* sounded like someone close to royalty and the term temporarily distracted her. But in a moment it was clear. "You mean to offer me a role as your servant?" Eeona could feel her skin burn, as though her blood were turning to saltwater.

Liva leaned into her tea, the rocker on its front tips, and did not meet Eeona's eyes. "Well, what else were you hoping for, dear Eeona? Truly now, what else could you hope for?"

Eeona stood. Her body was a crumbling stone, and her standing was shaky. She put her hand to her hair, intending, really, to simply adjust her hairpins. But with Liva not even looking at her, Eeona felt a great groveling need. She removed each pin bit by bit, right there in the parlor. Liva, hearing the singing of the pins, finally looked up and saw the hair go sailing. The servant was just coming to replenish the tea, but now he sent the tray he was holding crashing to the floor and the sugar on the tray spraying across the room. Eeona did not wait for Mrs. Lovernkrandt to shove her out. "Liva, may you lose everything you've taken from me."

And that was the last time Eeona saw Liva Lovernkrandt.

Of course, Lovernkrandt's illegal rum had been difficult to sell. Indeed, the Continentals' murder of our major industry with their Prohibition had been Mr. Lovernkrandt's justification for why he could not forgive the Bradshaws their bone debt.

During the Prohibition, the British Virgin Islands had made rum as they always had and BVI women smuggled over the sweetness in their panties. The U.S. Coast Guardsmen only sometimes managed to shove their bare hands into the rummy underwear. By the time rum was legal again, Lovernkrandt had already been forced to dismantle his mills and his business connections. He had tried to make do on molasses and sugar instead of rum. Molasses had never been a big seller. And now beet sugar was being more cheaply made in the U.S. For some time cane sugar had been sifting away.

Mr. Lovernkrandt had always said he

would never quit the Virgin Islands, but then there he was, bon voyaging on a ship with his wife. Gone, the both of them. Their sons married wealthy; they could settle into a Connecticut cottage. Not New York City after all. But still, they were heading to America. Despite his Danish parentage, Mr. Lovernkrandt was a native of the Virgin Islands, according to the U.S. declaration. A Caribbean man, but also an American all the same. We all were.

When the Lovernkrandts left, they were forced to sell their estate, for they could not maintain it from abroad. They sold it and everything in it. The rocking chair included.

27.

ANETTE

Don't mind I is a pickney. I still old enough to ascertain what the ass going on. Sometimes Eeona leave me with any old neighbor when she go on her outings. Riding that burro sidesaddle like it a steed. The neighbors kind enough, but they don't claim me. They feed me a little dumpling if I hungry. They give me a pot and stick to pung if I bored. But they don't love me. And though I can't say how I know, I know about love. I know my sister supposed to love me. She the only one supposed to. I know whatever else I get is by grace.

Eeona think that because I a child that I deaf and blind. When she went go buy the ticket for St. Croix, she take me with she because there was no neighbor to throw me by. I hear she say my name and not her own. One ticket. And I hear she call me Anette Stemme and not Anette Bradshaw, even though I don't know person one with the name Stemme. But I know enough. That I going someplace and Eeona ain accompanying me. And when I gone, I ain going to be her sister anymore. Different last name going to break that just so.

So see me. Since ticket buy, I trying bad to be good. Earning my stay. I sweeping the floor. I only eating a little-little bit of food so she don't worry about feeding me. I squeezing tight to the edge of the bed so she don't feel I inconveniencing her sleep. I barely sleeping at all. I keep to the corners of the flat when she sewing so I don't disturb. I even leave the flat and walk about, float sticks in the gutter water with Gertie and the other wild children. See, I staying out of the flipping way.

But Eeona still sending me. I know the day reach when Eeona pull a cloth bag with clasp from under the bed. Is something

144

fancy like maybe had belong to Mama. It swell up with clothes. And I know is for me. I sit down and watch Eeona stir up the soursop tea. After I drink that, I was so soursopped I could have walk on water. It to calm me. Keep me from saying my true name or from harassing the situation — like what they give children nowadays when they go on airplanes. But you ain know me. No matter what poison I been given, I still ain getting on nobody boat. I know boats mean I heading to dead. The soursop have me stupefied and that have me stupid enough to start up a wailing when we get near that boat. "I deading! I deading! Don't let me dead!"

Eeona looking around like she going to shrivel up with shame, her hand trying to cover my mouth to hush me. We ain even right up at the boat and already I bazadie. She gripping me like I is a wild animal but looking round the whole time to see who it is seeing. Is then I realize that throwing me away ain just a secret from me, but from everybody. So I really get to work then. I bawling about my own impending death so loud and intent that I start believe it my own self.

The captain he self had to come out and tell Eeona that I can't board unattended if I carrying on so. And since this man is a captain, he know we and call we by we name. So now if they didn't know before, everyone waiting for that boat know that the very Eeona Bradshaw attempting a sending-off of she little sister to St. Croix, and what the hell that could mean? The captain's wife come out and watch me in my face. "The child is sick," she say, and though she say it tough it have a gentleness. But Eeona recover fast. "She's going to family. Doctors. A family of doctors in St. Croix." The wife shake she head and step back. "The child is likely contagious."

Let me tell you. When that ship blare, I, Anette Bradshaw, am slumped on the dry dock watching the ship push off. Eeona is standing watching it as though it a man she love pulling away from she. But I have something else going on that Eeona ain catch as yet. I sick for true.

There on the dock my skin blazing like I have a fever. My eyes them watering but it ain water, is something thick like it going to blind me. Eeona march home and don't even watch behind to see if I following. I only stumbling behind her wondering how the ass I do this. I say I deading and look, now I deading. That next morning, I wake up on the floor. But I only know is the floor because I feeling it hard and cold. My eyes them seal shut like with a paste.

Eeona don't call no doctor or take me to no hospital. But a neighbor woman come. This a woman from the island of Jost Van Dyke. Same side of the Virgin Islands, the British, that our mama from. Everybody know that this woman sweet on other woman like how woman suppose to sweet on man. She ain fraid of Eeona. She fancy Eeona. So she think she doing Eeona a favor when she come by the flat. But even she quick make the pronouncement. Fever to the bone. Mucus stuffing every membrane. And yes, is true. I deading. I about to dead any blooming minute. Or maybe it might take a month. But I heading there. The Spanish influenza, she say, cross she self and back out the room. Contagious, no lie, and kill anyone it kiss.

But me? I live. And I know is not no Spanish flu that near machete me. Is me the machete. Is my own self saying something and then making it so. And no doctor ain heal me. Is me. I there spending days and then weeks telling myself that I going to live. Eeona have me worse than a leper, but that mean I get the bed all to myself while she sleep on the settee in the outer room. While she waiting for me to die, she still have to water me. And that Jost Van Dyke woman still come looking for Eeona and bring me broth. So I sustained enough to keep my thinking clear. I going to love and be loved, and it going to be all right, because those who to love me won't, but someone will and he coming if you just stay alive, Anette. Is my thinking almost kill me and is my thinking save me.

But let me tell you, all of that power, it scare me no ras! Speak-and-make-it-so is a easy magic for mistakes. I live, but I come careful. I live to not wish death on a soul for years and years, until I meet a man who give me a love like a tsunami. And I would swim to get to the deepest point and drown myself in him.

28.

Eeona

Beauty is a parlour trick. It is in how you sit in the light. It is in how you turn your head and how you breathe. A man will never see his wife with pure eyes after he has smelled the tiny space behind my ear.

Men may marry despite their inabilities. We women must seek a life based on our abilities. The ability I have always had is that men will love me. It is the magic I have.

It did not seem to me that I could choose my true self and still keep a child. In this way, my mother and I were alike. It is only that we had different ambitions.

I only wanted some land and a villa. I only wanted a ship. I only wanted a father for whom I was the favourite. That had been stripped from me too quickly, you see. Even I was aware that my beauty may not last forever.

Of course, I would have mourned my Anette dying. I mourned her living all the same.

■ ■ ■ ■

BELONGING

■ ■ ■ ■

All hail our Virgin Islands.
Em'ralds of the sea,
Where beaches bright with coral sand
And trade winds bless our native land.
— ALTON ADAMS, "VIRGIN ISLANDS MARCH"

29.
ANETTE

Nothing ever happen just so. It must be a story. But when I break from that fever, the first thing I see from the bed was a boy there watching me. At this time I had only know Ronald as a boy who I see sometimes with my friend Gertie when she dress up nice and ain running with me in the street. The smell of his mother's cooking more than once had me sitting beneath his window dreaming. But now this Ronald here watching my body before he catch he self and look up at my face. I ain self realize that I just laying there in my flimsy nightie and I been sweating out this fever so the whole thing wet like I been drowning. All what God give me there for Ronald to see. "Anette, everybody saying that if I kiss you I going to die. But I don't believe them."

"Believe them," I say scratchy and quiet because I ain use my voice in a long while.

He leave and come back with a glass of

water. I reach for it but my hands them slippery. Is the fever breaking? My chest and all busting water. But I ain care. Ronald put the water to my lips. It going down like prickles but it feel good enough. "Thank you kindly, Ronald."

"You going to be at school, Anette?"

I don't know what the ass this boy talking. When we was rich Eeona had a tutor and then get send away to Tortola for more tutoring. Me? I was too young for the tutor when Papa and then Mama gone. The free grammar school finish at fifth grade, so is a good while I ain been in school. Eeona don't have me in private school because she had say we can't afford the tuition and the books and the uniform. I know how to read, I know my numbers, I know history and social studies what people talk in the street. That's my most recent schooling. But I lie to Ronald, because now I thinking maybe if I say yes, then yes will make it so. "Yes, I will see you at school."

"It will be good to see you."

"But you seeing me all now."

He gulp. I ain care. He there in the doorway to the bedroom, and I wondering what to do to get him to go away so I could go inspect my body and see if it come nice or shrivel-up. But I can't just close the door in the boy face. So I ask him. "You want kiss me now?" His eyes pop open like he seeing me naked, which he almost is for how light and wet this nightie is I wearing. "I'll see you in school, Anette." And he spin round fast-fast.

See, me? I had never want what my sister want. Eeona want to have things. I had want to be had. I had want to be claimed. I ain shame, put it on my gravestone: *Anette get love up good.* And that is what my life has been about. Only not as I thought it would be.

That very week it come out in the paper and announce in the churches that public school expanding and now going up to the end of twelfth grade. Everything free, even the books. Is not a choice, is a big word: compulsory. American law in your bawna. Eeona have to send me. And she glad to send me away.

That Sunday Eeona want to take me to see the new American Anglican bishop and get a blessing because is only by the grace of God that I recover — so she say. In truth, I thinking her carrying on is just for show. But she insisting that is a real blessing that I going to school.

I think we walking to church but Eeona

hop on Nelson, the ass. I don't like this animal, let me tell you. And I don't like riding sidesaddle like as idiot. Eeona have the damn ass ears tie up in blue ribbons to match her own blue dress. Like we is a pappy show. And the donkey is a male, so I can't see how it could like the ribbons. But Eeona just swing she leg around so she can ride sidesaddle. Her hands so tight around the reins she knuckles turn bone color — and despite what she think, she ain a white woman, so this mean she holding them reins tight, you hear.

"I could walk," I say.

"Must you be such an obstacle, Anette?" Eeona there holding Nelson reins in one fisted hand and a frilly white parasol with the other like she a queen. "If you walk, you will miss all of Mass. Climb on the back of the animal." Is like she commanding me.

Now, I know how a donkey could be kitten in the front but tiger in the back. Nelson know that I ain like he. As I sit, he begin to adjust he rear, and I thinking the damn donkey going let go a fart and we going to end up in church stinking like ass of ass. Eeona clear her throat and hold her mouth tight, as though tightening up her own lips going make the donkey fart hold inside. But instead the donkey rustle and rustle and

156

then slowly lower he backside to the ground so that I go sliding like is the kiddie slide they have for Carnival. If Eeona ain reach out her foot, she would have been there bum first beside me. Instead, she standing over me looking vex and, damn she, more beautiful for it.

"What have you done?" she ask. I want to tell her is this fool-fool burro. Instead, I say, "Let me try again." Again and again I try but each time I climb on, Nelson just sit down as if he get tired. How the damn donkey know is me when he ain even look back, I can't say. I could see now why they sell this animal to Eeona for cheap. I sure ain no one could ride that beast but Eeona Bradshaw.

Just so Eeona leave me there in the house and ride that ass to Mass so she could at least catch the second reading. "I shall pray for us all," she say, as she canter away. Then she call back without even turning her head, "Fetch water from the standpipe for cooking. Please roll some dumplings for us. Go to the Hospital Ground fish market and fetch an oldwife. No other fish will do. Oldwife only. Now that you are recovered you must make an attempt at usefulness."

And let me tell you, Nelson never let me ride he. The problem is that Eeona always have chores for me while she gone to the Hospitality Lounge where she get a piece of job sewing and stitching, or when she gone riding to church to thank God that I gone school and give she some space or what have you. Fetch some sweet pepper and limes from the market, she say to me. Haul water from the standpipe for brushing our teeth. Get fish from Hospital Ground, never from Frenchtown. Eeona claim that I jumbie Nelson because I trying to get away with being dependent on my sister for everything. But I say again, I don't believe in these things — jumbie, obeah, voodoo. I believe in me.

And watch what I mean: I never even went walking that first Sunday for fish or water. For true. I just sit down in the tiny flat we renting and think of the fish frying and the water springing. It come like I procrastinating, but I wasn't a lick surprised when Ronald rap on the door again and say he just had an idea to pass with some fresh fish and he have some fresh water in this here bucket. Is the fish oldwife? Yes. He also bring the sweet pepper and limes for the fish. Man, Ronald even clean and cook the fish, you hear. He a boy but he learn it all from his mother.

What can I say for Ronnie? He was a good

boy and he come a good man. But I ain really that special to Ronnie. Is not me alone he would do things for. Anybody ask him for a dollar, he reach in his pocket and give them ten. Is good to give, you know. But Ronald give like he don't know when to stop. Man, Ronnie even friend with the tourists that walking about drinking rum like water and sweating like they is standpipe. He offer them rag to wipe off. He jump into the water when the tourists throw a dime — fetch it for them. From his own cup he pour them Coca-Cola for their rum.

But woy, the boy could cook. Eeona there thinking that maybe I might be worth keeping around because I learn how to make johnnycake and paté, red pea soup with dumplings. I like I learning in my sleep. But once she gone down the street on Nelson back, riding sidesaddle with that too-warm crochet shawl around her shoulders, I would just think on Ronald and then Ronald and Gertie would come and knock on the door to see if I need anything.

See, after that first time where he make the fish and dumplings, Ronnie never come by he self. Because really and truly it just ain proper for a young man to be in the house alone with a young girl. He come with my friend Gertie. And while he in there

159

fixing fish and fungi, Gertie and me there playing cards — go fish. When food cook, all a we eat.

Eeona spending all her time working in the Hospitality Lounge, planning some plan to get she self rich again. But she ain talking 'bout sending me St. Croix. And I ain going no how. St. Thomas come sweet. Besides, once I big enough I even start helping with the rent — working at the apothecary after school as cashier — those child labor laws from the States ain yet take proper effect for we. The food that Ronnie make every Sunday lasting the whole week. I barely seeing Eeona at all. Is like we sisters living each in our own land with the sea separating. But is fine with me. Is pretty fine. Is fine for years. But it only take a few years for a war change up all of that fineness.

30.

It was easy. There was war. We had to prove something to the nation, it seemed. Prove we were worthy of the U.S. passports they'd allowed us. Every man in St. Thomas knew he was going to be drafted. And every man who put on a uniform wanted to leave something behind. A wife. Something to

160

return to. They were in high school now, but Ronald had been in love with Anette for years; since on a dare he'd snuck into her flat to try and kiss her.

Ronald came from a decent family. This was not important to Anette. This was important to Eeona. It is true that Eeona did not take to Ronald. In fact, she thought his picky hair would surely sully the Bradshaw genes. But Eeona needed two things: First, to be free of her unwanted charge in a way that still kept the family dignity. Second, very second, though it should have been first, to keep Anette away from the wrong mangrove man with the McKenzie name.

But what Anette needed was to fall in love in such a way that she was hooked to that man as if with an invisible cord. A cord not unlike the one fastening you to your mother at birth. Only this is one you cannot see and so cannot easily cut away. Still, Anette thought she liked Ronald enough to go around with him. It was easy to think this. Many girls liked Ronald — he was likable.

Just after turning eighteen Ronald Smalls got the letter, which all our young men were getting, that said he was drafted. Instead of howling out of fear, he went to the beautiful Eeona. He told her the lie that he was enlisting, and the truth that he would like Anette to be his wife. He sat in their little outer room and answered all of Eeona's questions. "Will you love and obey her?" "Yes, Miss Bradshaw." "Will you promise to not die?" "I promise to try not to." "You do know that she does not love you?" Ronald did not know this. He sat there and blinked with his mouth slightly open.

"Young man, love is not everything." Eeona said this with authority. Poor Ronald. "It is fine, Mr. Smalls. You will do."

So Eeona gave her blessing for the marriage and began, as her mother had before her, to sew Anette a dress. Eeona also began to consider her savings, her possible means, the clearest trajectory, the shortest time frame to her backward escape. But there was one thing that she did not consider: that Ronald Smalls and Jacob Esau McKenzie would both end up as soldiers in Port Company 875.

31.

ANETTE

We ain really know it have a war. We there living good, you know. The Navy there in Sub Base, but who really studying them? The Navy boys just like to drink and cause

162

confusion. The Coast Guard repaint the Muhlenfeldt Point lighthouse and install bright lights that blink up the sea at night. But nobody ain really study the Coast Guard since the Rum Wars done. Me and Gertie try to get out to the lighthouse point for a picnic but the keeper, a old Yankee, run we off. And then all the sudden there was a war and they say they starting up companies just for Virgin Islanders. Army. Coast Guard. Even some special boys with good last names end up in the Navy proper. Everybody say that if the boys serve good, they going let we vote and let we have our own governor. The statesiders bring the Puerto Rican soldiers and sailors over to show our backsides they mean business. See those P.R. boys, sharp-sharp in their white uniforms. Walking in the street with some broad shoulder as if they is men even though most of them is seventeen or eighteen, like me and my classmates.

All a we went to Charlotte Amalie High then. Only one proper high school on the island so everybody know one another. It have a McKenzie in my class and his name is Saul. Them McKenzies used to get skip or hold back depending on whether the teacher think they brilliant or stupidee. Saul is a stupidee, so he actually older than the rest of us, but he a nice fellow. I hear he have a brother who younger than him but in college already. That brother, supposedly a brilliant, name Jacob. And one time, I open the yearbook and that selfsame Jacob smiling from the seat of a piano. But that's the most I think on that McKenzie.

Plenty girls had like my classmate Saul. He dull but still a McKenzie. But he ain studying none of we. It turn out he don't fancy girls at all. No matter, because when the war come, every girl in the high school had a Puerto Rican soldier or sailor boyfriend, even if only in she mind. Puerto Rican music now taking over the radio waves, Spanish boleros on everybody tongue.

Now it coming clear that Ronald, despite all that cooking and cleaning, wasn't no man to hold me. Ronnie ain even try again to kiss me on the mouth all these years we going school together. He ain fraid of no Spanish influenza, he just one of them too-proper boys. But still, he have people thinking we going around steady. But I was a fast girl, always spinning on my own axis, and I ain have no patience for Ronald who don't know how to hold on tight.

When the Puerto Rican boys liming in Emancipation Garden, me and Gertie go and lime, too. Manie, is what I call each of the soldiers them, even though I ain know if they name Manuel or Manuelito or any such thing. Is just that they really doing the man thing, you know? They say bold things in Spanish. Encantada. Bonita. Everybody on St. Thomas know enough Spanish to buy provisions on the Santo ships when they come in, or beg the Ponce man who own the movie theater for a Clark Gable. ¿Cómo estás? we say. Bien. Hombre bonito. Por favor. The boys know enough English, because they does learn it in school in San Juan. They ask if we have boyfriend before they even ask our names. When we exhaust the languages, the boys start taking we by the hands, walking about the garden like we going steady. When we walk, they leading; a little guide go that way, a little turn let we stop here in the shade, and a little dip let we sit at this bench. Smooth as water in a glass.

Now I ain thinking that sitting down on a bench with a boy is no big deal. But that evening I reach home and Eeona tell me, "Your suitor came calling." I only wondering how that Manie find our flat. I thinking Eeona going to yabba me good: *Who, pray tell, is this ragamuffin Puerto Rican who cannot even speak English knocking on our door?*

165

But then I thinking it might even end up okay. Eeona might like the young man because he light-skinned, you know, and we could all pretend he descend straight from Magellan or Columbus or something so.

Just as I thinking this through, Ronald Smalls knocking on the door. He ain wait to answer but he come barging in even though the sun going down and it ain really appropriate for him to be in our place so late. "I hear that one of the Puerto Ricans has been going around with my fiancée." He ain even looking to me.

"Fian-who? What you talking about, Ronnie?"

Ronald look at Eeona as though he and she have a pact. "I hear Miss Anette Bradshaw has been courted by a Puerto Rican from the . . . Navy." You could see it was hard for him to say the last part. Because it's true, them man in uniform was sweeping up woman like cobwebs.

"I ain your fiancée, Ronnie." And when I say this, Eeona open her eyes until her eyebrow mash into her forehead. "I don't see no wedding band saying who I for." I wiggle my ring finger at them both and go into the bedroom. I flop down on our one bed and fall into a sweaty sleep.

That very week me and Gertie strolling

166

down Main Street each with a little blue and red scarf around we neck because anything in the American colors is fashionable now. Somebody come running past. Then somebody else. I hold one of them. "What all you chasing?"

"A local boy looking to fight one of them P.R. boys in the Garden. They fighting over some girl," he call over his shoulder. Then he stop and turn to me. "In fact, is you they fighting over. You is Anette Bradshaw, right?"

Is a big running me and Gertie do. We reach down to the Garden. No big-big crowd, just a scattering of men. But is only men, because even watching a fight ain a lady thing. So me and Gertie, we find a place behind some bougainvillea and we watch Ronald there shouting and carrying on to nobody in particular. And his friends, who is our friends, because everybody in the same school, there holding him back. But no P.R. boy in sight. I don't want to see Ronald get beat up, so I considering going to him and telling him I'll be his girl if he behave. But just then a gang of Ricans come strolling in. I had feel bad for how scruffy our boys look. I ain even think the Manie who sit with me is among these, but one boy walk straight up to Ronald, and before

167

anybody could say begin or ring a bell or what have you, he put a cuff on Ronald so hard Ronnie there on the floor sprawl out like he dead.

Everybody flock around Ronald. Even the P.R. boys bend down to see if the boy okay. But next thing the military police come sirening in and everybody scatter this way and that. Somebody look to pick up Ronald and drag him, but they find he is deadweight so they drop him and gone. Is clap and beat the MPs knock about everybody until the place clear out. Only then me and Gertie sneak out from behind the bush to go see if Ronald dead or alive.

See me there kneeling by Ronnie side, I ready to cry and be a widow even though just the other day I tell the man I ain nothing to him. Is then he choose to open his eye. "I beat up that P.R. man for you," he say, alive as can be.

Gertie start one big laughing. I smile, but out of pity I nod and say, "Yes, I heard." He move until his head there in my lap and I thinking to myself that this man take after Nelson the ass, what with his big head.

"Let we get married, no, Anette?"

I watch the man bust-up mouth say those words, and think to myself, *He must be lose he mind.* "I going think about it," I say

168

because I feel bad I is the cause of this man going crazy. He smile despite his swole lip.

How Eeona find out about the ruction, I cannot tell you, but this island small. Eeona give me a talking to about the indecency of me causing a riot. Her face tight up like she make of dirt. I suck my teeth and tell Eeona is woman I is. Eeona ain miss a beat of she stitching, she just look up at me with her eye them sharp and say, "Well, finally. Perhaps you will use your womanly sense to marry this good man. You have been on my hands far too long."

Is then I really watch what she there sewing and I see it looking white and lacy and bridal for true. "You marry him, then," I say, and slam myself into bed again. In my dreams I hearing somebody playing piano and I there going up the church aisle in lace.

Maybe a next week later a bunch of us walking home from school and Saul report that his brother get drafted into the Army. His little brother who suppose to be immune from war because he been in college. Saul vex because his brother should have go to the Navy, because that's where their father Benjamin McKenzie used to be before he went Puerto Rico to dead in the rain forest. "You mean your brother who does play piano?" I ask Saul, and everyone give me a funny look because I ain never even meet the boy, so how I know he play piano? But I think of that boy from the yearbook with the mangrove look. He look like somebody. I think of him in a uniform. I think that, yes, he probably look good in a uniform. Navy or Army, no matter.

But imagine this. Next I see Ronald he have on a little triangle Army hat. I say, "What you doing in that costume?" "It's not a costume," he say. "I fighting fire with fire. I going to the Army." Fool-fool. But who more foolish, me or he? Because on high school graduation day he stand up for his diploma in the tent hat and I watch the man and think, *He ain look bad.* And when we there afterward drinking punch and Coca-Cola at the reception, he come to me and say, "You think about marrying me?" I say, "I still thinking." He say, "I leaving on that ship that in the harbor now. Shipping out in days." I look across the room and see Gertie there with her beau. A boy from our class who enlist in the Army, like Ronald say he do. Gertie Army boy ask her to tie the knot and just today she accept. So she have a man to put his hold on her. I say to Ronald, "So I must make up my mind in days?" I suck my teeth. "Go on your boat."

But Ronald say he ain going until I give

170

he the answer one way or another. I want to tell the man no, but I ain have the heart. I figure the military going take him and there ain nothing he could do to stop it. He don't have the magic to stop and start things like I do. But I tell you, that ship sail without Ronald. It have some paperwork he ain fill out or maybe that wasn't his boat in truth. But hear this. Just weeks later we get the news about the ship going down, all the sweet Puerto Ricans on it, plus Gertie very boyfriend. Bomb somebody say. Either way, they sink to the bottom. Everybody dead. Gertie hysterical. I in a damn daze. Like the only reason Ronnie ain dead on the boat is because I was considering his proposal. I undead him. Maybe the magic giving me a sign. So Eeona push the white lacy dress and I marry Ronald like marrying him is my duty. Just so.

Eeona hold a little reception at Lindbergh Bay because we can't afford a hall. Gertie come to the wedding despite her grief. I don't have no father to do the last dance with me, like is the custom in the States. Ronnie come dance with me. But he can't dance good at all. We sit down, feet in the sand, most of the time.

But still. I feel good. Ronnie here. And Ronnie want me. And it have a war. And everybody marrying like is the style. I move into Ronnie mother house, giving Eeona that relief she want. For a week, just a smallie week, everything looking like it in the right place. Then Ronald ship out.

And I ain miss Ronnie one ounce. In fact, I happy-happy. I is seventeen years old. But even I know that something wrong if I happy when the boy I just marry gone to war.

32.

The local boys were now leaving, but the tourists had been coming. The two seemed connected, like they could mean the same thing. The tourists were older men and younger women; they seemed immune to the war. Or they seemed to be their own type of war.

The first time Eeona had walked into the Hospitality Lounge there was a man and there was air-conditioning. Eeona had never known of such a thing as air-conditioning. The air was cool and stifling, and the man who ran the lounge was cool and stiff. The man's name was Mr. Barry. He sat in a low chair behind a counter that seemed to dwarf him. He had the radio on too loudly and it was blasting the voice of a young personality from St. John calling himself Mervyn Manatee.

The lounge was one big room with two water toilets, complete with running water, each enclosed by a door. One door said "Ladies" and had a small emblem of a yellow-haired woman shaded by a parasol beneath the letters, so everyone would know what a lady looked like. The other door said "Gentlemen," and the painted pale man beneath it wore a top hat. No one had ever worn a top hat on the island.

In the lounge there were soft chairs for the visitors. There was a copy of the islands' newspaper weighted down with a sleeve of wood. Mr. Barry served hot bush tea in the morning and cold rum punch in the afternoon. His job was to cater to the island's new tsunami of visitors and real estate developers.

That first day Mr. Barry bought everything Eeona showed him — hats made of palm leaves with the initials USVI threaded in, crocheted toilet-paper covers in the island's own colors of yellow and blue. His voice tripped prices higher than Eeona had hoped for. Then he asked her to come again when she had more wares. She returned with coasters made of lace and napkin holders made of seashells. He wandered to the

173

end of his audacity and requested that she stay. He wanted the pleasure of simply looking at her. He served her a salary for this pleasure.

For Eeona, just sitting in the Hospitality Lounge was a little return of the luxury that was her birthright. In the air-conditioning her hair did not curl up at the temples. Her lipstick settled on her mouth without flaking. Sometimes in the AC little beads of cold would rise out of her skin like miniature volcanoes, so she crocheted herself a shawl. She flounced it around her shoulders and even wore it to and from work. And since she lived in Savan, and the Hospitality Lounge was on the first floor of the Grand Hotel, Eeona cruised the entire length of town in that shawl, despite the heat. Yes, let them see. She worked in air-conditioning! Mr. Barry was her employer in the Hospitality Lounge but it looked to any of us as though she was running things.

Mr. Barry was not a U.S. Virgin Islander or a British Virgin Islander, and not a Puerto Rican, which was most of what we had known for so long. Eeona barely realized that he was a human being. For months and then for years she'd treated him as though he might be a dried-up tree. When she spoke to him, it was only an excuse to speak to herself.

"Mrs. Lovernkrandt lost her house and the rocking chair. Indeed, one could say she lost everything."

"I am so sorry, Miss Eeona," he said politely, because he didn't know the Lovernkrandts at all.

He did, however, know about the sinking of *The Homecoming.* Even on his home island of St. Kitts it had been an important ship. He knew the many stories. One was that the captain had not drowned in the surprising surge onto the reefs, but had simply walked off his ship before they had even entered Anegada waters. Mr. Barry knew that Eeona was the captain's daughter. Eeona had been a debutante and the darling of the island. She was the kind of woman who, without her sad history, would have been beyond Mr. Barry's station. But now Mr. Barry fancied himself as her almost beau; he even asked her to marry him — more than once. She had not said yes as yet. But Eeona still worked for him and so there was still a chance.

At the time of the boys leaving for war, Eeona was arriving at the age of thirty. For a woman in her time this was the age of desperation or resignation. Eeona had given in to neither. Besides, an old maid and a free woman might be the same dangerous witchlike thing. It was just a matter of choosing the correct way to view things. It was, indeed, nice to be sought after and not just ogled, even if the man was beneath her.

The Tourism Commission funded Mr. Barry's Hospitality Lounge and funded Eeona to smile at the white American women who spoke slowly to her. Eeona kept her hair pinned up and wore blue to ward off the randy American sailors, soldiers, and tourist men. All day she gripped straw tightly as she forced it into braids for baskets. She held her needles as if they were surgeon's knives as she looped them through the yarn for purses and shawls.

Several times each day the bells hanging from the door jangled and then hot air blew in. A woman and a man, faces pink and sweaty, would burst in smiling. Sometimes it was two men. "Hi, there!" the man would say to Eeona. Which was inappropriate on many levels. Still, Eeona would stand to pour them some tea.

Servitude was not necessarily a step back, she told herself. It was all in the angle of vision. This wasn't at all what Liva had stooped so low to offer. This was more like being a hostess of a fine home. Eeona was simply refining all the skills she would need when her life came gushing back. She was ready. She had taken care. Hadn't she found Anette a husband? Hadn't she watched out for Esau?

33.

Jacob Esau was a sand-colored man with long mangrove legs and, as far as anyone could say, a McKenzie. Studying eugenics wasn't something he wanted to do. His eldest brother, Adam, was in dentistry school. The second brother, Mark, was going to be a lawyer. The next one, Saul, wasn't very bright and was held back, challenged with the McKenzie daftness. Saul became an architect — the very first black master builder on the Virgin Islands government payroll, though he'd never thought of himself as black before. Doctor was really the only thing Rebekah had left. The study of genes, that is what she wanted of her favorite son. She believed that to be the magical element of medicine.

Jacob displayed an early brilliance, and so his mother sent him to first grade at three, ensuring that he would miss Anette in school. Rebekah told him "doctor" with her long hand wide open toward his face as if in offering. Her hands and arms were lean and long and beautiful. She always kept them bare, attracting her husband and eventually flinging him away — though she didn't know she was sending him right to Eeona Bradshaw. That would come later.

It was almost scandalous the way Rebekah always wore long dresses but then never failed to expose a slice of her shoulder or a rounding of elbow. Her skirts swept the ground and collected a respectable film of dirt at the hem. Jacob had only seen his mother's animal left foot once. He'd been too young and too sleepy to even remember. But he knew she was powerful. She offered him doctor. She told him he would be a great golden man if he knew what went into making a man.

Jacob would have chosen something academic, something artistic. He would have been a professor who played the steel pan. He would have been a professional traveler, joined the Navy. Daddy Benjamin had been in the U.S. Navy. Daddy had lived in Puerto Rico and then had disappeared for good into El Yunque. The McKenzie uncles now sent some meager money for college but didn't really interfere, and so they were not available for emulation. If Benjamin had died for sure, one of them would have taken the boys, like they took any fatherless cousins. They would split them up amongst themselves and tell Rebekah to go back to her family. But Rebekah would not have it. There had been no funeral and so who could say that Benjamin McKenzie was dead? Maybe he would return any day to be father and husband.

Actually, Benjamin McKenzie did not die. Even though that had been Rebekah's obeah intention. Scatter his two legs in many directions, she had canted. But instead, Benjamin had grown six more metaphoric legs, eight in all. She'd sent him into the rain forest of Puerto Rico's El Yunque to be taken by the wilderness. But instead, he ended up in The Rain Forest of St. Croix and became the wilderness. Rebekah had stuffed tiny shreds of American licorice and Caribbean stinking toe fruit into the waistband of her husband's underwear before he left for P.R. The licorice so people would want to kill him and the stinking toe so he would be easy to find. But instead, he was invisible. Flying from Puerto Rico to St. Croix and even eventually to St. Thomas without anyone making note. And people didn't kill him. Instead, they put their lives in his care. Her obeah seemed to have worked, even though it didn't. When it came to love and marriage, Rebekah often had it exactly wrong.

Mrs. Rebekah McKenzie was a woman of roots and incantations. But this is the Caribbean and so no one is one thing; no one is pure. Rebekah was an obeah woman who might sell limes in the market square, but she was also the most sought-after piano teacher to debutantes. This was another way she was unlike the other McKenzie wives, who were whittled away under their husband's hands.

Did Rebekah collect money from the piano teaching? It could not have been enough to keep her independent, for the McKenzie uncles would not have knowingly allowed that. There was a limit to how working-class she could be. They allowed the selling in the market: a gardening hobby, they assumed, with the daftness of men who only know other men. They always reminded Jacob that though they'd been absent when he was a child, it was they who financed him through college because his father never came back from the base in Puerto Rico.

But Rebekah always seemed to have more than enough to send a package of stewed cherries in the mail or a new jacket she bought in one of the nice stores built for tourists. Jacob would hide the stewed cherries — a sweet too island for his Yankee friends to understand — and he would flaunt the jacket, demonstrating that even a West Indian boy could be worthy of the bachelor's degree they were all slaving for. But it was Rebekah, a eugenicist of sorts herself, who made all her boys into these remarkable professional people.

In the end, and not without its irony, Jacob was the only one who would continue Benjamin McKenzie's line, though it wasn't really a McKenzie line at all. He would fall in love with that little brown girl, but she was a divorcée with a child. And to make it worse, she was from a fallen family. Marrying low or lowered would be an anomaly never heard of among McKenzie men. And then, of course, there was the thing neither he nor the girl knew.

We'd all heard it before, "That one is your second cousin. This one is your young aunt." The island so small that parents had to be vigilant to prevent intermarrying, and in the government nepotism was the only way anything got done. But Rebekah did not tell her boy why not Anette; she did not tell him about Anette at all. If Jacob was deemed illegitimate, he would lose the McKenzie respectability and the McKenzie money. He needed both to get through medical school.

Jacob's mother could make dust out of bones and blood, and blow it into faces that would crack to pieces the next day. She could send a serpent into your dreams as you slept in the valley even though she was mountains away. Jacob was the last son. "Doctor," she said, and thought she had settled it all.

Jacob's brothers played the tuba and the saxophone and the upright bass long before jazz became fashionable on this island. They were McKenzies. Ultra-manism made them odd and standoffish, but because it was manly, it made them odd in an acceptable way. But Jacob wanted to play steel pan. He loved the way the notes sounded like water. He wanted to jump in Carnival come April. As McKenzies, they danced awkwardly down the parade route with the Tiny Chinee troupe. They did not play pan — low class as that was. Instead, Jacob was made to play the piano. He played his mother's piano. And he became a doctor, which was quite suitable for a McKenzie. But he didn't do it the way his mother wanted and so in a way he would still be hidden behind Saul's mysterious buildings that poked out of the St. Thomas soil; behind Mark, who told jokes in court and never, not once, won a case; and Adam, the dentist brother who was too bizarre in his methods to be trusted even with a loop of floss. Jacob Esau was a doctor because his mother told him that was what was left for her to give. But before Jacob could become a doctor, he had to meet Anette, and before he could meet Anette, he had to live through the war.

34.

Whether it was the longing for belonging or her crippling fear of boats, Anette couldn't say. But when the other Army wives headed to the base in Bayamón, Puerto Rico, where there was free housing, she did not go. She stayed there and lived with her husband's mother, which was fitting enough, and tried to figure out how to make babies, even though her husband was across the water.

She met up with Gertie and the two went around like girls again.

Elder sister Eeona stayed alone in the old apartment. She spent hours staring at the mirror taking her own breath away. Then she read the paper and sewed grass-stuffed dollies for the Hospitality Lounge. Thrice in one week she went to the library and picked up a novel. She plowed through the books until the gas in the lamp burnt down. Every now and then, Anette came by bearing a stew that her mother-in-law had made, passing it off as her own. Eeona critiqued the intensity of the pepper, the color of the broth, and the texture of the taña. But the truth is that she was enjoying Anette's company. The truth is that they had been together, only them, for a long time.

"Fish and johnnycakes were your specialty before," Eeona said, by way of praising Anette's hand.

"Oh, please, Eeona." Anette smiled downward. "That was too easy."

After many months alone, Eeona found herself one evening sitting and looking at her hands. The blue veins rising through her wrists. She slipped her own hand into a pair of lace gloves that had been her mother's; she had tried and failed to copy them. But now she saw how neatly they fit her own hand. She sat at her dining table and faced the two empty chairs. They were cheap chairs, not the kind she'd had at Villa by the Sea.

Anette had said that she would visit more often than she ever did. Eeona noticed her own disappointment and was disappointed in herself. Her episodes worsened. She would find herself staring off into space, sometimes saying silent things to herself. Then the urge to wander would wash over her and she would rise up and walk out the door, despite the time. She would walk to the sea. She would walk to the mountains. She would return home and it would start again. Perhaps it was good that she lived alone, so no one could witness.

This lonely evening, it seemed to Eeona that the air might suddenly materialize a person. It seemed that someone might be hiding beyond a door or waiting on the other side of the window. Anyone. Anyone? Eeona rested her hands in her lap in such a way that it would look natural, despite the deliberateness of their positioning. She breathed but made sure that her breath did not come heavy and collapse her chest — for though she was beautiful, she had to fight against her body's any betrayal. A feeling came on her like a drowning tide. An episode of longing like Mama Antoinette's? But Eeona was no longer trapped and yet . . . she needed a push. She should just stand and jump and maybe leap out of the window. She wasn't journeying to her big true life, whatever that was. Would she even know her life when she found it?

Eeona did not remove Antoinette's gloves as she ate the soup she had prepared for her solitary dinner. She did not realize that music was playing from afar until she found that she was tapping her foot. She stomped it to shake the rhythm off, for the music was only a common calypso. The half-empty bowl of soup was before her. Her gloved hands now rested beside the bowl.

The feeling of waves, of water, of walking off a ship came up to her neck until she stood up in the little living room. Stood up to save herself from the drowning in her mind. She only had one friend who she might go to for talk and help, but he was not even a friend.

35.

In the Hospitality Lounge, Eeona had fallen in love with Mr. Barry's air-conditioning. She had fallen in love with his pursuits, for he did nothing all day but listen to the radio and read the paper and court her. She did not fall for the man. It is true that Mr. Barry gave her almost half his own government salary for the privilege of watching her sit across from him in the Hospitality Lounge. But she had been working for him going on a decade and he had become quite bold. Certainly, Eeona was still beautiful, but something had changed. Mr. Barry was a man without a landed name and still he felt bold enough to try her. He didn't know, being from St. Kitts, how our island men had always adored her from a distance, her beauty too dangerous to be trusted. Or perhaps she was no longer quite as beautiful. Either way, by the time Anette was married, Mr. Barry had already asked Eeona to marry him seventy-something times. Each time he offered her a flower. He began with hibiscus.

He went to his knee four times with hibiscus and each time he would reveal a new color: red, yellow, orange, and white. When these failed to entice, he moved to orchids: drown-me-in-your-love orchids, dagger-in-my-chest orchids, I-will-cry orchids. Soon Mr. Barry had a pattern. He proposed to Miss Eeona every third Friday evening. Mr. Barry was one of these dull men who believe in wearing a woman down. They never consider that a woman worn away by insistence is not the same thing as a woman swept away by love. By proposal number forty, he was on anthuriums, and she had dumped hundreds of flowers in the small yard behind the flat where she tied up the donkey. Such a dune of beautiful dead flowers was reminiscent of her last days at Villa by the Sea.

One evening Mr. Barry was fastening the big windows at the front of the building. There was glass fastened into the window holes so that he and Eeona could have both the air-conditioning and the daylight. Eeona was taking her time. As always, she knew what she was doing. There was no one to go home to any longer. There was no one who invited her for tea. It was a Thursday and there had been no beseeching with flowers. Eeona was a human being after all, despite what else she may be.

Mr. Barry had closed the door and all but one window before Eeona cleared her throat. He turned as though her voice had grabbed him from behind. "Dear me. Miss Eeona, I thought you had left. I apologize. I didn't mean to close the windows on you." As he was saying this, however, he was closing the final window.

Remember, it is the 1940s and it is the Caribbean. Eeona had never been inside an entirely closed building before, a building void of any natural light. At Villa by the Sea they had kept their windows open even in the evenings, cracked even in the rain. The starlight and the moonlight rushing in to mix with the kerosene lamp. Suddenly, Mr. Barry and Eeona were in a closed building with artificial light. It was frightening, even to Eeona. It made her feel brave just to sit there.

Mr. Barry's thick body lumbered about his desk as he shuffled papers and packed other papers as if he was leaving, though both he and Eeona knew they were not going just then. He was the kind of man that, had he been younger, many women would have found attractive. He was a big man. He was called towering. But he always seemed small to Eeona, drowning in the huge chair behind his desk. It is true, of course, that when she most often noticed him he was kneeling at her feet.

This evening Eeona sat erect, her hands curled like tree roots in her lap, and watched him. He did not look at her as he asked, "Miss Eeona. What, if I may inquire, are your plans for this evening?" He was folding his newspaper carefully into his leather briefcase as though the paper were made of something stiff and heavy.

Eeona smiled softly to show him that he was foolish. "I have no plans, Mr. Barry."

"Well, then." Perhaps he wondered why he had not brought some hibiscus on this odd Thursday. Perhaps tonight Miss Eeona would say yes. He was not in the crude habit of wearing his hat indoors, but now he placed it on his head. He adjusted it carefully, as though it held his dignity. "Miss Eeona, since you are not otherwise committed, would you care to join me at choir practice? I am a Moravian and that is where I am heading now, as I said, to practice for the choir. I am, you may not know, but now you shall know, the head of the Moravian Men's Choir, which is renowned across the island. I am, indeed, the men's choir leading baritone and the director. By which I mean that I also play the organ."

"Well, that is fascinating information, Mr. Barry. However, I would like to stay here for just a little while. My feet are positively aching." She was not telling a lie. Today she had rented Nelson out to someone she hoped would buy the beast. This was a move toward her real life, for she had decided to purchase a car. All the landed families had a vehicle or two nowadays. Besides, she could roam farther with a car than by burro. However, not having Nelson was quite the sacrifice. The kitten heels she wore today were not sensible at all.

Mr. Barry knelt beside her. This was nothing new. At proposal twenty-eight Eeona had felt generous and allowed him to hold her hand while he salivated his entreaties, but he had never touched more than her fingers, the palm of her hand, or, once, her wrist. When he did touch her hand, she could feel the paths of his fingerprints. She could feel the stones of his hangnails. Afterward, she would soak her hands in mint water to relieve them. Now she prepared her hands by willing them to relax. Instead, Mr. Barry gently lifted her foot and took it out of its shoe.

She was wearing an ankle-length skirt and now Mr. Barry lifted his hands up her calf with the expertise that suggested he had done this before, found the tip of her calf stocking, and rolled it down past her toes and off her feet. She could feel his hands grow sweaty even in the air-conditioning that was now snorting irregularly. Mr. Barry's breathing, too, became irregular. He leaned down and brought Miss Eeona's foot to his nose. She could feel his breath between her toes. She could feel his hand cradling her heel.

Mr. Barry was a man who was the age Owen Arthur would have been. He was a man who had made a business for himself. He would not be a bad man to settle with and for. He had a decent house up Garden Street, not a grand estate, but still.

Oh, but there was the hair sprouting at his knuckles. Eeona wanted a man who was bare, as smooth as Papa had been. Eeona looked up to the ceiling.

One foot now rested in this man's lap and she could feel his manhood growing taut. Her other foot was cupped in his gripping and releasing palm. She could feel his warm breath and then his cool tongue suddenly slipping between her toes. She felt his mouth open like an underwater cave. Jesus. She was alarmed and then anxious, and then she leaned back slowly into the chair and felt herself turn into something other than a lady.

When Eeona left that evening, Mr. Barry remained kneeling on the floor, as though in supplication or repentance. He had not removed even his jacket or his hat. He had missed choir practice entirely. As she slipped on her shoes and pulled down her dress, she could hear him softly chanting Psalm Twenty-three over and over again. When he said "the valley of the shadow," she knew the part of her that was the valley. When he said, "cup runneth over," she knew which silver part of her had run over. Though all she had seen during the whole lusty affair was his hat bobbing up and down as though it were floating.

What great ignorance had she just done? It was already dusk. Eeona walked home quickly, her feet chafing for she had forgotten her stockings at the lounge. She knew she would never make it to the flat before night fell, and she hoped that her transgressions were not obvious to everyone she walked past. Mr. Barry was now the only living man to know her silver secret in her secret place. Yes, she fancied the air-conditioning. Yes, she fancied the check he signed over to her every fortnight. She even fancied his flowers. She did not fancy him.

He had hair coming out, not only out of his knuckles, but out of his ears and nose as well. He wasn't even an American, she thought, but someone from a small colonial island where they still labored over sugarcane. Now perhaps he would spread a true rumor of her around her own island. Was she so resigned or so desperate that she was handing herself over so easily?

Eeona walked into her apartment just as the sky was turning purple and opened the door to a hollow feeling, as though the apartment were a deep water hole. She walked in and sat at the table across from the two empty chairs — Anette's chair and an extra for a guest. She put Antoinette's gloves on slowly.

Elder sister Eeona sat there and thought what she should do. What she should do and what she wanted to do were different things. Perhaps she was having another one of her mother's episodes of wanting. She wanted to lower herself to the floor and bang it with her gloved fists.

Tomorrow, instead of accepting Mr. Barry's mouth as offering, she would pass by her sister's. She had told herself that she would never venture to Anette's new abode. After all, Anette's leaving was just the freedom she'd been craving. It made no sense to haul herself down to see the sister who'd held her back all these years. But she didn't allow herself to remember any of that now. Anette's husband had been home recently from his basic training and had already left for the States. The man hadn't even paid elder sister Eeona the expected and respectable visit. She hadn't cared. No, she hadn't. Well, a bit, but not much. Now Eeona told herself that Anette must be needing some family company after being there with her in-laws all alone.

Ronnie's mother was the real Mrs. Smalls. Her husband was a professional philanderer and so never spent more than a few minutes at home, where Mrs. Smalls served him limeade she had made from limes in her backyard and coconut tart — she had grated the coconut herself. It was known that she was an excellent cook, but even her cooking couldn't hold her husband. All it had done was produce a son who was as good as any woman around the kitchen.

Eeona could see now that Anette had been eating. Sitting there on the couch in a housedress, Anette looked positively plump. Eeona observed that Anette might even look a bit pretty. Eeona's hair had been pinned up, but now she loosened it, feeling the need to assert herself before Anette's comeliness. Poor Mrs. Smalls, used to abuse, stood up and left the room as though Eeona had just stripped naked.

Though Ronald had returned from basic, he'd immediately been called back to P.R. and then shipped off to Louisiana. Anette leaned in close to her sister and told her what Ronald had managed before going to the mainland. "I'm pregnant," Anette said excitedly, as though it was she receiving the news. "I know, I ain think Ronnie had it in him either."

Eeona, who had never desired a child ever in her life, felt the slightest feeling of challenge.

Anette, so full of herself, didn't notice the sudden change of gravity come over the room.

36.

Sudden changes in gravity. Bright flashing light. Loud clanging noises. The usual hot and cold. All this, his brother, who was a dentist, had said would make the pain throb in Jacob Esau McKenzie's tooth. Why light? Why noise? Teeth couldn't see or hear. But like a sense he hadn't learned to harness, his teeth could feel sound. Could feel darkness and be comforted by it. This was America, his brother insisted over the phone. Strange things happened in America. Jacob Esau had gone to Howard University, two years younger than his peers, and then finished in three. He knew firsthand how strange America was. How mulatto Caribbean men like he was, who were educated and high-bred, could go to American colleges and become Negro overnight.

The soldier boys all knew some things, but Jacob, younger than all of them and more handsome than most, seemed to have a bit more. Jacob was college educated, played the piano, and knew how to swim. In the Army the officers had thought the other Caribbean boys were useless, born surrounded by water but having nothing to show for it. But Ronnie Smalls had thought it through. "I walk over a mountain without flying. What's the big deal that I walk in the water without swimming?" So swimming was like flying. Something witches could do.

The mistake was made. The Virgin Islands men were put together. Only West Indians in companies 872, 873, 874, and 875 on the base in New Orleans. Over meals in the food shack, the boys discussed this. Ronald Smalls slurped on rubbery pancakes. "It's for cohesion," he said between his moving teeth. "It's so we don't get lonely for home." Ronald was very lonely for home. He was a good man who did all he could to be the opposite of his philandering father. His wife was pregnant with a baby he dreamed would be the first of many. But Ronnie's dreams were only dreams.

"No, Smalls," said Jacob, "it's so we don't break free. It's so we watch one another and keep one another in line." Jacob knew what he was talking about. His mother was a woman who was expert at watching and keeping people from breaking free. She had warned Jacob about the toothache. She'd told him to use certain herbs to ward off the pain and wait until she herself could take care of it. But Jacob had defied her; he'd consulted his brother who was in dentistry school at Meharry, way in Tennessee. He wanted a real doctor and his brother was almost one. Jacob knew also that he would become a real doctor. Not a witch doctor like his mother. But still, it was she who had warned him that the Caribbean-only company was a curse.

Spice was from Grenada. He respected Jacob McKenzie because with all that learning and ability and sand-colored skin it was hard not to. Spice thought Ronald Smalls was naïve for thinking the Americans could mean them well, and pitiful for pulling out the picture of his nice titi wife if anybody even mentioned pum pum. Spice knew that it was these Americanized ones from the USVI and Puerto Rico who couldn't seem to understand America. "Listen, man. The Yankees don't want to be with us." Spice was Grenadian trying to become an American citizen. He knew things that no else knew . . . and not because he'd been to school. He was the eldest of the bunch, but his father and mother had been dead since he was six. He had lived bouncing between distant family scattered on different islands. He knew Spanish and French and Dutch and English. All the Caribbean languages. So even though he was already the eldest, he seemed elder still. He knew the Caribbean. And so he knew the world.

"Why wouldn't they want to be with us?" Ronald asked, thinking about how the Puerto Rican soldiers had beat him up. Thinking that perhaps the separation by region and language had to do with women.

"The Yanks think we smell," answered Spice with authority.

"Bad?"

"Yes, bad, you coconut head."

"But is they smell like uncooked meat."

"True," said Spice. He was known for his conspiratorial views. He wouldn't even eat the food-shack grub. He ate the rations instead. He poured water over the shrunken steaks and dried packs of peanuts. They fed this to the guys on the line. It was stay-alive food.

"I don't know why they don't want to be with us," said Jacob, answering Ronald Small's earnest question. Ronald sighed, took out the picture of his wife, and thumbed it gently. Jacob pressed his fingernail into his gums where the pain was. In college Jacob had experienced the condescension of white Americans. Those who visited campus for lectures were sweet but syrupy. And yes, he'd heard the dismal stories from his schoolmates. But those students didn't study as hard as he did. They didn't have the good name that he had. *Niggardly,* Jacob knew, was a real word. It meant stingy and mean. Some people were niggers. Jacob just wasn't one.

Before they'd left for America, Ronald Smalls had made love to his wife for what would be the last time ever. Then he'd sailed to Puerto Rico and joined the rest of the company, which was also Jacob's company, on a boat for New Orleans. His first time in real America. His life was a dream come true. All he had to do was keep living. He didn't want to believe in anything that could mean maiming or death or trouble even a bit.

"See, Spice," Ronald shouted, when they were all in the back of a tented truck heading toward the base. "If they had hated us, they would have sent us to the Nazis."

Spice had shaken his head. "You scunt. This is Naziland, U.S.A."

Jacob, who felt protective of Ronald, slapped the Grenadian on the back. "Give him a break. Just give him a break, old man." For it was true that at his college job waiting tables Jacob had been called boy. But he was a boy. Always had been. Youngest in his class. Baby of the family. He was a boy even now in the Army among all these men.

When they had all first arrived, their

superiors had told them that New Orleans wasn't so different from the Caribbean. That was when they'd hoped the Caribbean boys would be helpful in the water, but only Jacob among them could swim. The truth was, however, that the city was below sea level, like Atlantis. Like they were all underwater but somehow still breathing.

Jacob's tooth pulsed dully and constantly. His brother had sent him a paste, so it wasn't so painful. Still, each time he breathed deeply, a sharpness lit though his face so that his lips twitched. Other men began to see this as something stylish and self-assured, like holding a cigarette or pulling out a comb to run through your conch-straightened hair. Soon Jacob's twitching became a mark of West Indian Company 875. The lip-twitching making them look ready, just ready for something. This made the real Americans, the officers, watch them closely.

The company stayed in for the first two weeks, fixing and cleaning and following orders. Ronald Smalls whistled and twitched. America! Land of freedom! It felt good. There was no ocean around telling you to stop. There was just land and land. To be roamed. And admired. To be conquered and tamed and called one's own.

Ronnie was so happy he wrote to Anette telling her to name the child Ronald, please, Anette, please. He was sure he would create a legacy during this war. He was too happy.

We were at war. Happiness wouldn't do.

37.

The music from Jacob's little wooden box sang loudly because Jacob's tooth didn't mind the blues. A woman was crooning. My, my. A woman could croon. A woman could sweep a man from his feet. The world was changing. Yes, indeed. The boys pomaded their low-cut hair. Spice had a conch and his hair was pitch-black. Like the pit in Trinidad. Jacob creased his own uniform pants. They all shined their shoes. They had leave that night. They were going out on the town. They were gonna drink. They were gonna dance. Maybe meet a few nice pretty women who could sweep men off their feet.

Ronald's lips were full and soft. Anette had come to enjoy pressing her own mouth against them. His hands were smooth despite his job of washing dishes. He was a regular man in every other way. He knew this. He felt that regular was something to be proud of. Spice was thick bodied and dark and angry with straight hair that grew like weeds. The French Quarter women loved being forcefully seduced by him. They had only to catch him in their eyes like a speck of dust and he was in them until he alone wanted out.

Jacob's body was lean and tall, like the trunk of a coconut tree. He always had a mist on his upper lip, which made women want to lick his mouth. He trimmed his brown pubic hair with delicate scissors. His underarms were always moist and his body gave off the smell of soil. His skin and eyes and hair were all the same wet-sand color. Even the white sergeants could not explain their own desire to root into him. In her letter his mother had reminded him that "there is more schooling still. Do not settle."

Well, he was getting out tonight. Going to trawl Tremé and the French Quarter. Going to dip his hands into the Mississippi. He was a handsome man and he had the will to do just about anything. He was going to be a doctor if he outlived the war. And he would live. His mother watched over him and his soul was huge. Someday he would marry someone as desirable. But now: "I want to find out which of these Creole ladies going be the mother of my children."

"Not me," clarified Ronald. And he took out the picture of Anette that he was always showing around. Held it now beside his face as if the woman were there beside him. Coming with them into town. Jacob smiled at sweet Ronnie but squinted his eyes at the woman in the picture. He wanted to say, "I feel as though I know her." This would not have been a big thing. St. Thomas was still a very small place. But instead Jacob said, "Put your wife away."

Together, these three island soldiers made a perfect beautiful man. When they were dropped off at the edge of town, they all stopped to wipe their shoes. Tall and coolie haired and soft lips. The three of them walked puff-chested down the boulevard. And people watched them. Men gawked with approval. They tipped their hats. Even the night women slinked by them, only to stop and look back at the way their muscled buttocks pressed again and again against their pants.

The men were belly hungry for something besides rations and rubber pancakes. So they didn't wait to reach the fancy of the French Quarter. The door was flung open. The smell of frying pork reached out. It was a charred smell, a greasy and smoky and bloody smell. The sign said MAMA'S PLACE. The name of the joint was all that was needed for Jacob to nod at the two who were his right-hand men. Spice Grenada and Ronald Smalls nodded back. All three walked in. They sat down at the only empty table.

All of a sudden the jukebox was playing too loudly. The lights were dull, except over their table where a solitary bulb shivered, its brightness landing on Jacob again and again. The counter with the hefty lady serving drinks was never empty. The patrons spoke in screams. Pots were banging somewhere. The walls were painted yellow, giving off a noise of their own. Jacob's tooth threatened to jump out of his mouth. Now his eyes twitched, too, and he held his hand thoughtfully to his face. Spice was cracking mean hearty jokes, but drumming his fingers against the table, making it shake. The other tables emptied and filled. They waited.

"Excuse me, miss. We're ready to order when you're ready."

"Excuse me, ma'am. I see you're busy, can we just tell you what we want?"

"Miss? A bowl of gumbo. One of them poor boy sandwiches. Please, miss."

She was thin and middle-aged. Her hair was under a scarf but her eyes were a bright sea green, a disturbing contrast to her milky and sagging skin. She wore a worn-out white uniform. It was short and graying.

They felt bad for her. She was kinda pretty with those mossy eyes, and she smiled at them as she rushed by again and again. None of them had a watch, but after what seemed like an hour she finally took their order. "It's gonna take a real long time," she said. "You sure you want to eat here, soldiers?"

"It's Mama's place," Ronnie remarked with a hungry smile. The woman nodded and repeated that it would take some time and wouldn't they want to eat somewhere else? Maybe deeper down in the Quarter?

"What is exactly going on?" Spice said this directly to the mossy waitress who stepped back and looked afraid. He was pressing his fingers into the table now, trying to fight the urge to slap her, trying, instead, to leave his prints in the wood.

Jacob interrupted. "We're sorry to bother you, ma'am." He fixed his pretty eyes on her. Commanding her in the way he could always command women. His tooth was aching. Perhaps hunger made it hurt, too. "Just bring us some chips and some drinks to start. We'll be fine."

"You boys not from around here," she said, and nodded.

Grenada watched her walk away. He watched her give the meal ticket to the large woman at the counter. Watched them whisper. Watched the waitress's head nod again. The big one was Mama. This was clear. And Mama stared out at Grenada as if he indeed were his island and she was the *Pinta* or the *Santa María,* her big boat self, come to eat him alive. He should keep an eye on her, but his staring was rude and she was his elder. So he turned away. He suggested out loud to Jacob that it was time to leave.

Ronald Smalls rubbed his palms and belched. His belly was beginning to fill with gas. "Nah, partner. We about to get serve right now. We'll go somewhere else and wait a next hour."

The gray waitress moved back and forth. Now she didn't smile or even meet their eyes. They called her. "Miss." "Excuse me." Finally, Spice elbowed Jacob to go and then Jacob did something. He whistled at the waitress to come.

Sure, Jacob had had some awareness of Jim Crow when in college. But he'd never really believed it applied to him; and he'd been working too hard, isolating himself so well that he'd never had to find out. Sure, his school was all Negro and the shops he frequented were all Negro and the waitstaff at his job was all Negro, but that's how home was, too. There was no American Jim

Crow in St. Thomas — Negroes, light and dark, were the majority and he assumed that's what it was back in D.C. and now in New Orleans, too. And how could Jim Crow apply anywhere now that they were here in uniform, pledged to die for everyone in this joint? Besides, New Orleans was so like St. Thomas — the verandas, the ladies smiling at him, the music thrumming in the streets. How could he be anything less than the coveted mangrove man that he was?

But when he whistled, it was as if everyone, every single one at every single table at Mama's, had been waiting for that signal. It was as if the show had now begun and Jacob was an unexpected player, because the place went quiet except for the box playing something loud and eager. Jacob's tooth pulsed with each rush of his blood and he wanted to cry out because the pain had become unbearable.

"Hey, now. Niggers can't be whistling at white women — not in the state of Louisiana." A big man with the omniscient words stood. He wore his hat even though they were indoors. His clean white shirt was belted in by suspenders. They held up plain but pressed black pants. The big man was dressed old-fashioned, but he was younger even than Ronnie and Jacob. He walked over to them calmly. And though he was only a few yards away, during this walk a few couples managed to scuffle out of Mama's joint. The big man also managed to duplicate himself so that by the time he reached their table there were seven or eight who looked like he did standing just beyond his shoulders. In the eyes of the soldiers, the suspenders gave a comical look to these men — only young schoolboys wore suspenders back home. Ronald Smalls thought hopefully that this big fellow was the owner's son and they could make him apologize for the bad service. Jacob didn't twitch. He looked at his men. Ronnie's eyes were open wide and watering. Grenada looked ready, just ready. "Did this youth just call me a nigger?" Jacob was incredulous, not even meaning to be bold.

The big guy put his big hands flat on the edge of their table. He was smiling. "Let me clarify for you. I don't think you soldier boys are in the right place." He looked at each of them one by one. "You giving Mama a hard time." His words were steady but there was a bit of shrillness to them, as though his voice had just broken. He gesticulated toward the big lady at the counter, but the soldiers didn't move their gaze. They were trained well. They kept their eyes on the talking enemy. "We're all American patriots here, but we ain't going to stand for disrespect." How old was this youngster in small-boy suspenders? Who did he think he was?

Jacob was in charge. Jacob was the leader. He felt something warm and moist worm its way around his mouth. "We just want to eat, man."

"This ain't your eating place, soldier."

They didn't move. But then there was a sudden change in gravity as the white man-boy spoke again. "If you niggers leave quietly, me and my friends won't drag you out by your dicks and throw you in the river. Are you understanding?"

Yes, Jacob Esau McKenzie understood. Here was a story like his schoolmates had told. Here it was. And here he was. He was going to be a doctor. Could play piano better than anybody. Could swim like he came from the ocean. This kid in suspenders couldn't see all that. But surely he could see that they were in uniform. That they had shined their shoes.

Still, Jacob Esau McKenzie, with his so big soul, pushed his chair back slowly. It made an achy, grating noise against the ground. A sound like something ill being exposed. The others followed. The big boy leaned back and let the soldiers who had

pledged to die for this America walk out on
Mama. And Jacob didn't pause. Not even
for a minute. Just walked straight out. And
the men followed Jacob out into the street,
where he spat thick dark blood onto the
pavement.

They walked until they found the water.
But the river wasn't the sea. So they kept
walking in their darkness until a truck of
military supplies passed and made room for
them among the fresh white linens.

38.

ANETTE

Plenty woman does marry safe and then see
the shadow of regret on their children's
faces. It was the 1940s. And for a good
while I had believe I was happy enough. I
save Ronnie life, in a way, and now Ronnie
give me a life. See, is just me and Ronnie
mother cooking and keeping house and my
belly there growing big. And me talking to
her or Eeona about my dream, which is to
be a history teacher. And his mother challenging me that maybe I ain know much
more than nothing about being a homemaker, how I going to go be a teacher? Or
Eeona challenging me that maybe I need to
go pass teacher and be a professor and go

America. Them woman. They think that their dreams supposed to be mine. I ain studying them. I know what I want.

Before Ronnie leave for New Orleans, he had come home from training in Puerto Rico. I have a sense for arrival. I put on a red dress that I know fit to make me a siren. Those short weeks that he on leave with me, we go out and have fun or stay in and have fun. We don't see Eeona. We barely see he mother and she right there in the house with we. I know for sure that I was every husband's dream wife for all the ruckus I there making in the bedroom. The next morning his mother would be all hide in she bedroom like she shamed of us. The boil eggs and tea on the table like we is guests in a motel.

Eeona never forget that she a lady from a genteel family. Me? I forget all the time. I laugh with my mouth open wide-wide. Life was easy, let me tell you. I could make it so. Then when the Army drag Ronald to New Orleans, I discover I get myself pregnant by him. Eeona start coming over late in the evenings. I live on the other side of town now but still she showing up in the evenings to rub my feet with olive oil. Sometimes she even come and stay late until after Ronald mother done gone in. When I live with my sister, she never pay me so much mind.

I am one of those woman love being big with child. It easy for me. I is at my best. When I pregnant, everything have me happy. I pick mangoes from Mrs. Smalls's mango tree and they taste sweeter than sweet. I walk to the grocery store at the head of Pave Street and my legs feel strong and my belly feel tight as a muscle. A milkman and a fisherman come down our street every morning carrying icebox on their backs and they always come to me early, so I get the fish and milk freshest. People rush to help me even with a bag of plums. Man run down the street to open a door. Me and Gertie liming and though she belly flat, is still me getting watch. Everybody serving me, even the trees bending to me with their fruit and flowers.

I get some dye slap on my head, and though my hair ain turn black-black like I hope, the red now hide beneath a nicey brown. My skin moist and soft. My nails grow. I looking pretty. My belly big but I look the best I ever look. It even come like me and Eeona might get close. Be like real sisters. After all, she coming to where I live just to rub on my foot and spend time with me. We talk 'bout things.

In fact, is really she bend my ear. Even though later she act like she so surprise

when I reach back from the ship without
Ronald. Is *she* turn my head. She act like
she forget.

"Anette."

"Yes, Eeona?" I lay on the sofa chair with
my head fling back. I there staring at a high
part in the ceiling, studying its curves and
bumps. My sister's fingers slipping around
my ankles. She rub rough, it had hurt but
feel good at the same time. Then she move
to my heels. I feel the squeezy motion travel
up my calf and settle warm in the bottom
of my spine. I sinking into the chair. Oh,
Eeona was good with feet, I tell you. Where
she learn that, I can't say.

"Anette, you seem quite happy in your
marriage."

And is true. I was happy. How much of
this was my marriage, I can't say. Ronald
ain barely there for we to have a marriage at
all.

Now Eeona speak slow, as if she need me
to hear every word good-good. "Do you
think you will be an adequate mother?"

I raise my head to get a good look at my
elder sister. She ain look up from my foot
in her lap. She seem to be concentrating,
working both her hands them into my heel.
Doing some obeah on me is now what I
thinking. But I ain succumbing. "I'm going

214

to be a perfect mother."

"How will you love the child?"

"How? Like how everybody loves their children, Eeona."

I rest my head back. Eeona move to the arch of my foot. The oil she using slippery, wetlike. She at the ball of my foot, digging in. We sit there quiet-quiet until she switch and begin massaging my next foot.

"What I mean to ask, Anette, is how will you know how to love as a parent? You did not have parental example."

But this a odd thing she telling me. Ain she been my example? "My husband love me. That's the example I'm going to give the child."

She drop my foot hard onto the floor. I feel the baby in me tense up, even then Ronalda was so sensitive. Eeona reel from me as though I a piece of bush on fire. "Anette Bradshaw Smalls. Love between husband and wife is not the kind of love you give to your children. This is what I am hoping to have you see."

I feel the laugh come out of me like a cackle. Then I swallow it back in my chest when I see is serious she serious. "You sincerely harassing me with this?"

"Speak proper English, Anette. I am only asking you how you will love your child.

How will you make sure you do not communicate an unhealthy love?"

"But Eeona. Love for your spouse is like the love for your child. There ain no such thing as unhealthy love."

Then she stare at me as though I is a real stupidee. She stand up, wipe she hands on she dress like she wiping she hands of me.

"Eeona, what the ass?"

But she ain study me at all. She turn away and walk out the house. Just so.

Really, I can't say is all Eeona fault. I can't say she rub up some obeah on my foot to have me wanting to walk across the water to kill or save my marriage. But them simple question she questioning do me something. Because in truth, I don't love my husband. I never get the chance to figure the love thing out with him. He gone for the most of our marriage. Now I sit in the room, this baby punching me up from the inside. My foot aching because Eeona just slam it on the floor. My husband gone for what he tell me going be a undisclosed amount of time. I really wasn't planning on missing him. What the hell love I going to give Ronald Junior or Ronalda for true? What the hell I know about love? In my head, I imagine falling in love supposed to feel big and safe, like a soak in the calm ocean at sunset. And

I know, in truth, that Ronald ain never make me feel like that. It ain his fault. Is just so.

I want to shout after Eeona that is *she* was so pushy for this marriage and now that I in it, she just jealous.

But that very night when I there in the bed by myself and not missing Ronald at all, I start thinking maybe I done read too much history love book about Napoleon and Josephine and Caesar and Cleopatra. Because really, what the ass I going to do if I leave Ronnie? Move back with Eeona? So I make up my mind. I going to fall in love with Ronnie. I going magic myself into it. I going learn it on my own, just like I keep myself from deading of the fever.

I plan it: We going to have to live just we. Without he mother snooping behind the door and timing how long we spending our husband-wife fun. We going to install a phone in the house and tell Eeona she have to call before she come.

When Ronalda born, Eeona bring nappies and spit rags and all that. She being a good sister again. But she also talking funny — having what she does call her episodes. She say she get these from our mama. Talking about how we need to be free women and how we think we free but we not. Doting off into space when she talking, as if she telling story to people who ain there. But I done with listening to she.

All this time, the rumors been coming about how some of our boys cause a ruction in New Orleans and get in a heap of trouble. We know is over some racial stupidness and we proud of them for all that. More proud than if they been fighting in Germany or Japan. When we find out that war done, I already know what it is I going to do. Radio say the boys coming back on a big cruise ship, like tourists. I start watching Ronnie mother so I could see how to make the red pea soup like he like it. I watch my figure so I could stay thin and nice. I love baby Ronalda. I mean, I love her like any mother love a child. I choose to live. Why I can't just choose to love? All I have to do is focus on the love that coming on that boat.

I going to be there on the dock with half of St. Thomas waiting for the boys. I going see that Ronnie step off the ship and stoop down to kiss the ground. See me there, my heart open and ready like a mouth for the Sacrament.

39.

"So what the hell is the plan?" Back in their bunk, Grenada was mad and hungry and full of gas.

Jacob took off all his clothes and dropped onto his cot as if he were a felled tree. "We'll do it tomorrow. I swear on my mother we'll do it tomorrow."

Ronnie pulled out his softened picture of Anette. He sat beside Jacob. "Look here, Jay. I'm swearing on her."

Now Jacob held out his hand and Ronnie relinquished the photo to him easily. Anette was looking out as though she were reading his mind. "Can she cook?" Jacob asked.

"She can't boil water."

Jacob smiled and pressed his sweaty thumb into Anette's neck. When he passed the picture back, there was a slight discoloration on the photo, as though Anette had become hot around the collar.

That night Jacob lay in his spare cot of a bed in just his socks, while the other men went to the shack to eat rubber in silence. Even Spice Grenada ate, not caring about contamination. Ronnie had sworn on his own lovely wife and Jacob had sworn on his mother. But were they brave enough? Were they soldiers after all? Jacob stayed behind and thought of his mother and of the mama at the restaurant. He thought of the waitress and he thought of all the New Orleanian and Virgin Islands women who didn't know him. Didn't know his potential, his worth. In his dreams that night Ronnie's wife appeared before him in a red dress, wet as though she had been swimming. I know you, she said. He stood before her and felt his very teeth begin to crumble. He opened his mouth and they fell at her feet like seashells.

Jacob fasted all the next day, as if he were holding his breath. They were underwater after all, fighting for their piece of air. After spitting out pus, his tooth had stopped hurting but it retained a soft pink color so that he did not smile broadly until years later when his dentist brother bleached it white and Jacob's soul shrunk to a normal man's size. But that whole day in New Orleans everyone stayed away from him. The news got around the West Indians quickly. The American officers sniffed the air but could not locate the source of the new stench of blood. They watched their island boys. But no one would have suspected young college-graduated McKenzie of doing wrong. He was lighter-skinned and polite. He could babble island to the boys and yank American to the officers. No one would have thought he would sneak into the armory and carry three rifles out. This felt like a real war now. They would be real Americans, finally.

The three of them now made their own way into town. Jacob prayed Hail Marys in his head. He was a McKenzie and all McKenzies were Catholic, even though his mother had never allowed him into the cathedral. But children will have their rebellions. For this battle in New Orleans Jacob had sworn on his mother. Now he prayed to Mother Mary.

Smalls and Grenada walked and nodded at each other intermittently. A silent encouragement. Jacob had not explained the mission. Jacob did not know the mission. He went on intuition. And he would do this for everything until his mother rose like a wave to knock him down.

When they walked down the street, the stares were different now. Some bowed at them. The tall guns over their shoulders meant they were keeping the peace. Protecting everyone from the evil Nazis and the lunatic Japs. An Anglo husband whispered deep into his wife's ear as the men crossed the street: "They giving the niggers guns now? They'll be using them against us, you know." The woman, who was a passing octoroon herself, giggled at her husband's silliness.

This time they noticed the sign outside of Mama's. It was black with bright white letters. Anyone could read it, even in the dark. How could they have walked in and sat down and not noticed it before? NO COLOREDS ALLOWED. They were the coloreds. But they walked in again, the rifles stiff at their sides, and they sat down with the rifles between their legs and the muzzles to the ceiling. "Mama," Jacob called to the heavy woman behind the counter who was picking her teeth with her fingernails. He spoke tenderly as though he were talking to his own mother. "We made an order, Mama." He felt his soul glow amber and expand. "We come to get what we ordered."

Spice tapped the butt of his rifle on the floor three times and like a spell the food appeared. Every single thing on the menu was put before them by the same graying green waitress. She didn't smile or look pretty anymore. She didn't look at them at all. The plates crowded the table. Spice licked the bread of the prawn poor boys. Ronnie chewed on chicken legs and spat out mush into napkins. Jacob gargled with the liquor — letting it slosh around his mouth, cleansing that tooth, before releasing it back into the mugs. Not one of them could eat. All three massaged their rifles and looked into one another's sinking eyes.

Five weeks in the stockade for each of them. They'd disturbed the peace; they'd stolen guns. They were lucky they hadn't been given years in prison. After his time, Spice Grenada was deported back to his navel string island of Grenada, where he reclaimed his birth name, Michael Worthingham V, and joined the Grenada Revolution.

For their American Caribbean Negroes, the Army followed up stockade time for McKenzie and Smalls with some sessions of reason and reform for the entirety of Port Companies 872, 873, 874, and 875, just in case. They brought in the Olympian who had raced in Germany and won and won, and had then been hired by the American government to lecture the darker soldiers.

"I understand your frustration," the gold-medaled hero had said to the West Indians. "But this is the way America is. You do a service for your fellow countrymen by fighting for your country. Don't make waves for the U S of A. You show them that you are . . ." But the hero hadn't finished. Because these men who were dark like he was didn't understand bowing and smiling and surviving. They screamed out, "Ass licker," "No-souled," "Slave-minded." But Jacob had sat there quietly, wondering what really was happening.

Jacob was still brave enough to be aware of his own fear. And Jacob was afraid that his world, the one that belonged to him, the one where he was handsome and loved and a future doctor and piano player, was being smiled and bowed away. So while the others jeered, Jacob stood up and threw his shiny black boot onto the stage, smacking his country's great Negro Olympian in the head. Just so.

After that incident, they split the West Indians up. There never was a West Indian company again. Ronnie was allowed to stay in Creole country because everyone knew that on his own he wasn't much harm.

But after the boot smacking, Jacob had been put in solitary for two solid weeks, where he had to keep his hands on his own face to know that he still existed. Then they'd sent him to Sand Island in Hawai'i, to be killed by Japs he figured. Sand Island for our sandman was just another kind of jail, for on that island all his dreams were of

St. Thomas beaches and shells and girls in stewed-cherry dresses.

When the war was over, Ronnie was demobed to Puerto Rico with a batch of Puerto Ricans, where he drank rum with them as though they were brethren and sang "The Star-Spangled Banner" like any American. A tropical storm blew through and so for more than a week he and some other St. Thomians kept the party going while their boat to St. Thomas bobbed on the P.R. dock.

But as soon as the second bomb fell, Jacob had been given his demob and was sent home early on an ocean liner shipping supplies and a few St. Croix soldiers. "We docking first in St. Thomas," one of them said. "Imagine, we part of the same U.S. Virgin Islands but I ain never been to St. Thomas before. It sweet?" Jacob had nodded. "Too sweet," he'd responded, but he didn't lime with those boys. He found out that the war was over while lying on his cot feeling the Caribbean Sea already beneath the boat. He went among the commotion and celebration of his fellow soldiers, his fellow Virgin Islanders, but he couldn't bring himself to raise a glass with them. Jacob Esau thought only about arriving to his mother island and to his mother. He thought about going to medical school. His thoughts were incomplete.

40.

St. Thomas was such a strange place now. The island was not the same, and its native sons returning would not make it the same again. The owner of Eeona's flat had up-rooted Eeona's back garden to make room for a pavement so the neighbor woman from Jost Van Dyke could park her car. This woman not only owned and drove her own car nowadays, but also had her own busi-ness — a restaurant on the waterfront.

There were still some known Savan fami-lies living up on Frenchman Hill, but as one traveled down the hill, the area became less familiar. Eeona really didn't know her neighbors now, who were mostly British Virgin Islanders passing through the win-dow from Tortola or Jost Van Dyke for work. Most of them rented the flats in ninety-day shifts, as the law allowed. They worked all the new jobs that had been discovered. Bartender. Waitress. Cook. Chambermaid in the hotel. Calypso singer at the airport. Welcome to the island work.

Eeona was still seeking her way out and up. She knew now that she must go where no one would know her history, her losses, and her transgressions. No Anette. No Mr. Barry. No Villa by the Sea and its ghosts just there in Frenchtown. It seemed clear New York City would make sense. With the war ending, the big city would need citizens of class such as she to help revitalize. Besides, Savan was becoming a place where a lady of class should not live — especially if she lived alone. Whereas before there was only Lettisome's Corner Grocery, there were now three small shops. They all stayed open past dark and sold cigarettes by the pack. Eeona would quit Mr. Barry. She would sell Nelson the donkey, not to buy a car after all, but to buy passage. She would take out the money she had been saving in the St. Thomas Bank. But first she needed to plan for what she would do in New York. She was not going to arrive with dreams and no way to reach them. She'd thought it all through — not like Mama who'd sailed on a whim.

Freedom was not the same as loneliness. No, it was not. It was not. Eeona had a strategy for her freedom. One that would take her to the people she was meant to be among. She carried a tiny coconut tart to the Jost Van Dyke lady restaurateur. This was the same woman who had nursed

Anette to health from the Spanish influenza so many years before, and she still went out of her way to regularly wish Eeona a good morning. She seemed to have some class and intelligence about her. Jost Van Dyke was one of the *British* Virgin Islands after all. Eeona was offered tea and then she and this woman spoke at length about the Stemme family, among others. Stemme was still a known Anegada name and Antoinette Stemme was still known as a native daughter of the soil — bless her soul and rest her in her grave. When Eeona's talk turned to business, the restaurateur offered her some hours cooking or waiting tables at her restaurant. But then Eeona let her hair down and the BVI woman understood how valuable Eeona could be. "I been thinking," started the woman, "about setting up rooms on the top floor. Too much work for me alone. I'll need an assistant manager."

Even though Eeona was quitting him, she managed a reference letter out of Mr. Barry — one she would take to America. Then she walked out of the Hospitality Lounge and straightaway began working at the restaurant that also let rooms. She was so lovely to look at, walking among the tables or sitting up in the office going over the bills. She made people hungry, so the restaurant business boomed. And she made people horny, so the rooms boomed louder.

As Eeona gathered her letters and her money and gained her experience, she knew that Anette was fine. She knew that she would never leave Anette if her sister needed her. So Eeona told herself.

But come now, the signs were quite clear. Mrs. Smalls would stop Eeona in the street to whine about Anette running out to the grocery at eight or even nine o'clock, leaving little Ronalda behind. Couldn't one wait until morning to buy a tin of condensed milk? When Anette came to visit with little Ronalda, Eeona saw that Anette now admired her mirror. Eeona of all people should have known the sin. And then just before Eeona was due to heave off, there was Esau McKenzie's image there in the newspaper, like a warning. But Eeona ignored all that as best she could. Had to.

Besides, Eeona told herself, Anette had a baby now to take care of. Eeona did not. Anette had a husband to take care of her. Eeona did not. Never mind that Eeona had chosen against marriage and the children it could bring. Or, at least, she believed she had chosen.

Eeona had been the assistant manager for two months when the first ship with the soldier boys docked in. That ship was the very one that would turn and take her away. In the meantime, she was learning the new work. When she arrived in New York, there wouldn't be a job she couldn't hold. All she needed was one job, any ladylike job, her beauty would do the rest. She would lie about her age if she had to. She would call herself Creole or Portuguese if she must. Whatever it took to find her way back to her deserved fineness. Watching out for her siblings was no longer Eeona's concern.

41.

Red was not a color Anette wore often, given her own disdained red hair, which she hid by lathering it with black dye. But red had worked well for her and Ronnie before. Made him make a baby. It was a "Look at me" color. A color that made the newly arrived down-island men look a little longer at the St. Thomian girls walking by. So Anette wore her one red dress when she went to meet Ronnie. She wanted to be like a lighthouse above the sea of all the other waiting people.

Anette, with Ronalda hoisted on her hip, passed by her sister's apartment to let Eeona know that she was heading to the ship of soldiers. "I going to my love. But I going pass him here first, if you don't mind. Drop Ronalda while we have a bit of husband-wife time." Eeona noted that Anette's hair was coppery, glowing almost. Perhaps she needed more dye.

With Anette and half of St. Thomas down at the docks, Eeona walked quickly down Main Street and sold the earrings out of her ears to a jeweler whom she did not know. The jeweler's fingers were moist as he leaned over to press her earlobes between his thumb and forefinger. "Thank you," he said, and passed her twice the money she was asking. "You are an angel, aren't you?"

"You are mistaken," Eeona replied. "I am a Bradshaw." She snapped her purse shut and walked out into the street. She stood there for a moment and breathed.

Anette's husband was coming home. Now Eeona was finally going. She would start a business in New York, conceivably. She would make her hats and shawls and lace doilies; she would manage her own hospitality lounge or perhaps a rooming hall for ladies. Perhaps she could claim her father was a rich general, dead in the war. Anything at all until a man with a nice last name walked in. Rockefeller. Carnegie. Ford. A railroad man, perhaps. It had to be good if it was going to replace Bradshaw.

Eeona had bought her ticket for the ocean liner with her pay from the restaurant. She was leaving in three weeks. Eeona stood on Water Front and saw the very vessel easing into the other side of the bay. Anette was there with a clutch of other wives and mothers and half of the island waiting for this first batch of soldiers to disembark. Eeona stood and watched until the huge boat seemed moored, then she turned back to Savan to sew the last pieces of Mama's lace gloves into baby underpants for Ronalda. She would wait for her sister and the baby and the husband this one last time.

But when Anette returned from the dock, there was Ronalda but no Ronald. Eeona was only a little concerned. Perhaps it was the wrong ship. Perhaps this one was full of medics and medicines or produce or even bones. Eeona did not put down the pieces of lace that were no longer Antoinette's gloves. She was almost finished.

Anette held Ronalda with the baby's face to her shoulder. She leaned into Eeona and shielded the child as though from a secret. "Eeona, boats been doing me wrong since I born. Now this boat have me divorcing Ronald."

Eeona's teeth clamped down hard inside the privacy of her mouth. She waited a few seconds before releasing her jaw. "You shall do no such thing."

"Watch me."

Eeona fastened a thimble to her index finger and did not look at her sister. "What has happened, Anette?"

"Nothing happened."

"Is your husband not on this ship? Have you no patience?"

Anette turned from Eeona to lower Ronalda down on the bed. The child was awake now but had not made a sound. Her eyes were open and staring at her mother.

"Eeona, you was right. I ain love that man. I never did."

"That is a very selfish reason to leave him."

"Well." She walked across the room, her hips now with an unmatronly sway. "It was the right ship, but Ronald wasn't on it."

Eeona still didn't look up from her sewing. "You are a Bradshaw. You are not a loose woman who becomes a divorcée simply because her husband is daft enough to miss his ship home." She bit the end of her thread. "You will end up an old maid, Anette. You will end up alone." She offered her sister the lace. Anette took the gift cautiously, as though Eeona had just presented her with a riddle.

"Eeona. I don't know what game you playing, but I won't stay with a man because I'm afraid. You have your beauty. I only have my sense of things. And I sense that my man was on that ship, Eeona. The problem is that Ronnie was not on the ship."

Now Eeona found Anette's gaze. "Little sister, you have no idea how foolish the women in our family have been over men and ships."

Then Ronalda made a sound as though she was deciding whether or not to cry. Anette gripped the lace diaper cover, as though it was a rag to ring out her frustration. She couldn't make this decision holding Ronald's baby.

"I'll be back just now," Anette said. Then she rushed out of the flat. She left her sister and her daughter there to each other.

42.

History records that, despite everything, Jacob Esau McKenzie was the first one off the big boat. He was the first returning soldier to shake Governor de Castro's hand. It was in the papers. There was proof. He was the hero at the Grand Hotel ball held in the men's honor.

But there really wasn't anything grand about being the first; if the newspapers really knew, they wouldn't have said "hero." His had been a dishonorable discharge, after all. He was the first off only because he couldn't wait to eat from his mother's hand. He'd been in solitary and he'd been on Sand Island. He was most afraid that St. Thomas wouldn't be real. The boat, which was also for luxurious island-hopping, now did its patriotic part. But it didn't dock up fast enough. Its hulking body slid and bounced against the dock, kissing the island tentatively. Men who had saved each other's lives, men who had cried into each other's laps, now pushed and bit at each other before the door was opened and the plank was lowered. Jacob had pushed the hardest. He had broken through with all the people there watching. He had taken off his Army cap and kissed the ground as if it were a lover or maybe as if it were a thought-dead mother. And he had stayed there, his mouth to the ground as though to a woman, until the governor came up to him, bent down, and said, "Son, I admire your passion but this is indecent," and Jacob had risen slowly and shaken the governor's hand for the pictures.

Really, Jacob was a hero. Because he had been fearless when other men of his same country had treated them worse than any German. He had been the one to steal the guns and demand service in the New Orleans restaurant. He had been the only one put into solitary. The one shipped out to Sand Island to die in the war that was ending.

But there were times when he wasn't so brave. When he was hauled off to solitary where he became a dreamer in order to not lose his mind. When he was sent to Sand Island where he hadn't been killed by the Japs after all, but had weeks of wet and mud with his gun between him and the earth wondering what made a man a man.

And then the war was over. And he was alive. And his mother had written saying that the heroism was in that, his surviving. But Jacob wasn't so sure.

On the day he arrived, he kissed the ground, he shook the governor's hand, and he saw in the crowd a woman in a cherry-red dress looking at him as though he were something she had lost. At that moment he didn't think of the wife from Ronald Smalls's picture. He only thought that he wanted to reach out and touch the woman's coppery hair. Nothing strange in that; he hadn't had a woman's attention in so long. But that night as he lay on his back, his reddish tooth still pulsing dully as though it were flesh, all he could do was think of that woman in red and how she had looked at him as though he was truly heroic just for walking off the boat. Even his mother, who had three other sons after all, hadn't looked at him that way when he walked in her door.

In his dreams that night he was following that woman and only then did she merge with the wife in Ronald Smalls's picture, who, in fact, she was. Her red dress flickered around buildings and into doorways. Jacob followed her down the road to Coki beach, the one famous for its undercurrent and infamous for swallowing people whole. The woman appeared before him in a red dress, wet as though she had been swimming. Once again, he felt his teeth begin to crumble. He opened his mouth and the seashells fell at her feet.

43.

ANETTE

I was glad to have Ronalda. Don't mind I didn't want her father. Is just that on the day I gone to see the boys return I see the tall lanky one walk off the ship and not

Ronald at all. The mangrove man look like someone I done been loving. When he stoop down to kiss the ground, it like he own the land. And I want to be that land, you hear.

Eeona mouth gaping at me when I declare divorce. So I leave Ronalda and fly out to Gertie mother house, where Gertie still living. I knock on her door and tell Gertie right there in the threshold. "You won't be the last," Gertie say. "At least your husband's not dead. At least this is your choice. At least you been married at all."

Gertie pour out two tiny glass of guavaberry from a crystal decanter — even though it wasn't Christmastime. We drink until we couldn't look at each other without laughing. My feet bicycling in the air as Gertie make imitations of Ronnie earnest character. Me choking on my own laughter and then suddenly collapsing into tears. "Oh, Gertie. Don't make fun of the man," I say, with my head in my own lap. "It ain he fault."

That very day I leave Mrs. Smalls house and take myself back to Eeona, just like before. When I had start packing up, Mrs. Smalls had turn from me saying, "You always thought you were better than he was." Which wasn't true. Is really that Ronnie was too good, but how to explain that? Just so, that woman wash her hand of me.

The day after the ship arrive, the selfsame man I see stepping off the boat is there on the cover of the newspaper. Well, hello! It hit me that this is Saul's younger brother. The piano-playing one. I buy the paper and cut out the clipping of the man shaking the governor hand. When I come home from taking Ronalda to visit her grandmother, Eeona there sitting at our little table with the clipping clench up between she fingers. She wave it in my face like a rag. "Why do you have this here?" She suck her teeth when I tell her is nothing. I ain never seen my sister suck her teeth. It was not a lady-like thing to do, and Eeona always a lady. I squinch my face at her. "Is just my classmate brother."

"Let that be all you ever know," she say. But I think she having she weirdness, what she call episodes, and I does find is best to ignore she then. Plus, what I know about the man? Not a thing. Instead, that very day I go to the library and rent the typewriter for a hour. I myself type the letter stating that is divorce I looking. One copy for Ronnie and the other for the court.

Must be two weeks again before Ronald arrive in St. Thomas. But he too late. He gone to his mother's looking for me. She tell him that I leave the house and that I leave he. Ronald arrive to our flat, hat in hand, as though he courting again. I kiss him on the cheek like a sister, passing him his daughter with one hand and the letter with the next.

He take baby and letter both like a punishment he deserve, which I glad for, 'cause it make the whole thing more easy. But when he leave, I find the letter outside in the street, neat, like he just lay it down on the ground for a second to tie he shoe. But I had give Ronnie that divorce letter, you hear. Don't mind what bad behavior I get up to in the future. We is Americans and I don't need my husband permission to leave he. I is an independent woman.

44.

EEONA

I was not against divorce so much as I was against Anette being unwed. I should have told her: "Do not trust your own emotions." I should have told her: "Do not love yourself too much, otherwise you might fall in love with the wrong man." I told her no such things.

After telling me of her intentions, Anette

dived out of the room with the end of Mama's gloves. I never saw that lace again. My simple magic was averted. Instead, across from me was Ronalda. The baby had just learned to hold herself sitting up. She was staring at me with huge hopeful eyes that reminded me of Anette's the morning our mother died.

The next day I saw my father's face looking up from the newspaper. The name was not a match, but still I suspected that this soldier was our brother. I believe I made my disdain clear to Anette, but I had never quite understood Mama's warning to watch out. I knew, however, that our Bradshaw name had been lowered enough. How far would the name and reputation sink if it was revealed that my father had been with a woman who worked obeah? A married woman, at that? I needed my name. I loved and respected the man who had given me that name.

Before leaving, I intended to do all I could to prevent Anette's divorce. Still, you must understand the strain of this. Family can be like an anchor. An anchor may tether you. An anchor may also pull and sink your ship.

45.
ANETTE

Gertie mother thinking I is still a well-married woman, and so she ain fuss that Gertie going with me to a dance down by the Catholic school. I leave Ronalda with Eeona, saying I just accompanying Gertie. It ain raining as yet. Just the smell of rain, crispness in the air that any fool would think is hope or a new beginning. You see, the war over. And even though is the church holding the dance, Jeppesson start up with that silly calypso just as soon as Gertie and me walk in.

The sandman wasn't there in the dance hall. Is ain yet a month since his ship land, and so though it like I feeling him coming, I ain really believe is he coming. Not so soon. In fact, is Saul come in and dance and add rum to the Coca-Cola, like the calypso song say. Saul always mischievous like the McKenzie he is. They done saying that Saul does be building house only so he know how to sneak in and out with the man of the house in such a way that the wife don't suspect. Yes, Saul always been a nancy man.

Let it be known that I was already settled on the divorce before I meet Jacob. Jacob wasn't looking to be a home wrecker — not as yet. "Rumors fly," as the love song goes. Jacob ain thief me away. Try and remember, I wasn't wearing my wedding ring that night. I done pay for the divorce with my own money that I get from my work at the apothecary. I telling everyone to call me Miss Bradshaw from here on. I wasn't even at that party looking for a man. I was there with Gertie. I wasn't trying to impress a soul. Is true. Yes. That I had want a man who going to grab me up and hold me tight, worship me like a fat golden calf. I had the man who come off the boat and kiss the ground in my head. But I have my sister's warning to be a lady rinsing out my ears. Eeona think is shame enough that I divorcing, she ain want me to flaunt myself on top of it. So, I ain coif up my hair or anything at all. I wearing flat shoes. I wear only a little light lipstick.

Rum and Co-caaa-Co-la. That was the song Jeppesson was singing and Saul McKenzie was there pouring the rum. I know this song from Lord Invader scratching it out over the radio. Is much later we hear 'bout the Yankee Andrews Sisters thiefing the song. But now nobody vex with the Americans because is America win the war. The Caribbean is the rum and America is

243

the cola and we in the Virgin Islands is both, so everything sweet, sweet, sweet. Not like now with the Americans all bury up in their own school, living out East End like is Little USA, drinking at their fancy bars that only play their music. It wasn't like that then. In my time, the Americans seem like they actually come to we island to be with we. Man, that night I feel something was special in the air, but I sure is only happiness at being on the winning side. Happiness at being an American.

See me. I moving through the party. I chatting with everyone. When they ask for Ronnie, I ready for them. I smile and flip my hand. "He's well, he's well. We're divorcing, you know, but he's well." I ain want to announce it in hushed tones, like I shame. I don't want people's pitiful look. I know thoughts have power. I had want to declare the divorce and then dance. Not giving anybody a chance to even think sorrow for me. Some of them woman who there with their husbands even give me a look like they impress with me.

Now at the party, I feeling the man coming like I feeling the mist from the rain coming in from the balcony, but I ain know what I feeling. We win the war! We is winners! The thing I feeling seem like patriotism, but now I know that loving a man and loving the country he fight for might be the same thing. In the rum and Coca-Cola song they singing 'bout the GI boys loving up the native peaches. And I know I is the peach and I waiting for my GI.

Listen close. Saul McKenzie and I had been classmates. I knew he have a heap a brothers, but I was never one of them girls who deading for a McKenzie man. Saul he self handsome and fun but he duncey. And besides, it turn out he only interested in getting romantic with other man. Me and Saul dance for a little bit, and I grabbing him every now and then to settle him back into the right beat because, like every McKenzie besides Jacob, Saul ain have no rhythm at all. "Rum and Co-caaaa-Co-la!" I sing the song in Saul ear to keep us from moving to the rhythm of the rain or whatever it is he listening to. Gertie with the first man that swing she to the dance floor.

That night the song say we supposed to swoon when we hear Bing Crosby croon and so we girls all put the backs of our hands to our foreheads and pretend to stumble a little. The song say tropic love, and we giggle, 'cause we know that mean the kind of love only we island girls can give. Even though we ain have sense enough to know that love is love is love. I finally sit down after roaming and dancing. I keeping a eye out for Gertie because I ain see where she gone, and her mother make me cross myself and swear to watch her. I ain no cross-myself Catholic, but I still looking out for Gertie.

The band taking a break but I hoping Jeppesson play the Coca-Cola song again, even though they done play it three times for the night and that's unheard of. Lord Invader from Trinidad looking to take New York by storm with this calypso, but we ain know this on St. Thomas, because the radio pouring us American songs about the Caribbean and West Indian songs about America and to we it all seem like another way to be the same. And that night I loving the song because I loving being out of Ronnie mother house and I loving being a single island peach. But Jep ain play it again. And the next time I hear this song is years later at that stinking Gull Reef Club. Is then they have these three white woman singing it on a record like is their song and we all realize Lord Invader is the one who get invade.

But now a man sit down on the bench beside me. And when he do that, the weight of the wood push up against me. Is the rain must be chase him in because as I feel the bench take he weight I hear the rain really pelt down on the roof. Since the school only go up to sixth grade, the benches them low, which perfect for me, but he too tall. He looking foolish there with his leg them bend up and rising into he chest. He ain in uniform, but he have that sand-colored skin. Is him.

What get into me to say something? I don't know. Maybe is the song so sassy it make me bold. Jesus, I can't lie. I know the power I had. I know I dangerous. So I say something, but in Spanish: "Anegando en mis llanto." I am drowning in my tears. "Anegando." I say again. Drowning.

Is just something from a Puerto Rican bolero that was ruling the radio year before last. I guessing this man ain know the song because he ain been around. Boleros ain in style no more; now we want only American tunes. But I remembering because this man have this yellow-brown color like sand, and plus it raining outside like rain could drown. I say it while staring down into the cleavage of my own dress. Is then I realize that I exposing myself. My brassiere all peek out from all that dancing I been doing, and my sleeve hanging to reveal the strap.

"Anegada?" the man ask, like he need help with the translation. And just as he asking this, the first thing the man ever say to me, he also reaching his hand over to adjust my blouse. Like he done already know me.

We hear the rain really start coming down and it steady-steady, like the sea coming to we. I ain answer the sandman question about Anegada or drowning in tears, but it like he still fully feeling what I say. I feeling his fingers on me even after he stop touching. Them is Army-boy hands. Hard and knowing. They is piano-playing hands. Long and able. The man look to Jeppesson like they know each other from dog days and Jeppesson catch the cue and his band curl into a new song. One I ain hear before, but now every time I hear it, even in my old age, it causing me to lose my breath like I underwater. The Irving Berlin song "They Say It's Wonderful." And it was. I telling you. Maybe is magic or maybe is God or timing or fate — all of that is the same thing anyhow. The man stand up and I follow him onto the dance floor like I already his.

I would never have guess that he was a real McKenzie, because he know how to dance. He hold my hand and my waist with those hands of his, and he guide us to the music. He was decent, not like the young people nowadays with your grindup-grindup. We lean on our feet. "I know that

falling in love is grand" — Jeppesson crooning nice and this man moving me with his
hands. Gertie appear to whisper something
in my ear about leaving with some boy and
I just nod without turning my head to her.

The man ain ask my name at first. I
remember. I remember, because it was so
wonderful and strange. He ask first, "Are
you real?" I like that he coming to me with
questions, not no arrogance. But still his
questions bold.

We dancing and he have my hand curl up
in his, against his chest. I say, "Pinch me
and see I real." He squeeze a piece of my
shoulder between his music fingers. I feel
that what happening here is magical and
dangerous and not just timing. Not just the
music or the rain rushing down. Not just
chance at all.

"Well, I'm Jacob McKenzie. I'll be walking you home this evening."

His voice don't sound like war. It don't
sound defeated, which is how Ronnie always
sound even before the war, even before I
pass he the divorce declaration. Jacob sound
like piano playing and white guayaberas and
hibiscus in the hand.

I bend my neck back-back just to look this
man in the face. "Call me Nettie." I give
him a nickname, one nobody ain never call

me, but it come like it my true-true name. I stand flat again and stare into his chest. I just start talking to his heart with my mind: *You will be open. You will be full of me forever.* And before my thoughts finish, Jacob Mc-Kenzie say these words to me out loud: "Isn't the beginning of love wonderful?" And I nod yes, even though I ain never been in love before. Even though he just steal the words from Jeppesson singing mouth. But I nod yes, because I feeling it, too. The song now coming to an end, the piano notes dropping like drizzle. And I feel foolish. But I want to be foolish with this man.

Really, I ain known chick nor fowl 'bout Jacob McKenzie before. He was a full two years ahead of me at school even though we born the same year. He just one of Saul's brothers that I see once in the yearbook playing piano. But then he went to war and he come back a man. And then he was the man of my life.

The rain ease and before Jeppesson could start in on a tune by the King Cole Trio, the janitor come sweeping through the dancers with his broom. Everybody skipping to avoid him, the boys calling out, "Come on, Stumpy, one more song!" But the janitor ain studying us, and when he reach to the other side of the room, he flick the light off and say into the darkness, "Dance done!" And then he flick the lights on and off like a storm until we all drain out.

In front of the school Jacob standing close to me while we wait out the rain. He brother Saul stroll up to us. He say to Jacob, "Treat Anette good, you hear. She is my classmate." Jacob nod, as though this was a command. Then to me Saul say, "Anette, this young man is my baby brother. You best give him a damn hard time." Then he turn and leave we. I remember, because is the approval we never get from Jacob's mother or from my sister.

The song say the moon above supposed to be wonderful, but I ain know. Was there a bright star guiding us? I ain remember. It perfect but not a kind of perfection I can explain. I hear a merengue coming out an open door. We walk through the back streets and the step streets, so even though I only live just maybe five minutes from the Catholic school, our walk take a good half hour. It come like even time ain real.

We turn onto the hill in Savan where my and Eeona shack of an apartment close to the bottom. The wind blowing the curtains open. There is my daughter sleeping in the bed. I ain realize before that if somebody

251

just stand up on the hill street they could lean and glance in the bedroom window. Ronalda's arms out straight in front she self like she reaching, her legs curl up tight to her belly because she already that kind of child.

I come accustomed to men commenting on Eeona's beauty. But is my daughter there. In only a nappy. Her uneasy beauty circling round her like it about to land. I turn to Jacob because I ain sure if he know that this my daughter he watching. I desire to jump through the window and cover her, claim Ronalda hard. To say "mine." I want to say that if he want me he going have to want her, too. But Jacob just turn to me and say yes. As if I had ask him a question. "Yes."

I take his face in my hands, I telling you. Right there with my daughter inches away and me not quite divorced and Irving Berlin in my head. And I kiss him. And this kiss run through my whole body until I feel it punging like a heart in the arch of my foot.

Nobody used to lock doors back then, so I just open the apartment door. Before I walk in, I turn and see Jacob there, standing at the bottom of the hill. Watching me like he a guard or like he my father. Then he shout "Love is grand!" into the night, just like the song said he would. A rooster screech in response. And I know it. I know is over for me. I pitch myself into the flat and close the door. I lean against the door and believe I could feel it pulsing. Like the building have a ocean waving through it.

This too wild and fast to be love. But it is. Like in the movies, only for real. These things happen, I telling you. Not always with songs playing, except for the one singing in your own skin. People can need each other like water. It can be wonderful.

Waiting in the dark apartment, Eeona voice slice like a machete. "You are late, Mrs. Smalls." But I ain Mrs. Smalls no more.

46.

Eeona was not there to reel Anette in by her hair when the man kissed the ground as he left the ship or at the party when she and the man spoke of Anegada and drowning. Eeona was not there. And what could she have said to Anette, anyway? That man is our father's son. That man is your brother. Eeona would not have been able to bring herself to do it. And it was nothing anyway. Should have been nothing. How could Eeona have known that it would boil everything? By now Eeona would have convinced herself that such a sinful thing was hers alone.

Let us be fair to Eeona. The morning after Anette came back from that dance with Gertie, Eeona was on her way to refund her ticket to New York. She didn't know that Anette had met Jacob Esau the night before at the dance. But she did know that Anette had clipped his picture out of the paper. Eeona was on her way to do the right thing, for heaven's sake. She would delay her emigration. She would delay her freedom. She would stay in St. Thomas just a while longer and prevent Anette's divorce. But then out of the air came McKenzie. Another McKenzie. Rebekah's McKenzie. Eeona's McKenzie. A damn McKenzie who was supposed to have disappeared in a rain forest years ago.

Now we old wives know that a woman's beauty is not in her looks alone. Her power is in the way she lies in the sea. The way she fixes her footing on the earth. Eeona has always been a beautiful woman. But then this man sailed in on a seaplane. Consider how obvious it was, after all. A plane is a thing of transport. A plane has a captain. A plane is no different than a ship. And a seaplane, well, that's a ship but more. He was the age Owen Arthur would have been. He already had a history of loving the same woman Owen Arthur loved. He had been Rebekah's husband. Technically, he was still Rebekah's husband.

The white cruise ship was sitting there in the harbor like a fat rich man, just waiting for Eeona. It would leave in a week. Eeona walked past the big saving ship and didn't even give it a treacherous glance. She was heading to return her ticket, get her refund. But near the terminal, where the tickets were sold, there was a little gathering of people. They weren't there for the boat, they were there for something better. A seaplane or airboat, or whatever it was called, was flying in from Puerto Rico. When it arrived, it would take off on St. Thomas water, fly in the air, and then land on St. Croix water. St. Croix! Where Anette was to go to the orphanage, but she had wasted Eeona's money and fell ill instead. No known Bradshaw had ever seen St. Croix. Even Captain Bradshaw had never had the opportunity. But history was happening now and Eeona stood to witness.

At the dock, each seaplane passenger was made to step on a scale to be weighed. There was a stoic lady who held her hat on her head with one flat palm even though there was no wind. There was a scrawny young man who beamed out at the crowd as though he had invented air travel. When the count neared the maximum pounds, the others were turned away. Eeona, waiting for the ocean liner desk to open for her refund, watched the chosen six stare at the horizon and then she, too, watched the horizon as the seaplane became a dot, then a bird, then a machine skidding along the water, like a thing of Jesus. The seaplane roared as it slapped against the dock. The hatted lady released her hat for a second and it jumped off her head like an animal. She let it fly, her hair swelling into a cloud above her. The plane's engine quieted. As the door opened, the young man backed away slowly, clutching his one leather bag to his chest.

When the boarding began, no amount of coaxing would get what had been a young man and was now a frightened boy onto the seaplane. They needed another body to balance the weight. Eeona was already at the front of the crowd because crowds have always had the effect, like water, of parting for her.

"Last call for Freedom City," roared the ticket man. For Freedom is what the city in St. Croix was called. Freedom is what Eeona wanted. And so anyone could read what would happen.

Eeona raised her hand. Her hair was safely in a bun. Her pale blue dress was cinched only a little at her waist and bust. Her beauty seemed simply admirable instead of terrifying. The man in charge of the ticketing nodded at her. Eeona had no bags. Her bag for her trip to America was in the back of their apartment's closet, fully packed for weeks. Now she passed the man her New York ticket. It cost five times what the seaplane cost. The man accepted it as payment for Freedom City. Just like that.

Eeona sat in the back of the plane, which suited her because she enjoyed seeing how the other passengers scrunched their bodies toward or away from the windows, depending on their bravery. Eeona wasn't afraid, nor was she brave. She was in a reverie. It was so much like being on her father's ship. Only she was flying over the ocean. Like one would in a dream. In the air, she strained her head towards Frenchtown and, without considering it, found herself searching for Villa by the Sea. And there it was, now owned by wealthy Americans. Never burnt down, of course. That had been what Eeona told little Anette, so the girl would not home back to it. Now it was being turned into an inn, so Eeona had heard.

She stared at the villa, focusing on it as though it were a bull's-eye and she an arrow that might dive toward it. But then the seaplane curved. Now Eeona saw Lindbergh Bay where the American, Charles Lindbergh, had landed and left his name. Then Eeona saw St. Thomas dip away.

She hadn't left the island since she was a girl. Not since her father was alive. She hadn't seen Villa by the Sea since she'd left it. Now when they saw St. Croix rise off the skin of the horizon, a Crucian passenger began to bawl above the scream of the engine: "Look my island! Look me, look me!"

To Eeona the island was the back of a man whose head was under the sea. She saw an eight-sided house at the shoulder of a little cliff, rising like a keloid bruise. But then it was gone from view, a foam of water crashing against her window as the seaplane skidded across the water. Eeona touched her own face and found that she was weeping.

Her McKenzie was there as Eeona stepped off the plane. He had been on the seaplane but in the cockpit, and so she had not noticed him. He looked like a white man, but any island person would know he was not.

He would tell her he was from Anegada,

because that is what he told everybody. That
was a lie. But it was the perfect lie for
Eeona. And he would tell her that he was
the captain of the seaplane. That was the
truth. It was the perfect truth for Eeona.

47.

So Eeona freed herself of the island the
morning after the dance. But that same
morning Anette was still back in their flat.
She was only now waking because baby
Ronalda was stroking her face. Anette was
so tired from all the dancing the night
before. But also she awoke smiling, for she
had met Jacob.

48.

One more thing happened that morning
after the dance. Over breakfast, Jacob Esau
told his mother that he had met Anette
Bradshaw. At this, his mother's hair, cut just
below the ears since her sons had all reached
puberty, stood out straight as if it were a
den of snakes she carried hidden in her
scalp. She hissed at Jacob Esau. Her tongue
flicked out long and she stamped her foot
like a steed. Though he was afraid, he had
presence of mind enough to think to himself

that she did this expertly.

And then Jacob remembered seeing the hoof. Remembered the man who had danced with him as his mother played the piano and remembered then that she had seemed to be the happiest she'd ever been and ever would be again. And he, now grown, stood up and turned his back to his mother and said, "This is not real," a crooked version of the question he had asked Nettie. And when Jacob turned back around, his mother was just his mother and she said calmly with her hands out in offering: "Not that girl."

And that evening he didn't bring Anette to meet his mother — he never would — but he imagined that their love grew into something alive, something to be smelled and touched and tasted. And when he bit into this love, it was sweet, like the stewed cherries his mother sent to him during undergrad at Howard. In the bed that night Jacob reached out for this love and clenched his sleeping brother instead. But Saul, deep in his own dreams of flying buttresses and bookshelves that opened onto secret rooms, didn't allow the groping fingers to spoil his sleep. So Jacob plunged into this love like a feast. The food of this kept coming until he bit hard on the candied seed and he had the dream again of his teeth loosening one by one. His teeth rattled around his mouth, clanking against one another like tiny shells — filling his mouth and making a chiming noise. He didn't want to spit them out this time because the woman was not there to give them to. And so he woke up instead.

He dressed and then walked out of his house. Past his mother who sat on the settee in the dark and watched him go. Past the goat who always bleated at passersby. Past the big mango tree that didn't bear anything but fungus. Up the small hill. And in the middle of the night he looked through her window. The shutters were open and he could gaze at her face sleeping beside her daughter's. The elder sister was nowhere to be seen. He reached his hand through the window and brushed aside a bit of her hair from her face. He noticed that the roots were red in this light and he told her out loud: "I love you, Nettie." Because this was the woman who would save his soul, and being saved isn't a bad reason to love. It's a better reason than many others. He wanted to tell her about his dreams: the crumbling teeth, the cow foot, his fears in solitary, the gray-eyed papa who had danced with him.

His fingers brushed Anette's forehead and she opened her eyes. And she thought that she saw the sand-colored man with the moon behind his back. "Don't let me go," she said, as if she were casting a spell. And then she smiled in her sleep because her spell now meant that she would always be had. And for a girl who had been orphaned, this was not a bad reason to fall in love. It's better than many others.

As Jacob McKenzie walked home, he no longer thought on his real-real father, who was also Anette's father and who had been a sea captain and who had known that magic was real. Jacob knew only that he wanted this woman and more, wanted her to want him, respect him, know him as a man.

And when Anette woke up the next morning, she knew that she would slide her dignity aside for that man.

Their knowing was not fully understood.

His mother was home waiting for him, but he did not go home that night. He knew she was angry enough to put a spell, make his charlie shrivel like an earthworm, make his heart run like water. Instead, he went to a fancy rum shop owned by two American ex-servicemen. He sat down at the empty piano and told the room, "I'm a veteran. Get me drunk." He started playing something sad and then realized that his mother had taught him only sad songs. Still, he kept playing, and the bartender passed him firewater as long as the music poured on.

49.

On Jacob Esau's birth certificate, where the question was "father," the answer "Benjamin McKenzie" was written in bold caps. But Benjamin McKenzie did not go by that name any longer. Now he called himself Kweku Prideux, and when Kweku first saw Eeona Bradshaw, he was sitting at a canteen by the dock in Freedom City, St. Croix. He was still in his Powsen Passenger Seaplane captain's uniform. Eeona had stopped to buy some crackers in a tin. She did not know what she was doing or what she would do. But Eeona was calm and controlled, and she looked for all to see like a woman who had landed where she belonged. To all, that is, except Kweku. To Kweku she looked arid and severe. Her hair was pulled back, poking out defiantly at fierce angles like branches. She walked stiff and straight as though she had bark for spine. He did not see what other people saw. He didn't see the beauty. The obeah that had been done on him had stripped him not of life but of love. Which is the same thing, really. All

Kweku saw was Eeona's skin muddy because life had been a steady rain on her body.

She was not walking toward him, but she was walking his way. As she walked, she unbuttoned the top button of her blouse. She felt hot. She had done something wild and intrepid by getting on that seaplane.

Kweku stood when she walked by. He stood so that he was in her way, not because he wanted to take advantage of her, not yet, but because he recognized her. Well, not her exactly. He recognized what she was. An escapee. Like himself. A woman who was running away from her family or herself or her island. Same thing.

She spoke to him quickly and easily. "Either I can hire a burro or you can point me in the direction of a boardinghouse appropriate for a lady."

"Burro?" he said, and opened his mouth to laugh, but did not. "Are you such an old-fashioned lady that you still ride an ass? Welcome to Freedom City, St. Croix, in the United States Virgin Islands. I'll give you a ride in my automobile." And because it was the late 1940s and because he was still in his captain's uniform, Eeona trusted him. And because she seemed to him like a thing he'd been taught men should conquer, and because he had tried and failed to conquer Rebekah, he decided to take Eeona and never bring her back.

She introduced herself as Eeona Bradshaw, and though his people were actually from St. Thomas and though he knew what a Bradshaw was, he had been a sought-after McKenzie, so to him her surname did not impress at all. He introduced himself as Kweku Prideux. The first name was West African, but Eeona didn't know that and didn't know its reference. The last name was French and Eeona certainly knew what it meant: man of the sea, or something so.

Either way, it was all so easy.

Eeona had had her first plane ride and her first car ride on the same day. That was more than enough magic. On the St. Croix soil she felt as though the land had come rushing to her instead of her to it. Like a wall to lean on. Like a father to hold you up. This man beside her stared her down as he drove deeper into the veins of Freedom City.

She sat in the passenger's seat as he commanded his very nice and on-loan silver Chevy. During the drive, Eeona decided St. Croix might be another kind of Anegada. Or perhaps Anegada another kind of St. Croix. Both islands of coral and openness.

Both islands separated from their virgin sisters by the Anegada Passage. And so beautiful. And so unknown. A place to be beautiful where no one would have to truly know you.

From the sky she had seen the shape of the island and the dips of the ocean into all the bays. As the airboat left St. Thomas, Eeona had even seen her Villa by the Sea, but the first house she saw on St. Croix was the one with eight sides. It turned out to be Kweku's house. And that would reel in anyone. It is funny, the way freedom works.

Because who was Benjamin McKenzie anyway? A man who could not keep his wife in love with him. A man whose wife had cuckolded him and had a son with a ship captain. A man who could not beat his wife like a pestle to its mortar because she was a woman who could be the pestle and the mortar and even the salt and pepper within. So he left Rebekah his picture on the wall and left their sons unfathered. He had paved away Benjamin McKenzie of Solberg, St. Thomas. He was Kweku Prideux of Anegada, even though he had never been to Anegada. But to Crucians the atoll was remote and its people remoter and anyone on St. Croix could claim Anegada, and there were never enough true Anegadians on island who could securely say it wasn't so. He was a man who had lied about his race and education to get his seaplane license. He was a liar, all over.

It had been decades since anyone had called him Benjamin. He barely resembled that man at all. Benjamin had died in St. Croix's Rain Forest, though Rebekah had wanted Puerto Rico's rain forest. But her spell hadn't worked most ways you put it. Benjamin McKenzie might be gone, but here was Kweku Prideux in his place. And Kweku was the first man who saw all Eeona was and was not afraid. Well, the second. Owen Arthur had been the first.

Let us also be true in this history: This new man had become a myth.

His octagon house was neat — but only because it was so large and empty. There were chests in corners and rum bottles on the counter. Buckets and cans served as tables and clothing drawers. The house had appeared overnight like a spider's web. One had the feeling that Kweku Prideux was a man who had not yet moved into his mound of a house at the edge of this beautiful earth.

It wasn't an orphanage but it might as well have been. Eeona walked into Kweku's house, the house her dignity would live and die in, but not really live in after all. She looked around and then she looked up.

"Dear me, there are spiders everywhere!"

"Spiders does eat mosquito. You scared?"

He was mixing her a warm rum and Coca-Cola, for he, too, had heard the song. There was no ice in the box today because there was no electricity in the house today — it came and went. He did not pay for it and did not need it.

Eeona, who was thirty-something, was still a child in some ways. Today, magic was filling in her. How could she know that magic could fill you until it overflowed and left you dry? "It is just a ceiling of webs," she remarked now. "No spiders at all, Monsieur Prideux." Already she enjoyed saying his surname. Wouldn't she enjoy hearing it after her own given name? She sipped her warm drink. She knew he wasn't a pure European man. He was not speaking like a European man. But she easily let this prejudice go, for he looked so familiar. It felt so familiar. And besides, here was a large house, a villa one might call it, and the large piece of land it sat on and the expansive sea it overlooked.

The drink seemed all molasses on her tongue. Proper Eeona had never had a rum and cola in her life. She did not go to the dances and so did not know the song the Andrews Sisters would steal. But the drink was good and she was half finished with it by the time he poured his own.

"Those who know me call me Kweku."

"For the time being, I shall call you Monsieur Prideux," Eeona said, for she was aware of the naming power. "I prefer it."

"Yes. Call me that." He said it with such an authority that Eeona knew he had taken a bit of the power somehow. He stared at her, one of his eyes drifting so slightly that she could not be sure if he was staring at her or just beyond her or directly into her.

He brought her onto the balcony, through huge hushed glass doors. The ocean opened up. The breeze was like eight hands groping gently at her buttons. She looked out at the ocean and felt warm and overcome. Perhaps she was inebriated. Perhaps she was in love. What is the difference? She was free.

Kweku Prideux took off Eeona's clothes easily.

This was dangerous for many reasons.

They were on a balcony on a hill overlooking the ocean. There were not many hills on St. Croix, yet there they were. And though he still had on his pants and shirt, and even held his glass of rum in one hand, she was suddenly and completely naked. There was also the silver that no living person but herself and sad Mr. Barry had ever seen.

She felt her silver grow moist. She felt, with a sudden tearing, that maybe it was not her beauty all along, but maybe it was this silver that was her magic. This petrifying silver thing that Prideux was now cupping with his whole hand as though it were something he could break off from her and treasure away.

There was another house on the hill, smaller, but not far away. Muffled chattering came through the bushes while Kweku eeled into Eeona on the balcony. Those people might spy them, an unwed man and woman nasty for all to see.

There was also the ocean far below. Steel in color but moving and waiting to accept wholly whatever should fall.

His mouth was now sucking her there where she shined like a jewel. It felt to her as though he were drawing blood. She held her breath and watched her diamond hair glinting around his mouth.

The first time she had been kissed on her silver was on a ship and that man had been her father. And now she felt the remembered magic first as a withdrawal of air, a skip in the pattern of her breathing that she could not control. Then her self burst out of her and her head leaned over the ledge, her hair stumbling behind her toward the sea as she

270

screamed, the demons or angels inside her slipping like oil down her thigh. Now he seemed to be holding her with his arms and his legs, even as he buried himself into her and calmly sipped his drink. Now all of her body was taut. All of her mind was on self-preservation.

Her back was scraping again and again on the hard narrow railing. He turned her head to the side, so he could spill rum and cola onto her shoulder and then suck it off. She saw through the bushes, Jesus Lord, the neighboring balcony. Another man and woman moving against each other like the slamming of the waves. That woman was looking at Eeona. That woman was looking like her. And that woman was grimacing, her naked back to that man's shirted belly.

It was then that Eeona realized that she still had on her shoes. She scraped her heel into Kweku's back and in response he released her. He did not watch her hit the sea. She did not even fall over the balcony. Instead, they crumpled onto the balcony floor. His glass shattering about her face and head.

"The bed," she whispered, though she had not meant to whisper it. She had meant to demand it, to say it with strength. She coughed, but her voice still came out whispering something less than she knew she had been capable of. "Prideux, I want the master bedroom." He picked her up as if she were a skeleton, revealing a thick rug of dark hair bursting from the collar of his shirt. The hair would have repelled her were it not already too late. Now he carried her to the mattress on the floor that would be theirs.

50.

ANETTE

Hear me good. I have a talent for sensing arrival but not for departure. So I don't know what to think. My sister gone a full day and night. Leave a packed bag in the bedroom closet like she on a planned adventure but just forget the luggage. I wonder if maybe I send her away with my mind. I sure she done try that with me already. But in truth, having my own place for a bit seem like a gift, since Jacob living with his mother and she a salty piece of woman. And besides, Eeona always crazy talking about how she want she freedom. And just upping and going seem like something she would do. Like Eeona she self say Mama used to do with her episodes. Dreaming and then escaping, just so.

So I admit that I ain look for my sister at all until two days past and the stories start streaming in. First 'bout how somebody see she fling she self over waterfront and swim to St. Croix. A next that somebody see she walk into Western Cemetery, dig out a hole, and then toss she self in like a seed. Other people even talk 'bout how she gone to the old Villa by the Sea, a place Eeona always tell me been burn down long time ago. They says she flow past the Frenchies who working and the tourist them who guesting, and just jump off the villa balcony. All kinds of thing I hear. People come to my window and my door just to give me the deading stories. It come like deading is our family story.

I realize I don't even know who Eeona's friend them is. I ain even sure if she have friends. I go to Mr. Barry in the Hospitality Lounge, but when I say I lose my sister, this grown man just bust out in tears saying he lost she, too.

I couldn't do a thing, I tell you. I had Ronalda to keep my mind on. Even though Ronald helping watch her every now and then, and even though he still treating me sweet like I might change my mind and be his wife again. But I also have something else. I have Jacob.

We first meet at the dance on that Friday night. On Saturday he come to my window in a dream, like the sandman in the American song. On Sunday all three of we — Jacob and me and Ronalda, walk from town all the three up and down miles to Magens Bay — the beach what shape like a heart. On the walk, I hold Ronalda for a while and Jacob carry our bags with blanket and lunch and my books. After a while, he carry her also, the bags on his back. My child, looking to the world like his child, natural in his arms. Like we done belong to him. And he crooning all the way. Singing the Irving Berlin.

Let me tell you. How young and happy he was when he was just a man with rich dreams. He wealthy now — money does that. Make you stingy and mean. But back then, with a disappear McKenzie daddy, he almost poor and he ain care.

As we rounding the corner of Magens Bay road, he make a dash up into Brown Estate. I keep walking, now holding Ronalda, who twisting her head to see where the sandman gone. Jacob say he coming as he slink away. When he reappear, he have a bunch of frangipani petals in he hands like they just float from the sky. He offer the bunch to Ronalda, who is a baby but can still reach out her hand to grab, and when she do, she pick just one, just one. She always been the type that ain sure if she deserving. Then my sandman open his palm over my head. "It's raining flowers on you," he said.

"Is so you does bringing me flowers?" I say. We keep walking, the petals slipping down to my shoulders.

"Do you know how pretty you are?" he ask. As if that is an answer.

I know I ain the pretty one, but I like what he saying. "Always bring me flowers," I say, picking a petal from my tongue.

"I will always bring you flowers." He take the spitty petal and put it into his mouth, like we doing obeah on each other.

I have my books at the beach because I studying for a teaching position in history, even though I know they don't want to hire no divorcée. I readying myself anyway, because you never know. Waking up that morning with the sand-colored man on my mind, I decide I ain want to know the future. Knowing the future does ruin it. I have a gift for that, but I ain want it no more. What I want to know is the past. As far as I could see, that ain never ruin nobody yet.

While I studying, Jacob building a fort with Ronalda in the sand. He instruct her to crawl all over the fort when they finished, he cheer her on as she knocking it down. "That's the enemy," he bellow. "And you're the hero!" he shout, like they at war and he the commander. Later, when we in the water hugging up, he whisper: "Another way of loving you . . ." And point he chin to Ronalda sleeping on a blanket up on the sand. And I know what he mean. That he going love my child because he love me. And I think this a man who know about love. Hold-on-to-me love.

There at the beach he pull out a jar of stewed cherries for us to eat. I hate them things but I eat one or two because is a gift he bring. When he see I ain like them, he laugh and put them away. He say, "I won't bring them again. You will be my cherry." And then he kiss me. And he suck on my lips in a kiss more than a kiss; it a grasping, a sexing with tongues doing the work. I know I sweet. I know I belong. I ain faking at all when I hold him back so tight.

Only after that first beach day, when Jacob leave and I had slide into the bed next to my sleeping daughter did I notice Eeona brassiere there on the cot. The cups round up like hills. It give off a eerie feeling. Like there used to be a woman lying there, only she gone away suddenly and all she leave behind on the cot was her breasts. And is then I remember again that my sister missing. I get up to go fold down the bra so it don't be there haunting. But is when I tuck it up under the spare sheet that I see the itinerary for a trip to America. The ship stopping in Puerto Rico, then Santo Domingo, then making its way up to New York City. I ain find no ticket so I put two and two together. Eeona gone to the mainland to pursue she dreams, like Mama.

And let me tell you, that fine by me. Ever since I leave Ronald, Eeona ain giving me no peace. I need to keep something to myself. Secret. In truth, I ain even telling you everything.

51.

What Anette is not telling, because she will never tell, was what happened only a week later between her and Jacob Esau. It was night; that much is very important. The sun had set. The sandflies had swarmed and retreated. Down in the city up a small hill in Savan a young woman who had never known her father and had little memory of her mother had just nursed her own baby to sleep.

Anette sat at the head of the bed where

she could lean on the windowsill and hum quietly to herself: "Mister Sandman, bring me a dream." Her blouse was unbuttoned, but she could see the street and could see if anyone was coming. Besides, the lights in her flat were off and no one would even know there was a woman at the window unless they were right on top of her. Anette took in the breeze and thought about how she would pay the rent without Eeona's half. She had already gone without getting her hair dyed longer than was decent. The red at the roots was beginning to show. But she could manage. It would mean she would have to spare a new outing dress. She would do her own hair dying at home. She would ask at the apothecary if she could keep Ronalda there in the back. She might even have to ask Ronnie or his mother for more help.

Now the sandman came up the street humming. It was a quiet song, but Anette knew it because it was their song. She buttoned up her shirt just as he was saying, "It's me," from the darkness of the street. She edged out of the bed and went to the door.

"What you here for?" she asked, with the kind of cut eye and push mouth that made it seem she knew exactly why he was there.

"For you," he said, reaching to her head and combing a lock of hair back with his fingers. "I here for you."

They stood in the threshold for a few moments until Anette heard a sneeze from a neighbor, and then she let Jacob in and away from prying eyes. "It's not appropriate for you to be here," she said, but she meant nothing by it.

"I'm not staying. I'm taking you with me."

"But you crazy. Where we going at this time of night? Ronalda done gone sleep."

"Is a secret."

Anette smiled and waited.

He smiled back. "Nettie, as a good West Indian woman you should offer me something to eat or drink."

"Well, Mister Mac, we don't have anything to eat or drink. Plus, you quite fast and forward to come here after all of nine o'clock looking for eat and drink."

"Let we go then."

"You going to carry Ronalda?

"I going carry you if I have to."

He carried the baby over his shoulder. She was still small and light, and not yet a burden. Anette wore a dark dress and bright lipstick. It was too late and this was too ridiculous, but she was going where he wanted her to go. The only other thing they had with them was his small cloth bag, which she held. She'd rummaged through it with propriety as soon as he passed it to her: a bedsheet, a flask with water, and nothing else.

They walked out of town in the quiet darkness.

"That's where I was born," she said, when they passed the road going down into Frenchtown, even though it was nothing she had ever said to anyone before.

"I didn't know you had Frenchy blood."

He couldn't see her smile, but he heard her short, sharp laugh and then her slapping her own mouth for making noise. "I ain no Frenchy," she said with a sly whisper. "It's just where I was born. I ain been down that road once since we left."

"Not even to visit the radio station?"

"Not a once. And now you know the family secret," she said.

"Well, Nettie, then let me tell you something you don't know about me."

"I listening."

"I can play the piano."

"But I know that already."

"For true? All right. Then my best color is red."

"Is so easy you is? I know that already, too."

"Then you know me."

"Come again. You have me and my child here in the dark of night walking to God knows where. You best give me a proper secret before I scream out."

Before the war, Jacob might have still continued with silly things. He might have told her that his middle name was Esau. But he didn't. His middle name seemed like something trivial, though it was not trivial for either one of them. Instead, he told her the thing he hadn't even yet told himself. "I been wanting you since I seen you in New Orleans."

"Look here, mad man. I out in the middle of the night with you. My only child in your arms. Don't go telling me that you have me mix up with some woman you meet in America."

"No, Nettie. A fellow in the Army had your picture in his pocket. Carried it every-where."

Anette thought of silly Ronnie showing her picture around. Thought of both of these men looking at her face and feeling like she was something to stay alive for. It was sweet to think. But also it seemed so slack. Did Jacob fancy her because of a

281

picture alone? But then again, didn't she fancy him because of a picture in a yearbook and a picture in the paper? Anette and Jacob kept walking, the moon was up, but it wasn't clear at all where they were going.

"This one time," he said, "I touched the picture." He stopped speaking and they stopped walking. They had arrived at a lonely beach. Anette knew that another woman would be afraid right now. This was either a major mistake or this was the man of her life — that these two things could be the same thing did not occur to her. "It was like I could feel your face," Jacob continued. "And when I went into that restaurant ready to shoot up the place, I did it for you. I mean, I did it for myself. I even swore on my mother. But I did it for the girl who I was going to love. I knew you was Ronald's wife. But is like you were my girl, somehow."

They laid Ronalda down on the sheet on the sand. She squirmed a little, for the ocean was sending in a breeze. Jacob took off his jersey and covered the child. He was only in his white undershirt now and it lit him up like a glow. They sat on the sheet and he held Anette as they looked out toward the sea. They were on Lindbergh Bay, where later Americans would build a hotel for its close convenience to the new airport. But for now there was no hotel and there was only the Navy plane hangar down the road. The waves were rhythmic as a lullaby. The trees were rustling like whispers. The beach was speaking and singing.

"I lived through a war," Jacob said quietly. "They say there might be a next coming. But when this one come, I don't plan on going."

"So what you planning on?"

"Us. Me and you. You're what I'm planning on."

Ronalda was already asleep. Jacob undid his pants and shuffled quietly out of his shoes. Anette slipped off her blouse and skirt and slip.

"Can you swim?" Jacob asked, as they walked into the water.

Anette didn't look at him, for she didn't like her answer. "I never learned."

"Lean forward into my arms," Jacob said, once they were waist-deep in the cold water. His arms were lit up by the glowing worms of phosphorescence. Anette could live in those hands. His palms were up in a way that meant he would be touching her. Very much so. She was scared. It was too dark. Who knew what was in the water. What would claw her at the ankle and carry her out to sea. The water was cold. So cold.

"You can do it," he said. "I'll make sure." Assumptive, like the way he put his hands on her.

Actually, he didn't know why he said something so sure and foolish. Something he couldn't honor at all. But Anette leaned into his arms, his palms at her belly. He felt her stiffen and yelp but she swallowed the noise. Her feet were going furiously, but not in that big splashing of his fellow island soldiers when he'd tried to teach them. "Kick," he told her, but she kept her legs under. "Harder," he said. He felt himself growing unsteady because of her propulsion. Then she stopped. "It's too dark, I can't see," she said. "That's nothing," he said. "You don't need to see to swim. Your hands are out in front, they see for you." He stood and demonstrated in the air. Then he stooped and showed her, his arms slicing slowly through the water. "And more splash," he said, because that was how he had been taught.

"But splash will wake the baby. Bring the sharks."

He smiled and cupped his hands around her waist. "Sharks don't come out at night." Was that even true? He didn't know. Maybe they would drown together. But he wasn't thinking of sharks or the baby sleeping, abandoned on the sand. He was thinking of wanting and not getting. He was thinking of cooling and relaxing and not wanting to cool or relax.

"We trying again," he said.

Anette felt the sand coming and going beneath her feet with the waves. She didn't like standing in water where she couldn't see the bottom. And just then, as though the sky had read her thoughts, the clouds swam apart and revealed the moon, bright as it could be. At Anette's feet she could see the sand now. See the silver of tiny fish.

"This time hold on to my waist," he said. And when she did, she was right there where he, it, was. She could imagine the thick outline of it inside his wet shorts. When she lifted one foot and then the other, she couldn't just hold his waist with her hands. She had to pull until she was hugging his waist, but then her face was at his belly. Then she could feel him. The coarse hair, that announcement. That trail of welcome. Her cheek at the hair, where it would leave an imprint on her face. "Let's try a different way," he said.

This time he held her by the waist and she smoothed her arms in the water. Smoothed her feet. Her feet were pushing so hard and yet they were barely moving at all. Slow motion. Like she was stuck. She felt Jacob's hands around her waist. Holding her up. Holding her. She kept pushing.

She pushed, but then her legs fell, so heavy she would never fly. Again. Same. Then he stumbled back with the force of her effort and that caused her legs to lift a little higher. Until they realized together that it was his moving away and her following that kept her afloat. Or perhaps it was her pushing and him never going too far. There is more to think on this, but that time will come. For now she was learning how to swim and he was teaching her.

Soon she reached her toe down and there was no sand. And instead of giving in to the depth, she turned to look for her child, as any mother would do at her death. But then she felt that his hands were no longer on her and she knew she was swimming. She looked to Jacob. He could still stand where they were and now his hands were at her waist in two seconds. "I have you," he said. And she wrapped her arms around his neck and her legs around his waist, and he was grateful he could stand, because if not, she would have brought them both under. "You swam," he said. "I swam," she said. As if it were a magic he had given her.

Though we old wives know it was her

mother's magic.

Still, for Jacob and Anette this was exactly what they needed it to be. She loosened her arms and legs, and swam a few strokes toward the shore. Then stopped, putting her hand over her mouth, laughing quietly. "I can't believe it would be so easy."

Because it was too easy. Easier than it had been for the boys in the Army. So simple and so fast. Like with a baby who has taken its first steps when the mama wasn't looking and so surprises everyone when she simply gets up and walks. A genius baby. Or a miracle.

They had already made their private vows and already Anette's wet panties were off when Ronalda awoke. It was the time when the child usually awoke to nurse and be changed. Anette released herself from Jacob and slowly undid the child's buttons, slowly unfastened the wet cloth of diaper. Anette stood, right there in the big moonlight, and her body was like a shadow standing before Jacob. The naked mother and child went to the water. The water was cool and Ronalda gripped her mother tightly but did not cry. She was not that kind of baby.

Anette eased them in until Ronalda's little bottom was submerged. From the sand,

Jacob looked on and knew that this was his life. Anette had wanted him so immediately, believed in his love so instantly. So, yes, that was his confirmation. He felt a valve turning in his body. He had reserved this honor for his mother, and even now he thought of his mother, and though the thoughts were all crossing together, he still felt the tight burn between his legs.

When Anette came out of the water, she and Ronalda were both shivering but everyone was quiet. Anette and Jacob did not know for sure if there wasn't someone else taking a sleep way down on the beach; they weren't sure if there wouldn't be someone walking by to set up early in the market. But they felt ancient and natural, like they were, just tonight and just here, alive in a time before Americanness. A time before any kind of ness.

Anette lay her own wet body and Ronalda's small, wet body down, and Jacob wrapped them and himself in the embrace of the sheet. Ronalda rooted into Anette's chest until she found the breast and the swollen ready nipple. Jacob curved his body to mold Anette's. And he rooted into her until he found the other ready swell. And it was all bodies and all together. "Claim me like a country," Anette whispered. He didn't hear, but it didn't matter. He already felt they were native to each other.

The waves receded. The moon receded. The sun spied from the horizon. Anette held Ronalda, the child's mouth on her breast, and Jacob held Anette, his mouth on her shoulder and neck and arm, and Anette felt the rise and the wrongness of having both these things at once, and the knowledge that she wanted, wrong and all. And Jacob held on, one hand grasping for brace in the sand, the other feeling for stomach and finding her stomach and finding Ronalda's little girl toes and the heel of her little foot and her soft baby calf and still touching and gripping, and it all feeling ancient and right until the sun burst out from the water like sin or a sign or perhaps just like the sun, and showed Ronalda's eyes open and seeing. And Jacob opened his eyes to see as he came to and there were Ronalda's eyes looking at him over her mother's body and it was exactly as though it was her he was making love to. And he felt her little plumpness in his hand and he released himself and never again looked that Ronalda in the eye.

They all three lay there. And Anette knew and felt that it wasn't right because they'd all, even the child and the sun, been in on the lust and love. Jacob gathered himself, and because he was still a man with soul, he dressed them both. Buttoning them up awkwardly because, as the youngest of his mother's children, dressing someone else was nothing he'd ever done before.

"This is our real life beginning," he said, because as the man he knew he was the one to say it first.

52.

In Freedom City, Eeona saw the extent of Kweku's back hair on the second morning. After all, during their first storming only she had been naked. The hair swathed most of his back and it disgusted her over breakfast, but then it thrilled her later when they went to the mattress again. That is how it would be with them. During their loving, she would pull on his back hair until he wrapped his hand around her neck, choking her into releasing. But then again at breakfast she would avert her eyes when his back was to her. The rest of his body was deceptively smooth.

Eeona felt that it had all been decided. She would make herself the mistress of this eight-legged house and it would be grander even than Villa by the Sea. Eeona saw the hibiscus growing wild and wonderful in the yard. And then all she had to do was see the rest in her mind. A grand house. A captain as master. Her as madame.

But Kweku was no regular man. He was a rejected man. His chest, and the organ in it, had closed like a seawall and no sweet water would wear it down. He wasn't a man at all. He was a myth. He could fly a plane. He could trick an obeah woman. He could steal the stories from any lady of the sea.

After a week of Eeona, he began staying away. Some nights he wouldn't arrive to his arachnid house until after dark and then he would come in smelling of rum and saltfish, which were also the scents of sex.

He was a man of stories. And that was the only way he could live, in other people's mouths. Down in La Grange he would sit in a rum shop and listen to stories about his other self. "You hear about the Navy man from St. Thomas who leave his obeah woman, run way to Puerto Rico, and get lost in the rain forest?"

"Yes." He would nod. "I hear he disappear for good, man. But I hear he used to give it to she good, too. And he only make he self lost because the obeah wife was too nagging, man."

"But Kweku, where you hear that story?

It ain smallie Anegada you from?"

"Even on Anegada we hear things. But watch, no. I ain think you drinking enough."

In order to stay alive as Kweku Prideux, the Anancy, he needed to hear stories about himself, needed to be the mélee. And in this way he isn't unlike other humans who find themselves unexpectedly in the Americas.

Kweku also knew that Eeona might reveal him, his pre-spider history. And so he kept her away from other people. He only let her leave for drives in the country with him. She would dress in something nice that he had brought for her. Something earth-colored, no more of her Virgin Mary blues — he wanted to be constantly aroused around her. He made her go barefoot — to keep her from roaming too far, though he told her it was because he loved her feet and always wanted to see them. By then Eeona would have gone naked for him. She was a lady, but she was also in love. When he left, she would sit in her seat waiting for him, legs crossed at the ankle, like a woman of wealth.

53.

Freedom City, St. Croix, was some forty miles from Charlotte Amalie, St. Thomas. It was double that from Anegada. But still, it was close enough. After all, Kweku had told Eeona that the atoll was his homeland. After a few weeks of Kweku, Eeona began to think of her father. Her father stepping off the ship. Her own words like a sharp knife at his belly. Her father drowning for love of her.

On St. Croix, Eeona didn't know a soul. Some Americans lived in the houses nearby, but there was no occasion to visit them and, besides, she needed to be official to do that. She needed to be Kweku's wife, not just his live-in concubine. Kweku wasn't falling easily, after all. And so many other men had! What was taking this man so long? Perhaps she had given too much too quickly. It made her wild to think of it, made her want to jump off the balcony.

The first half of every day became full of thoughts of her father. She had once asked Papa if he had ever put his mouth on Mama like he'd done with her. Now alone in a quiet big house Eeona remembered that Papa had looked at her as though she was a grown woman and had said no. And she had thought, good, his mouth is mine. But then he had kept staring at her and said, "But I have done it. With the one who taught me. Rebekah, the mother of your half brother,

Esau." And it was as if they were not discussing intimacy, but discussing something like sugar or molasses — like business. And Eeona had wanted to kill Owen Arthur right there. For wasn't it clear that there would be nothing for her? There was a son, even, a son who might get the land and the house and everything due to Eeona. And she wouldn't even be left with Papa's love, having to share not only with Mama but with this Rebekah woman, too.

In this Anancy home Eeona obsessed over these sad recollections. Visions, really. Papa walking until there was no more walking, only falling and falling and then sinking to the sand.

But now wasn't Kweku Prideux better, best? He was Eeona's alone. In the mornings, she would sit to write with the paper and pens Prideux brought her. This was her transition time. Each day she wrote a letter to her sister, explaining where she was. Explaining that she was happy. That she had a house, despite the cobwebs that kept reappearing. Soon everything would come, she wrote, soon all would return to her. She reminded Anette to avoid that Esau, that fellow from the newspaper. Despite the sea between them, Eeona was still watching over Anette, still keeping her safe.

Eeona would give the letters to her Prideux to mail, but Anette never wrote in
return. Did Anette just not miss her at all?
Perhaps Anette had figured out that it was
Eeona's own fault that they were orphans.
Eeona's own fault that they'd lost everything. Eeona thought on this blame for the
first time in her life. But then, because she
is still Eeona, she didn't think on it too
much.

Eeona spent the second part of each day
readying for Prideux. She swept the floor
and the cobwebbed ceilings. She wiped the
cans and counters clean. Then she began
readying herself. Bathing in a bath of bay
rum leaves. Lotioning her body with avocado pear and rainwater. Conditioning her
hair with the mash of coconut jelly. Eating
honey with bits of mint leaves. All of this
growing wild right outside the house. The
readying would take hours. Which was good
because sometimes Kweku didn't come
home for hours and hours. All this she did
for him out of her own free will. If she was
lucky, Kweku would honk the horn when
he arrived, making it bray like an animal,
and she would walk out to him — bare feet
and all. They would go on drives. They
would go to the edges of the island. They
would go to cliffs. They would go to the

Rain Forest, where he'd first come to his senses when his wife had cast him away. They would make love in the car, he pressing so hard against her chest that she almost passed out. From the love of it, she supposed. They never visited other people. Never needed to, he said. They had each other. The rest would come. Was coming any minute now.

Besides, Kweku kept bringing her notepaper for her Anette letters. "One day we'll put all your writings in a book and sell it." But it was just something he said. Something to make her feel treasured and therefore vulnerable. She stared at the page of whiteness with hope, as if it were a frothy ocean. With the black-ink pen he gave her, she wrote epistle after epistle to the unresponsive Anette.

"But you must forget your sister," Prideux said one day. "You need to write bigger things. About we V.I. people. Write about me flying beyond the blue horizon, why not. Not no stupid letter again. Even your sister ain care about that."

Eeona was sensitive, as women from the class she was born into were raised to be: Anticipate when an elder would like more tea. Anticipate when a young man would like to speak with you. But this meant that

Eeona could also detect even the mildest disgust and disfavor. This man was one who didn't land at her feet like every other man had done. And this was so confusing, so painful, so human that Eeona felt it must be love, the real thing.

She knew, by now, that she was going to have a child for this man — her man. And wouldn't their child adore the stories Mama Antoinette had told? Eeona started writing the Duene. She began with the Anegada women, those of great beauty with backward-facing feet. It was not long, however, before . . .

"My darling Prideux. Have you seen my writing?" For days she asked Kweku Prideux, three and four times an hour, where the story she had written just moments before had disappeared to. Sometimes she was angry and firm, like her old self. Sometimes she was very sweet, begging if he knew.

"No, baby. You know I don't read plenty."

"My story has just disappeared."

"Stories about important things, baby girl? Tell me what they name?"

She had renamed it so no one would suspect it was really just a childish fable, so Kweku would not suspect she was really just a child herself. "Drowning," she whispered, as if the walls might hear.

"That there sound like it ain appropriate for a lady," he said. "Maybe is good it gone. Maybe I shouldn't have buy all that paper. You ain ready. We need the real St. Croix stories. Like Anancy or Cowfoot Woman. But modern, for now times. So people know we real."

By now even he knew that she was pregnant, even though they did not speak about it. She was slowly nesting into the small room off the foyer. She kept it clean. She ripped rags into nappies and kept them in the closet. She thought on how she would ask her Prideux to purchase her a needle and thread to start the layette. In this small room there was a small desk and a small chair and from that position Eeona could study any person coming before they even knocked on the front door. But no one ever came. Her man sat now at the little child's desk he had hauled home for her, a gift. His body was still, only his eyes darting around.

She looked up to him from the floor where she sat, tugging episodically at her hair. "Please help me find it."

"I don't know where it is, baby girl," he said. "Maybe it fly away like me." And with a hand he mimicked a flapping.

Where was the story? The same place as

the letters to Anette. Not in the attic, for there are no attics in the houses here. Not in the bottom drawer, because there are no sets of drawers in the octagon house. He did what buccaneers had done a generation before. Used the mother earth as a safety deposit. Buried all the writing like treasure. But as they were not in a chest or a sealed jar, the leaves of paper would disintegrate and become part of the earth and then the earth would erode and sift into the sea. Kweku didn't intend to kill the story. He wanted it to live. But he wanted it only for himself. He didn't realize that one does not allow for the other.

For Eeona, the impact was erosive. She stopped with the story writing. She didn't sew or stitch or make hats of palm leaves. She eased into this new lack of control. This must be the longed-for freedom. She began to live inside her episodes. Walking the house as if she were on a pilgrimage. She let the cobwebs collect, though the spiders never appeared to claim their creations. She picked bay leaves and avocado pears. The grounds were a kind of Eden that way. "This is what I wanted," she explained to the listening walls. She knew she could escape so easily. She could jump into the cistern and drown. She could tip over the balcony and drown. She could walk into the sea and keep walking until she drowned. And wasn't that the greatest freedom?

With the child in her, Eeona would never be a child again. Kweku was not her father. Her father was dead. The child in her was not yet a child and so not worth staying alive for. Drown. But then Eeona finally felt the baby inside her swim. Clearly a stroke, not gas or one's mind getting the best of one. There was a living thing splashing inside her. Yes, yes. Of course she wanted this. She must double her efforts. Work on her beauty. Convince Prideux that loving her for all his life was the thing he needed. That was the story she wanted in the end. She was an adult now and could see that even freedom came with its own binds.

With this clarity came renewed thoughts of little sister Anette, and how Anette was newly unwed and might yet find herself faced with the danger that was Esau. It was Eeona's first conscientious moment in months. And she resented it completely.

But that very night Kweku lowered his mouth to her, because he was the worst kind of man, the kind who knows just what a woman wants and uses it against her. He whispered into her silver, "You're my diamond little girl." She felt his words vibrate on her as if she were a wind instrument and he were playing her into the horizon. And who would not want to be wanted this way? Besides, it was a sign that her efforts were having an effect. And so it was easy to forget about a sister in need of being unfreed.

Kweku held Eeona in the bed as though she were his skin. She hadn't felt so loved and so drowned since she was a girl. In the morning her beauty flooded the room.

54.

ANETTE

Eeona gone for months now. It ain that I forget about she. Is just that I been an orphan all my life. I always getting left. Eeona been wanting to leave. I figure her time just come. Yes, I worry that she ain write and I even worry that maybe she dead, but I ain really worry 'bout she at all. Eeona good. She take care of she self always. Even if she there in heaven, she likely seducing St. Peter and running the heavenly show. Besides, I now have Jacob. He done tell me that he ain never going to leave me. And I believe he.

You see, is a perfect time to be alive. In the middle of the century, in safety. No apocalypse. Two great wars behind, plenty smaller wars ahead. But in these islands — not quite American, not all Caribbean — we living in the eye of the storm and know only the peace. I leave Ronalda with Ronnie mother and I lie, tell she I gone looking extra work to help pay the rent. But I gone gallivanting.

The car we was in had not a door. The roads was loosely paved — mostly gravel and pound-up dust. Me and Jay in the backseat. A group of we driving up to the Muhlenfeldt Point lighthouse. Trying to lime there for the view. Dirt and rocks was flying all around us. The turns spring out of nowhere at all and on every bend we almost fly out.

Gertie and some American fellow in the front. The American is our ticket to the lighthouse, since me and Gertie have try to get there before but get runaway by a military Yankee. This American fellow say he know the lighthouse keeper and could get us to the lighthouse and even inside the lighthouse, where we could watch the sea. Gertie ain have a regular beau but her American man seem like he like a little lick of the tar brush. Now he shifting gears as if he know what he doing. "Americans know how to drive," he keep saying loud-loud. Every few minutes the car seem to go faster than before. It like a Carnival ride.

In the backseat with Jacob, I holding on to him as my stomach tighten and my mouth open wide. Damn it to hell, I felt like braying, like that awful donkey that we don't have no more. But my noises just fly back in my mouth with the speeding air. The piece of trash car careening about.

Jacob focus on guarding me. He arms all about my shoulders and legs as if he alone could have protect me from flying through the space that should have held a windshield. That how he was then. Always touching and protecting. Always claiming me hard.

The gravel kicking up. Clanking into the bottom of the car. Slapping my calves when it force its way through the holes; flying at us in a steam of dust. I close my eyes but that make my stomach sway. We come to a big ditch and the American fellow ain brake but instead shift and shift and slam right in and out of the dip. Woy! The fellow go flying into the hood of the junkyard Dodge; not *onto* the hood because his elbows and head was forced through the holes. His legs jut back into the seats and one of his ankles crash onto my shoulder, knocking hard against my head. Through a fresh rip in his pants, I stared right into the poor boy's exposed white backside.

Gertie start up a screaming of the man name, "Ham! Hamilton! Ham!" and it sound like she demanding food. But the American fellow just there laughing. Laughing! I crawl out from beneath him as my man guide me away. "Let's get from here," Jacob say. "That fellow is drunk." Gertie look up to the sky and suck she teeth.

"We can't just leave," I protest. "We ain even reach the lighthouse."

Jacob argue back. "You shouldn't be dealing with any rough driving. Is too much for you." He put his palm on the small of my back. I know what that is. Is something he does do when other man is around. Is an announcement. Like to prove that I is his. Now there don't have no man around who care to notice. And so I know his hand on me is secret speak. I have you, it saying. You go where I go.

That work on me like a charm, but I still digging my nails into Jacob wrist so he could know I ain happy with his direction.

"Nettie," he say, when he guide me a bit away. He always call me that. "You must take care."

"I ain a doll, Jay," I say, even though I loving the way he talking, like he going to take care of me. "I ain a baby."

"Yes, yes, you is." I see his chest rise up. He make it sound like I precious. I turn to Gertie and she wave me away. She going to stay with the American. Ham now standing on his own and leaning against the car, smoking a cig and chuckling like he ain almost dead. So I let my man walk me back down the way until we see a car and hitch a ride.

Jacob only take me halfway down the street to Ronnie's door because I ain ready for Ronnie's mother talk or anybody's talk. When I pick up Ronalda, her baby eyes them big like the saucers and have bowls beneath. Is like she been awake looking for me all day without a bit of shut-eye.

For the most part, I been paying for the flat in Savan on my own. But Jacob helping a little. He stay with me sometimes, but with his mother more often. We waiting to wed. I waiting to see if Eeona returning. And he waiting for his mother to come around, because it turn out that Rebekah don't like me just by the sound of my name. I know is 'cause I a divorcée. Them McKenzies was big Catholics, my child. Knights of Columbus. Catholic Daughters. The whole horse and carriage. I ain what no McKenzies thinking for one of their own.

But is okay. It only been a few months.

Jacob and me, we know we for each other. We don't have to rush-rush and ruin the thing. When time come, our love going to be clear like water for all to see.

I put Ronalda to bed and I lay there beside her. Sometimes when Jacob don't sleep over, he does come to my window and push his hands in my hair. That night I dream of fish and then newborn lizards. I wake up in the twilight, not to Jacob hands on me, but to the knowledge that I pregnant again. And there, in the moonlight, like something staking its claim, is my belly rounded. Claimed overnight, like the Europeans pulling to this shore of peaceful Arawaks. As if Jacob saying "Yes, yes, you is" make it so.

I still breast-feeding Ronalda and is Ronnie mother she self tell me that that suppose to prevent pregnancy. So I know that who inside me must be powerful. I had make this sandman fall in love with me by speaking some bolero words at a dance, now he give us a baby by saying so.

The rest of the night I toss between dreams and I deep in the feeling of arrival. Something coming. But the feeling don't seem like seven or eight months. It feeling like just now. Like I more pregnant than I even looking. In the morning I look to get

306

out of the bed and figure out what the ass I going to do now that we have a baby coming too soon to make it look decent. But there in the bed beside me is the thing that now arrive and is my very sister. Motherscunt!

I start breathing short and heavy because I just know that this is my dead sister lying in bed, haunting me for not staying married and respectable as she had command. But then this Eeona open she eyes and I scream. She jump on me like a witch on a broom and say, "You will wake the child." And even though I know she meaning Ronalda, who scrunch up like a worm at our feet, it come as if Eeona mean the one in my belly, too.

When she release her palm from my mouth, I pounce away and go stand by where Ronalda sleeping. Ready to grab up the child and scrape out. "You real?" I ask my sister or the ghost of my sister.

"I do believe so."

55.

EEONA

I never could bring myself to tell my sister the true story, but I shall deliver it here and now.

For many months I did not leave the

house without Monsieur Prideux. Everything I did, I did with him. If you were there, you would have understood. Freedom City, it was called. It was quite lush and lovely. The house he lived in was grand and overlooked the ocean. It was difficult not to be in love and therefore desperate. One evening we were returning from a scenic drive when I leaned across the front seat and beseeched my Prideux. "Let us go to the beach," I asked, for that was one thing we had never done. He shook his head as though he was scolding me. "It's too late, my baby. The no-see-ums will get you." Still, I believed the beach would be the place where I would finally win him over. The beach had convinced even Louis Moreau to propose.

The blue air of dusk surrounded the car. The wind was gathering in the darkening clouds. It would rain presently. One could hear chimes dancing loudly. The music was uncoordinated, as were the thoughts in my mind.

By the time Monsieur Prideux parked the silver Chevy at our door, the sky was a deep blue. I was feeling a sense of freedom, as our drives through the country were wont to make me feel. I felt what was inside of me. St. Croix was so like Anegada, flatter than St. Thomas. Made of coral. Sitting there on the Anegada Passage. I wanted the beach. I must have the beach.

I went into our great house and put on a pair of my man's rubbers and changed from this leaf-green dress he had bought me just for drives, into the blue dress I wore when I walked onto the seaplane that first day. It fit tight around the bust and barely fit around the belly. I announced that I was going for a walk to the beach with or without him. I had not been so bold since I first arrived.

"There ain no streetlamps and it getting dark. You can't go."

"I am going." I decided this in the same manner in which I had decided to board the seaplane so many months earlier. I had secrets from him. One such secret was that for weeks I had been attempting to lay a plan for myself, but my confusion was such that there were fish swimming in my mind. I had hoped that my maternal condition would hasten my Prideux's commitment, but this had not yet been the case. If I went to the water at night, perhaps my mind would clear and I would discern my options. More important, if I ventured out, he would grow scared of my not returning. Perhaps my leaving, even for a short time, would convince him of me.

"Eeona, girl. No one's going to watch for you when you walking."

I carried a lit kerosene lamp when I departed. I felt safe as I began down the driveway. I had to walk through the bougainvillea bush to get around the latched gate built to keep out cars. Why was there this gate? Someone could easily sneak in and steal anything we had. Though I knew even then that there was not much that we had. Still, they might take my honour. They might kill my man. They might burn our house to ashes. They might throw us over the ledge to drown in the sea.

As I walked farther, it grew dark quite quickly. I could hear the conversation of a father and a young daughter. The familiar sounds were floating from a house just above. They spoke with proper American inflections. The sound of their laughing pooled in my head.

I began to see that what I was doing was quite nonsensical. Prideux was right, no one else was walking. It had been months since I had set out on my own and here I was doing so at night on an island that I did not truly know. A vehicle raced by with headlights on. I pressed myself against the side of the hill. It was a flashy car and the driver honked his horn in surprise at me. There was an American woman in the passenger's seat. With great speed, she stuck out her manicured middle finger. These Continentals coming to our islands have turned out to be so uncouth.

As soon as that car disappeared, I felt very alone. I felt then that Prideux should have lashed me to his chair and prevented me from leaving. I was losing my mind, like it was said always threatened Mama. I had already been gone for half an hour or more. He should have come just then with the car. He should have been worried.

As the road curved, I saw the water.

It would not be like the bays of St. Thomas. On St. Croix the shore will be narrow. The sand will have chunks of seashells in it. The water will have slivers of seaweed. From where I was standing, the waves looked frozen. The bay seemed dangerous and distant.

I remembered night swimming with my father. We would strip off our clothes and dive into the cold dark water. Our bodies would light up with the shining phosphorescence that swam around us and *The Homecoming* in reverence.

"I curse you," I now said out loud, though I did not know to whom I said it.

I thought about my sister and wondered if

perhaps she had found her way back to her husband. It seemed like years ago that I had gone to return my ticket and instead found myself heading here, to Freedom City.

I turned down the long road leading to the beach. The lamp in my hand was dimming. It was vital that I show Prideux that I could be worthy of nighttime beaches. It was vital that I show myself. I am Eeona Bradshaw and men have always thought me to be more than worthy. I am the daughter of a captain and I can swim and dive and direct a boat out to sea.

I walked all the long way to the bay. When I arrived, the air at the ocean was cool. The sand waved like water under my feet. The moon was out in a sliver. The sound was just the waves and my feet moving towards them. I took off all my clothes slowly and elegantly. Maybe Prideux could see me from the house. I left my clothes on the sand. I stood at the lip of the ocean as the waves covered my feet. The water was quite frigid, but I walked into it anyway. I swam naked in the ocean as I had done with my father. The water felt as if it were a man claiming me. Beneath the water, the silver of myself was glittering like a jewel. I tended to it like any lady would her diamonds.

When I was relieved, I ran out into the

cold air. I hugged my belly with one hand and my breasts with the other. I stood at the water's edge and it began to rain. I sensed that I had called the rain. I found my clothes and dressed quickly. I held the lamp before me and I walked all the long way back to the gate of our large empty house.

I was myself again. I only needed that small escape. Now I will add my touch to our home. I must sew curtains. I must purchase us some decent pans for cooking. I do not need his proposal. I will venture into the city and see to our marriage ceremony myself.

There was my Prideux with a candle at the doorway.

"I was worried. I was coming to find you," he said. "Where did you go for so long?"

"I went to the beach," I will say. "I swam naked in the ocean lights." He will look at me as though I were some mythical creature who did what she wanted.

My dear. That is not what really happened. That was all just a story I told myself.

What really happened is that I went to the water's edge, but I did not even take off my shoes. I did not expose my private diamonds. I did not know myself in the water at all. I kept the failing lamp on the entire time. I was too afraid. I balanced the lamp in the sand so the light would ease out to mimic a full moon. The only sound was the ocean and the kerosene humming from the lamp. I walked to the water and splashed the coldness on my face. Then I retrieved the lamp. Prideux's rubbers were too big for my feet and I slid back with each step. This made me feel more afraid, as though the ocean were holding on to me. It wanted to take me like it took my father.

When I finally arrived back at the main road, I began to run. I ran harder than I have since childhood, for ladies do not run. I tripped in the large shoes. My lamp shone at wild angles ahead of me. There was a bit of rock. Here was a slice of tree. Everything ahead looked as splintered and as threatening as what I was leaving behind. I did not turn into a Duene or a soucouyant.

When I reached the big black gate, I was just a woman. My ribs were bursting through my chest. I wondered if what was inside of me could feel my ribs. I wondered if what was inside of me could feel. I was wet with sweat. I lay down on the ground and stared at the weak moon.

Finally, the lamp burnt down and I walked

the last bit of driveway to the house that was mine in my heart.

My Prideux was on the porch, leaning forwards. When he saw me, he rushed forwards with a bitterness that should have been my warning.

"You had me waiting here so long." He did not ask me where I had been. Instead, it began to rain. Still, I felt defiantly magical, like some creature who had seen a hint that she might do as she pleased. I could walk down dark alleys of beach road. I could kiss the ocean and run all the way back.

Oh, dear. Please accept my apologies, for that, too, was a story.

The very truth, my love, is that I did not even make it to the beach for the baptism I had planned. I did not even get halfway down the beach road. I was too scared and it was too dark. I was not a shadow nor was I a bird nor was I a mythical creature. Instead, I simply stood there and imagined myself going to the beach and swimming and then drowning or drowning myself. Then I turned back to the house. My lamp was dimming. It began to rain and I began to run back. No, no. Let me be true. I only walked back up the road through the rain.

315

The cold rain beat down hard on my eyelids. I felt an abiding shame.

When I arrived at the gate, I had to rake through a dewy cobweb. I walked up the driveway and pushed myself through our door. Prideux did not even look away from the spiderweb he was tearing from a window.

I knew then that I would never return to what I had been.

56.

The end of Kweku and Eeona is a real story, for true. Kweku had three days to convince Eeona to stay and bear the child in her belly before she would climb onto a boat or a plane or what have you, swimming herself toward her family. And her family, as far as she was concerned, was Anette and Anette's offspring and no one else at all. Kweku already had children — boys and boys for Rebekah. But he loved this Eeona. He loved her the best his history had taught him how, but the best he knew was bad. He did not know that he had three days. He expected her to leave at any moment or not at all. He didn't believe in her packing. But for a crazy woman, she was packing meticulously. She was folding her muted cotton bra, rolling her bloomers into a ball.

Now Kweku stood in the doorway of the bedroom. Inside his mind was flipping because he did want her to stay.

"Drapetomania," he said. "That's what you have."

Eeona refolded the blue dress she had arrived in. It was too small for her now with her belly. "I suppose you want me to ask what that is," which was her way of asking, because even then she could not admit to him that she might be less then perfect.

"It means you wanting to run away, even though you ain have a cause."

So she said nothing aloud, but she thought in her head that he was right. She had a runaway sickness. But there was a cause. There was a whole history of causes.

Perhaps if Kweku had tried "I love you" instead, he might have won her over and she would have been lost with him in mind and in body until she died — wife or concubine. But the spider man thought that "I love you" could never be enough. That had never been enough for Rebekah.

Though she wasn't full-term, Eeona's water broke the second day of her packing. She kept folding. It seemed as though she were folding all the linen in the world, even though all she had was the dress she'd come in, the nappy rags still in the closet, and the few frocks he'd bought her as her belly swelled. Now Kweku brought her sea grapes and tea, and left them at the door while he sat in the living room drinking rum, waiting her out. She took the food without giving him any attention. Then she napped as though there were not contractions crashing and waving and crashing again through her. The mucusy water seeped out of her and onto the bedsheets — just his bedsheets now. She awoke to see Kweku Prideux standing in the doorway, his pale skin glistening with the shower's water. Though she couldn't see it, she knew that the big patch of hair in the center of his back harbored a thick fuzz of bath soap. It was the one place he could never reach. She looked up at him; finally, she looked up. "I still cannot help but believe that I deserve it," she said to him. "Then again, what is 'deserve'?" In the throes of labor, Eeona's beauty was receding like a wave.

In the doorway Kweku felt clean and empowered. When Eeona was too beautiful, it made him feel weak. When she was less beautiful, it made her feel weak. When she was weak, it was good for him. He would be good to her if she would just stay weak. "Eeona, my baby girl," he said to her

318

sweetly. "Your water broken. Come on. We have to go to the clinic so you can have our baby healthy." He thrust his arm into the room toward her. It was the first time in all these months that he had acknowledged that she was pregnant. When they made love, which they still did despite her packing, he would fuck her from the back or the side so he could avoid her stomach, the mass between them.

But now Eeona closed the suitcase and stood up. "This baby will go where the water goes."

Kweku considered letting her be. People who are crazy have a logic that can be convincing. *But it is a wrong logic,* he thought again, *always wrong.* "Eeona, that baby going to drown in there." But she wasn't listening to him. Perhaps her water hadn't broken at all. Kweku didn't know what else to say to her. He had tried, hadn't he? He walked through the living room to the balcony. He lowered himself and lay down on the floor. He stayed there until the air grew cold and goose bumps raised on his arms. The sky turned orange then purple like a bruise. He listened to the ocean beneath him. He fell asleep.

He dreamed of himself as a better man. As a McKenzie. As a father to sons. As someone brave enough to love a woman as he'd loved his Rebekah despite what the family men warned. What had happened to him, Benjamin McKenzie? Only in his dreams did he dare to ask himself this question. Perhaps he hadn't tried hard enough with Rebekah. Perhaps he hadn't given enough of himself to her. It was just that now, in exile, he couldn't find the him of himself.

In the morning Kweku awoke on the balcony. He felt emptiness in his house. Perhaps Eeona had just walked out. Perhaps she'd killed herself. Kweku thought maybe it was time to move again and this time farther away. Someone was bound to recognize him soon enough on a flight to St. Thomas. He'd hoped for that, hadn't he? But no, it was too late for hope. He'd fly to America perhaps, where no one would even have heard of the Virgin Islands. He smiled. Perhaps it was he who had the runaway sickness.

In the kitchen he opened the pantry and stared into it. There was bread and cheese, but Kweku did not see anything. He opened all the cupboards one by one and left them opened as he walked out of the kitchen. He went to the bedroom, thinking he would bury his face in the bed where Eeona's smells might still remain. But there was Eeona, laid out across the mattress heaving with the swells of childbirth. Her suitcase, which was really his suitcase, beside her. Her eyes were open and watching the ceiling.

"Eeona," he called quietly. "You leaving me? Go, then. But know is your own fault. You expect too much of me." None of this was true. But how could he say the truth? How to say I am a fable? I am in need of you. I am in need of us. But I cannot bear my own need. How to say any of that?

He stepped into the room. The room was bare and white. Only the mattress and the nightstand as furniture. He and Eeona hadn't even been married. They hadn't even bought real furniture. They hadn't talked about their child's future, hadn't sat on the pot while the other took a bath. There had been no relinquishing the radio station as a tiny gift, no frying the fish with the right pepper sauce for the other's palate. They hadn't really been lovers at all.

Eeona did not know why she was leaving. He had slept with other women since she'd arrived. This she knew, but even that was salvageable. He had stolen her, but it wasn't that either. Hadn't she, in a wild way, wanted to be stolen? Now all she wanted was for him to say the right thing. That he would put her name on the deed. That he would love her and this child, and put the land in their names. That she would be a lady with an elegant last name. That they would go into town together and be respectable. That he would not die and leave her. That he would let her call him Papa.

But how could she know all this, how could she say it? Instead: "Be my husband," she beseeched him now. Right there on the mattress, hard into a too-early labor. Her face tightening and releasing like a heart.

And then, as if he did not know how this could kill her: "My love, I is somebody else husband."

She must have known. Yes, it was true that he shaved the kinky hair on his head and arms and legs. But still. Despite his mythical chosen name, he was clearly a McKenzie, what with his skin so light he could pass easily for black Irish or Jew. And wasn't it obvious which exact McKenzie he was — the lost one, Rebekah's one? But Eeona was knowingly begging away her last grain of sane self-respect. "There is such a thing as divorce, Monsieur Prideux."

"A man don't leave his wife." And because he was cruel, he said this kindly.

"You have already left her, Prideux."

"She the mother of my children, Eeona."

"I am about to be, as well."

He looked at her and saw her face like a fist against the pain. "But Eeona, baby girl. That ain your role in my story."

What lunacy was he talking? But it made a kind of lunatic sense to her. She had tried not to think about the time she'd seen him, his body covered in shaving soap as if it were a sweater. He'd taken the blade first to the knuckles on his toes and clean shaved his body of all its McKenzie hair. Shaved the parts he'd directed her never to shave on her own body. She tried to conjure the memory now so it would repel her. So she could convince herself that this spider man was not her man. Could never be. But the baby was coming regardless.

Afterward, her own silver hair was everywhere, matching the sheen of the new spiderwebs. It was beautiful, as though she and Kweku and the whole house had died and been sent to the lining of clouds. The baby was born still. Not alive. Dead. It was a boy, of course. Kweku Prideux was, after all, a true McKenzie.

Eeona did not cry. Instead, she held the lump of boy child to her chest and thought about her mother. Perhaps Antoinette had been right to return so many children to

God before they were born. There was no one else to tell, so Eeona told Kweku that the child was named Owen Arthur. The name would not do for a living child, but the child would not have to live with the name. And no one knew the child had almost existed except for the two of them. Kweku took Owen Arthur's baby body and flung it over the balcony. He did not look to observe if it hit land or sea.

Then Eeona laid on her back until she could sit up. Sat until she could stand. Stood until she could walk. Walked until she found a boat. And did not stop until she was in bed with her sister.

57.

ANETTE

After Eeona reach back to St. Thomas, I had to warn Jacob. I tell him that she more than pretty. That he going to think she the most pretty woman he ever see. But he say that he know all about she. That every man raise on this island know of her, but that he don't want no woman who every man fall in love with. He just want the one he love.

But he still talk a little funny about she. "I heard that she a little wild," he say, like is a question he asking.

"Wild? She only wild by mistake."

"Well, I've heard that she does get a little twist in the head. Go wandering when she get ready."

"Just be a gentleman and you going be fine."

He arrive at the door with a bunch of anthuriums.

But here is the thing. Eeona eyes them looking like empty shells since she return. But from the minute I tell she that I going around with somebody new, her eyes them now squinching up like they full of sand. But she ain ask no questions. She behaving strange. Like she drain of energy. She ain saying where she been these months or what she doing back or what she going do now. She just find she itinerary to America and rip it slowly into pieces as tiny as dirt.

When Jacob come through the door, she watching hard as if she know him and know something bad. When she ask his background, he speak in his Yankee English, explaining that he is a McKenzie and who he for, who he come from. But is like he name alone reach out and strangle she. Jacob face watch Eeona and he come like a piece of stone. Only when he look at me do his face soften, though it soften in a kind of confusion because Eeona like she hate he on site.

She ask what he know of his father, and he tell she he ain seen he father, Benjamin McKenzie, since he small and that his mother alone raise him and he older brothers. Then Eeona stand up and speak loud so it come like she talking to a crowd of people, "I regret to inform you, sir, that you are no longer allowed to court my sister," which is the most words she string together since she appear in my bed two nights before.

I stand up. "Eeona, what the ass? You gone crazy?"

She twist her head around at me in such a fast way it seem she a iguana. "Yes, I have gone crazy. Now I have returned to tell you, Anette, that you will do as I say!"

And this is such a strange thing that it stump me. I ain have time to gather myself and slap she in the face before Jacob stand and said, "Nettie." Just my name, as though this rigamarole was what he expect. After all, is he tell me that she wild. With the tips of his fingers, he pat the air down as though is water he testing to see if it hot or cold. Simmer down, he trying to tell me. Is okay. Is okay. Then he back out of the house like he can't turn around. Like he must keep he eye on the enemy. Eeona stand there in the doorway blocking me from following, like she a mountain.

But I ain really bother with she. I go to the bedroom where Ronalda there napping. I crawl on the bed, careful not to wake my child, and I ooze out the window. Jacob going up the hill and I catch up to him as he turning. He look at my neck and at my hair, but I reach up and grab his face to make him look in my eye. I feeling the tears like a stone in my throat. I feel I can't speak.

"That's not a beautiful woman," he say finally. "That's a soucouyant. That sister of yours best put her skin back on every night or I will salt it for her." For a long few moments we let that sit between us. My sister a ugly witch living in a beautiful woman skin. But then he finally reach out, grab me, and swaddle he arms around me. We high up and we look down over the roofs, down the streets that leading right to the sea. I look with he at the sea and we hold each other as though we might go swim away this very instant. Then he turn and hold my face in he hands, like it belong to him.

"My mother will not allow us and your sister will not allow us." Now he put the flat of his hand on my front, pressing my dress 'til he reach the small rounding belly.

When I walk back down to our flat, I can't help but think about John Smith and Pocahontas, which I know all about because I studying to be a history teacher. About how they end up with other people. But still, I so stupid and so catch up in this romance that it seem romantic. It don't seem impossible.

I start in on my sister as soon as she in earshot, while I still in the street and she still there in the doorway. "Every girl want a McKenzie," I shout at her. "Even you, Eeona. A McKenzie would do even for you." She standing in the doorway looking at me as I cross the road to her. I keep expecting that she going fuss with me for putting all our business in the street, but instead she just stand up there until I feel like maybe I should shut up. She don't even speak to me until I get inside the house and she sitting down in that rickety rocker that she pick up from some garbage heap.

"He's a good match for me," I try again.

"You do not know the half of him."

She speaking slowly and quietly, like she trying not to say the wrong thing, even though everything she saying sounding wrong to me. Then she lower she eyes to look down at she belly like she have something hiding in there. This I ain never seen.

I mean, I ain never seen my sister lower her eyes to anybody for any reason.

"Eeona. I know all I need to know," I say gently. "He's good to Ronalda. He will be a good father."

She look up into my eyes now. "You have no idea what a good father is." Now, that's my Eeona. Getting riled up just by mention of Father. "Anette, this young man does not know what a good father is."

I can't bear to stand over her while she seem so softy, so I sit on the settee. Her moods like they all over the place and maybe she gone crazy for true. Maybe them episodes finally become more than episodes and become what she is.

"His mother is not a decent woman," she continue. "His McKenzie father" — she say this slowly as though she reciting something she just teach she self — "was a poor example of husbandry." And now she look up at me with her usual stern Eeona face. "Do you understand my meaning, Anette?" And her face is finally fierce, as if she know these people good.

I confuse, so I just say what I really mean to say. "Eeona, you too late for whatever it is harassing you so. I done love him."

She lean forward, her back straight as a board, looking like she might ram her head into mine. "Anette Bradshaw, did I not warn you against a McKenzie called Esau?"

"His name is Jacob, Eeona. You thinking of the elder brother, Saul, maybe. I understand your worry. I know Saul is the sweet one who don't go for woman. But mine is Jacob. Jacob McKenzie."

She watch in my face like she casting a spell. "He is Esau. Ask him if he is not Esau."

But why I going ask the man such a thing? Not on he Army badge or he driver's license, not what he friends does call him. Why I going ask the man such stupidness when I know what it is really going on? Eeona jealous. She think I can't tell that she run away and reach back sour, and that it must be that whatever episode she having is over some man? I done had two man already, so I can easy put two and two together. Must be she finally give that cherry away, but then the man wasn't so sweet.

It ain my fault, I want to tell she. It ain my fault that the reason Eeona gone bazadie is that she heart get break. "Eeona. I sorry you taking issue. I real sorry, but he the one for me."

"Not this one," she say firmly, with her hand them tight like she have my Jacob there in she fist.

I stand up and walk to the next side of the room because I realize that I 'fraid she might lunge at me, though this ain nothing she do before.

"We have to marry, Eeona. With or without your consent." I put both my hands on my belly, where the baby there blooming, so she can understand my meaning. Just then Ronalda wake up in the next room with a screaming.

58.

Jacob had known who Anette was from the moment he'd sat down next to her at that party. Well, he knew she was the wife from Ronald's picture. He even remembered seeing her at the dock in that red dress when he kissed the ground, and she was there staring at him as though they already had a history together. But he did not remember running to her on the beach when they were both eight years old, her red dress swimming around her, her queen conch shell crooning in his ear. That was like a dream. And dreams, like all vital things, have to be written down to be really remembered.

When Anette was nine months pregnant, and clearly growing weary of waiting, he told her his plan. "Once the baby is born, we'll marry. My mother will support us once the baby comes." Anette had nodded with eyes facing the sea. She had thought they would be married and living together already. Perhaps she didn't understand his mother-love because she couldn't remember her own mother's love. Or perhaps sister Eeona was right, in a small way, about him. That he couldn't know how to be a father. Anette wanted to ask Jacob about Esau, but she'd become too reticent to ask him anything.

She and Jacob walked into the water and made love to each other with their hands. The contractions kept coming hard until she finally walked out of the water and noticed that her own water had broken.

Eve Youme saw Jacob's face first, before she saw her mother's. This is why her mother couldn't save her from what she became. The only one who might save her was her father.

He called her Eve, for she was the first female McKenzie anyone had ever known. And like the biblical Eve, she would lose her father. But Jacob wanted the baby when he saw her, even though he let her go. She really did look like the first thing ever created. Jacob was God. Anette was Earth. Eve was of them both. And Eve went wild, of course; what other choice did the first woman have?

But naming is a voodoo all parents do. Anette listed the child's second name as Youme. She'd spent hours in the island's library looking up baby names instead of studying for the teaching certificate. The name didn't mean "ours" as she'd first hoped. It meant "dream." But that also made sense and perhaps what was ours was all a dream anyway. Something to keep striving for or something all in our mind — depending. And as these things go on island, the child was never called Eve. She was called Youme early on, but in the islands' history she will simply be called Me. History could do that, change a person's name. History was something so simple and insistent that none of us has escaped it. History even derailed Jacob and his Anette.

You see, another American war was brewing, this time in Korea. And it turned out that there was only one way for Jacob to avoid being swept into that one. And that way was not sinking into the woman he loved. Despite Jacob's vow to Anette, his mother had still not approved. Indeed, she had told him he must never bring the new child to her house. Rebekah told him that she could see in his future that he would end up in a Korean ditch if he did not listen to his mother very carefully. So, being the mama's boy he was fighting and failing not to be, he listened.

"She already has one child. And a girl at that. You have no business raising another man's child."

"We will have help. And it's not just some other man's. It's my mate's. He'll help, too."

"Do you hear yourself, son? You can't be a father to a daughter. You will get in trouble with girl children. And two of them? Never. Even the one you think is yours can't be yours," Rebekah said. "Remember, you're a McKenzie and McKenzies have only boys."

"Maybe I'm not really a McKenzie," he said, remembering the man with the sea eyes.

Rebekah did not even pause. "That woman has put a magic on you. Don't you dare forget who you are. Then you'll never be a doctor and you'll never be anything. Do as your mother says and you'll be blessed. Go to medical school and don't marry that Bradshaw girl. Really, son, you don't want to be in Korea for just eighteen hours before you are taken hostage by the enemy and they strap you to a wooden board, tilt you backward, and pour the sea down your nose and mouth until it fill up your chest because you drowning. Or perhaps you will only think you drowning, which is worse, because you will lose your bladder and you will lose your tears and you will be cowed worse than a soldier in a segregated Army. So, to avoid losing your life and, more important, your manhood, you must go to medical school and become a doctor with the money those McKenzie uncles of yours provide because they believe you are one of them."

Jacob heard his mother. He heard the parts that sounded like savior. He told himself that as a doctor he would be respectable. And as a doctor no one would tell him what restaurant he couldn't eat in. As a doctor he would be responsible for life, like God. Then he would be able to save himself and his woman and his child . . . and, if possible, his woman's first child, too. He wouldn't wed Anette now. He needed to get strong enough on his own. So he made another plan. As soon as he got back to America, he would go to his other brother who was a dentist and finally get his reddish tooth bleached white. No more dreams of crumbling seashell teeth. Then he would grin his way through.

He would come back for Anette when he

was a man. As soon as he was free of his mother's premonitions. He'd taken Ronnie's wife. He'd fathered a child with a divorcée. These weren't very gentlemanly moves. He wanted to do right now and doing right meant he must survive and become a man. Then a husband and a father. He tried not to think of his own McKenzie father who'd left and never returned. Tried not to think about his mother finding another man to love. He tried not to think that maybe that other man was his real father.

But Jacob always knew Anette like a hibiscus that closed in on him at night and made him feel like sand alone. For years he would slip his hands into other women and search for Anette.

59.

EEONA

It is my belief that human beings have children because of a need to love. This is not a sentimental position. After all, is it not so that men fought two great wars because they loved their big countries or their tiny string of islands?

When I returned from Freedom City, I found I could still love a child, despite what I had lived through. Indeed, it is the least I can do. I have loved Anette's daughter, Eve Youme. Yet it is in her that I have watched my sins row before me.

60.

On the day Jacob left for America, Anette wore a white cotton dress. As a farewell gift, or rather a stay-behind gift, a promise of sorts, Jacob had bought this simple white cotton for her, along with yards and yards of an extravagant red dupioni with yellow flowers. He imagined her in a long skirt, like the kind his mother wore. Red being his favorite color. The yellow of the flowers, he had said, was for the island's ginger-thomas and bananaquit — the national flower and the national bird, respectively. He wanted Anette to be the island — waiting for him, unchanging in the sea. The white cloth he thought she might make into a wedding dress someday. But Jacob Esau, being male, didn't understand that a divorcée could not wear white to her second wedding.

Eeona had made the white cloth into a day dress for Anette, but had refused to make anything in the dupioni. Eeona believed it was a harlot's fabric. The white dress had classy embroidery at the bottom and at the end of the sleeves.

Jacob was in gray trousers and a matching blazer even though it was too hot for the formality. His shoes had been shined. He was holding Ronalda's hand; the little toddler's hair was full of tiny wild flowers that he had picked for her mother. Eve Youme was in her mother's arms, swaddled in the remains of the white cotton cloth. They were all standing in what had been the Navy's hangar but was now the island's sweaty and loud and dark airport.

Passengers were arriving, checking in, waiting, picking up luggage from mountainous piles in the corner; some were dragging the heavier suitcases by leather ropes. A clutch of tourists stood chatting so loudly it seemed as if they were in a quarrel. Their faces were pink and slimy. The ceiling was too high even for birds to have their nests, but it was still humid inside. There were bats in the high corners, but they were too far above to bother anyone with their blind diving. Some light came from standing lamps that stood not much taller than a man. In the mix of people, Jacob and Anette and the two children might have been a legitimate family.

No loudspeaker had told them it was time to go, but being there waiting was worse than leaving. What does one converse about in such a time? It's over. Good-bye. Will we see each other again? Pray. Believe in God or something. So they walked toward the exit, toward the airplane. In the heat Anette's white dress stuck to her legs. Jacob was glad for this. He didn't know when again he would see the imprint of her thighs.

"I going to be back soon," Jacob said. "Soon as I can."

They reached the end of the walkway. Out there was just open space and big planes, the air feeling wound and spinning. They moved aside for others to walk by.

"I love you." Jacob said it to remind Anette that he wasn't leaving her. He was just leaving. And there is a difference. He thought to explain the difference to her, but he knew, he believed, that she understood. Anette hugged their baby to her chest. Eve Youme's face peeked out of the swaddling cloth and stared at her father without blinking.

Anette hadn't said a word. Her man was leaving. He was going to medical school, he told her. He'd come back soon, he told her. And then he could work a real job and not be dependent on his mother or his uncles or anyone. And Anette had smiled and smiled to keep from cracking apart.

On the day Jacob left, she'd worn the dress from the white cloth he'd bought her. She'd let the red in her hair come in a bit, which he liked. She'd allowed him lovemaking that very morning, despite that the ban after giving birth wasn't yet over. She had brought her daughter and his daughter. She had even managed to convince him that the right thing to do was to say good-bye to his mother before going to the airport — so that she would have him in his last island minutes. But he was leaving Anette anyway. Medical school wouldn't bring him back just now.

Anette had left a husband who loved her. A husband who would have been a doting father. And now the man she loved was leaving — not on a boat, but on a plane . . . but still. There in the hangar Anette was busy doing the opposite of thinking. She was forgetting. Forgetting the seduction magic the Bradshaw women were rumored to have. It was all old talk and stories.

Jacob leaned over and kissed his daughter — his first child who later would be left out of the family photos. But now she was a baby who knew only that love, like food, was given to her when she cried for it. Eve Youme smiled at her father, for she was an early smiler, as her mother had been. Jacob leaned forward and kissed his Anette — in public — owned her — in public — was her man — in public. Kissed and held her to wake her up, to make her speak. She couldn't hold him back, their daughter in her arms. But he put his mouth on hers. It felt as if she were giving him strength — even though she was too unherself to give anything.

He eased Anette's left hand out of its cradle, the hand that he had not put a ring on, and passed Ronalda's little hand into it. Then Anette watched his body disappear into the plane.

And that was the first side of their saga.

A Freedom

61.

After Jacob had walked away, Anette waited in the airport for another twenty minutes. She had two girl children now in her solo care. It wasn't until Jacob had gone from her sight that the announcement was made that it was time to board. Anette watched the clutch of American travelers break apart in loudness. They had been drinking, it seemed. As far as we could see, that's all the Americans seemed to do — drink rum and buy up land. One half of the group sloped toward the plane. The other half was staying. These were not Frenchies or American politicians or military personnel or old Danes who hadn't quit. They were the worst kind of white. They were tourists.

Anette cradled Eve Youme and led Ronalda past the wall of luggage. The American whites who had stayed behind were now climbing into a car almost as big as a truck. They honked at Anette as she crossed in front of them. She nodded, as was the courtesy. They started talking loudly at each other. She was sure they weren't speaking to her, as the Americans didn't often speak to us unless doing business. Anette kept walking slowly so the toddler could keep up. Lindbergh Bay, where she and Jacob had first been together, was a long arm of sand and sea at her side — beckoning or dismissing, she couldn't tell. But she didn't look to it. She would walk down this street with her eyes straight ahead. March down to Savan to sit with her sister and wait for Jacob. Even though she knew she must not wait. Even though Eeona would make that waiting a misery. But the big car of Americans seemed to follow Anette down the road. And then they were, most certainly, following her.

Anette stopped; perhaps the newcomers needed something. There was a woman in the passenger seat, but it was the man who spoke to her.

"Yes, hello. I own the Gull Reef Club over on Water Island." Anette blinked and tried to smile. She hadn't heard of the club and she had never been to Water Island. "We're looking for a chambermaid. Ours, it seems, has just been deported back to Antigua or Anguilla or somewhere. You can imagine we're in a bind. If you're free, we could take you right now, tykes and all." The woman in the passenger seat nodded vigorously to this last part and gestured toward the large space of the backseat.

If Anette was not at present in mourning over Jacob and if at that very moment Jacob's very plane had not roared above them, she might have done the fiery thing — which was to release Ronalda's hand, reach over the driver, and slap the woman in the face. A woman should have known better than to allow such an insult in front of the children. But Anette was too broken-hearted for heat. Instead, she and the woman looked at each other and then the other followed Anette's eyes up to the roaring plane.

"Cat got your tongue?" asked the woman, using an expression Anette had never heard.

"I'm so sorry," she said finally. "You've made a mistake with me."

That night Anette lay on the bed. Her daughters stacked there between her and Eeona. Eeona had a satin mask over her eyes. They were in the same place they had been. Just the same. Only now there was another child. Only now Eeona, protecting her beauty, wore a satin mask as she slept. Anette lay there and she thought, finally, that she had been a fool to love that man. But she knew, and hated the knowing, that she would be a fool for that man again and again.

Anette tried not to think about the Americans in the big car and their Gull Reef Club on Water Island. Weren't they the ones who had really tried to make a fool of her? Anette would never have imagined that a year later she would find herself over on Water Island at that very club.

62.

In America, Jacob went to his dentist brother and had his red tooth bleached white and his wisdom teeth removed. When he woke up from the gas, he was screaming and screaming. His brother stood by and held Jacob's head down so he wouldn't flail and break anything. And what Jacob was screaming was something very strange.

"I am real! I am real!"

And he screamed until he grew tired and calmed. His brother told him that such screaming was normal. Really, quite normal. Though it wasn't at all.

63.

As a babysitter, Eeona was strict and full of
old-time manners, but the girls enjoyed her
enough because she let them play with her
hair. Even as Ronalda was braiding neatly
and Youme, just a baby, was pulling out the
braids, Eeona would sit with her back
straight and face set. Eeona did not have
smile lines around her mouth — she was
never in danger of those. But there was
something around her eyes now — they
were called crow's-feet — that revealed she
was no longer quite as stunning. She would
never marry. That still baby was the only
child of her own she'd have.

She had not been around to watch out for
Esau. But now she watched out for Youme.
She felt as though it were her fault Eve
Youme existed at all. Sometimes Eeona
would brush Youme's hair. Sometimes she
would braid it and then she would whisper
into the child's head. A special chant for
each strand as they plaited into each other.
My own, she thought. *My own.* She never
braided Ronalda's hair.

For the months after Jacob left, Anette
had waited, though she knew better. She
could tell when people were coming and
she could tell Jacob was not. Still, she

waited for a letter on a ship from America or a long-distance phone call from America. Any sign from America. She waited for a surprise visit or a package at her door. But since he had left, she had not heard cat nor dog of Jacob McKenzie.

She cornered Saul in the street one morning. "He's alive," Saul said stupidly, "Mama's always sending him stewed cherries." And so Anette stopped waiting — at least outwardly. She started going out to dances. She thought, in a backward, magical way, that if she went to a dance the band would play "They Say It's Wonderful" and then Jacob would appear. Anette left her girls braiding and unbraiding Eeona's hair.

On this particular night Anette did not go to a church dance; for by now, even a short time later, St. Thomas had changed. There had been a war and then rumors of another. All the men smoked cigarettes. Everyone drank rum and Coca-Cola. Every family had a relative in America. There were Virgin Islanders and Americans on island, but imagine, there were also many, many people from other Caribbean islands! The down islanders were making beds in the hotels. In the market they were selling coconut water straight out of the nut. They even owned things: businesses, houses, cars. Everything was different. The Catholic dances had always had competition with the Seventh-day Adventist game nights, the Lutheran skit series, and the Anglican bowling alley. But the fête Anette went to with hope of summoning Jacob was one of the newest types — this was something secular. She went alone.

The dance was held in a restaurant after serving hours. The tables pushed to one side, the chairs lined up all around the walls. There were too many chairs, really. Too many excuses to sit and be shy. Anette was sitting now. Not because she was shy, but because she was tired out from dancing all night with various men who were new to the island from other islands and surely didn't know that she was a divorcée with two daughters from two different men. Gertie was on a dinner date with Ham, her American fellow, and so there was no one to help Anette mind her manners. Anette was sitting, cooling out, and trying to feel for Jacob when a dark-skinned man came up to her. "Good evening, Anette."

She didn't recognize him, but she had the grace, the Eeona brought-upsy, to be cordial. "Good evening."

"May I have this dance, Anette?"

The fact that he knew her name and she

didn't know his was a problem. If she said yes, then she would be dancing with someone who knew her and whom she was supposed to know, which was something all together different from dancing with perfect strangers. And this man was quite dark-skinned, something Eeona would give her grief over if it was ever found out Anette had even danced with him. Besides, she was tired and her feet hurt. "No, thank you," she said with a high-class smile, and turned her head so he might know he could take his leave. She was not anybody's chambermaid. Her sister had raised her to hold a teacup as a lady should. Besides, she had a fiancé, didn't she? He was in the States. He hadn't even written her all these months, but still . . .

This man leaned in closer to her, speaking to the side of her face. "Anette, you should dance with me, yes." And there was something like a premonition in his voice. As if he were a ghost and not a man, which is, in a way, what he turned out to be. She was taken aback by his forwardness. Offended even, though his forceful voice intrigued her. *I should dance with him or else what?* She thought this to herself but said to him, "I believe you are being rude, sir. I do not know you." She gave him her Eeona English for spite.

The man didn't draw back as he should have. He leaned forward into her face. "Anette. You remember a boy who made you a tin house once in grade school? Your sister wouldn't let you keep it because she thought I wasn't your kind."

Well, hot diggity damn. Franky. Franky Joseph, who'd made her that doll-size living room set. He'd made her a home. Of course she remembered. She pictured that silvery aluminum dining set. Resting on the very same old table that she and Eeona still ate their meals on. In the very same rented apartment that had been nice twenty years ago but was now, well, twenty years older. Of course she remembered. Hadn't he left school early? Hadn't he disappeared during the war? She put her hand out and he took her to the dance floor. She had not remembered him having green eyes, but there they were. Bursting out of his dark face like a promise.

The next day, the blue-collar man with the green eyes and green Cadillac leaned over the counter at the apothecary after accepting his change and asked Anette to the movies.

"Yes," she said. "But my children will have to come along."

But what did that matter? Franky had been in love with Anette since he was a child. He knew this was his time and his chance.

64.

Franky Joseph was no obeah man or magician. He was simply a disciple to his love of Anette. Had been for years and years. He had been learning this love and studying this love like history. During the war, he had worked for the Coast Guard. That history made all the difference. His war had been spent in mess duty on a cutter. He hadn't gone to Germany and he hadn't been on the mainland. He'd been on the ocean. Now that they took colored boys for more than just cleaning and cooking, Franky was in the Coast Guard proper. Hailing foreign ships, mostly from other islands, checking their papers. He also served as the assistant to the keeper of the lighthouse up on Muhlenfeldt Point. Not many of us even had the opportunity to see that lighthouse up close. But Franky knew all the Virgin Islands, the lands and the seas in between.

Franky had heard about the movie dance over on Water Island before anyone. But he waited until the buzz. Yes, the Americans were making a movie. The Virgin Islands itself was going to be a star. Franky had only been going around with Anette for a few weeks. Their outings were chaste and nostalgic.

He took her on a picnic with the children up at the lighthouse. A place she and Jacob had tried to visit but had nearly been killed when Gertie's Hamilton crashed the car. Now up at the lighthouse, the wind didn't whisper; it shrieked. The view was wide, as if they were in the center of it on a ship, except Anette felt safe. But Franky cooked all the food himself, which reminded her too much of Ronnie. Next they'd had a predawn breakfast on the beach with the children, and when the sun rose, that had reminded her too much of Jacob. This movie filming over on Water Island would be their first going without the children and without him doing the cooking. Franky needed something to make himself original for Anette. She'd never even been to Water Island; this time wouldn't conjure images of anyone else at all.

On the radio it said to wear bright colors. Dresses that fly when you spin. Most of the men wore their finest white linen. A few came in American-style shirts and suits. These men had lived on the mainland and

knew that Continentals didn't really understand the formality of the guayabera, so they
didn't trust the request for "island formal."
Everyone wore their best shoes — the worst
kind for dancing.

Anette, who was still working at the
pharmacy but had recently begun working
as a teacher's aide in the Anglican school,
was going to the dance despite her fear of
boats and despite her waiting for Jacob. She
was working hard at being respectable. What
else could she do? Unwed and a single
mother — she couldn't be hired as a full-
time teacher. She needed to keep up ap-
pearances. All over town, there was the meté
of how a McKenzie man had served her up
a girl child and then left her. No one could
believe it — McKenzie men only had boys.
Anette was likely a liar. Who would want
her now?

So Anette went to the movie filming over
on Water Island at the Gull Reef Club
because everyone was going and she wanted
everyone to see that she was fine, just fine;
and look, green-eyed Coast Guardsman
Franky had offered to escort her in his dress
blues uniform. And Anette, like the island,
used revelry the way other people and other
lands use cough syrup or the confessional.
Bacchanal was the cure for all personal and

social ills.

Besides the fact that Franky was still not entirely acceptable, what with his dark skin and unlanded name, Anette was generally doing what Eeona wanted for her. She wasn't making love to Franky. She hadn't even let Franky kiss her.

But it must be said that Anette was also going to the dance because she'd met Jacob at a dance and who could deny that it would be just like the sandman to row a boat across the channel to the Gull Reef Club, appearing out of the fog to reclaim Anette hard?

But Franky Joseph had other ideas. He was wearing his dress uniform, seaman's hat and all. Franky knew that Jacob had wooed Anette at a dance. After all, Franky had attempted the same. Their little relationship, Franky knew, was as fragile as a baby. What he wanted was to give Anette a memory that would wash out any others.

65.

JACOB

May I interject here? I am a doctor . . . I have saved many women's lives. Perhaps when I die they will name the St. Thomas hospital after me . . . I just want to give a word here. May I have a word? My mother . . . she had powers to stop and start so many things. Love, however, was not in her jurisdiction. All about the island it has been said that my mother, too, fell in love with a man she should not have. Perhaps that is the story to tell . . . my mother gave in to her love and she was never able to move anyone else's. I tell you, she didn't move my heart . . . which is to say . . . I loved Anette immediately and always . . . like my own flesh. Is only that . . . it is only that I needed to obey my mother . . . until I became a doctor . . . then I could be my own man. But Anette . . . she went first. Not me. I was waiting for her.

That's all I have to say.

66.

The crowd met at the waterfront. Boats had been hired to row them over to Water Island. Anette held on to Franky as the little fishing boat docked up. It was only a short ride, ten minutes, five minutes, maybe. Anette could swim, but it was the boat she didn't like. Franky, who was a Coast Guardsman and so trained to deal with both boats and frightened people, held Anette around the waist even as the boatman took her hand. Franky could feel Anette's quick breathing.

The Americans had built their movie set on the island in the harbor. Everyone who lived downtown, which was almost everyone on the main island, saw the movie equipment being rowed over to the little island. It had taken two whole days. Water Island rose out of the harbor like the back of a large underwater creature. The Gull Reef Club was on the shoulder of that rock.

There were hotels on the main island, which would have been more appropriate. There was the Grand Hotel with the austere Danish architecture. There was the Hilton, which boasted a waterfall filled with the fattest shrimp in the world. But the movie people wanted solitude along with a beach and a hotel owner who would let them have their way. The Grand Hotel was owned by locals, who the film people felt might ask too many questions. The Hilton was owned by the Hiltons and those sorts knew too much already and didn't need to ask questions at all.

Anette Bradshaw, who would always be a Bradshaw no matter what other name followed, wore a dress of red dupioni with a pattern of yellow flowers. It was the fabric that Jacob McKenzie had bought her. It was cloth that was supposed to take the place of an engagement ring. She hadn't touched the fabric for the months and months Jacob had disappeared.

But Anette didn't want the red fabric to hang in the closet and haunt her, so she'd decided she would wear it to the filming. Or perhaps Anette knew the fabric would always be about that Jacob McKenzie, who would always be a McKenzie because his mother had made it so. And so she wore the dress, like a siren, to call out to him. She wore it like any magic.

Eeona, with her still-fabulous hair bursting out, had declared to her younger sister that the dress of red dupioni was too risqué for the filming.

"Stop harassing me," said Anette. "I look like a star." She ran her palms down the bright red fabric.

"You look like a tart. You are the mother of two daughters." The older sister leaned forward and hissed, "What are you signaling to society?" Eeona knew about Franky, but on that she made no comment at all.

But it was a dress for American movies. Anette had also planned to wear her nice black heels, but Franky thought they didn't go with the dress. With his green eyes and green Cadillac, he knew about matching.

He took her to La Zapatería, the Puerto Rican store with the latest fashions, and bought her a pair of white patent-leather shoes with a thin silver strap and a tiny silver buckle. On her feet they shimmered like fish scales. Franky knew what he, in his dress blues, and Anette, in her bright red and white, would look like. They would look like a real American couple.

Their old boatman introduced himself as Mr. Hippolyte Lammartine, or Mr. Lyte, if you like. He offered Anette a taste from his rum bottle to calm her. "Miss Bradshaw," he called her. Anette smiled through her unease, though she didn't remember him. She took a little sip and felt the sweet heat. "I knew your father," he said.

"Thank you," Anette said, because she hadn't known Owen Arthur Bradshaw at all. She looked down at the water and then forward at Water Island. She could swim to land if the stupid pirogue sank. Franky's arm was around her like a lifesaving tube. Hippolyte Lammartine let the bottle be passed around to everyone as he began to row.

The Frenchy men, who would be classified racially as white but identified themselves ethnically as Caribbean, were the most suspicious of the white movie people from America. As he rowed, Hippolyte asked the question he had been soaking to ask since he'd been offered this boat job for the night. "Why all you think they ain want to make the movie at the Grand Hotel?" Passing the bottle from mouth to mouth, everyone nodded that it was a good question. Hippolyte, receiving the bottle and holding it tight between his knees, kept prodding. "Is a secret they have to hide, you don't think?"

Franky, who was a natural leader and wearing his uniform besides, was the first to offer. "Is because they want a hotel what have a beach. And this the only one have a beach, yes. Name of the beach is Honeymoon."

And since none of the others had ever even been to Water Island, much less the Gull Reef Club, they all nodded at this answer. Yes, a hotel on a sweetly named beach. That was a nice idea. Though it was also a strange idea. Didn't them Continentals consider the biting of the sandflies? Or didn't they consider how the hotel would manage its plumbing so close to sea level? Or didn't they consider that a hotel would block other people from getting to the beach? But Franky had only considered the name of the beach, Honeymoon. And now that he had said the name out loud, he also allowed himself to think the thought: *Might this evening not be the real beginning of him and Anette? Like a honeymoon?*

Hippolyte spoke up now with what he'd figured. That the movie people wanted sticks of fire as decoration. The Hilton wouldn't allow this and it would be too dangerous downtown where the Grand Hotel presided. Franky didn't think the fire on the beach was a good idea at all. There would be trees around for the flames to catch. Everyone else in the boat was thinking that maybe the flames would keep the sandflies from biting everything with blood. Otherwise they would have to really dance up to keep the bugs from leaving itchy welts that wouldn't look good on camera.

"That ain no worry," said Mr. Lyte. "Only them Americans going get bite. Sandflies like fresh blood."

The set was indeed out at the beach. There were a few tables in the center and they were decorated with glasses oddly half full and others more oddly turned over, which were draining onto black tablecloths. But the St. Thomas men in their white guayaberas looked smart beside their ladies in blue and yellow. But Anette was in bright red dupioni and Franky was in his seaman's dress blues. They stood apart.

Markie and the Pick-up Men were given matching shirts and short pants with a design of waves and surfboards. They protested the shorts, stating in vexed sputters that a real West Indian scratch band would never wear short pants to play a party. It would be shameful — they weren't little boys, they weren't working around the blasted house, they weren't going for a damn swim. The director ranted back: "It's a movie! You're getting paid to be authentic."

"I thought we was getting paid to be a scratch band."

The director seemed as though he was fed up with them all before any film had even begun to roll, but then the leading lady, yellow-haired with impossibly lean hips held tightly in a wrap skirt, noted that the musicians had all come in matching black slacks anyway. The director calmed and nodded. Markie and his men were allowed their long slacks. It didn't matter much anyway; not much camera time would be spent on the musicians. They wouldn't even be singing. The movie people had a record. The Pick-up Men would be phantom playing. Hadn't they read the contract? They were just for background. They were just for authenticity.

So it go. Markie never really recovered from being sent away from his microphone. Before, he used to do a little skedaddle dance up front and get the crowd really ready. That evening he was sent to play the cowbell over on the side, and he remained there ever after. The band never sounded the same again.

The record that played was the popular song "Rum and Coca-Cola." Only it wasn't sung by Lord Invader, as everyone knew, but by some white sisters named Andrews who were doing a horrendous job. The Pick-up Men held their fingers above their instruments and made ghost music, their bodies stiff like corpses, their faces stricken. The song was played over and over again. None of the Virgin Islanders had heard this version. We queried the director. But the American moviemaker said he'd never heard of the original version sung by any invader.

"But it's women singing and they have the Pick-up *Men* up there," a young esquire tried to point out gently. Everyone had thought this, but no one had said a word. "Hush, Attorney Fondred," we called. "Is no big deal." This was an opportunity for the island. We all, the band and the dancers, tried to look happy.

We smiled into the camera and smoothly forced our way into its vision. The nice shoes were more than just too nice for dancing, they were almost impossible for dancing in sand. We avoided too much grinding and bum jerking because that would cause a tumble; besides, there was a minister among us.

But it *was* a free lime and it was on a beach and that is all we ever need to enjoy ourselves. Husbands held wives closer and then farther as if they were courting, wives clutched husbands' shoulders as if this was juicy infidelity. Those going steady showed off their slippery foot action, sometimes with only fingertips touching.

Anette thought on that obnoxious couple who owned the Gull Reef Club and had mistaken her for a possible chambermaid. Were they here now? Could they see her so well dressed? She looked for them but didn't recognize them among any of the whites milling around. Perhaps they'd already sold the place and left. Seems like the Americans were always buying and selling, coming and leaving. Now Anette wanted to throw her head back and give a good wind-up, but she controlled herself, remembering that she was representing her

island and, just as important, she was showing everyone how okay she was. Everyone
was, after all, watching. There had been so
much talk.

*Them poor Bradshaw sisters. You ain hear
how the father dead and leave? Just look at
how the family fallen since! The elder daughter
used to be so pretty but then she disappear
and return a old maid. And that Anette one —
a divorcée! Gone and had a second child with
piano-playing-war-hero Jacob McKenzie — so
she say. He gone and left she and the child.
Gone a whole year almost. Now look how she
jump on the first green-eye man that come
along! Them Bradshaw women. Is a curse
they have. But they father and mother orphan
them. So what you expect?*

Anette knew and heard, and there on the
sand in her new white shoes and red dress,
she kept the smile wide and camera-loved
on her face. She felt the feeling she sometimes felt. That someone important was arriving for her. Maybe Jacob McKenzie.
Coming to claim her in this dress made of
the fabric he had bought her. But Franky,
knowing more than he ever let on, twirled
Anette and held her tight. For all to see.
Maybe Franky would be the man to banish
Jacob McKenzie from her head. They
looked special, they did. And even the oth-

ers stepped closer to them, to get a bit of their spirit.

But during the break, the chef of the Gull Reef Club charged out with her arms spread wide and hugged Anette. "Can it be? Yes, my Lord. Baby Nettie," she exclaimed loudly. Others stared because few of this group had been this friendly with the Bradshaw sisters, not since their parents left them paupers and certainly not since all the talk. "You don't remember me?" asked the chef, as if she really couldn't believe it. "Is me. Sheila Ladyinga. I used to work for your mother over by Villa by the Sea. I wiped your backside when you was a baby. You all used to call me Miss Lady."

Anette stepped back. Was this the person who she'd felt coming? Not her man Jacob after all. Mrs. Ladyinga searched Anette's face until it became clear that Anette did not remember her. Then it became clear that Anette didn't want to remember her, not right then.

Mrs. Ladyinga started to say more, to further explain who she was and ask the cordial questions, but then the movie people put on another record. This was a recording of drums, not steel drums or conga drums, but African drums. The Pick-up Men were told they were no longer needed. The dancers were called to form a half circle and to clap vigorously in time while a limbo stick was set up and then set on fire. "You, sitting," the director called out to Anette and Franky. "Are you in or out?"

Anette stood up without saying anything polite to the lady chef. *I am with Franky,* she said to herself. *I am here with Franky. I am here and I am with Franky. This is not Jacob. I am with Franky.*

"Well, little Anette," said Mrs. Ladyinga sourly. "I've got to get back to the kitchen. A lot to feed tonight. Not like when it was just you and your sister." She wiped her clean hands along the clean front of her chef's coat. "But if it wasn't for me, you wouldn't even be born. Believe it. So now let me give you one bit of warning." Anette could not follow what this woman was saying. She didn't even try to smile, but instead leaned back, making her distance. This woman was not Jacob. Not Jacob at all. How could Anette care about this woman coming and giving her anything? But the chef continued anyway, now a bit more quickly and quietly, as though they were conspiring. "I'm not certain that this here movie is your kind of movie." Then she left Anette Bradshaw, just as she'd left her before.

Franky and Anette joined the group in the

clapping and the dancing in the circle. Anette knew she had something to prove to these people and, really, mostly to herself. So she danced and clapped and smiled and laughed and in general seemed to be having fun, fun, fun. More fun than anyone. Jacob had not come. Jacob would not come.

Instead, the American leading lady, whose wrap skirt was too fitted for limbo, walked into the center of the circle. The lady chef came out to watch the performance. Now Anette tried to catch the chef's eyes, tried to give a smile — she knew she'd been rude earlier. But Sheila Ladyinga looked everywhere but at Anette. So Anette looked at the American woman and made a small wish that the American would catch a fire. She didn't have a bitter feeling toward this woman, per se, it was just that she had a bitter feeling. The woman was only there to receive it.

The limbo stick was placed lower and lower, and as the leading lady contorted more and more, the crowd of sixty, not twenty, roared in support. Franky shout-whispered, "Is a dancer she must be." Anette nodded and tried to keep her mind on the moment.

Then the stick was lowered, low-low. Jesus, Lord! It could be done. Those who walked on broken glass with their hands could limbo this low with fire in their face, but could this tourist do it? The camera waited while the leading lady breathed and breathed. "I'm only gonna do this once, so don't mess it up," she called to the air in a voice that sounded hoarse and older than she looked. The clapping stopped. Everyone waited. She hiked up her skirt and the flames reached out to her thighs. She bent her knees low, pressed the inside of her ankles to the ground, splayed her hands out in welcome, and tilted her torso back-back-back. Her knees first, then her palms.

Then there was the lady's exposed hips and crotch. The flames licked up. Minister Milford's eyes widened and averted. Then the lady's torso with her large breasts and then finally her head. It was her hair that caught aflame. All the stiffness of it simply unable to resist the leap of the fire. There was full-on screeching. And then there was the lady chef letting out a huge kyak-kyak laugh. Minister Milford rushed forward to save his sins, covering the actress furiously with his suit jacket and slapping down the fire.

Anette began to cry. She had done this. Anette had been wishing ill on the woman and Anette knew better than to wish ill on anyone. This was not going to help her get to where she belonged. Not going to help her get gotten by Jacob. She held Franky's arm and turned her face into his body.

"Is only a wig," Franky whispered to her like a savior. "Look, see." And Anette looked to see the leading lady freeing herself from under the minister's jacket, and emerging with black hair plastered down on her head and a charred yellow wig in the sand.

The lady stomped on the wig with her bare feet, but without the expected anxiety. Her face was calm and steady, and she kept stomping. "Cut!" someone called. "Don't you dare cut!" from someone else. And the actress kept stomping, her sandy feet pulping the curly wig into pieces that flew the hair and the sand about, until the leading man, who was wearing too-tight swim trunks, finally stormed through the crowd and grabbed hold of her in a hugging, containing motion. The actress told him calmly to let her go, and then she walked out to the water.

Left in the sand, the wig looked like murdered baby birds.

"That's a wrap," the director said into his megaphone. And the dancers, who were doctors and lawyers and pastors and educators and one Coast Guardsman, walked off

Honeymoon Beach, back to the dock, and boarded the little boats. Across the water, where words so easily carry, everyone could hear everyone else creating the story of the lady doing the limbo.

Mr. Lyte was not their boatman this time. Anette thought of the lady chef now and felt badly. She was distracted enough to forget her fear of the little boat, though Franky kept his arm around her. Anette didn't remember any Miss Lady, but how could she? She didn't remember her own mother. She thought of Jacob, but then kept pushing that thought out to sea.

Once they docked back on St. Thomas, Franky could easily have walked Anette home, but instead they slipped into his car and Franky let the roof down. Anette moved close to him on the front seat and rested her hand on his thigh — something she had never done to him before. "You a star, yes," he said. And with her dyed black hair blowing around her face and the moon big above and his fast Cadillac swimming them around the corners, Anette believed him. *Franky is a good man,* she thought to herself. If she still thought of Jacob then she must be a fool. Tonight, she would finally kiss Franky. He deserved that at least.

But sensing his time, Franky didn't wait

even a second. He pulled the car over, walked to the passenger side, opened the door, and got down on one knee. It was just a month into their chaste courtship. Anette put her hand to her chest as if she had been shot. Franky took the hand, isolated the finger, and pushed on an engagement ring with diamonds peaking like a volcano.

"Oh, Franky. Thank you. Thank you," Anette said, because she couldn't say yes, but she knew she shouldn't say no.

67.

Jacob Esau McKenzie hadn't just disappeared and left Anette unwed and with child. In fact, he'd appeared firmly in medical school in the nation's capital. If he was going to be a pediatrician, he would have to get through medical school and the years of specialization with focus. No women. No movie theaters. No liming or skylarking. Only child skulls. Baby intestines. The soup of an adolescent cough. These were his foci. And, of course, Anette and baby Eve. He was going back to them. No nurse, no lady doctor could move his mind. Just "be a doctor." One day — husband and father.

He did not write to Anette back on island. Writing would make it longer. Writing would be "I miss you." Writing might be "the love is fading." And also writing to Anette might be the end of him. His mother had said as much. And how wouldn't she know on that small island? Likely, she'd sweetened the postmaster by gifting him with a concoction that juiced up his wife's pussy. Something like that. So Jacob didn't write Anette or anybody — not even his mother. That was his one small rebellion against Rebekah. Though she kept sending him the stewed cherries, stuffed into tiny jars that had been used for baby food. Yes, the world was changing. Baby food now came in a jar. It was even being sold on his island apparently.

Instead of writing or calling, Jacob wound a single rubber band around his marital finger and imagined Anette wearing the white dress. He'd bought her the cloth for that dress, though instead of waiting for a wedding, she'd worn it the day she'd seen him off. But he dreamed anyway.

One cool D.C. day he swore he'd seen Anette's face on a movie poster. He stared at the poster for *Girls Are for Loving* and decided that it could not be Anette. Despite the familiar fabric of the dress and the familiar face of the woman. No, that was not the Virgin Islands. Not on that poster and not in that movie.

Still, the movie poster churned him enough that he broke down and wrote just a quick note to his brother to check on Anette and the baby for him. But Saul was distracted by his current architectural project and adjoining clandestine love affair. He had not visited the post office until the postmaster himself ran into him on Back Street and let him know that there was a letter waiting. So Saul wrote back to his brother too many weeks later: "Anette engaged to be marry. How you ain hear?"

68.

In St. Thomas, Anette and Franky had become celebrities. The movie posters were plastered around the island. GIRLS ARE FOR LOVING was written in red. And below the words was the scene at the dance over at the Gull Reef Club. And there were Anette and Franky, on the poster like they were the stars. They took up more than half of the poster. Never mind that Anette's dress was flying a little too much. Never mind that her skin was lightened up so she looked very much like a white woman and that Franky's skin was darkened and his green eyes seemed too green. Never mind, they were the stars! They were making the Virgin Islands known!

The newspaper interviewed them and asked when they were getting married. Anette, her ring finger glinting, held Franky's hand and said, "Soon." Franky was a good man. A fine man, really. In the Coast Guard. He was taking care of his old mother who had hair on her chin. Anette was being a lady — like sister Eeona wanted. No thoughtless thing like with Ronnie. No loveful thing like with Jacob. She had children to consider.

Franky had been giving Anette a ride on the days she volunteered as a history assistant at the private Anglican school. On the morning their interview was printed, Franky waited until she got into the car, and then he laid a copy of the newspaper in her lap. On the cover of the paper was a picture of them, her hand held firmly between his two. Her engagement ring shining like a promise right there on the front page.

On the ride to school Franky swore to build her a living room set and an entire house, one she could live in this time, with his own hands. "Anette, I been waiting to hold on to you since we was children, yes."

And this was all it took really. Because Ronnie hadn't seemed able to hold on to her for half that long. And because Jacob, her first love, now seemed like he didn't want to hold on at all.

Anette spent three hours grading sixth-through eighth-grade tests on Caribbean history and American history, which together now made up our history. Still, she stood three times to go atop the school stairs and look into the harbor to see if Jacob had arrived without her sensing it. It was silly, but she felt a sudden desperation. When the bell rang for lunch, her grading was over and Franky, not Jacob at all, was there waiting to pick her up.

Anette stood at the top of the school stairs to take in her final breaths and then she walked down. "Let we do it next week," she said. But Franky, who had a sense of timing, said, "Let we do it today, yes."

"But I don't have no dress," she said, looking around and noticing that a few of the teachers walking past were making a big show of pretending not to listen.

"Well, the court don't close until four and the shops don't close until five."

And Anette, with no time to sense the arrival that was coming because it wasn't yet coming, said, "Well, why not, then."

This was the correct, the logical thing to do. Franky was a man who would build a house. A man who would care for the girls. A guarding man. Jacob McKenzie had not come floating in. Well, then he was barely a man at all.

Eeona did not like Franky for Anette, but she had consented. Anette had two children. She was lucky to find a man at all. Even a yes man who only wanted to please. Maybe that was for the best. Either way, a low-class man was better than a blood brother, even Eeona knew that.

Anette bought a simple yellow dress. Green was his color and red was hers, but yellow was the island's and Anette needed this nuptial to be bigger than her alone. At the courthouse, Anette closed her eyes when the judge asked if anyone objected. When she opened them, she saw only Franky, and looking into his eyes, she saw only him loving her and only him staying by her side.

That week Anette and the girls moved out of Eeona's flat and in with Franky in his modest two-bedroom. He had moved out of his mother's house long before it was typical for island men to do such things.

Eeona stayed alone in the small one-bedroom apartment.

Now that Anette was remarried, there was no moral obstacle to her promotion and within the week she was called into the principal's office and told that a teaching position would be available for her in summer school. And if she stayed married, and there was an emphasis there, there would be something permanent when school opened in September.

Franky started looking for land where he could build a house to keep his promise. But before Franky could build the house and before Anette could become a teacher, some other things arrived. First, there was Jacob McKenzie.

69.

Jacob McKenzie did nothing when he found out about Anette's engagement. Nothing, really. He didn't study harder at medical school or eat less at the restaurant or reflect on himself or his past failures. He did not take official leave from school or work. Just took one month to gather the money from his earnings waiting on tables — his polished American accent and sandy skin affording him ample tips. Then he just bought a one-way ticket home to the island. Jacob did everything he knew how to do then — but not a thing entered his mind until his plane slid onto St. Thomas and he smelled the rusty hangar and realized that the last time he had seen Anette or his infant daughter was in that very airport.

Other passengers cut around him to get off the plane because he had stopped at the bottom of the stairs. Jacob stooped down and put his face to the tarmac. He didn't kiss the St. Thomas ground like he'd done when he'd returned from the Army. This time he licked it. He licked the ground that planes rolled on and hundreds of feet a day walked on. He licked it as if it were a woman. And women stared until the pilot rested his hand on Jacob's shoulder and told him that his land love was honorable but obscene.

Jacob didn't go to his mother's house. He was bold-faced and hopeless, so he went to Ronald Smalls's. Ronnie had stayed in the Army and had kept Anette's picture as his amulet. In Korea, where he'd most recently been deployed, he'd been as chaste as ever and seen no military action at all. Jacob went to him because Ronald had been married to Anette. Ronald had loved her. Ronald had lost her. Ronald would understand what Jacob was now feeling.

"I had wonder if you would come," Ronnie said, when the two of them sat down in the parlor. Ronnie's mother served them guavaberry rum, for it was the Christmas season. She felt bitter on behalf of these boys. She'd never liked Anette for her son. Those Bradshaw sisters thought they were too good for anybody. Hah. Now look at Anette. She was a tart and the whole island knew.

Jacob nodded at Mrs. Smalls to fill his little rum glass to the brim.

"I don't know much, Jay," Ronnie began awkwardly. "I wasn't there."

"There where?" Jacob asked, as he felt the rum burn down his throat.

"When they get married."

Jacob coughed rum back into his glass. "Mother Mary! I hear she *getting* married. I only been gone a few months, man."

"America eat your brains, Jay? You gone near a year." Ronnie shook his head sadly, for he understood Jacob's loss. "Is a nice fellow she marry. In the Coast Guard. Not many of we in the Coast Guard, you know. He does keep the lighthouse. I even went with him for a drink the other day."

Now Jacob gulped his rum and put the glass down loudly on the table. "Ronnie, you soft in the head? The man marry your wife and you had a drink with him?"

Ronald sucked his teeth and poured more rum. "But Jacob, you make a baby with my wife and I here drinking with you."

Jacob nodded. In his chest there was a swelling of humility and a tightening of pride and the sweetness of the rum. "Just don't tell me no more about what the new husband does do. Or what he look like. Or about he character. I just here to make Anette marry me."

"So you ready for marrying now?"

Jacob shook his head. His hair was knotted into little nappies. His clothes were wrinkled. His eyes were bloodshot. "I just ain ready to see her married to someone else." His eyes started to water, but then he stood up quickly and walked out of the door. He left his bag and his scarf and winter coat on Ronnie's bachelor couch. His rum glass empty on the coffee table.

Finally, Jacob went to his mother's house. He knew his mother wouldn't be home at this time. She'd be in the market selling her mesple and limes and spellbinding teas. He didn't want her to see him, for fear she would spin an obeah that would keep Anette and him apart for life. But Saul might be home and might be able to help.

Jacob opened the door and saw no one. He looked in the two other rooms — the boys' room and his mother's room. No one. The piano had been moved to the center of the hall. The sofa had been raised on concrete blocks and sat in front of the piano keys as the piano bench. Jacob sank down into the sofa.

He didn't really play something. He just played anything. Harmonies of this, melodies of that, humming something different, stamping his foot to his nodding head. To him, it sounded like American blues music. To those walking by the house, it sounded haunted.

Jacob played, feeling the sweat gathering underneath his thighs and the tears running down his face. He was melting. The music slow and dirty. No neatness like a love letter, nor like "I do." It was messy, like "I'm giving up on medical school and manhood," like "I know I'm late but I'm here now." Messy with Anette's two daughters and now a new husband. But Jacob didn't actually hear any of that, though that was what he was playing. He only heard his fingers on the piano keys and his foot stamping on the piano pedals and his own mouth bawling. He only heard himself. So when his brother entered, early plans for a new housing development under his arm, Jacob didn't see.

Saul heard the music and began dancing around the room to a beat that was not of the music. When Jacob heard a man's steps, he turned his face and he stopped playing. A childhood memory of a man with sea-gray eyes dancing with him in that very spot pulled in before Jacob's watery eyes and then receded. He wiped his face with the back of his hand.

"I come for Anette," said Jacob to his brother.

Saul stilled. "I know."

"You must give her a message for me."

Saul fixed his face as if he were receiving a disease. "I ain want no part of this. Mama will maim we both."

"Just help me, nuh."

"All right, Jacob. I going handle this thing just now."

"Why not now-now?"

Saul looked at this brother. They had shared a bed growing up, but they did not often express affection. It was not the McKenzie way. Now Saul walked up to Jacob and touched his streaked face.

70.

Anette smiled tightly and pretended she didn't know why Saul had come. She knew; she had a sense for knowing when someone was coming. But it was an awful knowing, for it was all too late. Here was a magic that had turned out useless because someone didn't always come when you wanted. But she knew Saul was coming and she knew Jacob would follow. In the living room Saul spoke to her about their other former classmates and the children — Eve Youme, after all, was his niece.

"Beautiful girls," he commented, without looking at them.

"Get your uncle Saul some guavaberry rum," Anette directed her daughters. They had half a decanter that Eeona made for selling during the season. Ronalda went for the little glass, but her sister didn't follow. Eve Youme, still a toddler, refused to waddle out of the room. There was something off about her even then. Saul looked hard at Eve Youme, who looked calmly back at him. Finally, he gave up hoping for privacy. When Ronalda returned with the glass of rum, he took only the napkin from her. He pulled a fine ink pen from his pocket and scribbled his message. Then he took his leave. Ronalda saw the door close gently as she stood beside her sister with the guavaberry she was too young to drink, the fumes of it rising into her face.

Anette didn't open the note then. Not with Ronalda standing there with a glass of rum in her hand. Not with Youme staring at her as if she were reading Anette's mind — the child's hair snaking around her head.

Anette went to her closet for her outing hat and saw her red movie dress. She gripped the fabric in her fist, as though demanding something of it. Then she smoothed it out with a forced calm and went to brush her hair. She left the house, and left the girls, to go read the napkin.

With her mother gone, Ronalda was in charge. Instead of pouring the guavaberry rum back into its decanter, Ronalda sipped it slowly, then poured some more for her sister.

Anette walked for a long time. Her heels clicking. She was a proper married woman again. The movie starring her and Franky was coming out in just a few weeks. And then there was the other thing — the child within her, who would be coming within the year.

How far did Anette need to get from their apartment before it stopped being betrayal? She walked toward the harbor, where there were boats unloading and a few white sailors smoking cigarettes. There was even a large passenger ship docked. In the middle of the harbor was Water Island, where she had danced with her now husband Franky at the Gull Reef Club with the movie cameras filming. She stopped on a bench on the newly paved Water Front. This place had all been sand and rock, and now it was concrete, and cars could park here, and sailors and tourists could walk here, and women could sit here to contemplate infidelity.

Meet him by Lindbergh Bay at dusk. He say bring baby Eve and only whatever else you need for Stateside.

Anette was still young. Still Julie mango juicy and still knowing it. But she also knew that her grown-up life was finally beginning. Not this back-and-forth, running-behind-some-man, driving-in-a-car-without-doors life. But a real life with a house and children, and a husband whose mother did not obeah his life. Anette was now teaching history and she'd been taking classes through the mail. Getting her bachelor's so she could get the higher pay and prestige it would afford her. She wanted to be a real woman, finally. How ironic that now *she* would be the Bradshaw running away and ending up in America.

The sun was bright and hot, but there was a smooth trade wind cooling her neck. The world seemed to be open and opening.

Anette looked out at the ocean. She looked past Water Island and didn't think of the movie. She thought instead of the man and woman who had thought she was a chambermaid. She looked out at the possibility of the horizon. The dusk was arriving.

She shouldn't have looked that way. She should have looked back at the cars or the people or the buildings. But instead she faced the sea. The sun was reddening the sky. The sea air was filling her. This moving and big and overwhelming blue sea. This active and passionate and relenting blue sea. And she thought of the first man she had really loved. The way they knew each other's bodies, even in the dark — like they were aboriginal to each other. How even without a wedding ring she had still felt like Jacob's own. And when she was screaming and pushing out their child, he was screaming, too. His face right beside hers. Until the midwife threatened to kick him out, saying this was not how fathers were supposed to act. He'd pushed the midwife aside and held Eve Youme's flaming head when it arrived. Like the doctor he would be. How he loved Anette as if she were something worthy of nighttime beaches. How they made love there at night. How they did things that she knew she should be ashamed of. How he said she was so strong that her little body could make him kneel. How she rubbed the gum of his aching tooth and made the pain go away. How he pushed his fingers through her hair and massaged the roots, telling her he could feel the red. How he touched her like he owned her. And how she had felt more belonging with him than she had her whole life. Being with him was being claimed. She had been a fool not to wait for him.

But now she was married. Now her husband cooked for her and drove her around in his green Cadillac and took her dancing and took care of Ronalda and Youme as if they were his own. But Franky did not feel like kin, despite the marriage that said so. That was Jacob.

Anette walked back home to get ready. She wanted to belong. She was going with Jacob.

Jacob had not asked Anette to bring Ronalda. He had only asked for Eve. So for now Anette would have to leave Ronalda with her sister. It would be for the best. At least until they settled. Anette didn't think about what she knew. That Ronalda would not do well with Eeona. Or that there was another baby on the way and that the baby was Franky's.

Anette passed no less than six film posters featuring her and Franky. She was determined not to see the posters at all. People called out to her, famous Mrs. Joseph, and she responded out of courtesy. But she kept her mind tight. Thinking on nothing but her future beautiful life. Her heels clicked on the pavement. She needed to hurry. Hurry.

71.

Jacob waited at the beach. Beneath the sea grape tree that she and he had shared on that night he had first made love to her. But it had not just been them; Ronalda had also been there. He breathed and tried to remember that night, but he tried not to think on Ronalda. He could not bring her with them now. He could manage his tiny rent with Anette; it would be a struggle with Eve, but he could handle no more. Not money-wise or mind-wise. Ronalda was his old friend Ronnie's child, anyway.

He thought of Anette and the ocean; he thought of them as the same frightening, enticing thing. Behind him was an army of coconut trees. There was the thump every now and then of a coconut hitting the ground. He didn't turn away from the waves for that noise. He would only turn for the hushed movement of the sand. For the swish of a leaf. He wanted her to come up on him. He wanted her to touch him before he saw her. He wanted it that beautiful. He wanted to just sink back into her chest, her arms circling him. He wanted her to keep him and his soul together. He wanted them to begin again, both looking out at this sea.

This is not how it happened.

72.

Anette opened the door to her and Franky's apartment. Her husband, the man with a sense of timing, was home early from cleaning the lighthouse. Anette heard him banging around the pots. She smelled onions and garlic and hot canola oil. She entered the kitchen and there was his bare dark back facing her. He was leaning into a pot and stirring it, then stretching to a cupboard to find a spice. "Franky," she said.

"Greetings, Mrs. Joseph." He turned to look at her, his screaming green eyes, and offered a wooden spoon filled with sauce.

Anette shook her head and stepped back. "Franky, we have to talk."

"I know we do. I come home early because I have something for you. But the girls sleeping like they dead, yes. And you ain here." He spooned the sauce into his own mouth before rinsing it off in the sink and drying it cleanly on a kitchen towel. Anette just stared at him. *This was a good man,* she thought. *A good family man.* "Anette, you okay? You looking . . ." He stepped toward her.

She had always been a small woman. Short and thin and tart. She held up her free hand to stop him now, her purse dangling from her wrist. He was thick and muscled, but he stopped for her. "Franky, what would you do if I left you?" Franky's upper body shot back as if he had been hit. Slowly, he returned himself back to an upright position. Without a word, without a curl of his lip, he turned back to his cooking. For a long few seconds, for almost a minute, Anette knew it was going to be okay. She had made a mistake rushing into this marriage. She'd done it out of necessity and not out of love. And love was, she knew now, the only true necessity. Franky would be fine. He deserved a woman who loved him wholly. There he was cooking, after all. There he was, moving on — in his own gentle way.

Anette watched his strong back but was already thinking about the things she needed to pack. She thought of Jacob and knew he was at the beach already. Waiting for her. Anette lifted her heel slowly, but it was then that she realized the food was burning. She let her heel drop with a click. And then like a switch, Franky was turned on. She saw his hand in slow motion . . . and then pots were flying and hot oil was splattering across the walls and glasses were breaking and he was a hurricane crashing into her shore. And he was howling and cursing and spinning and kicking, and all she could understand was "I here" and "I been waiting for you all these years" and "I building a house for you." "I ain going nowhere." He stormed past her, pulled open the front door, and slammed it, leaving it swaying on its hinges before it crashed onto the front steps. Anette stood there in their kitchen. Onion skins settled quietly to the ground.

But it was a simple act of Franky's impeccable timing. Because after Franky roared out, Anette hurried to the room to pack her and Youme's things. Hurried before she came to her senses. But there it was. Hanging in their room like a piece of art. The thing Franky had come home early to give to her. The poster of them in the movie. Framed and all. Above their bed. An American movie, realer than a wedding ring. It was only a matter of timing, not of love, but it was life.

73.

Jacob's second message came the very next morning. It was stuck in the unhinged door that had been propped up into the doorway for the night. Anyone could have seen Jacob wedge it there. Franky could have come home from wherever he had been all night and read it. But Jacob's note was so small, metaphorically and in reality, beside the picture that now hung above the bed. Jacob's note was so small and Jacob was so late. Anette plucked the note from the door and knew she was watched even as she read it deep inside the apartment, on her and her husband's bed, beneath the picture that sealed her to Franky. She was aware of the infidelity. *Anegando en mis llanto,* she thought, and then did. Afterward, she burnt the note over the stove.

74.

Jacob was in Puerto Rico that evening. He slept in the San Juan airport, waiting for any flight to the States to take him away. Away from the memory of Anette at dawn, pushing her unhinged door aside. He'd watched her as she peeled his note from the door in her bare feet. He watched as she turned without looking around, without even looking for him kneeling there in the street, the note in her hand loosely like she might only be carrying it to the garbage bin.

When Jacob Esau McKenzie returned to medical school in America, he seemed perfectly normal. No one thought much of anything could have happened to him. But he did two Anette-driven things. First he snapped the rubber band wedding ring off his finger. Then he changed his specialization from pediatrics to gynecology. From children to women. He would put his hands into other women and dig for Anette.

But remember that Jacob was not the only thing to come. The second thing was the movie. *Girls Are for Loving.*

75.
ANETTE

That *Girls Are for Loving* movie was meant to make us us. To make us real. Franky and me make it to the advertising poster. That poster was a magic. It was a sign. Forget about Johnny-come-late Jacob. Because there was me and Franky. Like we belonging to each other. So proper a couple that we make it to the poster. Jacob and me, we was never a proper thing outside of our own hearts. Never proper to anybody else at all.

That movie make me and Franky seem real-real. Jacob so far away, seem fake. Then Jacob come, begging me back, and is only me know that I have a baby in my belly. And the baby is Franky own. But a child, like a poster or a movie, is a thing for all to see. A child is a real belonging. Nothing you can do about it. And I know that Franky going to claim all my children. I can't say the same for Jacob. Stupid-ass Jacob. My stupid-ass Jacob. But forget he. Forget he. Forget he.

Now listen. Before the baby born, *Girls Are for Loving* arrive in St. Thomas. Crucians seaplane in from St. Croix and Johnians ferry from St. John. It ain just about me and Franky. It about all of we. Tourism gearing up over here and even people from Tortola and Anegada regularly passing through the window to come work. This movie was going to make us the finest piece of land in the region. A place of culture. Worthy of Hollywood.

The line long for the theater. Yes, we had a real indoor Apollo Theater own by a nice Puerto Rican man. We had nice things, then.

Our own hotels, banks, cinema. Besides all the people, it was a very regular movie evening in every other way. No one had priority seating or anything. But me and Franky still feel like we is big celebrities — not just extras.

Even though I pushing out of it, I still wore the dupioni dress. But I wear modest flats this time and a little jacket to keep off the night dew and protect the plumpness of my baby belly. And I ain shame. In the dress, everybody recognize me walking in. I get smiles and nods. Inside, Franky hold me close. It feel like the whole thing is for we alone.

The cinema man yell to quiet down and the light go soft and the movie crackle on and is no waiting. Our scene is the opening scene! See us dancing and shuffling smooth calypso style, seven-step, two-step, dipping and all. There was the Pick-up Men looking happy enough. And there was all of we sure looking good, my girl. Close in on Franky and me and my red and yellow dress. My husband up there looking so handsome. My husband! I is his wife. Imagine. I feel scared and excited like I about to win a prize. I watching Franky spin me first nice and slow and then fast so my dress fly a little. I squeeze his leg in the theater darkness. His

leg tense under my fingers and I feel powerful. I watch the screen and see all of we
becoming real. Seeing my marriage, this
marriage, becoming a real wonderful thing
that even the Americans can see and know.
I ain thinking of Jacob McKenzie at all.

Then the limbo scene. Just as it was. All
the leading woman thigh and thing showing, which had seem okay when she was just
doing the limbo, but ain seem okay now that
we seeing it so large up there. But they show
it all, right up to her panty and when she
wig catch fire on the limbo stick. Then a
cut. A cut to the skirt of my dress, the very
one I wearing self — waving in some wind.
Not a body you know, just a piece of the
dress. It make me feel uneasy, like my flapping flame dress was to blame for the hair
on fire. Like the movie people was reading
my mind. Then there is the whole scene
with the woman stamping she wig and acting crazy, with a cut to my red, and then us
dancers there gaping and curling into our
men not thinking we acting, and then a cut
to my dress flying about now in slow motion, a piece of my leg showing, then back
to the leading man taking the woman in his
arms and then a cut to my dress. And I in
the theater wishing it would stop, wishing I
hadn't worn the stupid dress to the opening

after all, knowing that the fire is my fault. And then back to the leading couple, though now . . . now they was naked! And all we could see was the man sweaty bumsie moving forward and forward and the woman oily legs coming from either side of him and moving like a broken machine. And flash back to my dress. And then a close-up on their faces all tonguey kissing, and then my dress, and then a solitary breast wobbling vigorous-vigorous — and then the pastor's wife scream in the theater like she 'bout to dead. And all the people in the theater start to flood out.

I crying. No tears. Just a sobbing thing, holding my belly and rubbing it. Me saying again and again: "My dress, my dress." Now on the screen — groans of the two Americans just doing it for real as if we ain watching.

We spill out into the street but can't look at each other. This how we get put on the map in America? This me and my husband debut to the island and the nation? Is what they call pornographic. You hearing me.

The governor issue a formal complaint to the studio on behalf of our Virgin Islands. His letter publish in the *Virgin Islands Daily News.* "The people were innocent," he write. But the movie people ain even respond back. People quarrel up with the Gull Reef Club and finally the American club owner get his American lawyers to write in a note claiming no violation. "No one did anything against his or her will," the club put in the paper. "There were no secrets. Not our fault no one had bothered to ask. Besides, those people were not in the sex scenes."

But ey, ey. What the hell he mean by "those people"? I was those people.

But the Gull Reef Club make good money and they want the whole thing hush up. So they go back to paying us no mind at all.

I often lay in bed thinking that we was so foolish to pappy show ourselves for them Continentals. I lay in bed beside Franky and I wonder if he going stay positive like he is. Or if he going to cool now. I would think how I shame for myself and I shame for my island and I even shame for my marriage. Sometimes while I there brooding, a shadow cross our window. I don't think thief. I think Jacob. Think how with him there was no shame. Then I turn and see Franky in bed with me instead.

■ ■ ■ ■

A BELONGING

■ ■ ■ ■

76.

But once the boy was born, the family of Mr. Franky and Mrs. Anette B. Joseph settled in and became a sort of something. There were three children now — the last was named Frank, like his father. He was never called Franky, but always just Frank and that was how they were differentiated.

The Navy was lessening its presence on the island and so Franky was promoted to head keeper of the lighthouse, no assistant needed. He went to the point every day, cleaning the fixtures so they kept shining. Replacing the lights even if there wasn't a need. If the rain was heavy, he might even stay the night there, watching for ships that never seemed to be in distress.

He and Anette had never, not once, mentioned what had happened that day in the kitchen when she'd almost left him. He had come home the following night and fixed the door quietly. A few men walking by had offered to help, but Franky had only shaken his head. Then Franky had slid into the bed beside Anette and held her tightly, as if to say thank you. But he never said anything about it at all.

Nor did they ever talk about the movie again. About how after the film came out Anette had come home, torn her clothes off, torn the poster from the wall, and pleaded that he swim into her. Again and again. Until he was sore and she was sore. And it had been like that for weeks until her belly bloomed and he began to worry that they'd hurt the baby.

For years they lived with Ronnie always calling before he appeared and with Jacob not appearing at all.

But Eve Youme's father, Dr. Jacob E. McKenzie, did return to the island to practice as a lady's doctor. Youme was no longer a baby when he came back again. Then she began regular visits to his apartment and then later his and his wife's house. The wife was a sweet woman handpicked by Jacob's mother. Papa Franky never drove Me there or anywhere close to her father. There was something about Jacob McKenzie that made Franky Joseph feel small. He noticed that Anette did not drive Youme out to her father's either. Nor did Jacob himself come. A maid was sent to pick up the child. Franky was thankful for this careful avoidance.

Eeona seemed to warm to the new family. Not only did she babysit, more than once she'd brought the children to work with her. Showing them off, it seemed. When she'd returned from her Freedom City episode, she had taken up a government job administering loans. She offered to help Franky with the money to build Anette's house. Eeona wanted this marriage to stick. This wasn't because she'd come around to liking Franky. That wasn't her way. In exchange for helping them, Eeona asked that Franky help her choose a car to buy and teach her how to drive.

77.

Once upon a time, Eeona's father had told her she'd never want for anything, and then he'd left her nothing. Moreau had promised to make the whole island of Anegada into something for her, but then he'd ran off to France. Kweku had planted a child in her womb, like building a house on a piece of land, but he hadn't even been willing to promise her marriage. Even Liva Lovernkrandt had let her down. Eeona had been foolishly depending on men and women to take her and take her away. Now she would have her own car, her own captaincy. At the car dealership, she tried not to think of Kweku Prideux teasing when she'd asked for a carriage ride during her first minutes in Freedom City.

"I think this one, Franklin." Eeona gestured to the blue Datsun.

The car salesman was the only car salesman on the island. He nodded and smiled now. He was selling the Datsun brand-new, though he'd been using it in the country to teach his son how to drive. He also smiled and nodded because there was the great Eeona Bradshaw walking before him. *A nicelooking woman for true,* he thought, and followed them closely as they inspected the vehicle so he could smell her. The car salesman was from Anguilla, though he had been on St. Thomas since he was a teenager. He'd heard about Eeona Bradshaw's beauty. He'd only glimpsed her once before, when he'd gone to the Department of Finance to ask for a business loan. They didn't keep her out front, for surely people would traipse in just to catch an eye of her. But he'd spied her walking from one room to another. He'd recognized her by her blue nun clothes it was said she always wore.

Franky walked around the Datsun. "I don't know, sis. You should get you a light-color car, something people could see you in, yes. In this dark blue you going get lost if you ever in the country at night. No one going be able to see you self."

"Well, that sounds lovely, Franklin. Why would I want to be seen if I was driving around at night? Clearly, I would be up to no good. Besides, blue is my color."

"Good for learning to drive on," pitched in the salesman, who was standing too close beside Eeona.

Franky patted the man on the back and smiled. "How you guess? I teaching my sister-in-law here how to drive."

"Salesmen know these things."

Eeona pursed her lips.

The salesman watched her and thought, *Yes, Eeona Bradshaw was very pretty, but there were whores on the island now who were just as beautiful.*

Back at home, Franky joked about Eeona being invisible in the nighttime hills. Eeona, as she often did now, was joining them for dinner. Anette lifted little Frank to the sink to wash his hands, but looked hard at her sister.

"For true, Eeona? All of invisible?"

"Please, Anette. Use proper English."

Ronalda looked away with embarrassment — her mother had been scolded. Anette cleared her throat. "Is that how you wanted it, sister Eeona? Do you want to be invisible?"

"Indeed."

"You always take the risks you never want me to take." Anette didn't say this with angst, she only said it like it was true.

"That is what elder sisters are for, dear."

Youme was the middle child on her mother's side, but would be the eldest on her father's. "Auntie Eeona, you'll be like a witch flying in the night."

Eeona pulled gently on Youme's big wild hair. The child wasn't yet beautiful, but Eeona could feel the possibilities. Now she leaned in to whisper to Eve Youme. Her soft breath sifted out like sand. "Me," she said. "Me, we are witches." Youme didn't betray this secret by smiling. She only stood still to hear the whisper and feel her aunt's breath on her ear.

But the blue Datsun was never the thing it was supposed to be for Eeona.

With Eeona in the passenger seat, Franky drove the car out to the golf course by Brewers Bay. A golf course was supposed to be Eeona's in Anegada, now she would drive all over the golf course in St. Thomas. Like it was hers. She would mash it down with her wheels. She would destroy it to get her freedom.

But actually, student drivers practiced on the golf course all the time. Indeed, a more private one would soon be laid in the countryside so tourists could hit their white balls with brown sticks in peace. There was talk of building a college on the current course site. Soon one might learn how to be a nurse without having to leave the island or get a teaching certificate without having to send away for the tests. For now, it was Eeona's idea to use the golf course in order to learn how to drive. She sat in the passenger's seat, resentful that this Franky Joseph had to teach her anything.

The idea of Anette and Esau being romantic had been simply awful, but at least that Esau was of good stock — of course. But this Franky Joseph. A regular black man. Couldn't Anette have done better?

But Eeona needed this black man to teach her how to drive. She longed to be racing around the island in her fast car. She had her hair in a tight neat bun for the driving lesson but she already saw herself driving and letting it flow out of the window when it was just her alone. She didn't care if she was too old now to have her hair flying.

Franky was speaking. "See what I'm doing here? I turning to avoid this dip and I letting the steering wheel slide like so. Inch it, yes. Easy. Clutch, brake, then gas. Yes?" She looked so he wouldn't keep yesing her. But really she was looking through him. She was seeing herself running alongside the beach that flanked them now on the left. Seeing herself like a beautiful animal with hair flying behind her. She was galloping. She was something to be feared. She loved herself most like that. She also hated herself most like that. But no matter, because she missed herself most like that.

The car smoothed over the grass. Franky turned the engine off and stepped out. He walked around and opened the car door for Eeona. He didn't do this chivalry for his own wife, but he knew he had to for his wife's sister. This sister was a real harpy, but she was the woman who had raised his wife. He had to give her the respect of a mother-in-law. Besides, she was still pretty. Older than he was by far, but he did, sometimes, only sometimes, picture he was riding her when he made love to Anette. It wasn't a betrayal or anything, not really. He loved his wife in a way he never knew a man could love anything that wasn't God. But Eeona's

412

ocean hair and that mango-colored skin —
well, there was still something of God in
that, too. Even though the dryness around
the eyes. Even though that bit of gray in the
roots.

Eeona walked around the car and eased
her way into the driver's seat. In the distance
there was one white flag sticking out of a
hole. It waved at Eeona and she decided
she would aim for it. Crush it. But behind
the wheel she seemed small and frail, like
this machine would move her instead of the
other way around. She furrowed her brow
and turned the key in the ignition. Nothing
happened. There was not a sound. Not even
a vexed skittering.

"Pump the gas," said Franky calmly, as if
nothing out of the ordinary at all was happening. "A car is like a woman, yes. You have
to be gentle with her." He realized that that
might not be the right metaphor for a
woman driver, but then again. He'd been
suspicious of Eeona. She'd never married
after all, and as far as he knew, she'd never
even been with a man. Perhaps she was one
of those women who preferred women. "I
taught Anette how to drive," he said now.
"I'll teach Ronalda and Me and Frank, yes.
Everyone thinks it's impossible at first. But
remember it's like a woman. It can be

moved." He could tell from her face that this wasn't, after all, the best thing to say. His metaphors were scarce.

"No," she replied. "What you are saying is not true." It wasn't clear what she meant. She tried again anyhow. Still nothing. Franky got out and walked around. He opened the door for her and let her out and then he sat in the driver's seat and turned the car on easily.

"We going practice turning on later," he said. Then he scooted over to the passenger's seat for her to take over. When she sat down, the car rumbled. She jerked at the wheel and the engine cut. He went back around and went through the same motions of turning the car on for her again. She sat down again in the driver's seat. "The pedal, the clutch," he said. "Soft-soft, yes-yes."

Eeona rested her foot on the one he said was the go and eased off the one he called the clutch. The car shut off.

But Franky had been thinking of metaphors. "A car is a like a ship," he said. "You have to ride it easy over the waves." He looked at Eeona for approval.

"I understand," she said, staring out of the windshield and studying that white flag, the solitary stander on the green.

"Yes, now try again. Gentle over the

waves. Your Papa was a boatman, you'll know like instinct how this is to be done."

"I know that I will never drive this car."

And she never did. The car never started for her. It never went for her. They tried again and again. They tried for days. Anette got into the Datsun and took it for a spin to the market. Even Ronalda, a child, could at least get it to start.

The last mode of transport that Eeona had been able to direct was a stubborn burro named Nelson. No, she had not won out over the golf course. She had not outwon Kweku, a car driver who'd made her his powerless passenger. Some people would have taken this to mean they were destined to be pedestrian. Or destined to stay and be still and not wander, not be free. Given all the failures, Eeona would be forgiven for giving up.

But Eeona is not some people.

78.

The house Franky built was on the lower part of Garden Street. But it was still in the prime area. Right there on Bred Gade step street. Not too far from the Crystal Palace and Villa Fairview. If you just walked to the top of the step street, you could have the high-class view Eeona would have killed to cling to. It was only a short walk from the Anglican church. When the house was finally built, Anette, full of her married respectability and her position as history teacher at the Anglican school, had the priest come and bless it. This wasn't her mother's actually Anglican Anglican priest, but an American Anglican who laughed loudly and spoke quietly of ordaining women.

The day of the blessing was the last time anyone on island ever ate sea turtle, as the Americans had begun a conservation effort. Gertie's engagement ring stood on her finger like a lighthouse, and, indeed, the man who had put it on her finger was the selfsame American who'd drunkenly driven her almost to the lighthouse so long ago. Hamilton chatted with the priest as if they were kin back on the Continent.

During the blessing, Eeona, who still lived in Savan, stood beside the priest with her body tight and straight. The priest, who was married, took a small step away from her when he bowed his head.

Eeona didn't notice. She was caught in considering that she had finally done her duty — overdone it, actually. Little sister Anette now had a house and some land.

Anette had even resisted Esau in the end. Eeona's freedom time must now, certainly, be coming. Either that or it would never come. So Eeona made no one privy to her thinking this time. Already she had taken a boat over to the island of St. John, where she'd quietly eyed some land.

But this day of the blessing Franky unveiled his final domestic gift. It came in a box and it was heavy. He hauled it up the step street himself, from where it had been hiding in the back of his truck. He perspired in his suit as he heaved the box, for a home blessing was a suit occasion. Anette smiled and smiled and could not, despite her powers, figure out what this arrival could be. The children gaped just because it was a heavy box, though they could never have guessed what it was either.

Hamilton whispered into Gertie's ear knowingly. Gertie's face opened with surprise.

Eeona knew, as women who can make others worship them always know, that in the box was something that would gain as much attention as she ever had. It was something as dangerous as she had ever been. Franky rested the box down in front of the priest, took out his pocketknife, and sliced it open.

It was a TV.

"I knew it!" said Ham, punching his fist into the air.

The priest, who himself had seen TV in the States, laughed and laughed. He didn't own a TV since moving to the island but how nice to have neighbors who did! He blessed the TV with more reverence than he'd blessed the house. Then Franky plugged it in and turned it on.

So television came to the Virgin Islands in the 1960s. An American named Joe West was selling the TVs for cheap and soon the entire island had them. Everyone could afford a set and the two stations West offered — a Spanish channel from Puerto Rico and an American station with a variety show and the news. It was the news that did it.

79.

The islands had been isolated for so long. The radio waves didn't fly in anything past Puerto Rico. The last major contact with America had been the Second World War, when the boys came back with their stories of segregation, and with sharp chips on their shoulders. Some privileged few, like Dr. Jacob McKenzie, had gone to black colleges in the States for their degrees and come back smoking cigarettes. But TV was the worst America yet, and everyone had one.

Anette was cooking saltfish in the kitchen and it was stinking up the whole house. "Ronalda, see that Me and Frank ready for lunch."

Anette continued cooking. Ronalda was the kind of child, for better or worse, who always obeyed. Anette added more of her husband's pepper sauce. He would have to make a few more bottles soon. Anette didn't know how to cook saltfish without it. Franky was at the lighthouse and she'd drive over later with the lunch. But as Anette was thinking this, she was suddenly aware that something was not right. It wasn't that her house was quiet. It was that every house in town was quiet. Not that there wasn't noise. There was screaming and water rushing and the sounds of a crowd. That, too, seemed to be coming from every house. She looked out of her kitchen window and into the living room of the neighbors. Mrs. Rockwell was sitting on her settee staring at the TV and chewing on an empty wooden spoon. Anette left her fish to burn and walked into her living room, where her children were also staring at the television.

There was a crime happening right now on the news. Men in uniform, official-looking men, were beating actual people with batons. Was there a fire? There were hoses blasting water. The hoses were blasting actual people around the street. Actual people were hiding behind trees, screaming, crying. Men in uniform grabbed at the people, detached them from the trees, from each other, from their purses and their hats.

Anette's children were watching this. Ronalda, who was almost grown, was not blinking. Instead, her mouth was opening and closing silently, like a fish's. Youme was sitting sideways as if she wasn't really watching at all. Little Frank was patting Me's hand, looking from her face to the TV.

Then the newscaster came on. "Downtown Birmingham, Alabama. Our men in uniform are attempting to restrain Negro protesters."

It wasn't until then that all of us anchored to our televisions realized that it had been white men in uniform against dark-skinned people. It hadn't been clear what those people had done wrong. This wasn't because we were feebleminded, it was because of the land we lived on. Because we were Frenchy and Danish and our white people hadn't seemed capable of this behavior. Sure, the Americans we'd met were rude. What with their gatherings where they never invited us. But this was something else. The word *Negro* had never meant much to us, since even the darker of us claimed a mixed lineage. But now we could see that even those who looked as mulatto as anyone were there being blasted away.

Anette, to be sure, needed the newscaster to verify what even she couldn't believe. Jacob had told her his New Orleans story. But did people really treat each other like this even when there wasn't a war going on? Look here, brown-skinned people were doctors and lawyers. Look, she was a brown-skinned woman herself and she was a proper married lady. A teacher of history at the Anglican school that even some of the American children went to. Her husband, it was true, was a black man, but he had built this entire fancy house with a balcony wrapping around it. He was a Coast Guardsman and he was the keeper of the lighthouse. And he had green eyes.

Anette shook her head. Thank God things in the Virgin Islands weren't like that. Those Continentals were crazy. Anette stepped around her children, turned off the TV, and announced that food was ready. Longtime ready.

Anette left to take her husband his over-cooked saltfish. She tried not to think much more about the news, but as she drove down the street, she could hear it blasting from the other houses. Negroes. Blacks. Whites. Freedom. When she left town and cruised up into the hills, she thought she was done with it. But when she reached Muhlenfeldt Point, a clutch of native Guardsmen were gathered outside the lighthouse. The men, in their casual uniform of khaki and dungarees, were in the uproar of a heated debate. It was clear that they, too, had seen the news. "Ask Mrs. Joseph," one of the men said, gesticulating to her. "Her people from there. Ask her about the Anegada man who fight for Virgin Islands freedom. Ask!" He thrust his hands out to her.

But no, she had not heard anything about Anegada. "Really, Mrs. Joseph? It ain so that your people from Anegada? You must know 'bout that fisherman who just the other day was giving lectures 'bout all of we needing rights. You see the TV? America ain giving us. Them Anegadians went and take it from their British owners. We think we free 'cause we belong to America. But is them Anegadians and BV Islanders that have a taste of free."

"I ain know my British side like that," Anette said. She had never even considered that side before. "I never even been Anegada." She couldn't quite see how the Virgin Islands, British or American, connected at all to what was happening on the news.

"Mrs. Joseph, the Anegada protest man is probably family to you. Is because of that man that the British Virgin Islanders own their beaches and the land and the sand and the mangrove and the everything. Look we over here in the USVI. We think we free. But the TV, just look at the TV, and you seeing that we is the United States V.I. and that mean we don't have nothing."

It wasn't true that the Anegada man protesting had happened just the other day. It was years ago. Some said it wasn't a protest at all, but a melancholy lobsterman with a chronic broken heart for a woman who had left him for a sea captain. But it was true that he was a kind of fisherman and it was true also that the man was family to Anette. He was a distant cousin and he was also the man who Antoinette Stemme had left behind. Anette was a history teacher, but she hadn't studied this history, despite the fact that it was only next door. There was no course where she could study Anegada history or Virgin Islands history at all. She taught American history and a general Caribbean history that focused mostly on the pirates of Jamaica. That is what there was for her to teach at the Anglican school.

Now Anette waited and listened to the men discuss the Belonger laws being pressed and passed in the British V.I. Though they all seemed to be on the same side, the men were quarrelous. Why we can't have law that say this place belong to we? Laws that protect we, help we belong here, help we keep the V.I. the V.I. Why we can't have first rights to buy land? Why we can't have first rights to set up a hotel? Just like the BV Islanders could leave, go back, and still belong, and nobody can't tell them different, we need that, too. You don't think, Franky? You don't, Fullmore? Mrs. Joseph, what you think?

"It's an interesting discussion," Anette said, but she couldn't say much more. She'd been an orphan since she could remember and nothing had ever belonged to her except herself and now her children — but even the children were a temporary ownership, for they would grow and belong to themselves. The only thing she belonged to was Franky and even that . . . well, she knew that could be undone.

When Franky finished his lunch, he decided to drive her back into town, taking the long way through Barracks Yard, which was a seedy area with calypso blaring. But Franky felt good taking his wife through there because he was there keeping her safe.

Back at the house, Ronalda had served her siblings. Youme had brought a book to the table and only nibbled her food. Frank was busy stuffing himself so that he would for sure throw up. Ronalda could not eat at all. When their mother and father walked in, the children seemed uneasy.

You see, Papa Franky was in the Coast Guard. Papa was a man in uniform. His dress blues, the ones with the sweet silk tie at the front, were hanging right now in the closet. The idea that people who guarded you could also be the people that you needed guarding from was nothing anyone should have to learn, but that is what the children learned that day. What the islands learned that day — the Coast Guardsmen included. The same thing that makes a man dive into the sea for your rescue can make him hold your head underwater.

Ronalda could not eat the tough saltfish. She could not be an example for the younger ones. She chewed and chewed, but the saltfish would not go down. Of course, she never ate saltfish again. Which was confirmed for Ronalda as the right thing to do when in college at Howard University, she learned the history of the salted codfish, brought from New England cheap to feed the Caribbean slaves. She would think of how Caribbean folks ignorantly sought out the slave food as a delicacy and thought nothing of eating it along with some dumplings and green banana. Ronalda would never think lightly of things again. She would let the world eat her from the inside out.

As Ronalda saw it, Papa Franky was a Coast Guardsman, but he was only Frank's real father. Youme's father wore a uniform, too. A white lab coat with a stethoscope around his neck. Youme said he even sometimes wore it at home, walking around his house, like it was his skin. One father was supposed to guard the people, the other was supposed to save them. But Ronalda's father wore the worst kind of uniform. One like the men on the news. He was in the Army. When Ronalda's real father came to visit, he would pat her on the hand like a stranger. He would drink a beer and laugh with Papa Franky. "That's my wife serving us drinks, Franky. I never signed those papers. I just loaning her out to you." As if he could just steal Mama away.

80.

Eeona didn't believe in living on loans, though she'd lived in this unbelief most of her life. But times were changing fast. Unlike the new islanders coming from all over the Caribbean, Eeona was an American citizen. By birth, we all were. This was all that was needed to qualify for the public housing designed by our very own Saul McKenzie. "Are you suggesting I live among the common public?" Eeona had said with disdain when Franky suggested she buy into the housing project.

"Eeona ain never leaving Savan and don't try and make sense of it." That was Anette, dismissing and misunderstanding. Because soon after the housing development was filled, the homeownership loans were offered. Eeona quick-fast left her government job and took her savings and her pension and left for the sister island of St. John. Within the year, Eeona's inn had risen out of the ground like a manifesto. She was gone. Well, just an hour away, but still. Now Eeona owned the land. She owned the inn. In that way, they belonged to her. She had made her own inheritance. Just so.

At three stories high, Eeona's inn was, and is, the tallest building on the side of St. John known as Coral Bay. For now it was attracting tourists from the Dominican Republic and Trinidad and even the mainland of America. Much later it would be listed in *Gay & Lesbian Outings* as a safe place for lovers of all kinds to room and board.

St. Johnians were of a different sort. Though they were Virgin Islanders, they were also from a tiny island where most people could still remember when the first white man arrived to live. In fact, the first white man was still alive and still living there. More than half of the island was now U.S. national park, which was supposed to keep out the big hotels, but this hadn't quite turned out the way St. Johnians thought it would. The hotels couldn't come, but neither could one go for a swim in the waterfall down by Reef Bay or sleep on the beach down by Caneel. Those places belonged to someone now. The United States Federal Government, to be exact. Which meant it didn't belong to we.

St. Johnians were understandably protective and private. But they liked living in homes where the trees eased over, the branches bursting into the doors like welcomed guests. They welcomed Eeona like she was a part of nature. They called her "Madame Bradshaw," because that was how

428

she introduced herself. Now she was exactly who she wanted to be. Who she told people she was. She had learned to do this from Kweku Prideux. On St. John she was the daughter of Owen Arthur Bradshaw, whose death and sunken ship were still major points of reference. But she had also taken the title of someone who might have been married to the captain. Neighbors quickly shortened Madame to Mada. Which sounded so much like Mother.

81.

Mada Eeona would only leave Coral Bay, where the ghosts of her own long-dead deeds were welcomed into her spinster bed at night, to return to St. Thomas and visit with the child that made her forget her other almost child. She always arrived unannounced, and if she stayed, she always slept in the same bed with Eve Youme.

In their one bed together she would tell Youme the real, but not true, stories of the Bradshaws. Things Eeona would never tell to anyone. She would not even tell them to Youme, really. She waited until the girl was asleep so that they went into her dreams: Antoinette's perfect sewing skills and Owen Arthur's perfect handsomeness. The tables made of St. Croix wood and the rocker made of mahogany. The fish caught right on the water that swept toward the house stairs. The beef brought to their yard, still alive as cow, from Tortola. The eight-legged mansion on the hill and the spider man who lived in it. Eve Youme would know the stories and not be sure quite how she knew them.

Ronalda, in the bed over, would lie still and strain her ears to capture bits and pieces that Eeona whispered into Youme's ear. There was never enough for Ronalda to put things together and know the stories. There was never enough for Ronalda. Ronalda, of course, would be the one who left for America. Just one body on the boat of us who left, because things had not been passed down to her, things had not been passed her way.

And then there was Anette. Standing just beyond the doorway like a spy. Listening to her sister's hushed fables. Villa by the Sea had always been forbidden to her, even in talk. And now Eeona was just spilling it. Anette was thinking she should stop her sister. Thinking maybe that her sister was a kind of danger to her family, there whispering stories about their kingly history. Anette and Franky were trying to instill a sense of equality, especially given the seeming lack of it in America. But Anette just stood trying to hear because she wanted to know. She stood there until Eeona's story voice was replaced by the steady breath of sleep.

Anette approved when Eeona told the children more fantastical stories out in the open. Anette had begun to keep the TV off more often, because now she didn't want any of the children watching the glass-and-flimsy wood box without her supervision.

Eve Youme had just become a teenager when Eeona told the story, out in the open, of the Duene. The children were all in their regular orbits: Eve Youme at Eeona's feet, Frank just beyond, and Ronalda running errands for her mother. Auntie Eeona had arrived, like she always did, without announcement. She would call at the door, "Inside," and then she'd be in. Sometimes she would bring a nice thing to eat. Sometimes she just brought the stories. Eeona sometimes told of the Cowfoot Woman and of Anancy, but not today.

"The Duene are the ones of us who protect the wild places. The women live in the ocean and the men on the land. Their feet are turned backward, so you cannot tell if they are coming or going. They are capable of slicing you to pieces with their thoughts alone."

Eve Youme concentrated hard on her breathing. She wanted it to match the rhythm of her aunt's words. Ronalda came in the door and stood by, listening. Now Auntie Eeona was speaking of a male Duene who had a smooth bald body. He'd fallen in love with a female Duene with winglike hair. "The Duene were allowed to mate, you understand," said Eeona, though the children didn't really understand, "but love had been forbidden to them. The secret Duene lovers loved with abandon. However, this love tethered them to the bay, for their worlds met there on the beach. They made children who could swim and walk and love, but had to keep their love a secret."

Anette, listening above her onion chopping, sat up straighter and arched her head. Eeona sounded winded, which was not like her. "Your grandmother," Eeona said to the children, "told me this story when I was a child."

But as Eeona said that, she felt and then she knew it was not true. She'd never heard that part of the story before. A bald boy Duene and a wing-haired girl Duene falling in love? It seemed Eeona had just made up the story. Just right there. Just like that. Now Eeona couldn't remember what her mother had actually told her. Instead, something was happening to her, something like a little storm brewing in her brain. She thought she'd escaped her episodes since claiming her land and building her villa-inn. But now Eeona reached behind her own neck and released her hair of its pins. She did not do this for the children. She did it to regain her strength, for something was not right with her. Not exactly right.

"Now," Auntie Eeona began again, "who protects the wild things?" She asked the room, even as she moved her head in such a way to feel her own hair waving along her back.

But the children did not answer, for a kind of spell of thinking had been cast over them, which is another thing stories can do. Youme leaned back onto her elbows, her face disappearing into a shadow. A rooster crowed at the moon from a neighboring yard. Out in the street a man called to a friend in greeting. Franky came in from keeping the lighthouse and greeted everyone, stopping to blink at his sister-in-law with her hair down like a deep well a man could jump into.

Anette came out into the parlor to greet her husband, but then went to her sister instead and gathered the elder woman's hair back into a bun. Eeona allowed this then looked at her sister without meeting eyes. "I shall go lie down," Eeona announced.

The three children had heard the story of the Duene lovers, but they interpreted it differently. And it does not matter, ultimately, what they heard or even what they knew. It is how they interpret the story that will make all the difference.

Ronalda didn't think protection of the wild things was needed. *People* needed protection. Just look at what was happening in the States. Ronalda, who was heading to college in just a few months, made up her mind to leave all this island foolishness behind.

To Frank, the Duene were martyrs to their love and to the wilderness. They were heroes. They were like Superman, like on TV.

To Eve Youme, the Duene were in conflict with what they were. But perhaps it was an honorable conflict. One that allowed for abandon. If so, then they were something like herself.

And this is all that is needed for each child to become what he or she will become. But first Ronalda left. Then Mary came. Then Eeona disappeared. Finally, the Joseph family would gather on a beach, as lovers do.

■ ■ ■ ■

Drown

■ ■ ■ ■

It may seem so simple to say that it is
sea. But it is the sea.

— DEREK WALCOTT

82.

Ronalda left for college in the States. There she found things to be much worse than she'd expected. When Ronalda arrived, the States was outright racist and outright sexist and outright everything that it could be, and Ronalda was an outsider. True, she'd always felt that way. But in the States feeling that way was righteous — not belonging was a way to belong. And American blacks seemed real to Ronalda. They were on TV. They were in the newspapers. They were in magazines and books and movies. And there they were. Real for all to see. The Virgin Islands barely existed at all.

83.

Then Mary came. Some hurricanes were numbered. Others were named. The latter had an identity, a persona. For years, the named storms were only women, which seemed fitting. They could be in love, they could be envious. Whether this hurricane was the Virgin or the Magdalene, no one knew until it was too late.

The islands had seen storms. The houses were built for them. But the radio made it sound very serious. Why was this happening? What had we done? The cousins over in Tortola, which the storm was set to ignore, snickered: Those American Virgin Islanders were getting their due punishment for their relentless excess. After all, the dubious spoils of tourism had been flooding the USVI for years.

Hurricanes, like all important things, happen by the generation. Youme and Frank thought they were a thing of Caribbean folklore, like pirates and mermaids, or of Caribbean myth, like Eeona's Duene and Anancy. But because they were mythic, Eve Youme had also known that they would return. She believed in all the stories.

As the radio directed, the family put up a map distributed by the government and drew a line from where the hurricane had started off the coast of Africa. They gridded in the latitude and longitude. This was a game that the community played collectively. We watched Mary grow, a mutant baby, as she traveled across the Atlantic.

438

Then Mary was there, knocking on the door. Everyone was nervous and a little excited. No school! Early off from work! All the bustling about. Mervyn Manatee announcing on the radio, "Get Ready! Get Ready! Hurricane Mary coming!"

Franky was a Coast Guardsman and so he was the type to prepare. He sent Anette out with Youme to buy batteries to keep things working, and nice things to eat in case the storm made anyone morose. Franky and his son heaved a thick sheet of wood and nailed it over the windows at the front of the house. He called over to St. John and made sure that someone would pass and check on Eeona's inn. After he'd secured their home, he went to check on the lighthouse. The Coast Guard had relieved him of lighthouse duty until after the storm, for it would be too dangerous. All the ships in the area had been alerted. When he returned, he ordered everyone to move all the valuables up onto the highest shelves.

But then what a sham it all seemed at the start. Mary arrived and she was just measly rain and a little blow.

Dr. Jacob McKenzie and his wife were friendly with some Continentals and had been invited to a hurricane party. He took his pretty wife to the party in the hills that were now called Peterborg. Once upon a time he'd ran up into these hills and plucked a fistful of flowers to rain over Anette's hair.

Now with his desirable wife and American friends, he looked over Magens Bay and saw the Atlantic Ocean grow very rough and then settle down a little. The Americans had been right about the storm. It was best to throw a bash and enjoy the time off from work. Jacob's wife clinked flutes of champagne with a homemaker whose husband was in development. In Jacob's mind the only disaster was that their Santo Domingan gardener might have to replant the roses.

Anette was a historian after all, and though she didn't really teach Virgin Islands history — because none of the schools thought it necessary — she still listened for the local stories. Anette had heard about the long-ago tidal wave that swam the waterfront and washed up at the Anglican church. She'd been told about the ancient earthquake that had knocked down the Peterson Building. She knew about the old cholera that had taken a son from every family, like a proper plague. She even knew about the sinking of *The Homecoming*. That was all history. Now at their house Franky was telling a story about the one time he saved someone from drowning. In all his honorable years with the Coast Guard, this was the only time he'd saved anyone.

Everyone said that Mary was an angry woman storm — either a jilted lover or a desperate mother. With a name like Mary, we should have known that she would be the worst ever. No one was prepared. How could we be? The hurricane had seemed a storm and then it had not. And then it was, this time for real. We'd underestimated her.

The sepia portrait of Owen Arthur and Antoinette was off the wall and packed up. The cruise ships had just turned away and headed for Jamaica. Ronalda's dorm was called and called but she was at a Student Nonviolent Coordinating Committee meeting and didn't get home until curfew, which was seven p.m. Phone curfew was nine. At eight forty-five she finally returned the calls and said, "But there's nothing on the news here about the V.I. at all. It's going to be okay."

Then Eeona called from St. John and said, "Listen clearly, Anette. It is not going to be okay."

"Then get over here, Eeona."

"There is no time. Anette, the entirety of Anegada is being evacuated. The atoll may go under."

"What does Anegada matter?"

"It matters."

Perhaps we have forgotten Anegada, but Eeona had not. What she knew to be true was indeed true. What would Anegada be like without its walk-through-mountains people? What would happen to the few trees? Eeona, strangely, found herself more concerned about that land than about her own inn.

"Eeona, just make sure you take care. Is anyone with you?"

"Our grandparents' graves are in Anegada. That is our history there."

"Oh, Eeona. A whole island can't be taken by the sea." As if no one had heard of Atlantis.

Youme and Frank were sleeping with the depth of teenagers. They didn't even notice when the electricity went out.

84.

The rain was fighting to come into the house. Then pieces of galvanized tin were knocking on the door. Then the wind sounded like a woman howling out her broken heart. The radio station stopped its mix of American soul and island quelbe.

Frantic men and women and children started calling in and screaming that their roofs were tearing off their houses. That their children had gone out into the rain that we'd thought before was just a little drizzle. Help! We live in Tutu. We live in the new housing development. We live still! Save us!

The call came over the radio that all emergency personnel were needed. All. Police and doctors and firemen and, of course, the Coast Guard. Report now. Immediately.

Jacob was still in the hills of Peterborg and the folks at the hurricane party were beginning to get the hint that this wasn't a lark after all. The host burst into the dining room and hollered, "They need the doctors!" Jacob rested his wineglass and took his wife by the elbow to their car. They lived in Wintberg, so though the drive home was treacherous, it was short. As soon as he arrived at their house, he began to pack his medical bag. Seeing his hands trembling, his wife turned to him and said that he mustn't go. He might die. She didn't say what her real fear was: that he might find himself dying in Anette Bradshaw's arms.

Besides, Jacob was afraid of the storm. Hadn't he done enough? Fought for his country? Withstood racism? Lost his soul and lost the love of his life?

He resisted his little wife for a little while but was grateful for her big fears. When the radio called again for doctors, he turned it off. Then Jacob and his wife lay in their bed and listened to Mary screeching. And then, so he could feel like a man, he rolled onto his wife, hoping they would make a boy child.

When the call for emergency personnel came over the radio in the Joseph house, Franky looked over at Anette. "I have to go," he said. Franky was in the Coast Guard, but he'd never dealt with a major emergency. When he'd joined the Guard, there hadn't even been formal training for that sort of thing. Most of his work was keeping the lighthouse, for goodness' sake. And despite that, he'd never even seen a ship wrecked. He wasn't a surfman or even a coxswain. He'd once saved a drowning person on Coki beach when he was off duty. That was it.

But he was going anyway.

Anette watched him dress. Her husband was a seaman, in a way, but the sea seemed as though it had swiveled upside down. Was coming down on top of them. They would soon drown. Anette watched how Franky put on the heavy boots and jacket that he wore when they'd all gone to the States just a month ago to see Ronalda settled. They hadn't thought much of America then, it had rained in the morning and the afternoon and into the night without even one break for sun. Who had ever heard of such a thing, raining all day? But now it was indeed raining all day. And Anette was glad that at least one of her children was away from here. But Papa Franky wished that Ronalda was here. She was the child he most trusted to be in charge.

"I'm going to be fine, Annie. Is a man I is, yes. *You* be safe. *You* don't give me cause to worry."

Anette nodded and felt the tears behind her cheekbones. Her husband had never called her by a nickname before. It seemed too intimate for the time, as though there were something grave between them that must be given a sweetness.

The rain was knocking hard against the back windows. In the living room Youme and Frank had gathered, unable to sleep anymore. It was one in the morning. Franky didn't like the idea of everyone there saying good-bye to him. He wasn't going to his death. He was going to save lives. He would be heroic. He would return.

Anette didn't like it either. Her firstborn child was safe but so far away. Her sister safe and closer, but not close enough. Anette wanted most to be with the ones she loved and who loved her.

Frank hugged his father. Then Franky went to Youme and tapped her head gently as though she were a small child. Finally, he kissed Anette on the mouth, which was not something the children had ever seen them do before. Franky opened the heavy front door with a fierce push. The rain came sleeting into the living room. They all gasped and stepped back. Franky stepped forward. He slammed the door behind him. Anette looked at the closed door, still seeing her husband's back and the storm before him.

Then Anette wished Franky would die.

Just a simple shocking wish. Just a desire that Franky never return. Wouldn't everything be fine if Franky would drown? A hero's death wouldn't be so bad. Then wouldn't Anette have done her duty? Stayed by him these years because he'd stayed by her? And then she would be free. And then Jacob McKenzie would arrive instead. Well. How strange to discover that Jacob was still among her best beloveds — and not even among, but above. Anette hadn't wished anyone dead in so many years and here she was wishing it on her husband.

Youme looked at her mother standing at the door and knew exactly what Anette was thinking. She found her mother's thoughts peculiar, for hadn't she and Papa Franky just kissed? Why would Mommy think such an awful thing? That she could read her mother's mind did not strike Youme as peculiar at all. It seemed to her something that anyone could do. Something family should do for each other.

It struck Anette differently. She felt the intrusion in her thoughts as though someone had broken a window in the house. There was a crack and then a moment of fear. Then she turned slowly to look at Youme watching her. They stared at each other until Youme's eyes watered and she felt she was doing something wrong. *Me?* Anette said in her head, and Eve Youme heard her pet name echo in her own ears. Then the child did what she would only do for her mother. She turned away.

Besides, Anette didn't really want Franky gone. He was a good father to all the children. A good husband to her. She would be devastated. She wouldn't know how to be a sensible woman. How would she cook saltfish without his pepper sauce? She barely knew how to cook at all. No, no, she didn't want Franky dead. It was just that she wanted Jacob. That was all. She just wanted Jacob to come. To take her and hold her and be her husband like he had promised. She hadn't felt such foolishness in years. And it was foolishness. She was just scared. She was just feeling abandoned because of the storm.

Anette focused on the door again. She stood staring at the door for a long time. Conjuring the image of Franky's back at the threshold. Keeping him alive. Overriding her earlier heedless thoughts. Jacob is married, she now reminded herself. Not free to claim her even if she were free to be claimed. Who says he would be a good husband to her anyway? Who says they would still be in love now if she'd been his attainable wife? *Leave that alone,* she told herself. *Franky is your man. Franky is who you need.*

She walked to her daughter and pulled Youme's face to hers. "You be careful in other people's heads," she said out loud. Then she released Youme and went to the kitchen to gather a supply of candles and matches. The candles that had been lit were already melting.

At five a.m. Anette picked up the phone

to call the lighthouse and check on Franky. She found her phone line dead. Frank Jr. turned the transistor radio on high. Mervyn Manatee was declaring that everyone should open their windows. This would prevent implosion. This would prevent the pressure inside the house from rising and blowing the roof off. Frank opened the windows in the back of the house. The photo albums were sopping wet. They all felt their ears popping as they watched the roof.

This was now a wild-woman storm.

Frank kept checking on the latches and locks as his father had instructed. Even though he was the youngest, no one told him to settle down. He seemed professional and military-like. Anette observed him with a mother's secret pride: that mix of attraction and protection.

The radio, on the other hand, was spewing horror. The hurricane had slowed down its movement. Had stopped altogether and settled over the Virgin Islands, dumping destruction like something premeditated and biblical. Police were radioing in. This home is gone. That roof is gone. Then the directives of meek advice: Hide in the bathtub. Pull a mattress over your head.

Afterward, they would hear the stories of entire families who stuffed themselves into bathtubs with mattresses over them as their houses fell in. Help us! Help is coming. The Coast Guard is coming. Police are coming. Where is the doctor? Where are you? What is your address? Hello? Hello?

The eye of the storm finally passed over. The eye. A perfect metaphor for so many things. There was quiet all over the land. A peace. A light rain. Sunshine coming from the unboarded back windows of the house. The radio warned not to leave your home because no one could know how long this calm would last before Mary started up again.

Frank, who was baby-faced but almost a teenager, wrapped blankets around his body. Anette pretended she didn't notice he was heading out. She didn't think she could stop her son, so she didn't want to try and fail. There was something determined in him. In this chaos he seemed to suddenly be a man. Later, when he was fighting for the revo in Grenada, she would tell this story of him going out into the eye. But now Frank pulled the door that Franky had left through and had not yet returned through, and went out into the stillness.

Youme and Anette laid sheets in bundles under all the doors and at the base of the windows to keep out the water that was seeping in. They didn't put any at the front door until Frank returned. When he did, a half hour later, he looked scared and brave. "I looked into the eye of the storm," he said. "Now the bumsie coming."

The front of Mary had been bad, but her tail, like any Caribbean backside, was worse.

85.

Hurricane Mary lasted for two days. Mary was pissed. Then she eased away, sassy and slow and satisfied.

In the afternoon after the hurricane, Youme and Anette waded through the neighborhood. The ancient mahogany tree had been uprooted and thrown down in the gutter. There was an actual Maytag refrigerator lying on its side in the middle of the road. Most curious of all was the neighbor's at the bottom of the step street. In the middle of the debris there was a bed still standing — its headboard and all. Its sheet was still tucked tightly, its pillows were still plump at the head, while the entire rest of the house lay in splinters. If the bed had been a cross or a saint's statue, everyone would have said it was God's miracle. Instead, Anette looked at it for a long while.

But Franky's house had, oddly and completely, survived. When retrieved, the ancient picture of Antoinette and Owen Arthur seemed fresher than it had before.

Life was changed on the island. It was not something new. It was not something opening or awakening. It was an expired life — even though only three people had died between all three islands, and they had been tourists. We had to climb over people's lives to get down the street. There were kitchen tables in the road. There were dressers crashed up against cars.

And worst of all, those living in the valley could see the bare hills. There were houses there. So many houses! When had these been built? Who lived in them? And why were they so huge?

These weren't homes that connected to the step streets. These were way up. The townspeople just hadn't been paying attention. Yes, they owned their land and their houses and yet, it was something to realize you were looked down upon. To realize, all of a sudden, that they didn't live in the prime location anymore.

Twenty-four hours after he walked out of the door, Papa Franky came home a hero but not dead. He picked up his wife and spun her around and told her, "Thank God for life."

Later the islands' mantra was belted over the radio, sung in the breadlines and phone lines and taped onto packages of mosquito spray sent from Ronalda in the States — "Thank God for life!" It was declared that neighbors had saved each other. It was declared that the island community was returning to its old-time roots. We'd come together. We loved each other again. We knew each other. Like we had before. "Thank God for life!" The island was months without electricity. Months with the toilet-flushing water drawn from the cistern underneath the house. Months without tourists or the revenue they'd brought in.

But secretly, no one wanted normalcy to return. Secretly, everyone felt this push backward in time was a savior, worth the sacrifice. We were looking to the past for the first time in a long time. And we were seeing something. Thank God for this life.

Anette pressed everyone's clothes by heating the iron over a small fire in the yard, protecting the clothes from charring by laying them under a tablecloth. Instead of watching the TV, the family told each other the stories Eeona had taught them. In young Frank's version Anancy always shared everything equally with everyone at the end. In our usual version Anancy is tricky —

453

would never share a thing, not a piece of fruit, not the deed to his big house on a hill. Papa Franky told about the seductress with a hoof foot, who, so the myth went, could sing like a piano. They had forgotten exactly how the myths went, but they told them anyway. Was the La Diablesse the same thing as a soucouyant? Was Anancy the spider man a Duene himself? Eve Youme listened and could feel the tingle in her toes. Her feet sometimes ached, as though they were trying to run away from her.

Eventually FEMA stopped handing out bread and started passing out boxes of military rations — the food they'd given to the Army boys. Jacob, in his house that was now without rain gutters and without a balcony, poured water over his meat to inflate it and remembered eating similar trash many years before when he'd been bold and righteous. That was when he'd known he wasn't second to any man. Now Jacob and his lovely wife ate at their large candle-lit dining table. They had a pricey generator that ran their necessities — the water pump, the lights on his wife's vanity.

Youme, in Frank and Anette's house, ate her inflatable fruit cocktail and felt as though she were eating a sugared sponge. Me, who since she was twelve had always slept in shoes and socks and a panty even if she was naked otherwise, would save the fruit cocktail and bury it in the backyard while everyone slept and the whole island was dark. She thought maybe it might grow into something. If it didn't, then it wasn't fit for her to eat. She didn't like the way it made her feel numb.

As if out of respect for a woman as forceful as she, Hurricane Mary did no damage to Eeona's inn on St. John. But the storm did flatten an octagon house on the forehead of a hill in Freedom City, St. Croix. The spider there crawled out and quickly webbed a new home, as Anancies do.

Franky had offered to take a Guard boat over to check on Eeona, but Anette didn't, really didn't, like the idea of her husband going anywhere that wasn't work-required without her. Not after she'd almost killed him with her mind. And with her fear of boats, she didn't want to go with him either. Besides, there had been no reports of injuries or fatalities from that love island of St. John. The ferries were mainly taking dry goods and medicines back and forth so it was more than a month before the family had word of Eeona — and then it wasn't word, it was Eeona herself arriving at their door.

By the time Hurricane Mary reached the continental United States, she was much weakened by her travels. But the hurricane still brought the hurriedly built wood-and-sheetrock Continental houses down like so many dominoes. Mary killed many people in the U.S. But hurricanes do start off the coast of Africa, following a kind of triangle trade of their own.

■ ■ ■ ■

THE BOMB

■ ■ ■ ■

I rather walk and drink rum whole night,
Before me go ride on LaBega Carousel.
You no hear what LaBega say?
"The people no worth more than
fifteen cent a day."
— "LABEGA CAROUSEL"

86.

Somewhere on the scalp of a mountain on an island with a city called Freedom, a house with eight sides lay flat as though squashed by a foot.

And somewhere deep in Frenchtown a boutique hotel with a restaurant on the ground floor revved up its generator and started cleaning oldwife and snapper that had been caught in the harbor. After the hurricane, many Americans on the island had been cradled off to civilization on the mainland by the federal government. It didn't matter that the native islanders were also Americans — no islanders were welcomed on those flights out. But there were a few Continentals who did not leave — like Gertie's new husband. Those were the ones who would later bristle when called outsiders and respond that they had survived Hurricane Mary and had stuck it out and that fact alone surely made them belong. Right

459

now they were not sure about their decision to stay and right now they were eager to pay well for a decent meal and electricity and someone serving. The generator at Hibiscus Hotel and Restaurant roared like a monster and the fish sizzled in the pots.

In Garden Street the Josephs had not heard of airplanes taking the real Americans back to the real nation. Only those meant to hear had heard. Kerosene lamps and battery-powered lamps worked together to cast geometric webs of light into the corners of the house. The radio said it would take many months for the islands to be reconnected to light and running water.

Anette would wait for electricity as had Antoinette and Owen Arthur. She would wait for it like it was magic.

Eeona arrived a month or so after Hurricane Mary had come and gone. When asked about her inn, Eeona said it was fine, just fine. When asked how she'd managed through the storm and how she'd managed on her own this month and half afterward, she'd answered the same.

"I am here now because it is actually quite nice to be in St. Thomas without electricity. This is how it was when I was a child."

Everyone sat in the living room waiting for it to darken so that there was nothing left to do but sleep. Everyone was exhausted by seven, the whole island in bed by eight. Sitting in the dusk and kerosene lamplight, Eeona thought of her father coming home and telling her about the little girl whose hair rose to the sky when she held the magic balls of electricity. Anette remembered when the janitor had turned the lights off at that dance, remembered standing there in the dark, the sand-colored man beside her. And then she was remembering the dark night she lay with both her child and her lover. Then she looked out of the window and tried to conjure the appropriate shame.

Youme, for whom electricity had not been a luxury but something accepted as natural — no different than the sun, really — lifted the rug in the middle of the living room and opened the cistern door. A generation ago they would have each gone to the public standpipe, and it was true that some were doing that now. But the Joseph cistern was huge and held enough water to spare them the standpipe queue. Eeona and Anette watched Me draw out her water. The girl was wearing white socks and black patent-leather shoes. Not only was Me wearing out a pair of clean socks, an excess now that everything was hand-washed, she was also dirtying the floor with her outside shoes.

But Anette had allowed each child their little post-hurricane comfort. Young Frank was allowed to climb the one high coconut tree in the neighborhood that had survived the storm, pull down a nut, chop off its tip, and swig all the water and nyam all the jelly. Tree climbing was dangerous. But so was leaning over a hole in the floor and pulling up a heavy bucket of water.

The family watched Me and held their breaths. But so what if Youme fell in? Couldn't everyone in this family swim? Yes. But what if the cistern wasn't quite full, and then falling in meant busting your head on the concrete bottom? Or what if there were scorpions or sea snakes at the base that would slither into your hair or, and this was what Auntie Eeona was thinking, slither into your vagina? Then what? Anette had repeatedly asked Youme to leave this chore to Papa Franky, but the girl insisted on this independence.

Eve Youme fished her bucket carefully down until it was weighted with water. She heaved it up. As she stood, her brother came forth and closed the cover gently. He swathed it with the fake Persian rug. Even he felt that she should take off the stupid socks and shoes. Who wore such things in this heat, anyway?

The cistern door in the middle of the parlor floor seemed inconveniently placed now that they drew water from the cistern for every bath, for every teeth brushing, for every water everything. Before, there hadn't been much thought given to the cistern. But their water pump had dislodged and blown away, and how could it pump without electricity anyway? The pump was the family's one casualty. It now lay intact in a yard two miles away, where another family would sell it and then they would sell it and then they would sell it and then when, weeks later, Franky went to Market Square to buy a used pump he would pay full price for the same one that had been his own.

But for now Eeona was watching Eve Youme haul the bucket of water carefully to the bathroom. She had a kind of crooked gate, sexy almost in its openness. Her legs, thin but shapely, were like the limbs of trees that live at the neck of the ocean. No one criticized how much water Youme had drawn. It was evening, but it was really too much water to simply wash one's feet, face, and teeth — which was all, really, one needed to do in the evening. They each took proper bucket baths in the late morning with water that had been left out in the sun to warm.

But perhaps the water was to pour down the back of the commode, to flush away heavy waste and the smell of it. Though rainwater was scarce, ironic after all the flooding from the storm, no one minded a full bucket if it was for flushing. The bathroom now smelled of humanity. Though Anette scrubbed it down every two days, it was perfumed with stale water and fresh backside. At its best, it smelled of eggs boiling. But it had been many weeks with this smell and they had all become accustomed to it. Even just-reach Eeona, because the smell was familiar. They had used chamber pots when she was a girl.

Eeona, who had a sense for her own, followed the girl to the bathroom. Eeona quietly twisted open the door and was not surprised to find Eve Youme squatting completely naked in the tub. The girl was dipping the washcloth into the bucket of water. With her aunt entering, Eve Youme stood in the expected surprise and the more curious defiance. Her own glinting pubis shone like a shield.

Eeona was not surprised to see Youme's special brightness. Nor was Eeona pleased. She herself had not fully figured out what the curse or the blessing might mean. "Me, you are silver at your private part," Auntie

Eeona said.

Eve Youme, who was sure she had locked the bathroom door, nodded. Eeona, thinking the child wanted privacy, stepped in and closed the door behind her. This is not what Youme wanted. The girl wanted to be alone, to polish herself into a glory. But she was also hiding something else. She stood there guarding something that could not be seen.

This boldness was so different than the hesitation Eeona had felt when her own mother discovered the silver, and yet this made it easier. "My dear, how long have you been like this?" Perhaps the words were not right. But what could be the right words for something so strange and wonderful?

Eve Youme was not sure which thing her aunt was referring to, but she answered anyway, since the answer would be the same. "Since I was twelve."

"Does your mother know?"

"No one knows."

"Not even your doctor?"

For by now it was hard to hide a young woman's body. Doctors could strip them naked. Doctors could even spread their legs and go tunneling inside. This was considered good health care.

"The only doctor I know is Doctor McKenzie — my father."

The two women, one not a woman as yet, faced each other as though a mirror. There was a still intention in their forms. Eeona stepped forward. Eve Youme's back was already to the shower wall.

"Me, you are my special one. You may tell me anything. Has there been anything inappropriate in your relationship with that McKenzie?"

No, Youme wanted to say. It's not that at all. But instead she unfocused her eyes and stared at the door, willing her mother to come and save her. But then she remembered that this was all still a secret from her mother as well.

A lesser woman than Eeona would have not noticed the dulling in the child's eyes. Eeona noticed. "I understand. I understand, Me," she said. But Eeona did not understand.

The young woman, the child, started to cry. Her body did not reveal this. Only her face was suddenly flushing maroon and then a tear seemed muddy as it slipped down her face.

"Shall I come to you, or would you rather step out? It is okay." But it was not okay.

Eve Youme stepped out of the tub. She looked down to direct Eeona's gaze.

Eeona could not help the intake of breath

as she saw that where the toes should be, there was instead the smooth stump of a heel rounding out the front of Youme's left foot. Then the girl rotated her leg and there were her five toes, elegant but pushing out frighteningly from where her heel should have been.

"My child, a clubbed foot is something that can be fixed. It is nothing so . . ." But the lady who was always resourceful suddenly had no words as her niece lifted the backward foot and the foot began to turn with a slow creaking of bones, turning more, and as it turned slowly and slow, it also shifted a grinding shifting so that the location of the ankle shifted backward as the toes turned forward. Auntie Eeona exhaled her breath. "Eve Youme, are you causing that movement?"

"I feel it," said the child. "But I can't make it. It just does."

"We must fix you," said the aunt.

The only doctor they knew was the child's father.

87.

When Dr. Jacob McKenzie arrived, Papa Franky left to drink at the corner. The rum shop was open all day and served warm single barrel for cheap because that was all there was. Franky went and ordered little glass after little glass. He left because he didn't want to be there in his own house, competing and losing.

Jacob came in smooth. Stepped out of his clean car that ran on actual unleaded gasoline, unheard of since the hurricane. He leather-shoed up the steps, still strewn with debris, because there was just so much of it that it would take months to clean up. Jacob wore his white coat, but he looked straight ahead so the neighbors didn't have a chance to ask him questions.

Jacob and Anette did not say a word to each other, not for the entire time he was there in the house that Franky had built for her. For the first time she was ashamed of her house, and not because of the little hurricane wear. It was a nice house, but the living room was so small and the kitchen was so crowded and the only thing pretty on the walls were the misty pictures of the parents she had never even really known.

But really, Anette was ashamed of herself. Her hair had been thinning since she had begun to dye it so many years before, and now it was no match for the luminous bush of Jacob's younger wife who had been sighted a few times over the years at the

American-style supermarket. Anette had heated the iron over the gentle wick of the lamp and pressed the old white dress into newness. Did Jacob notice? It was the dress she'd worn years ago in the airport when he left her. She could not help herself. It was there in the closet when she opened it. Well, let us be honest. It was at the back of the closet. But it was a dress she had worn the last time she was Jacob's. It was the dress she should have married him in. She still fit the dress. She fit into it too damn well.

But Jacob, in his own white, walked past her, even though he felt the static in the air as their breathing rolled toward each other. He went to the room where Eve Youme sat on the bed beside her aunt. *That harpy,* Jacob thought, seeing Eeona holding the child's hand. Anette followed but did not say a word. Young Frank watched his mother's figure as she closed the door behind her in his face. Frank felt an instant and sticking hate for the doctor. Not because Dr. McKenzie was the only man let into the room that he could not go into. Not because Dr. McKenzie was Me's rich father. But because this man had caused his mother to stuff herself into that graying dress that was too tight for her. It shamed the son.

Oh, but if Anette had worn the red and

yellow dress. Jacob had never actually seen her in that dress, though he had seen the movie poster. But Anette had not worn that dress because after the porn film she'd ripped the dress to shreds and thrown it out. Right now parts of it were disintegrating in the dump out in the Bovoni countryside. Other parts were being eaten by fish in the Caribbean Sea. But if Anette had worn that dress or any red dress, Jacob might have not made it back to his lovely wife that afternoon. He might have not been able to steady his firstborn's backward foot on his knee and watch it twist and grind forward, as though this was a regular abnormality. He would not have been able to examine her silver through the child's embarrassed weeping.

They had to half draw the curtains and twist the louvers open to let in daytime light since there was no electricity. Nothing about the exam felt intimate and precious, as it should have. Eve Youme was weeping because no man had ever looked at her there, despite Eeona's concerns, and now here was her father and her aunt and her tightly dressed mother, all in the room with the windows gaping, while the girl rolled down her sock and then rolled down her panties.

Jacob did not kiss his daughter on the

forehead as he should have. Eve was suddenly a patient and a thing to be cured, not loved, for he was small-souled and did not realize that these things were the same thing. He nodded tensely at his child-patient, snapped off his gloves, and slid out of his white coat. But instead of going to Anette, he went to Eeona. "I'm not this sort of doctor." He had no diagnosis, no cure.

But Eeona's hushed response filled the room like steam. "This is your mistake on the child's body. I told you." She turned to Anette and then to Esau. "I told the both of you."

Eeona walked out of the room, out of the house, and right out of that island. Then Eeona disappeared.

88.

Communication was more vital than light and hot water, so the phone lines were already being replaced all over the island. Jacob was thankful for this, because he did not want to visit his mother in person to discuss what needed discussing.

When Jacob told Rebekah, she breathed "Ahhh" into the phone, as though he called her often to discuss his patients — which he never did. He was afraid his mother would say what it seemed Eeona had said — that the child was a sin. But why a sin? Perhaps he would be bold with his mother and demand to know what was meant, really. Many men on the island had outside children. This was a minor sin, if a sin at all.

But Rebekah said "Ahhh" again and again into the phone. She kept ahhing and Jacob wondered if she was in a trance or if she was ill herself. She kept at it until he grew weary and was about to interrupt, but then she finally gave words. "I say you have two options."

Jacob took out his lean leather notebook, which had a pen looped in at the side. He slid the pen out and touched the fine smooth tip to the heavy white page. He kept the phone wedged between his ear and shoulder. "I'm listening, Mama," he said.

"First, you might consider throwing the child into the cistern of Villa by the Sea and closing the trapdoor and not opening it until two full moons have passed, but it might be hard to get around the new bakra owners. More of a rigamarole, but just as effective, would be stoning the child with seashells until she slept and then holding her head down in a bucket of sea-wet sand."

Slowly, Jacob put down his fancy pen and hung up the phone. He poured himself a full glass of rum and took two horsey painkillers. Then he called Anette, desperate for her to answer, for he always hung up if anyone else came on the line.

"We must talk in person," he said, when he heard Anette's voice. "Just you and I. We must figure this out together." He was trying, trying. Trying, perhaps, to earn his soul back. He knew of a public place they could go to speak privately. Hibiscus Hotel and Restaurant was deep in Frenchtown and its restaurant was open and serving fish to monied natives and the Americans who still remained since the storm. The generator would be growling loudly, but it was a nice place, a fancy place. He didn't know that it had gone, in his mother's time, by another name: Villa by the Sea. The exact place his mother had suggested he drown his daughter.

"This might not be a good time. My sister . . ." Anette started to say.

"I know, but this must be addressed promptly." But he didn't know. He didn't know that Eeona had gone back to her inn and now would not take calls even from Eve Youme. He didn't know that Anette still had never been anywhere in Frenchtown. The French village was foreign to Anette.

Still, Jacob Esau and his Nettie agreed to

meet there two days later. It was a public place after all. They could have met on a beach but that, though public, would have been an infidelity. Beaches are romantic places, family places. They are not places people of the opposite sex meet unless they are romantic or they are family. So the two would meet two days later at the restaurant of Hibiscus Hotel.

But even just two days hold a whole forty-eight hours. And so much could happen in those hours.

89.

In those hours the Joseph family would gather on a beach, as lovers do. Because Franky couldn't take Dr. McKenzie coming into his home, edging him out with his walk alone. Franky needed to do something. The island was still a sea of blue tarpaulins covering every roof. That is how the idea of a beach lime came to him. Franky, the man of heart and timing and patience, knew of a beach. He knew how much his wife loved a beach. How she loved to swim. How Anette sometimes went to the beach alone early in the morning just to walk, she told him. Franky had gone to this faraway beach when he was a child and he'd taken more than one woman there before he was married. He'd passed it many times on Guard patrol. So the evening after Dr. McKenzie left, Franky announced his idea. The candles were flickering, but instead of telling stories they began considering their beach outing. They would go tomorrow morning.

Frank, the young man of the family, loved the idea of exploring more of the island. The hurricane had revealed to him that other people, those in the hills, had a piece of the island he had never known. Anette liked the idea of discovering a new beach. A place to create new histories with the man she was spending her life with. Just the thought of a beach still held the memory of Jacob's body and her body. Anette wanted to be a good woman; she would like the Jacob thoughts to be undone. More undone than she had thought they were.

Eve Youme wasn't sure she should go. If her brother and stepfather were at the beach, she would not be able to take off her shoes and swim. They didn't know about her strange foot or her silver. Only Auntie Eeona, Mommy, and now her father.

The husband and wife woke before the sun and had lemongrass tea in the dawning light of the kitchen. They leaned into each other as they had when he owned a green

Cadillac and nothing else at all. Anette packed some mangoes. Some salted crackers in a tin. Franky packed towels and a big sheet for them to lie on. They worked together to wake Frank, who slept like a stone. Eve Youme was already sitting up in bed, fully clothed in her sneakers and jeans when Anette creaked open the girl's door.

They gathered into the Datsun and smiled at one another. For the first time since Ronalda had left for college they felt like a full family. Two parents and two children. The two parents looked at each other and then back at their children. The son, the only child they had created together from scratch, looked back at his mother and smiled. He seemed to be looking at her with a kind of wonder. Later, during the protesting, young Frank would remember this very moment as the dusk of his own innocence. He would also remember this day as the day the BOMB really began.

Franky had two cans of rough gasoline sealed in his trunk. Prepared, as always. It was more than enough to get them to the beach and back. Once they were out of town and away from the worst of the debris, the Joseph family drove with the windows down and the wind whipping about them and the sun rising at their backs. Anette thought

476

briefly about being in another car, without doors, with Gertie and the man Gert would eventually marry, him careening through where a windshield should have been and the man Anette would love her whole life holding on to her. And then thought again that that was so long ago. *Let it go,* she said to herself. *Let it go. The only thing you have with Jacob is a daughter.* Anette stuck her hand out of the window and let the wind keep it aloft. Eve Youme did the same, but on the opposite back window. Anyone watching might have said that their arms were wings and that the two were keeping the car flying through the hills.

Finally, Franky came to a turn down a steep rocky road. "This is it," he said with a breath. But as he said it, the car smacked right into a link chain that was the length of the cleared road. The chain came sliding up onto the hood, scratching it, and right up onto the windshield before Franky had a chance to brake. "A chain," Anette said, as though anyone needed clarification.

"Maybe this is the wrong place," said little Frank, who was actually bigger and taller than his father.

"This is the place. I know it like myself, yes." Franky's father had worked for a branch of the Hodge family, who owned the beach. One of the daughters, a woman he'd fancied, had married a McKenzie. He shook his head now at the unfortunate memory. The beach had been Franky's father's in a way. He'd kept it clean. And so it had been Franky's in a way, too. Though, of course, it always belonged to someone else. But that someone had never put up a chain.

Anette and Franky thought of their own separate specialness on beaches and then thought, desperately and together, that they must get to this beach. It was more than a family outing. It was essential to the family. They needed their own common beach history. But it was Franky who said, "Maybe the road is being fixed, yes? From the storm. That's why they have a chain? We can walk from here. Though is a long walk."

"Let we start then," said Anette.

They left the car at the side of the road and began their journey down into the crotch of the mountain. Frank held the mangoes and the crackers and the bag with the bottles of water. Franky held the bag with their sheet and towels. Eve Youme held nothing but herself, though she still walked as though she had a weight on her head, and maybe a pebble in her shoe. Hers had become a haunting swinging movement and girls at school sneered that it was a sluttish walk. Boys in the street hissed loving curses — "Pssst! You breaking my heart just walking by, sweetness."

Anette, walking downhill beside her daughter, noted the weight of something to come.

It was a long walk down with nothing but trees around and above them, and the tree roots below them to climb over. But it was beautiful. It was an adventure. Frank began to sing a calypso and everyone joined in. They saw no one the whole way down — more than a mile. When the hill began to flatten, they could smell the beach. They could see brightness ahead. Now there were sea grape trees around them. Soft ocean trees. Then there was something hard under Frank's foot that made him trip. "Motherscunt!" he said out loud. It was the first time he had ever cursed in front of his parents. He looked down and there was a gravestone.

It was not only one grave. There, scattered in the sandy grass, were three others. "Oh, these been here since I young, yes," said Franky, as though he were introducing them. One was marked 1830–1885. One was 1846–1907. The names were washed out. They were close to the sea, after all.

"Nah, Pop. This one that tripped me is marked 1952–1952. Is a baby."

Anette looked where her son was pointing. "A baby boy. He was called Owen. Like my father." She read on. "Poor thing. No last name even."

"Don't worry," Franky assured them. "It old. It been here since dog days."

"But this one isn't old, Pops. This Owen would be the same age as Youme."

"Look." Franky redirected. "Here's the beach, yes."

And yes, there it was. Franky took his wife's hand, Frank took his sister's, and they led each other out to a quiet stretch of white sand. The waves were smooth and calm. The beach had been combed of debris. There was not another soul in sight.

As the family walked out, Eve Youme noted that there were whole shells in the sand. Things to pick up later and take as souvenirs, for they each had the feeling as though they were tourists on vacation — complete with that small niggling as if they weren't sure they belonged. They laid out their sheet, and the parents put their shoes at the corners to hold it down from the wind. The wind was whipping the sand and making it sting their skin just a little. Franky stripped down to his bathing trunks and strolled toward the perfect water. Anette sat beside her daughter.

"You doing fine, Me?"

"Yes, Mommy."

"You can swim over there, past the rocks," Anette whispered. "I could come with you."

"No, I just want the sun today."

"We'll fix you up soon. Your McKenzie father want to meet with me privately to discuss —"

"Yes, Ma, yes."

Anette nodded, understanding that Youme didn't want to think on these things. Anette went to join her husband in the chill of the morning sea. "Is just woman problems," Anette said, shrugging it off to Franky. Her eyes slid away to the horizon where the sun was still rising.

Franky did not ask for the details. Not because he was cautious about woman problems, but because he knew that the other father, that McKenzie, was the doctor. Instead, he looked out to the horizon with his wife. "This is ours," Franky said. And that was the only possible response.

So Anette focused on Franky. She thought only of Franky telling her that she was a star that time they had done that nasty movie. She smiled to think of it now, for it had been a while ago and the pain of it was mostly gone. Though her just thinking on that, of all things, should have been a sign

481

that things were not right in the least.

While his parents swam and his sister read a dense American paperback, Frank looked around at the bay. It was one small strip of beach. He looked up and saw the hills where they had come from. And then he saw the house on the hill. And then he saw the white woman, her hands flailing into the air as if trying to signal them. Frank waved back but the white woman kept waving, as though she was directing a plane. Now that he was watching her, he could hear her faint shouting. He decided to ignore her. Something in him knew that he did not want to hear what she had to say.

Instead, Frank took off his shirt and sped into the water. He ran fast and hard, trying to make enough noise that no one would hear the woman. He splashed cold water everywhere and his father swam to him and they had a race — their arms flinging and legs kicking. The son won. His father panted, but his face shone with pride. His mother clapped and cheered. And when Frank again looked up at the balcony, it was bare.

It was when they were sitting down to suck their mangoes that another man came slowly along the beach. He hadn't come from the road but from some other private path. He was the first person they had seen in almost two hours. Franky stood to receive him. The beach was small, but it seemed to take the man a long time to get to them. He was dressed in cut-off shorts and a white shirt that plumped out with the wind. The man stopped some dozen feet before Franky. "You with the Hodge family?" he asked.

"No, we're Josephs. My wife's a Bradshaw."

The man nodded as though he knew this already. "That woman own the land." He pointed to the house Frank had seen. The woman was there on her balcony again, looking out at them like a queen, her house held together, despite the storm. "She don't let no one come out here except the Hodges, because they have some of those graves there. Some of the graves are the Hodges' but the land is hers."

"But we're not on the land. We on the beach, yes. Besides, I've always come here. I know the Hodges."

"The Hodges don't own it no more. It all hers. Even the beach."

Anette stood beside her husband. "And who she?"

"She an American. I just work for she. I just do the yard and other dirty work." He shook his head. "All you didn't see the chain? That mean *don't come in.* It don't mean *you are welcome.*"

The man glanced over at Eve Youme, there in her sneakers and jeans and bikini top. His eyes trolled her body and then back up to her face. She was very pretty. Very. Though no one had much noticed before.

Franky looked at the man hard. He couldn't place the man's accent exactly, but he knew the man was from another Caribbean island, one far down the chain. "You're not even a Virgin Islander," Franky began in his big Guardsman voice. "You come from whatever gyaso island you come from, yes, and now you helping the white people run us off our beach?" Franky's body tensed all over.

The man stepped back and put his hands out as though to calm Franky. "The white woman watching, eh. You lay a hand on me and she going call the police."

"Now, you watch me good," said Franky. "I am a military man. The police do what I say."

"Well, then . . . well, then . . ." The man looked again at Eve Youme, who stared right back at him. He looked back up at the house there in the armpit of the mountain. *What a rigamarole,* he thought. *Why the hell did I leave Antigua? To come here and be in the middle of these blasted Americans?*

Frank, who was almost a man, came out from the water like a previous life form. He stood silent beside his father, goose bumps bursting over his body. Then Eve Youme, who was almost a woman, spoke. "Let's go, Papa. We've been here for a while." But Franky had something to prove. Proving something was the reason they were here to begin with. He looked at his son standing beside him. He wanted to kill for his son. Wanted to be brave for his son. Braver than any doctor who could walk into his house. But then he looked at his daughter — he never thought of her as his stepdaughter — and nodded at her. He began to pick up their things. He did not look at his wife.

The walk back up the hill was long. The Antiguan man told them that it was the same on his island. Beaches that you were always allowed to go to were now bought up and the white people were now disallowing you. "Listen. Is how it is now. Just cool it." He was trying to be reasonable, but really he was thinking that these Virgin Islanders must think they're better than everyone else in the Caribbean. No other islanders could just lie up on a private beach. But he didn't say any of this as he escorted them back. For the most part they were all silent.

Both Franky and Anette thought of the porn film they'd been in but said nothing to each other. They didn't yet see the connections.

90.

ANETTE

Look what happen. We just had a hurricane and I just discover that my daughter have a curse and we just get run off a beach. And maybe them three things was all the same thing. I decide I going to make myself a witch and fix my daughter since I can't fix the other things. I don't tell Eeona. She done run back to St. John and she inn, and she ain even taking calls. She ain have to know that is Frenchtown I going to meet up with Jacob. It ain a funny-funny thing, anyhow. Is just doctor and parent business. So I tell myself.

Because gas scarce since the hurricane, I walking. But I still get lost in Frenchtown, because I ain never spend even a minute in this place since I walk out of it thirty-odd years ago. Never gone there to buy fish. Never visit a friend there. Never even study a ball game they does have in Frenchtown

486

field. But now I walking back in it, like backward into childhood. I opening my eye big to see if I recognize anything, to see if I get a memory feeling. But that house we used to live in was big. Like a abby or a mansion, and it was down a long dark dirt road. And nothing I seeing here seem like that. So maybe Eeona tell the truth. That it get break down or burn down or whatever. I there in Frenchtown and I wondering if I belong. But I going feel like a jackass asking somebody where my old house is. So instead, I ask a Frenchy fellow for the restaurant. The man suck he teeth but give me precise directions. "If you looking work," he say. "They hiring, but not island people like you and me."

The restaurant was called Hibiscus Hotel. I, for one, had never heard of it. A stupid name, you hear, but that's what Americans always doing. Naming things after island things that don't make no sense. Who want a hotel that sound like it fill with hibiscus? That's the kind of flower close up and dead when nighttime come. That's what you want people thinking when they fall asleep? But Hibiscus Hotel wasn't make for we. Is one of those places only the white people used to go before the storm. But afterward it come a place that any well-off people go because the left-behind white people alone couldn't fill it.

Watch me. I wear a red dress. Not the one I wear to that foolish moviemaking so long ago. That one done gone. But red always make me feel strong around Jacob. Is true that I want Jacob to desire me, but is really that I want to be toughlike and in control. Is a witch thing.

When I make a turn by the bay, I see the restaurant that must have been a great house back in slavery days. I start walking up the road and is only then I realize that by walking I feeling stupidee in this too-nice dress, walking on this crumbly old road. But then I hold my back stiff, like I does see my sister do, and that alone make me feel pride enough to keep walking, even when I see the tall sandman there at the steps waiting for me like is our house and I coming home to he.

He reach he hand to help and we walk up the steps. Jacob press against me as he guide me by the elbow. He always been like that. A stray hair in my face, he never fail to finger it away. My bra strap showing? He never let that opportunity pass. Franky would just say, "Anette, your blouse." Leave the adjustment to me. Ronnie? He would have look away, too polite to stake any claim.

Now, when we there at the table, I ain realize at first that Jacob for real pulling out the chair for me. This is something Franky ain never do for me because Franky ain been trained that way. But it feel correct and I feel like I could be Jacob wife, maybe. And then a more funny feeling, I feel like I *is* Jacob wife. As though it been me and he all this time.

It have a single red rose standing at attention in a glass vial. It have three menus and two of them was there in front of him. He open the skinny one as though this wasn't meant to be a meeting. An important meeting about our daughter. Beneath the table he reach his hand to my knee. "The wine selection here is the best on the island," he say.

So. He know the place. And he know the wine. And this place have actual wine, despite people on island who don't have actual water. Imagine.

"You grew up around here," he say, as though he feeling my critical feeling.

"Not so," I say. "Just born here. We had a house. A villa. Gone, I guess."

When the waiter come, Jacob order a wine with a fancy French name. Then he ask the waiter if he know about any villas around here.

"No, sir. I'm from Connecticut." Then the waiter bow like he is a squire and we in a castle. Then he run 'way.

Jacob now slide the rose out from the vase. He reach across the earth of the table and fasten it behind my ear. "A flower for you," he say. And I wondering if it had been a good idea to wear a red dress after all. It working too good, but I ain sure if it making me strong or weak. "I wanted to bring flowers the other night when I came for Eve," he say. "But I just didn't think it would have been correct, given . . ." But he didn't say given what. He left it there.

I try to think now on Franky, because that's the correct thing to do. I think on how I tell Franky I going to the doctor to talk about Youme, and Franky look at me with his face reflecting this red dress and he just nod and say, "Don't stay long." And I nod back. And then when I turn to leave I feel he eyes in my back like teeth.

But here I is. Not in no doctor office. The office mash up in the hurricane, so Jacob say. But I ain tell Franky that. Besides doctor office have bed and thing for patients to lie down on and door that close for privacy. If Franky knew the whole story, he would rather we here then there any which way. Now I watch Jacob sniff he glass of wine and slosh it around on he tongue before allowing the waiter to pour a little into my glass. Jacob raise his glass to chink mine, but instead of saying "Toast," like I know is the proper thing to do when you raise a wineglass, he say, "To family." And we stare at each other like our eyes have a cord tight between them.

And now I remember Jacob lowering his mouth and nose to me, like I was a flower. But before I could keep going on that thinking — "Good evening!" Is a white man with his face flush like he just come from doing hard work. "I'm the owner of Hibiscus. I hear you've been asking about our history." Which we hadn't. And now I wonder if we do something wrong by harassing the know-nothing waiter. "This wonderful property was indeed a villa. We've gotten so many questions about that since the storm. No one ever asked before. Yes, well. When we bought this, it was called Villa Antoinette. Yes! A fine lady in her time. So I'm told. Before that, it was called Villa by the Sea. We almost returned to that name. But the locals, you know, the Frenchies, they said that would bring a jumbie to haunt us! I don't believe in those things. But I do respect local customs. We've even retained some of the original staff. The groundskeeper is authentic. To be honest with you, my friends, the groundskeeper came with the place. He refused to leave. A kind of loyalty . . ."

All this the man was saying as me and Jacob there staring at him. "Excuse me," I say, before he could keep on going. The man pause, but I don't say nothing else. So he just look at we and then say, "Well, yes. I'll send the server right over."

When he skip away, I stay quiet.

Jacob look at me and smile, something gentle and worried. "Villa Antoinette," he say like it just a pretty name. "Like Villa Anette. Imagine if this was your villa . . ." But just then the waiter come again. He ain have no pad and paper in his hand. But he start pouring the specials over us in detailed detail. Garnish with basil, he say. Over a bed of baby spinach, he say. My mind can't focus. I don't want to look up from this table. I don't want to look around. I mean, really, Jesus? Give me a break. My daughter ill. There been a hurricane. Is only so much a woman want to suffer at once.

I take a few sips of wine, a thing I don't drink ever, because I know. I know what going on. This my house. This the house I born in. This the place I supposed to belong. It ain burn down. It ain get wash away.

"What are you having, Nettie?" Jacob ask me.

And nobody don't call me that. Nobody but him. Is a kind of voodoo he putting on me and I don't have strength to do magic back on him. I feel tears behind my face. I would really be good with just some conch in butter sauce, but that ain on the menu. Jacob order some fancy fish pan crust or pot crust or something. So I say, "Same," because I can't say more. But before the food could come, I excuse myself to go to the bathroom.

I don't have to pee or replenish my lipstick. I just want a minute to arrange myself into a proper married lady, because it feeling like I forgetting who wife I really is and what life this really is. Because I feeling scared and sad and sexy and a whole heap of *s* word and it all mix up like I was meant to belong to this place and maybe if that was so, maybe I would never have almost get send to a orphanage and end up nearly dead and then marry Ronnie and Jacob mother would not have protest about he marrying a poor divorcée from Savan and Jacob would have married me and maybe I would know how to spit my wine back in a glass and make a proper toast and then nobody would ever tell me to get off a beach anywhere on this island and then maybe my life would have been something simple and sweet. I now walking away from Jacob and I have a feeling like my chest steady filling with dirt.

I walk to the restrooms up a towering staircase. I trying not to look at anything else. I can't deal with anything else. At the top there a room of couches and a rocking chair in the corner, a huge orchid display on the center table that I can't miss even though I ain looking. The room open and welcoming like a mouth. And there is nothing at all familiar about it. Good. I settle a little. Maybe the white man wrong. What he know about we island? Nothing. The restrooms down two corridors, like tonsils. And there is a huge balcony spreading out toward the sea behind some lock-up glass doors with MEMBERS AND GUESTS ONLY write in large fanciness. It have tables and chairs out there, made of wrought iron. I need to sit down.

I go to one of the couches and that's when I see the old yellow-gray-hair man with thick yellow-brown skin. He hanging on his old broom like he just taking a rest from sweeping. He a Frenchtown man, but he seem familiar and I 'fraid of that familiarity. I feeling a bad way again, like I getting swallow up. But he just gesticulate with his chin toward the picture on the wall of a young man hauling in a fishing boat. "That's me," he say as if I had ask he something. Is then I see that the whole wall have pictures.

"Hmmm," is all I say. Go away, is what I thinking. Then a woman's heels click-click behind us, the sound disappearing down the restroom hallway like going down a hard throat.

"That's me, just coming in at dawn, fishing since four a.m." He point the handle end of his broom from the picture to the real ocean beyond the Members and Guests balcony. "Same place you in now." He look at me square like is only now he realize he ain been talking to he self. "I'm Hippolyte Lammartine. You call me Mr. Lyte. That there is Madame Antoinette Stemme Bradshaw." He point to a picture. "You don't know that story?"

Of course I motherscunting know. She the milky picture Eeona insist I hang up in my living room. Though the picture I have ain look like the picture on this here wall. The one in me and Franky house is of young and lovely Antoinette, sitting with her back straight in a long skirt beside our father. He handsome as can be. But the picture I seeing here is of a woman a little older. Standing next to she is a girl so beautiful that even I know she must be a soucouyant. In this Antoinette lap is a baby, sitting like a little ugly dollie. Rounding the baby's face is a bonnet with brocade so elaborate it want to be a sunflower. The ugly baby look back at me from the picture like it can't believe what it seeing.

"I'm a history teacher," I say, clear like I teaching even now. "I know all the stories." But I feeling the baby staring at my face. Now I get the feeling like when you hot and you drink cold water. You feel the thing spread in you.

"People lived where you standing," said Mr. Lyte.

"I know that already," I say. But what I really want to say is "Shut your ass." I have other things going on just now. I can't do this. Christ, who send me to Frenchtown? I avoid this place all my life. Is Jacob fault. Is this thing with me and Jacob. It ain right.

"I ain talking about the tourist or the hotel owners." Mr. Lyte cinch his face into a crease. His eyes narrow. "I talking 'bout the people who this place belong to long ago."

"It ain my business," I say. Though I know I lying.

But the old Frenchy man breathe heavy and sit down in the old-old rocking chair. Is then I wonder if I know him. If he know me? From when I was little? The rocking chair have intricate swirls that mimic lace. Is the kind of rocker I could tell ain need a cushion to be comfortable. He let it rock. He begin to tell his tale. I can't walk away just then. Even if I want to. But you know the truth. I ain want to. Despite my fraidy-fraidy self, I want to know. This is my history and is a historian I is, after all.

He point to the too-pretty girl in the picture. "He Own Her. That's the elder daughter. He Own Her because the father hold the girl first. And the father leave the mother right there after she give birth and take the girl romping all about before she even get her first milk. He clean she when she pass her first stool. No father in the world ever do that before, so of course the girl going have a problem, of course she going have something different about she. You get my meaning? He ask too much of the girl. He Own Her turn out witchy."

Mr. Lyte rest his broom to the wood floor like putting a beloved to bed. When I catch myself, I realize I want to lie down, too. "He Own Her, hey?" I pluck a piece of petal and rub it between my fingers. It become smooth and oily. And it come to me like my own words make it so: He Own Her. Eeona.

497

Mr. Lyte just keep flowing. "They say she still alive and she still amazing beautiful. She still have hair like the ocean. Papa and daughter would sneak to he ship at night. Swim naked in the ocean." Lyte point to a picture of the sea. "So the girl grow up. And she a witch already. Even she red baby sister is something. The baby learn how to swim before it could even eat proper food. I was there. I know for certain."

I put my hand to my hair. I been painting it black since before Ronalda born. And swim? But Jacob teach me how to swim. But then Mr. Lyte say something that make me forget myself.

"You see where the Inner Wheel does have brunch meetings now." He point to the balcony with his lips. "The Papa and eldest child used to go there and make glowing love like angels, though this ain holy at all." He sucked his teeth. "If your daughter lovely, you should know it, so you can fend off bad man, but you ain supposed to be the bad man —"

"Wait, wait, wait, wait," I say because I can't say more. "Wait a frigging minute."

"— but Bradshaw fighting that feeling and so decide to get a side thing."

"I ain want to hear this foolishness at all."

"But you must. Because Captain Bradshaw and he side woman make a boy child that look like a handful of sand. He name Jacob Esau. He passing for McKenzie." Mr. Lyte nod gravely like he know he telling me something that is the worse, really the worserest, thing he could.

Now see me. A fist of orchid petals bleeding in my hands. I raise back my hand and swing at the man to slice open he lip and shut he scunt up. He old but he sway away and then hold my hands with a gentle grip. "But wait. I just catch who you is. Anette Bradshaw, I know you from small."

Lyte release my wrists and I stay there like I roped in. Captain Bradshaw is my father. Like this story hook me. Same Bradshaw is Jacob Esau father. And I know is just now I going to get haul into where I can't breathe. Jacob Esau is Jacob.

But Mr. Lyte give me a calm look, like he reassuring me. "Sorry, child. But that's the story. We who from here need to know, even if it ain nice."

I stand. Finally, I move. I breathing heavy-heavy, like I fighting for the air. That's how it feel inside. I open my hand and let the petals fall silently to the ground, the mess of their guts sticking to my palms. My life just get ruin. Everything I love just get make a sin. Something coming like a wave and is to drown me this time.

91.

ANETTE

When I leave that Hibiscus Hotel I ain even stop to alert the sandman. I run out like I on fire. In school they used to say you could chant the Twenty-third Psalm when you was afraid. But what about when the fear-thing is a life-love with a sand-colored man sitting downstairs waiting for you to come eat fancy food? But what about when the fear-thing is inside you? So all I doing when I stumbling out of Frenchtown is saying what I remember of that psalm again and again. "Our ocean runs over. Though I walk through the valley and the waters, I fear nothing. You comfort me. You prepare me. Only beauty shall follow me." I running and hugging myself, my own arms like they trying to carry me away.

Just so praying I find myself all the long way home to the house that Franky build.

When I reach, I jump to the phone like it a child crying. I call my sister. The phone working even though we still don't have electricity. I want to ask my sister about what I just hear. I want Eeona to tell me what is true. I want to ask what to do with Eve Youme, because I know Eeona know something more than she letting on. Is she first tell me Jacob was Esau. I want to ask what to do with myself. I know Eeona ain want to talk, I called umpteen times already, but I going to force a conversation tonight.

I get Eeona housekeeper on the phone.

"Mada left, miss."

"What you mean mother left?"

"She gone."

"What you mean 'gone'?"

"I mean that Mada Eeona ain here at all."

"When mother coming back?"

"I don't know, miss. She ain pack. And usually it does take she days to pack even if she just going by you in St. Thomas."

"Well, how you know she gone, then? Call out. She must be there. I can't take this stupidness now. Tell she is a emergency."

"Well, she leave a note. I have it here. It saying she ain coming back soon. Actually, miss, I hate to tell you over the phone, but it saying she ain coming back for a long time."

"It say that?"

"Not exactly, miss. It say, 'I am more wild than Mama.' That's what it say."

"What kind of stupidness? It ain she they

501

does call mother? Who mama she talking about?"

"I ain know, miss. But things been unusual with Mada Eeona lately. Things been very unusual. She been telling everybody, even the paying guests, that some stories come back to haunt she. She get real funny. Funny like in the head. Episodes, she calling it."

When the phone ring that night, my son jump up like the phone is fire bell. "Good evening," he say. I can tell from the way he say it again and again that the person on the other end ain answering. "Auntie Eeona?" he say, hopeful because I already give the news that Eeona gone and ain say where. But I know it ain Eeona. I look at my daughter whose stare is busting through my forehead. She know it ain Eeona. My daughter and me we both know is her father, Jacob. Calling to see where I gone. To Jacob it probably come like I vanish out the restaurant. Leave the rose he slip behind my ear on the floor by the restrooms. But I ain go to the phone even though I know he won't speak unless he hear my voice.

I sit there hearing my son say "Good evening, good evening" and feeling Me's questions roaming round my head, and watching her unbelievable beauty come soaking into she face. And a feeling is coming over me. I watching my daughter. And I feel the sand beneath my feet. Franky walk in the door and we give each other the sliding look we been slipping on since we get kick off that beach on our very own island. Now I smelling the sea. And it ain that I drowning or that I in a net. I swimming like how Jacob teach me. And I know what I must do to make everything right. I need something big-big to belong to. Something bigger than husband or boyfriend or sister, even.

I have to haul my backside back to Frenchtown.

92.

The radio station was in Frenchtown. By car it was easy to find because all the paved roads in the village led to it. When Anette went on the microphone, she was introduced as Mrs. Coast Guard Lighthouse Keeper Franklyn Joseph and Senior Schoolteacher of History at the Anglican Parochial School, but you may call she Anette. Mervyn Manatee, the radio man, told her to speak clearly. Then she said what she had to say to all of the Virgin Islands, both the USVI and the BVI, and whichever other island could catch the reception waves: "We have had a storm. Our land and our sea have suffered, but now we must claim ourselves for ourselves. Is time that we claim where we belong." Then she paused to reveal her dramatic meaning. "Our beaches must be free." And the calls start flooding in to the station.

The BOMB began.

There were letters in the *Daily News.* People talked about it on the street: The beaches belonged to the natives. But what is a native? No, no. The beaches were for the tourists who were only just now returning since the storm. Beach violence would increase if beaches were opened to the local public. But the beaches were for everyone. They are our community parks. Our zoos. Our arboretums. Our places to marry and make love. But the beaches would be filthy with all the people. The bodies oozing sunscreen, the wrappers left behind. Was there nothing good left in the world for us, for them, for me?

The hurricane had revealed so many beaches. Ones that were hidden by bush and tree were now washed and revealed. The homes that had shielded them were blown away or flattened or gutted by wind and rain. Who in town had heard of the sea bath called Stumpy? Who alive had ever been to Botany Bay?

It went unnamed at the time, but let us call it something, for things without names do not really exist. In the history it will be called the Beach Occupation Movement and Bacchanal. In America the Weathermen and the Black Panthers were blowing up themselves and each other. In Vietnam a Vietnamese soldier who was on one side aimed a gun at a Vietnamese man from the other side. The soldier waited for the camera and then shot his quivering countryman in the head.

John F. Kennedy died. Che Guevara died. Martin Luther King, Jr., died.

And in the Virgin Islands we had the BOMB. We were marching on the sand and doing wade-ins and soak-ins and — for those who could — swim-ins. Running to the beaches in the middle of the night, past the guards and the dogs. By day, we pretended to be Afro-American tourists. We wore broad bright hats and cover-ups over our bathing suits. Sandals to walk in the sand. Gleaming sunglasses. But then we would reveal ourselves by turning on a radio and blasting some Pick-up Men or quelbe and then screaming, "We is the Virgin Islands!" as we stripped off our costumes

505

and ran to the water. We would stay in the water, dancing up and singing loud until the police come. We were being hauled off to jail. One person even got stung half to death by a smack of jellyfish. That's when the newspaper started sending reporters and cameramen.

Ronalda, who in America wrote slogans for SNCC, could not think of a good one for this thing getting on at home. It was the first time that she had come up short in her sloganeering. Over the phone she tried out ones to her mother hesitatingly: "Don't leech the beach" and "Take our shore? No more!" But Ronalda was not satisfied with these. Oh, this feeling again: that she was not good enough for home, that home needed a perfection she could not provide. It was why she had left in the first place.

But young Frank became heavily involved. His first swim-in was at night, and the island was still drenched in hurricane darkness, for only the government buildings had electricity. The people brought flashlights and started up a singing. Frank waited for the chorus on the calypso and then ran in so fast he actually made it past wading and was able to swim nine full strokes in the dark water before the authorities reeled him out. Usually the protesters were hauled away before they even got waist-deep, so Frank's full swim was heroic. Anette cheered on her boy from the shallows. That was her son. Hers and Franky's.

After that, Anette and her son led regular training sessions right in their living room. First, how to get your entire body into the water so that at least you were carried out soaking. Second, how to look like you'd been drowning, which was good for the cameras. She spoke while Frank demonstrated the headfirst dive, the full-body dunk, the flail, and then the dancing, so that the water sprayed everywhere.

But if the beaches were our place, our belonger place, then it seemed a real ridiculousness that most of us couldn't even swim. Like we wanted the beach, but we hadn't really yet appreciated the thing. Like a man who begs his woman to marry, but then steps out as soon as the wedding night is over. So we got serious-serious. We rented two rooms at the hotel owned by a local family where there was a private pool for every suite. Anette took the women, her son took the men. "Hold my waist. Kick, kick. Make a big splash." Learning to swim in the pool was unnatural, hard. The activists shared the room fees for weeks. But when these amateurs first tried in the ocean, the salt raised them up. They swam. Easy as eels.

This thing Anette was doing was the biggest thing she had ever done. Her firstborn had run off to the Continent, her second child had some unworldly illness, her sister was missing, and she herself wrongly loved the most wrong man. But, for a little while, the BOMB was larger than all those loves.

Slowly and quietly, the hotels received their electricity. No more growling generators through the night. Charging full price again. Then the airport, which had been operating on half energy, went full lights. The planes started carrying as many visitors as they did emergency supplies. The islands were more, well, obviously Caribbean now. What with people back to buying their provisions in the market every morning. This authenticity, which was really poverty, was pulling in the tourists once again. Then the wealthier parts of the island started getting electricity back. Then the retail establishments went alight. Then the BOMB really began, because now the tourists were on the beaches and we all saw how they didn't need passes, permissions, or protests.

We started bringing coolers of rum and Coke. It was a bacchanal. But it was also serious business.

Big Franky was as impressed as he was

worried about his son's activism. Suppose the boy was thrown in jail? Since Franky was in the Coast Guard, he couldn't actively protest. He worried that he would be sent to pick up the protesters one day. Even Anette worried, despite her position as mother of the movement. What if Frank actually drowned?

She was also anxious because she wanted to call Jacob. But she never talked to him now. That was through. That was over.

Oh, but it wasn't. Because they had a child between them. It could never be over. And when young Frank convinced that child to stop fretting over her foot and join the movement, things really began to move.

93.

The big protest was planned over on Water Island. It was the very beach that long ago Anette and Franky had danced on for that nasty movie. People hired or rented fishing boats and dinghies, and motored over or rowed over on their own. There was no restriction for boats in the water. The natives had to fish. So we all gathered, filling the channel between the big island of St. Thomas and the smaller Water Island. Honeymoon Beach had the perfect name.

Because on that day something sweet did occur. Then a month later, a moon, it was over.

The goal this time was to get to the shore. To get on the beach, either by diving over and swimming or by riding your dinghy right up to the sand. From the beach, we looked like part of the entertainment the tourists had paid for. Yes, the Virgin Islands was worth the money. The natives came with music! Markie, of Pick-up Men fame, was still alive and he brought his handmade ukelele and sang out loud like a bugle to war.

Anette, the one who had begun it all, did not attend this protest, despite the perfect symmetry of its backhand slap. There were two things that kept her away. The first was her sticking fear of boats. Without her husband, there wouldn't be anyone there to stay by her side and ring his arm around her. The second was that word had been coming from St. John about Eeona. About people seeing her. Anette needed to stay by the phone. So she stayed in her house, but kept the radio on for news from Water Island.

The morning of the big protest Franky kissed Anette on the mouth, like he'd done during the hurricane. He was wearing his official white uniform, which he never wore and which meant that he was heading somewhere on Coast Guard business. They didn't speak about it. Perhaps the children, as they do, might save them both.

We Virgin Islanders wore cut-off pants and straw hats. We carried banners and battery-operated cassette players. It was easily mistaken for a Carnival until one read the banners that had Ronalda's slogans on them. To the tourists, it slowly began to feel like an invasion.

Unlike the scattered and spontaneous swim-ins before, this was the best-planned and most major event of the movement. The history maker. It wasn't planned as a swim-in even. It was a lime-in. We were coming from the water this time. The plan was to get to shore and party there like we belonged. Youme was there, though she was wearing the strange new style of bell-bottom jeans and the old-style sneakers. As the boats got closer to the shore, Youme shouted with the best of them. From the boats they could see the tourists, pink like seashells and scared. They could also see the hotel security guards who had been hired by the Gull Reef Club. The security guards, who were all Caribbean people, we people, were waiting in uniforms of American dark blue.

Security lined up along the water's edge with six feet between them, as they had been trained and told. But as the boats came closer and the chanting became very clear, some of the security guards, overcome with love for the islands, stripped off their uniforms and swam out to join the protesters. They clambered into the boats, where they stood out in their white briefs and black shiny shoes.

But that is when the real police revealed themselves. Those men, better trained and holding jobs that earned them health care, stayed in uniform and filled the spaces where the hotel security guards were quickly evacuating.

When the boats started singing toward the shore and the people who could swim started jumping overboard and making toward the sand, the police put their batons up, but they did so only halfheartedly. They were amused and proud, even as they grabbed people by the shoulders and corralled them into one gathering, out of the tourists' way. "V.I. people crazy!" the officers shouted. After all, these people were their cousins or their aunts and uncles or, in some cases, their sisters and brothers, wives and husbands. "All you so crazy!" The police said it singing, like crazy was the best thing to be.

But that was not all.

The Coast Guard was federal and so they appeared, as colonizers do, in big ships. As soon as the little protester rowboats and motorboats had left the waterfront for their five-minute voyage to Water Island, the Coast Guard boats were dispatched. It took the Guard just about ten more minutes to arrive. Their vessels were now out in the water, facing the crowd of protesters who were held on the sand, bearing down on the little boats where the people who hadn't jumped, because they weren't yet confident in their swimming, now threw down anchors or cut off motors and tried not to look afraid. The white Coast Guard commander got on a bullhorn and told those on the beach they would be uncorralled and told the ones in the boats that they would not be sunk, and told them all that they would not be arrested — but only if they agreed to go home.

"We already home!" the people on the boats and the sand replied in unison as if it had been planned.

The tourists on the beach were frozen in their fright. They seemed like huge sand sculptures. Like Lot's wife, tropical style. They stared at the protest signs stuck in the sand and did not know that they were the leeches. A revolution? Oh, no! The natives were rebelling. But for what? Look how beautiful it was here. Who could not be happy here in this paradise? Who would revolt here?

With the Coast Guard there now, the tourists moved slowly, hoping that if they gathered their towels and sunscreen bit by bit that no one would notice them.

And no one noticed them at all. Because something else was happening not bit by bit. A girl who had slipped out of the protesting crowd was rushing toward the water. She was doing a swim-in, even though a lime-in is what they had planned. But still, this girl was right. To be able to go back and forth from water to land as you pleased, that was the thing. The back and forth was the beach. The girl was fully clothed, with strange pants ringing at her feet, but her hair was swimming behind her like an impossible school of barracuda. Though she was running to the water, it seemed as though she were running in every direction. She kicked off her sneakers just before streaming into the sea.

Her beauty was so disturbing, so unusual, and so unfair that even the protesters lowered their voices. Even the police now

514

policing the water slacked their arms and
saw her slip through them like a fish. And
then she was lifting her T-shirt off and flinging it to the surf and charging the ocean
like a reverse Athena. Sprouting inwardly
back to her creator. So many, many metaphors.

Eve Youme had not meant to expose
herself. Perhaps she was coming into her
gift. Perhaps she was out of her mind, having her own episode. We old wives can't say
for sure. Because when the T-shirt was raked
off, so went the bathing suit top that had
been underneath, and Jesus Lord, what pil-
lowy wonders her breasts were. As Eve
Youme dived under, every single person on
the beach was filled with an ancient urge.
They all flooded after her.

For a full minute everyone, tourists and
natives and locals and Coast Guardsmen
and even the ones who just before swore
they couldn't swim, now splashed like they
were children. Like it was a pure bacchanal.
Like it was Carnival Sunday and we were
all one at the last lap. Everyone swimming.
A miracle.

Finally, the Coast Guardsmen, finding
themselves unexpectedly steeping with the
others, regained their composure and swam
after the protesters, dragging them splash-

ing out of the water. Eve Youme resurfaced far out by a buoy. A young hero Guardsman stroked out to her; she waited until he was close and then began thrashing and screaming like a banshee.

In handcuffs on the shore, young Frank was dripping. He saw his sister being reeled out of the water and was glad he had convinced her to come. "Me!" he shouted at her, so she would know she was supported. "Me!" her brother said, until she found his face and locked on his eyes for assurance. Then a thought came over Frank in a singular way that it had not when he had simply joined the others in the dash toward her and the sea: His sister was stunning. Frank had seen breasts before; his popularity at school had afforded him the privilege. But his sister, Lord Jesus. Frank allowed the police officer to turn his face away.

When Eve Youme was being hauled out of the water by the Guardsman, she looked like something of the sea. The young Guardsman had not taken off his own shirt to cover her, as he should have. Oh, she was something beautiful and magical that belonged to another world or maybe to this very world in all its magic. The Guardsman, though he was supposed to be protecting the tourists from her, held on to Youme as though she were his woman, his sunburned hand gripping her high on the waist, right below the breasts. Everyone watched as her body was revealed. Everyone waited for the fish tail. Her legs appeared but her jeans, wet and heavy, flared at the bottom like fins. She did not hold her arms over her breasts to hide them. The photographer from the *Daily News* remembered his vocation and put the camera to his face. With all that blinding beauty, no one had bothered to study her feet, shielded as they were in the newfangled pants. But wasn't it strange how afterward her footprints seemed to be sending her in opposite directions? Backward, forward. But then again, there were many footprints, who is to say for sure which were hers.

The young Guardsman continued to hold Youme tight. "I'm sorry, it's just my job. I'm not from around here, but I'm on your side, Me. That's your name, right? Please forgive me, Me. It's just my job." He sank this into her neck like a lover's whisper.

A group of older Guardsmen who had stayed behind in their officious whites and watched through binoculars, now dinghied to the shore. One of them ran forward, his shoes slipping in the sand. He unbuttoned his shirt. He stood before Eve Youme and the brave blond Guardsman. "Seaman, get your hands off my daughter." Youme allowed Papa Franky to slip her hands into his gleaming shirt. After a moment, Franky also took off his shoes and pushed her feet into them. She allowed his stumbling fingers to tie the laces and button her in. And forever after, he never allowed himself to consider what he had seen.

"Let Me go!" someone shouted. And then the others began to shout, "Let Me go! Let me go!" And there was no difference.

Keeper Joseph — Papa Franky — released her, now clothed and shod, to the people. And she slip-walked, the shoes too big, to the crowd of protesters who were corralled in a big bunch in a corner of Honeymoon Beach. They cheered for her and made way, like a school of fish, simply opening and closing as one body to accept their own. She was more than a hero now. She was a thing to drown for.

"What's your full name?" shouted the reporter. But no one was hearing. And so in the paper her name was recorded as her brother had declared it. And that is how everyone would remember: Me save the protest. Me worth fighting for. Me is a beauty.

The people were corralled on the sand, but the officials hadn't taken Markie's ukelele and he was inventing songs on the spot. "St. Thomas people crazy 'bout the bay! We going dance and sing until Me have the way!"

It wasn't clear to the Coast Guard or to the Gull Reef Club management what to do with the people now. The idea was to get them off the beach. Was it better to hold them on the sand until they could each be handcuffed or send them back to their boats in the water and handcuff them then? They had to get back to St. Thomas to be taken to jail or questioned or what have you. Now what was needed was that they get off the beach. As long as they were on the beach, they were successful. But what was the beach? The land or the sea?

"I'm sorry, Me!" called the young handsome Guardsman to Eve Youme, as he stepped her from the dock to one of the Coast Guard ships. Franky, standing apart, sighed as this man lifted the plank, trapping her and the others.

We people were held on the Coast Guard ships, where we all chatted like it was Food Fair day, just with no food, or like on Transfer Day so many years ago, which most of us could not recall because we'd

519

not yet been born then. Only the organizers, who stood to give up themselves, were arrested. The others were docked at the waterfront and set free. It had been a little scary and a little thrilling and a little magical, but it had been successful and it had been entirely real.

94.

Frank was not with his sister when Youme walked into the door that afternoon to meet Anette. Frank was in jail.

Within the hour, it was reported by radio that young Frank Joseph was staging a hunger strike, Anette looked to the ceiling and shook her head. Her boy was already stick thin though he ate like a hog. He wouldn't survive a day on a hunger strike. She packed up some food, and she and Youme started off toward the local jail, which overlooked the sea.

"Mommy," asked Youme, her face betraying both eagerness and defiance. "What's the plan for me? What did you and Dr. McKenzie figure out?"

"Me, let's worry about your brother for now."

At the jailhouse there was a crowd, mostly of protesters from the lime-in/swim-in, the salt dried on their faces like war wounds. The people gave way for Me. They hailed her loudly, "Me! Me!" but she only smiled and held her mother. Franky was standing at the front desk, barefoot in a damp undershirt and his Coast Guard white pants. He was whispering with the police chief. He raised his arm so his wife and daughter could find their way toward him.

"The boy won't take food," Franky said.

"He will from his mother," said Anette.

"Don't do that to him," Franky said to his wife. "Let him be a man."

Here it was. And so quickly. Her son belonged to himself now. Anette passed the food to Franky. "Me?" she asked her daughter.

"We should go, Mommy," Youme said. She could feel the crowd getting thirsty just watching her.

During Frank's airheaded hunger meditation in jail, he thought only on his sister and Auntie Eeona. He didn't believe Auntie Eeona was dead, like they were all fearing. He didn't believe she had gone off to drown like it was said was the Bradshaw way. Without food, Frank felt high and he felt that he knew, really knew, that his women didn't just give way to slice of knife or wall of water or ceasing of a beating heart. They last. They rise like volcanoes, like a pustule on the skin. They explode and do their cleansing damage.

Young Frank was released, no charges pressed, before twenty-four hours even passed. Franky had stayed all night at the station to wait for his boy because the police officers would only release Frank to one of their enforcement own.

When Frank walked through the door that morning, he went to his sister. He turned the big ice vat over and sat on it while Eve Youme sat on the couch.

"Why did you run to the water like that?"

"I don't know. It just come over me."

Frank watched his sister in the face and saw Auntie Eeona rising in her skin.

95.

The Beach Occupation Movement and Bacchanal was in full sail after the successful swim-in/lime-in over on Water Island. Eve Youme's picture, the indecent one with her chest bare, the black strip of the censor like a dark slot for entry, appeared in the paper the very morning that Frank was released. The BOMB was over a month later. It didn't take long for the Free Beach Act to be passed. It was the time, after all. If lunch counters in the State of Georgia were being made to serve Negroes, then it seemed that Virgin Islands beaches would be made to serve Virgin Islanders. Not that history always worked this symmetrically, but this time it did. The last mean hotel and the last stingy family had to take down their PRIVATE signs and remove their chains. We lay on the beach and felt our self-worth rise with the tide.

Of course, the tourists kept coming and the hotels kept bursting. And imagine, not even months into the new freedom Franky came home and announced that the Muhlenfeldt Point land had been sold to a big resort chain. The lighthouse was in jeopardy, as was Franky's life's work. But in the grand scheme of things, that point was on a cliff. Not on a beach. At least not on a beach.

The BOMB all happened and was over within three months. A month to represent each major island — for St. Croix and St. John were in it, too. Or perhaps a month for each Bradshaw sibling. Or a month for each manifestation of God. No matter. Because after those three months, after the beaches were peaceably free and justly occupied, Eeona returned.

■ ■ ■ ■

LOVE

■ ■ ■ ■

My name is love
I am the beloved one
The last romantic
Coming out of the islands
Of the sea
Coming out of the mossed ocean

— HABIB TIWONI, "AL-HABIB"

96.
JACOB

If I may . . . once more. Please. I would like
to make it clear that I made an attempt.
When Anette left me at the restaurant, I
waited . . . I called . . . but I did not want
to disrespect her household. I was sure her
husband knew nothing of our meeting in
Frenchtown. My wife . . . per usual . . .
knew nothing.

Understand . . . I did see my daughter
there in the newspaper when she was a
protester. I cut her picture out . . . for her
decency the black strip of the censor was
across her chest. I kept the picture in my
wallet until it wore to tissue. Please,
know . . . I did not participate in the movement and bacchanal . . . Never in my life
have I been asked to vacate a beach . . . But
I understood the movement's concern.

During the dark months of the BOMB, I
had been writing fellow physicians about
my daughter's condition . . . My letters were

cast out but did not produce a yield. Fellow colleagues wrote suggesting other colleagues . . . I wrote to Puerto Rico and the United States, to England and Denmark. There was a French doctor . . . he suggested a Spanish doctor . . . he turned out to be a priest who had been a medic on the Nazi side in the war. "Bring her to me." The Spanish doctor priest wrote his epistle in medical Latin.

Believe me . . . This letter lay open on my desk. My good wife dusted my table and folded the letter, but I reconsidered the Spaniard's offer every night. Here it was . . . a doctor who had been a priest. His cure would be codeine, exorcism, surgery . . . prayer. I contemplated this possibility without anyone to consult with.

As I deliberated, I would take out the picture of my daughter from the paper. In it she is the symbol, like a statue of liberty for the Virgin Islands. She's wet and standing in the water . . . she looks strong and defiant despite the Coast Guardsman holding on to her. I would try to talk to this symbol of her. Ask this symbol of liberty and tether what was best for my daughter. I contemplated alone with that picture until I knew there was no option but to send her away. In a country like Spain there would be others like her. Know this . . . I didn't like my decision, but it was the only one I had.

I phoned the Joseph residence day after day . . . for weeks . . . until finally my daughter answered. The beach protests were over, and now any old common person . . . even those from other islands . . . could lie out on our best beaches. Yes . . . she had made that possible. For better or for worse. When she answered . . . well, I could hear the beauty in her voice.

"You wouldn't send me away," she said.

I had to admit it. "My Eve, I already have. I've called the Spanish priest doctor long-distance on the phone. He and I have agreed. You will be there in less than a month. I must talk with your mother about the plan."

And then Eve spoke to me in a very adult manner: "Dr. McKenzie," she said, "don't you think that, in a way, it is beautiful? Worth holding on to?"

I felt my fingers grasp hard and sweaty around the phone receiver. I saw myself making love to her mother. I remembered making her. Yes, of course, every bit of her was beautiful. Of course . . . but beauty could be wrong. "Eve. My first child. I don't believe that this thing is of God."

"And so? It's of me."

Yes. It turns out . . . yes . . . yes . . . I admired my daughter for her bravery. I made the . . . well, momentous decision . . . I let Eve be.

Understand. What I'm saying is that I remember. I remember myself singing in the middle of the street to a woman with red roots at the base of her hair. I remember playing the piano, and the photographer at school snapping me. I remember my mother bathing me in the sweet-smelling water . . . I remember . . . believe me. I remember shining my military shoes and stealing the shiny rifles. I remember choosing the fine white cloth and then the racy red and yellow. I remember that beauty can be dangerous . . . I don't know . . . perhaps even that danger is worth it. I remember that I have been niggardly. I never intended to be.

97.

The rooms at Eeona's inn were charged at a price better suited for 1935. Because Mother Eeona still hadn't returned, the Josephs collected the rent and, after paying the staff, sent a bit of it to help Ronalda in college. They couldn't spare their own funds now because Franky had been released from keeping the lighthouse. A political demotion, he felt, for being the father of a BOMB family. But the Coast Guard had said that there was just no more need for a lighthouse. A hotel was going up there. A Marriott hotel, to be exact. That would shine brighter than anything.

Franky wasn't relegated to mess duty or anything degrading. He would continue routine coastal laps around the islands, but he had nothing so special as his lighthouse again. At home he was his same self. Only he started polishing the faces of the flashlights. Checking and rechecking the batteries with the tip of his tongue. He was a nuisance, but Anette let him be. The island had won the beaches and it had seemed there were no casualties. But here was the casualty. Living in her house.

And the family also fretted about Auntie Eeona. Anette did not feel the coming feeling. Maybe Eeona would never return. Perhaps Anette would even have to get on a boat and visit the inn. Make a decision about what to do with it.

But the good thing is that the Joseph family was going, every Saturday, to a different beach now. Stumpy and Sapphire. Sugar Bay and Botany. Magens and Secret Harbor. Afterward they would spend the evening looking at one another over candlelight, reading books until their eyes were sore and telling stories until sleep took over. Some private homes on island had electricity, but the Josephs were still waiting.

Then one evening Anette was grading history papers by kerosene lamp and Frank could be heard singing kaiso from the tub. Anette had just cleared out her now reddish-gray hair, for she was letting the black dye go, and there were stray tufts of it floating around her. The phone rang and it was the inn's housekeeper who had been promoted to inn manager, what with Mother Eeona disappeared. Anette and the woman had a banal conversation about a backed-up toilet and a newlywed couple who seemed to have forgotten they had real lives and still, two months gone, made love loudly until three in the morning.

"Well, thank you for the news."

"News, Mrs. Joseph? But I ain give you the news yet."

And that is when Anette found out that Eeona had been reliably spotted in town. A whole two days ago. Her human self, with her hair flying like wings, seen on the road, wandering as though lost. Seen talking to herself, muttering — so one report confirmed — about lobster. More than one person had fed her saltfish, figuring she was

532

seafood hungry.

There was nothing new to rumors of Eeona sightings. People had been sighting her since she was a girl. But the beggar banality of this one caused Anette to believe that something terrible had finally happened. Perhaps Eeona had had her own Villa by the Sea fright. Or perhaps winning the beaches had now brought her ghost back.

Anette had never been to the inn before. She had never been curious. And after her recent Hibiscus Hotel visit, Anette was worse than uncurious. But now she prepared herself for the ferry ride to St. John.

Little sister, Anette. She did not like boats or ships or any vessel of the sea, but now she walked up the swaying plank without anyone's help. She spent forty eternal minutes on the boat, which included the time spent with the boat just sitting there, doing no goddamn thing but swaying and shuddering and preparing to sink — so Anette felt. She survived it all by standing at the railing and staring. This seemed brave, but it wasn't. She was focusing on the sea so she would know where to dive if the boat suddenly broke into pieces. Swimming was natural, she knew. She'd long ago decided that boats were not. It was a late-afternoon journey but there was enough sunshine for her to see a huge sea turtle gliding beside the boat. She saw herself jumping onto the turtle's back and coasting to safety. Her hands gripped the railing so hard that they ached.

She arrived at the inn in the evening because she had been slow getting ready, reticent really, and had missed the ferry's morning voyage. But it wasn't as bad as it could have been. The inn, unlike the Joseph house, was bursting with electricity. It glowed in the dusk.

The groundskeeper opened the door before Anette could even knock on it.

Eeona's inn was painted blue on the inside and the out. It was ornate with dark mahogany chairs that seemed as old as antiques. It was baroque, old-fashioned. There were elaborate trimmings where the high ceiling and the walls of the foyer met. Cream curtains made of light linen separated the foyer from the kitchen and the kitchen from the hallway. It gave the feeling of an old galleon. Anette felt a bit unsteady on her feet. On one far wall there was a picture of Eeona herself, proprietress, with its own little spotlight perched above and shining on it directly. In the painting the madame was quite young, seventeen maybe, and her beauty tugged all the attention from the room.

Anette sat in the foyer of the room and had the odd feeling again. As though she had been here before. Or somewhere quite like this. As the inn manager stood with her hands clasped at her belly, Anette trailed her own fingers along the windowsills. It was so familiar it was making Anette's head swim. Finally, she asked to be taken to Eeona's room, knowing, just knowing, that it would look more like Villa by the Sea than even Hibiscus Hotel had managed. But the inn manager said, with all her professionalism, that that was the one room for which she didn't have a key. And it was quite locked.

Anette left her one small bag in another room with a bed very much like the bed she had slept in as a small child. But Anette would never have remembered this. Then she hired a gypsy taxi to drive her through the town of Coral Bay and then around the whole island of St. John. She held her aching hands in her lap and called out of the taxi's window, "Eeona! E-on-a. He Own Her," into the homes of Coral Bay, and people came out of their houses to watch. The evening stretched out until Anette lost her voice.

Finally, the taxi took Anette to the Emergency Station on the opposite side of the island from the inn. The Emergency Station was the hospital, police, and fire station all in one. Strangely, Anette's polite words came out in a croaking whisper, though when she cursed, she found the crass words came out clear and brassy. The emergency personnel looked at her in bewilderment, for wasn't she the dignified lady who began the whole BOMB? Maybe not. They knew for sure, though, who Mother Eeona was. They had directed many a tourist couple to her inn. When last was she seen? Seen a few days ago, but before that, not for months.

Then Anette waited. A group of teenaged St. Johnians came into the station making noise. Their car had crashed into a tree, but they were still well pressed and coiffed. They looked healthy and excited. Anette envied them. Their youth, their togetherness.

Hours later, two police officers drove Anette back to the remote side of the island, back to Eeona's inn. The officers rarely drove to this side of the island and they were weary of being out here in the darkness, for there was not one streetlight for the entire journey. But the officers were also thrilled to have the opportunity to drive someone around instead of the sacks of potatoes and rice their wives made them transport in the backseat. Anette sat quietly in the back of the cruiser and dusted off the grains of rice. With the bars between her and the men, she felt like something dangerous. The only illumination ahead of them was their own headlights.

When they finally arrived at the inn, Anette had her mind decided. She gesticulated that they should open Eeona's suite. But the police could not bust the lock, as the owner had not given permission. "But the owner is missing," insisted Anette now, her voice feeling choked and meager. The inn manager went to fetch the deed. But no, Eeona had years earlier made Youme the official owner of the entire inn. Who knew? Well, Youme knew. But that was a secret between her and her aunt.

"You moomoos! The owner is my child," Anette shouted now. "She a motherscunting minor. So I have the blasted say." The police officers stepped back, like they'd seen something more dirty than they could handle. Anette looked down and started to weep.

But the police stayed around and asked the guests and staff questions. Anette heard that Eeona had been seen days ago wandering the roads at night like a ghost. That she had been polite and accepted a can of fake crab as if she were a cat. But that just last night she *was* a cat with long silver fur in mats and curls. Here was the mystery Anette had expected, but this was not the Eeona who was expected. Yes, Eeona must be having an episode. She would be found, she would be returned, she would be okay. Anette tried to pull herself together.

One of the officers turned to Anette and, putting his index finger to his temple and twirling it around, asked: "Crazy?" But Anette did not reply. She couldn't answer.

Maybe sister Eeona had finally gone crazy. No children. No husband. And all that nastiness Mr. Lyte had talked about. Imagine the secrets Eeona must have pooling in her head. Anette couldn't really blame her for racing away. Anette herself had sped from Jacob, now that she knew what she knew.

It was too dark now to even consider driving back to the other side of the island, so the officers called their wives. Then they asked the inn manager politely if they could each have a complimentary room, even though it was clear that they would need the room and they would not need to pay. They took to their beds and didn't stir.

It was night and almost everyone was in

bed so Anette went to the groundsman, who was in the kitchen prepping ahead for breakfast because he was the cook as well, and commanded slowly: "Open the door." He shook his head no. "Sorry, Mrs. Joseph. I can't do that." Anette set her fire eyes on him and then from deep in her chest she started growling. "Open the fucking door before I broke it down." It was an American curse word and the worst she could think of. And it was like it was a magic word, because the man scrunched his face into a ball and brought out a large key from the secret folds of cloth at his chest. It was so like Eeona, to give a man the key to her room. It was like so many of the women of her time and place.

Anette and the groundsman went up to the third floor, past the rooms of the inn now empty save for the police officers who were snoring and the newlywed couple who were too fogged with their love.

At the suite, which was more than a room, but was what people once called "apartments," the groundsman opened the door. When he did, they smelled an alive smell. It was something like molt and moss. Like someone had turned their own human body inside out. But it was cool, a wind was coming through. And yes, the room was very familiar. But Anette would never have remembered that it was a copy of her mother's room.

"Eeona," Anette called. But no one was there. Eeona's blue clothes, though, were everywhere. Blue pantaloons and long-sleeved blouses patterned with bluebells. There were also opened food tins and uncovered pots rattling slowly, as if they were alive. There was a sticky liquid on the floor. There were magazines, torn and moist, laying like a crazy carpet, their corners lapping. On the glossy covers were women in fancy American clothes. The bed, a large grand mahogany antique with gauzy mosquito netting, was sooty and unmade. Then there was the writing on the wall. Actual paragraphs of Eeona's script written in pen. Up and down the walls. Sideways or in columns, down close to the floor or up at eye level. But all neatly done as though the room were a cave and the writer needed to preserve this writing for future discovery. Once Anette stood close enough, she could see that the writing was scraps from Anancy stories and Duene stories and other story stories.

And there was a balcony, a very small one, but still. This is where the breeze was coming from. The linen curtains were plump, like the sails of a ship. Anette went to the balcony, but no one was there. There was just enough space for two people to stand and embrace. She looked over the ledge. But no one was there either.

The groundsman began to shiver. "I should not have, I should never have let you in."

"Is me," Anette said finally in her own sweet voice. Then she guided the man out of the suite with her own arms. She faced the rooms alone. She went to the tiny kitchen. There was expensive champagne. In the fridge there was milk in a glass bottle, juice with its hand-squeezed pulp. All gone rank and sour. In an old-fashioned bread box there was fine butter bread now hard as rock.

Anette began to make up the bed with fresh sheets. She swept the floor and folded the clean blue clothes. She dumped papers into the downstairs bins. Dumped the sooty laundry into the washing machine downstairs. She fastened the balcony door shut. And she didn't cry.

That night she lay in the room that resembled her childhood room. She rubbed her hands with the lotion she found in the bathroom. She wore a proper nightgown, knowing that Eeona would appreciate such a thing. It was new and felt stiff on her body. There was a rack for hanging the damp underwear she had rinsed in the sink. A small bureau where she rested her toiletries. A shallow closet where she hung the matching house robe. The bed was large and high with little steps leading to the mattress. Beside the bed was a phone. Anette called Franky and told him, her voice finally her own, of the futile day and the sad room. She did not tell him about the antique furniture, the curtains, or about the possession of her speech. She couldn't explain that.

"When you coming back?" asked Franky, without a hint of the desperation he felt.

"Is summer time. I don't have to teach for a next month. I waiting the witch out."

"You know something, a light just come on for me, yes," he said. And Anette wondered what he knew. It wasn't like him to speak in metaphors. If he'd suddenly realized something, it couldn't be good. Did he know, somehow, about her and Jacob? She waited silently for him to continue.

"You hear me?" he said.

"I listening," she said.

"A light come on. The house bright like daytime, yes. I surprise them children ain wake up, for how blinding this thing is."

"You mean the electricity? The current came on?"

"Yes, yes," he said. "What you think I mean?"

There was no screen on the windows at the inn and that night the bugs came at Anette like they had been starving. She kept the standing fan on all night, thinking the mosquitoes would grow tired flying into its wind and drop dead. The fan whirred an oscillating rhythm. Through the walls Anette could hear the newlyweds melting into each other in a great boiling.

98.

Baby sister Anette dreamed of waking up to her elder sister beside her when Eeona had disappeared for so long that other time. But when Anette awoke, Eeona was not there in the bed. Instead, the sun was coming through the louvers. Despite the nightmare and the mosquito bites bubbling on her legs, Anette felt grand. After all, she'd taken a boat and had not been drowned. She'd slept in this too familiar house and hadn't been sucked back into childhood. Yes, this island of St. John was nice as everyone always said. Maybe she'd even find a beach and go for a swim.

She smelled sweet bush tea and pork sausage coming through the windows. She put on lipstick and shuffled into house slippers and the matching housecoat. She walked down to the main room and saw the groundsman, the maid, the police officers, and the newlyweds all at the breakfast table like a family. A gathering of empty utensils and plates lay like new bones before them. The groundsman, standing to clear the table, looked at Anette and then raised his eyes upward.

Anette, who was not a young woman anymore, took the stairs fast, like a fish against the current. Ahead, at the end of the hallway, Eeona's rooms did not release a glow as though a witch were there waiting. The door did not pulse or make odd sounds. It was just the room of an old lady who had faced her past. Anette knocked on the door. Eeona did not answer. She called, "Eeona. Sister." There was no answer. Anette stared at the lock and thought perhaps there was a time when she could have turned the dead bolt with her mind. But today she stepped back and charged the door with her shoulder. "You motherscunt!" she yelled out, and gripped her shoulder with the pain. She was not a young woman anymore, and the door did not open. Anette put her face in her hands and moaned; it was not crying, it was just a sounding. Then she reached forward and turned the handle. The door opened.

"Sit down," came the elder sister's voice. The windows were closed, but the balcony curtains were fluttering. That door was ajar, allowing a little light. Anette sat down in a chair she found in the shadows, for she had placed it there last night during her cleaning. "Oh, Anette. Do cross your legs at the ankle, not at the knee like some common tart. If you insist on being a tart, my dear, you might as well be a classy one."

Anette could see that a big comfy chair had been pulled close to the small balony. It couldn't fit out there, but it was close enough. Sitting in the chair, Eeona looked small and regal. Anette pulled her chair closer and pushed her chin forward to face her sister.

"How are you, Eeona?"

"I am fine, dear."

The sisters stared at each other's bodies through the chiaroscuro.

"Where were you?" Anette asked, trying, like Youme had, to read minds. "America? That's where Mama went to run away from us. You've been to America? You see Ronalda when you there?"

"You think such foolish things." Eeona stared at her sister and right into her.

Anette grew quiet. Though she did not feel an intruder in her mind, she still tried to clear her thoughts. "Eeona, you went to Villa by the Sea?"

"Now why would you think such a thing?" Eeona eyed her silent sister for a moment. "No, little sister. I have my villa here. I went after something more."

99.

On Anegada there are more crabs than people, we say. More shipwrecks than crabs. Eat lobster for breakfast and lunch and dinner, we say. You can fish for shark when in need of variation. Submerged island, we say. The tip of Atlantis. Onegeda. Anigeda. Anegada. Perhaps you've never heard of this place. Perhaps that is for the best, because if you hear too much you will hear it calling, like *anegando en mis llanto* — your own tears drowning you. But we've come this far.

Besides, it called Eeona.

The truth is that Anegada was still beautiful. Was still bare and barren. The people lived in homes stacked on a gathering of loose rocks with sandy land around them.

The people who lived there were the people who belonged to the land. People who the land claimed as its own. There was no golf course. No all-inclusive hotel. Eeona had stepped off the boat and an old woman, a woman, for God's sake, laid her eyes on Eeona's lovely face and said: "You family to me." And she was.

There was one small inn on the island, which is where Eeona was heading, but this woman whose last name was Norman but had been born Stemme said, "Come stay by me. The best lobsterman on island is my man."

Mrs. Norman was an oldish lady. Old like a grandmother, maybe, but she walked with her back straight, and her legs were thick and smooth. And as the two women passed the water, Mrs. Norman poured her arm out toward the sea where her lobsterman could be seen. He was nothing more than a silhouette at the edge of a little dock. The black shape of a man against the setting sun. His backward-facing feet under the water where no one but the fish could see. The sea was waving at his shins as he raised his machete to the lobster and chopped it into pieces.

Mrs. Norman hollered at the shadow man. "One more, my love!"

Then the man stepped up the dock and out of the sun's darkening.

It was Owen Arthur.

Or rather, he looked to Eeona just like Owen Arthur. His hair was silver and his face was worn, but it was the same sand-colored skin. The same shape of nose. His same face uninterrupted by a mustache.

"What mood are you in, pretty lady?" called the lobsterman. "I want to know before I approach." Eeona thought she must be the pretty lady, but no . . .

"I in a sweet mood," said Mrs. Norman. "Come meet my cousin."

But surely Eeona had come to face her deeds. Surely her running away had finally taken her to a haunted place where the past greets you at the door. The man who was not her father but looked so much like him held a bucket of lobster bodies in each hand. His feet, on land, faced forward.

"Nothing new in family," said Mrs. Norman, as they walked to The Settlement and to her house. "People always coming back here trying to find out who they belong to." She smiled at Eeona with her mouth turned down, as though they had a secret. "Lyonel came back years ago. We's cousins. Third or fourth with thrice removal, but family still."

Eeona walked between the two of them.

She looked at the man. Then at her own hands. She felt dizzy, which was something that Anegada could do — make someone dizzy with its beauty.

At the house they ate lobster out of the shell. Eeona finally introduced herself. Gave her name, gave her parents' names. The lobsterman nodded at her. "You come to find your grandparents' graves?"

"Yes, of course," said Eeona quickly.

"They was good, simple people," he said to her. "And your parents are still remembered here, too. We still talk about the crash of *The Homecoming*." His mouth tensed for a moment and then calmed. "The ship still there. People always finding bones in the sand from that very ship. Ghosts like you always washing ashore."

Had she just been called a ghost? Eeona had the urge to reprimand this man, but how could she when his face was there looking like the love of her life. Instead, she cleared her throat to swallow her words. Besides, she needed to gain any alliance. This lobsterman might be her guide. She was here for *The Homecoming*.

Mrs. Norman stood to clear the dishes, but then the lobsterman, wary of Eeona's stare, took them and went to wash them himself. Mrs. Norman sat back next to

Eeona. "There is a beach here that is named after a girl who visited with her French sweetheart some years past. You know it?" Mrs. Norman said this with her face blank of any suspicion.

"I do know it," Eeona said.

"Good. Is where we always go for our evening dip."

Flash of Beauty had not been originally named after Eeona and Moreau, but that was the story told, and so now that was how it was. And it was the same beautiful thing it had been decades before. How was this so achingly possible? The white sand with flecks of pink, like baby tongues.

"I cannot quite believe that I am here," Eeona said, swallowing the "again" at the end of the sentence. She waded out in the water with Mrs. Norman as the old lobsterman watched them from his perch on the sand. The two women swam fully clothed as was the old tradition.

Mrs. Angela Norman, who was a Mrs. because she had been married to Norman, looked out into the ocean. Miles out where the reef began, the waves crashed without a sound. "Anegada isn't real," Angela said. "It's magic."

"I am not, perchance, dreaming, am I?" Eeona was being lighthearted, but she also worried about the extent of her episodes.

"Perhaps you are, Cousin Eeona."

True, Eeona was not herself. Not herself at all. Cousin Angela Norman did not seem to really understand or care who Eeona Bradshaw was. Angela only seemed to care about the fact of their relation. As if that was anything. As if that was everything. And that Lyonel, the lobsterman. The only time he'd looked at her, he'd called her a ghost. But *he* was the ghost. A man handsome enough to be her father.

Mrs. Norman and Eeona began to walk out of the water. Their clothes stuck to their older women's bodies in immodest ways. Eeona was not a woman to cry, but when Angela passed her the towel, she found she needed to dry her eyes. The lobsterman respectfully looked away.

That night Eeona slept in a large mahogany bed in the couple's cottage. It was the kind that Antoinette and Owen Arthur would have slept in. It was high off the ground, and when she sat on it, Eeona's feet hung over the side of the bed like a child's. That night she dreamed. Because she dreamed, she knew that this Anegada was not, after all, the dream. She dreamed about a school of women walking out of the ocean. Then she dreamed it again. And again.

Until in the dream she was finally one of the women.

The next morning, over a lobster omelet with seaweed, Eeona said to the lobsterman: "I should like to see *The Homecoming.*"

The man squinted his eyes at her. "It beneath the water."

"That is of no concern."

He looked at Angela, his woman, and she nodded. "You a water woman," he said to Eeona. "Is your father ship we talking." Then he shrugged his assent.

So Eeona went out to the ocean on a boat with the silver-haired man who looked to her like her father. It was an ill-conceived idea. But it was true that, though Eeona was a middle-aged lady who could not drive a car, she could slip on a mask and fins and slide into the water like any amphibian.

The water was dark with the bodies of the boats. It was a place of quiet. The old lady and the older man snorkeled above it all, unable to speak for the mask. But for Eeona's safety, they held hands. Like lovers.

Beneath them, the boats were skeletons of their former selves. How would she ever find hers? But then the lobsterman pointed. Eeona looked. She struggled to see but didn't see. He kept pointing and pointing. And then *The Homecoming* revealed herself there in the cemetery of ships. No longer painted white, there was a deep green to her shell. The seaweed of the ship's underbelly that had once made Eeona uneasy had now taken over her whole body. It still troubled Eeona. But she gulped the unease down into her belly.

Instead, Eeona flew, like a witch, above *The Homecoming.* She saw the galleon as though looking through glass. The boat that had been hers was hers still. She flew, with her lobsterman, around the molding deck. The fish flew with them. Eeona's hair had been tight and flat to help the mask stay in place, but now the hair fought until it released itself and then it, too, flew all about her like tentacles. The ship was drowned shallow enough to catch the sun through the waves. Eeona could see the deck and the mast. Eeona could see the ship, like a body, leaning over on its side as though it were just a beloved reclining. Simply resting and waiting all these years.

This was her father's ship. And this was Eeona's ship. And though she was no underwater expert, she now held her breath, let go of Lyonel's hand, and shot her body down, so at least she might touch the mast. Or maybe she might reach the ball of her foot to the deck. Lyonel had to follow her, for despite his age, he still made a living off of this very sea. He knew it better than she.

Oh, Eeona. She was not ready to be snorkeling and diving on a hot day in the sea for so long. She wasn't young anymore. But she was of a sea people. So she did not panic as she fell, up, up, up toward the silvery surface. And when Eeona's body buoyed up facedown, Mrs. Norman, waiting for them in the lobster boat, did not panic either.

When the lobsterman saw Eeona falling up, not diving down to the boat at all, he watched her for a while. Her fall in the water was slow and gentle and full of grace. He watched and watched through his own eyes, for he never wore a mask. He saw her fall back up and up.

Of course, the man knew who Eeona was and whom she belonged to. All that was so long ago. He had been trying to give some distance, but the girl, the woman, had been giving him a flirty look since she arrived and then she'd grasped his hand during the swim and he just hadn't the heart . . . So he just watched her now. Watched her go, go.

But then he noticed the loose way she soared, noticed that her body butted against a jut of coral and didn't tense but simply slacked and bounced and kept falling up.

Like she was dead. So he shot after her, sucking in fresh breath as he pulled her into the lobster boat. The same boat, it turned out, in which he had proposed life and love to Antoinette Stemme.

Eeona stayed in her cousin's cottage. She dreamed and dreamed. She was there in the school of women. There was no hospital, but the island medic who was not a medic at all but what the less Anglicized still called an obeah woman, directed Angela to pour garlic water and lobster soup down Eeona's throat throughout her unwaking.

And then Eeona awoke. And she was not herself. Not herself at all. She knew where she was. She knew how she had gotten there. She knew she had not made it to touch *The Homecoming.* But she took one hazy look at the lobsterman standing over her with a bowl of lobster soup and she realized that he did not look that much like her father after all.

Who the lobsterman looked like was her mother. He looked like Eeona's own beautiful mother. And Eeona saw how the lobsterman stared at her now as an uncle might have. Those were Antoinette's eyes. That was Antoinettte's mouth whispering her name. Eeona had never really considered how beautiful her mother was at all.

What on earth? Was everyone related in these Virgin Islands? Was that the strange secret to freedom and belonging? Eeona had never wanted, really, to be anything but her father's daughter. And she'd been her desired self for nearly two decades and then in less than a year her father had died and her family had been deadened. And she'd never really considered what this might really mean. Never before.

100.

In the inn in Coral Bay, Anette could see her sister's frame lean forward — as if for battle. But instead of saying anything, Anette just sat there with tears raining down her face.

"Come, Anette. Give yourself some air. I want you to see what I've finally done. Open the balcony wide."

Anette sucked her nose in and bunched her eyes. Then she stood and reached her hands to the balcony doorknobs. With a pull, she let in the light and the breeze. The curtains winged around them.

The scissors were in Eeona's lap. The dark and light tresses were already gone from her head, already gathered in her hands. Her head, with the fine scars of an old lovemaking in glass, gleamed in places like a cut diamond.

"Your hair. What the ass?" And it was true that it was intense. More — it seemed insane.

Eeona's face was not a young woman's face. She was an older woman now. Beyond middle age, really. Her mouth opened and released a breezing sigh. "I was a child and I only wanted . . ." But she shook her head. The words were not working. Her hands were full of her own hair. Those hands were now reaching toward Anette as in offering. Without her hair, Eeona's face was all there was to offer. And Jesus, she was beautiful. Only now she also seemed as though she were either wise or an acolyte. Both seemed as though they might be the same thing.

"Sister?" Anette asked in a quiet way that said all the shock and sadness. But still Anette stepped forward to meet Eeona, because she was the little sister, after all. She took the silver hair. The hair was heavy and soft. It was the weight of a child and Anette cradled it. Now Eeona dusted the small curls of the hair from her own shirt and lap. She did it with her fingers, shaking and slow. She regained her composure as Anette pressed the hair to her own chest.

"There," Eeona said finally. She wiped her

face with a kerchief. She nodded her head now. Nodded and nodded until finally the words came out. "Anette, we are selling the inn."

Anette's tears were storming out of her eyes. *Crazy witch,* she wanted to say to her sister. But she kept her composure. "Relax, Eeona. You've had an episode. Your mind is not true. This inn is what you've always wanted. You just said, it's your villa . . ."

"Nettie, I am moving to Anegada."

"No." Anette was still standing. The balcony was right there beside them. "I need you, Eeona. I need my family." She hugged the hair from the breeze.

"You have your family."

"But Eeona. Right now you don't know real from not real. But is okay. I going take care."

"Oh, Nettie. If only I had sent you to be raised on Anegada. Perhaps you would have been able to walk through mountains instead of carry them on your back."

Anette felt uneasy with the nickname Eeona kept using. Had she overheard Jacob use it? Anette's fingers slipped in and around the hair. "But Eeona, you can't just up and go. I need to know things. I need to know about what happened with Papa. What happened in our old house? Come,

Eeona. The truth. I have real frigging questions."

"Do stop cursing. It is quite unbecoming. Besides, I am taking Eve Youme with me. You may visit. We will write letters."

Anette felt the tightening between her shoulder blades. "You gone bazadie. Now go to hell. Nobody taking my child from me."

"She is not a child anymore." Eeona breathed out. Pushed her shoulders back. "To be frank, Nettie, Anegada needs her. I suppose I need her as well."

Anette couldn't catch her voice fast enough. "If you had just speak the truth back when we was young." Anette's voice was rising. The hair was against her breast. "And if you had, maybe I would never had get knot up with Jacob and none of this bullshittiness would have happened."

"Yes, Nettie. That is true." Eeona said this without her face releasing any expression.

"*That is true?* That's what you have to say? After I love up the wrong man. After our birth house come a restaurant and people throw us off a beach on our very own island . . ." The hair began to slip out of Anette's arms. This made them quiet for a moment.

559

"Nettie, do you know why they call it Anegada?"

Anette felt that maybe none of this was real after all. Right here and right now was a thing reeled in from her subconscious. So was that time in Hibiscus Hotel. So was Youme's deformity. Jacob himself was a dream. She was still a child in her parents' house. Maybe Anette was the one going crazy. She shook her head now, as if clearing her ears of water. "Eeona. I teach history. I know Anegada is the land of drowning because of all the ships that crash into it. Our father's ship included."

"That is good, Nettie, but you are wrong. It is because of the land itself. It is the land that is of the water and that is how it has survived."

Anette had never been to Anegada. In truth, she had only read about it in the "Pirates and Piracy" section of the world history textbook. It was also the only section where the Caribbean was mentioned at all. Hundreds of wrecks still soaking in its shores, she remembered. Anegada was not a place one moved to. It was a place people avoided out of fear. Anette whispered to her sister. "Youme sick, Eeona. She has that thing, you know." She lowered her voice. "That obeah thing. The magic thing."

"Nettie, on Anegada there are others like her. She can come to understand herself." Eeona turned to look at the beveled mirror fastened to the wall. "Isn't that the most you could want for the child?"

Anette turned with her sister as though the decision was there in the reflection.

There was Eeona's neck and there were her shoulders and there she was. And finally Eeona was a woman who was fierce and elegant and the queen of somewhere — a woman men would always swoon over. Anette shifted her eyes to look at herself. And she saw that she had that in her, too.

A wind washed in from the balcony. Anette opened her arms and the hair floated out and away like it was nothing more than air.

101.

He meets her on a beach that is shaped like a lover's heart. But instead of sealing off into a pointed tip, the bay is a heart that is open. The sea waves in and out of the heart, as with any love. They will always meet there in the morning. No one is silently picking whelks on the far end of the beach. Not anymore. Someone had actually been robbed right there on the sand recently. But now it is early in the morning. The sun still rising and the air blowing cold. The water is even colder. Everything is covered with the blue of the blanching dawn sky.

They are not the only ones on the beach. There are also two Americans who have lived on the island for many years, close by in one of the big Peterborg houses. They are jogging in a pair. There is also a figure doing capoeira bends and balances by the rocks. The manager and assistant of the beach concession are already there, speaking Spanish to each other as they unpack frozen hot dogs and veggie burgers.

The woman sits on a bench. She doesn't lean back provocatively as she might have done if she were younger and wanted to show off her neckline. She does not look about anxiously waiting for him, hoping he will turn up. She knows he will come. He always does. And anyway, she has a sense of arrival. She isn't wearing a white dress nor is she wearing a red dress with big yellow flowers. She is wearing a gray linen pant-suit, one that matches her silver-speckled red hair. In her hand she cradles a small bag of stewed cherries.

She has taken off her shoes. There are little hairs of silver glinting on her toe knuckles. The sand feels good running through and over her feet.

The man comes walking up the beach in his leather shoes. He is wearing a very fine gray suit, but with the jacket over his shoulder and his sleeves rolled up. He wears a suit every day even when he isn't working. And he still works, even now that he could retire. But there is no one to take over the medical practice. All his six sons have gone into Wall Street business where there is more money. They have left him and his wife alone in their big house in the hills. His sons are only phone calls from America. They are only the occasional visit with a new lovely girlfriend, and they never stay very long. Except for the youngest, he still comes home for Carnival. In college in the States, he has learned to play the steel pan. Jacob smiles, thinking of this son in particular. With children there is always the possibility of a small reincarnation or a large redemption.

Anette watches her feet dig into the sand. *Sand,* she thinks, *is a kind of land that flows like water.* Ronalda had called last night purring about her husband, an American from Florida. Together, they make peanut brittle for a living. Anette hadn't been able to boil water at the same age. Frank Junior is teaching in Grenada. He will visit soon, likely bringing one of his tough-talking Marxist friends. A letter from Youme arrived yesterday afternoon from Anegada. And though Anegada is just there across the ocean, all letters have to be routed through Puerto Rico, and so the letter has taken two weeks in the coming. Anette has it in her lap like something childlike or something sacred. Which are the same thing.

Jacob is carrying one anthurium. Not a rose or a lily. Not an orchid. The flower still has its long stem. Its thick petal is strong and pink like a woman's private flesh. The elaborate pistil surges from the crease in the heart-shaped petal.

Anette sees him coming and doesn't move toward him. She only watches him approach. After all these years she still loves the way the tall sandman walks. *Like a mangrove moving,* she thinks.

"Nettie," he says, when he is close and can see all the features in her face.

"Yes, it's me. Why you ain wearing your glasses?"

"This is for you." He hands her the flower. On his long golden arm there are fine silver hairs, sparkling in the new sun like glints of light. Anette wishes she could put the flower in her hair, but her hair is thin and the flower might slip out. Instead she holds the anthurium in her hand as he sits beside her, his long mangrove legs stretching forward. She passes him the bag of stewed cherries. He thanks her by grazing her shoulder with the tips of his fingers. Together they read their daughter's letter, as is their ritual.

She will be the first to leave that morning. It is her right; he had left her first so long ago. She will get up silently and walk to the phone booth and ask her friend Gertie to leave off nursing Hamilton and pick her up.

Some minutes after, Jacob will climb into his smooth car, push play on his cassette player for the old Irving Berlin tune, this version sung by Sarah Vaughan because Jacob likes to hear it from a woman.

They will go back to the homes with their spouses.

Jacob will kiss his wife's forehead before slipping back in beside her. He will close his eyes and see Anette's silver hairline where the red has faded and imagine he had kissed Nettie instead. Anette will go home to Franky who will be up tending to his papaya trees. She will start breakfast. She will fry his eggs with the right amount of pepper sauce that he likes. He will ask how Gertie is holding up with her husband's illness and Anette will nod, fine, fine. While the eggs are sizzling in their pool of butter,

Anette will think to herself that she doen't even know how Jacob Esau likes his eggs.

But for now, Jacob is with Anette, and they are reading a letter from the child they made together. Just two people who have been in love a long time sitting on a bench with their daughter's words swimming before them. And now Jacob and Anette are pressed together as the cool comes in from the ocean.

AUTHOR'S NOTE

This novel is, in some part, a response to Herman Wouk's novel *Don't Stop the Carnival,* which also features the Gull Reef Club and the characters Sheila and Hippolyte. In my novel the club is where *Girls Are for Loving* is filmed. While all of that is fiction, the film is not. *Girls Are for Loving* was filmed in the Virgin Islands and came out in 1973. It stars Cheri Caffaro.

I first knew about both the Wouk novel and the Caffaro film from my grandmother. I rented the film long after I'd written my scenes set at the club, but my sentiment still feels accurate to me. The film is soft porn, but the locals participating in the movie were unaware of the sexual element. The scene in my novel never actually happens in the movie, and there is no native couple in the advertising. In my fictionalization I have also changed the date of the filming, making it more than a decade earlier, in order to keep the desired chronology.

Both the Caffaro film and the Wouk book were early, and lasting, portrayals of the U.S. Virgin Islands.

I have taken some great liberties with names and times. Characters' names are drawn from names that would have been common in the Virgin Islands at the time, but they are not meant to be connected to any particular person or family present in the V.I. then or now.

Gertie's American beau and eventual husband is based on Hamilton Cochran, a U.S. diplomat who lived in the V.I. during the early 1900s.

Frenchtown, called so now, would have been called Carenage at the time. Nowadays Frenchtown is also spelled French Town.

Lindbergh Bay (often spelled "Limberg" or "Lindberg") during Anette and Jacob's time may still have been called Mosquito Bay. It slowly lost its former name after the aviator Charles Lindbergh landed on the island during his 1928 goodwill tour.

Eve Youme's name is borrowed from the author, illustrator, and all-around cool human Youme Landowne.

The reference in the opening chapter to rain having legs comes from the poem

"Noche de Lluvia, San Salvador," by Aracelis Girmay.

The herbal abortion techniques that Rebekah offers Antoinette are made up. These things do, of course, exist, but I am not privy to them.

Formal schooling in the U.S. Virgin Islands was started by the Moravian Church and then contined by the Anglican/Episcopal Church. Other church schools and the public schools followed. My telling of Anette's and her compatriots' schooling is fabrication for the sake of simplicity and is not meant to reflect our history.

Part of the University of the Virgin Islands sits on land that was once St. Thomas's major golf course. Golfers still practice on the Herman E. Moore Golf Course land there, which is close to but not across from Brewer's Bay (also spelled Brewers Bay), as I suggest in this novel. UVI is, in a way, bordered by two beaches. Brewer's Bay to the west (near where Franky tries to teach Eeona how to drive) and Lindbergh Bay to the south (where Anette and Jacob first make love). The course might be more accurately described as being across from Lindbergh Bay. In the novel, I avoid explaining the geography in detail so as not to distract the reader.

The Anegada protest mentioned briefly on page 260 actually occurred two decades before this conversation at the lighthouse.

The Positive Action Movement, a political and cultural organization in the V.I., is somewhat the guide for the BOMB.

The Free Beach Act won by the BOMB really does exist. Officially it is called the Virgin Islands Open Shorelines Act.

My great-uncle Sigurd Petersen, Sr., was stationed in New Orleans while serving in the Army. His story inspired sections of this book, though my story of the V.I. men in New Orleans has been passed down to me from numerous retired military men of Port Companies 872 and 873. In this fictional telling I use the number 875 to signal that it is neither the real 872 nor the real 873.

David A. Melford's words come from a pamphlet, "Ninety Wrecks on Anegada, 1643–1853," warning visitors to the Caribbean. Melford has since updated his research to now include 134 wrecks . . . and counting. Many estimates of the number of submerged ships on the Anegada reefs bring the account to six hundred or more.

The Alton Adams lyrics are from the "Virgin Islands March," considered our national or territorial anthem. Adams, a native of the Virgin Islands, was the first bandmaster of African descent in the U.S. Navy.

Derek Walcott is quoted from his October 11, 2012, lecture at El Museo del Barrio in New York City. This was the entirety of his response to the question: What makes Caribbean literature unique?

The eponymous protest song "LaBega Carousel" from which I quote is in the quelbe tradition of my fictional Markie and the Pick-up Men. In the Virgin Islands the song is sung by local musicians such as Stanley and the Sleepness Nights, Jamesie, Lashing Dogs, and others. It tells the story of an early-twentieth-century protest that arose because a carousel owner, Mr. La-Bega, paid his workers only a very small wage. In response, people boycotted the carousel by finding other opportunities for revelry — walking around the town and drinking rum. The song is generally credited as having no one single author.

Habib Tiwoni's verses are from the poem "Al-Habib" in his collection *Islands of My Mind.*

I am indebted to too many texts to mention here. The following, however, were indispensable: *Rum War: The U.S. Coast Guard and Prohibition* by Donald L. Canney; *These Are the Virgin Islands* by Hamilton Cochran; *Take Me to My Paradise: Tourism and Nationalism in the British Virgin Islands* by Colleen Ballerino Cohen; *Time Gone* by Lynda Wesley McLaughlin; *The Men of the 872nd Port Company and Other Stories* by Richard A. Schrader, Sr.; *St. John Backtime: Eyewitness Accounts from 1718 to 1956,* compiled by Ruth Hull Low and Rafael Valls; and *Fire on the Beach: Recovering the Lost Story of Richard Etheridge and the Pea Island Lifesavers* by David Wright and David Zoby. I owe much to the painting of Camille Pissarro.

Here's some personal history: My great-grandfather was a ship captain. His ship, the *Fancy Me,* went down off the coast of what was then called Santo Domingo (now the Dominican Republic). As was the tradition, he refused to abandon his ship until everyone else was saved. He drowned with his wreck. Families across the V.I. were affected, and the sinking of the *Fancy Me* is a major historical moment in the V.I. — our *Titanic.* My grandmother was the captain's youngest child. After her father died, her mother left for America, but she returned sick and died soon after. My grandmother was raised by her eldest sister. Eventually, my grandmother married, had her first child, and divorced. Then she had my mother. My biological grandfather was a young man who would eventually become a doctor, a well-known radiologist in the Virgin Islands, though originally he'd wanted to be an obstetrician. His mother, my great-grandmother, taught piano.

When my mother was very young, my grandmother married a fireman. Along with my grandmother, this man (my grandfather in all ways except the biological) raised me.

My grandmother's family is originally from Anegada. When she was in her eighties, I took her there as a gift to her. She had never been there, but she had always heard about that beautiful place. While there we visited Flash of Beauty and found my grandmother's grandmother's grave.

My grandmother was a children's librarian. A large part of her job was telling stories, which she did with us (her children and grandchildren) often. Most of the historical facts in this novel were initially gathered from her.

The rest is magic and myth — fiction, as we call it.

ACKNOWLEDGMENTS

Thank you to Penny Feuerzeig, Beulah Harrigan, Gretchen Heyer, Keith Jardin, Amanda Nowlin, Monica Parle, and Gemini Wahaj, who read the earliest drafts. Thank you to Cassandra Francis for the resources. Thanks to Jericho Brown, Kathy Cambor, Amber Dermont, Nina McConigley, Keya Mitra, Emily Pérez, and Giuseppe Taurino, who always challenged and supported this project. Thanks to Hosam Abu-Ela, Vincent Cooper, Claudia Rankine, and Lois Zamora, who asked all the hard questions that led me to the harder questions. Thanks to Chitra Divakaruni, my thesis chair, who has supported me in all the ways a writing mentor can. Thank you to Patrick Freeman, Laura Jo Hess, Paige Cohen, Andrès Cruciani, and Gilmarie Brioso, whose time gave me time. Thank you to the Bread Loaf Writers' Conference (most especially Michael, Jen, and Noreen) and The New School (especially Helen Schulman, Robert Polito, David Scobey, Luis Jaramillo, and my amazing students) for being supportive and inspiring communities. Thank you to the Enid M. Baa Public Library of St. Thomas, the Anegada Community Library, and the French Heritage Museum of Frenchtown, St. Thomas, where I did research. Thank you to Elise Capron and Sandra Dijkstra, who are always encouraging and fierce. Thanks to Sarah McGrath and Sarah Stein, who said yes to what needed yes, and no to what really, really didn't. Thank you, Riverhead! You've been my dream! I am in awe of the copy editor, David Hough, who patiently worked with me through all the complexities of language this book explores. Thanks to Eddie Bryan, Norma Bryan, Judy Bryan, and Judy Petersen Rabsatt for the conversations. Thank you to the late Dr. Andre Galiber, Sr., for vignettes of his youth. Thank you to my mother and my aunts, who read the manuscript and then decided to love me despite, or support me because. Thank you to my brother and my son — my solstice boys who have been patient. My heart's gratitude to Moses Djeli, who is my partner in all things.

My life, much less this book, would not

have been possible without my grandmother
Beulah Smith Harrigan.

The employees of Thorndike Press hope you have enjoyed this Large Print book. All our Thorndike, Wheeler, and Kennebec Large Print titles are designed for easy reading, and all our books are made to last. Other Thorndike Press Large Print books are available at your library, through selected bookstores, or directly from us.

For information about titles, please call:
   (800) 223-1244

or visit our Web site at:
   http://gale.cengage.com/thorndike

To share your comments, please write:
   Publisher
   Thorndike Press
   10 Water St., Suite 310
   Waterville, ME 04901